After the Fall

After the Fall

RYAN PHILLIPS

Destiny Image Fiction

An Imprint of

Destiny Image® Publishers, Inc.

P.O. Box 310

Shippensburg, PA 17257-0310

ISBN 0-7394-6258-X

For Worldwide Distribution

Printed in the U.S.A.

Dedication

For Rachelle Hood: My Heart

For Suzanne Eustache: My Strength

For Jeri Dotson: My Joy

For Gloria Hood: My Love

God cannot give us a happiness and peace apart from Himself, because it is not there. There is no such thing.

– *C.S. Lewis*

1. The Fall

Abby slanted the rearview mirror left and examined her appearance one last time. She ran her fingers through her dark, silky hair—every strand was in place. Her makeup, she thought, as she slowly turned her head from side to side, was expertly applied.

"Perfect!" she chirped and puckered her lips seductively at her own reflection. She returned the mirror to its proper angle. "And now for the finishing touch."

She rambled through her newly purchased Fendi clutch and pulled out a small bottle of his favorite perfume. Carefully, she applied a little behind each ear and on each wrist.

Abby stepped out of her rental car and smoothed out her designer jeans. The air was raw. It was well below freezing. Any sane person would've been bundled up in layers, but it was impossible to look dazzling in a puffy down jacket and a skull cap, and she didn't drive all the way out to his mother's house to look like the Michelin man. She had an agenda and a key part of getting what she wanted—which she almost always did—was looking good.

Despite her usual immunity to guilt, a wave of it washed over her as she tiptoed up the snow-covered walkway, careful not to stain her suede, kitten-heeled boots. She knew she should be at her sister's house with her aunts and her mom and grandma. It was a Walker family Thanksgiving tradition. All of the men—husbands, brothers, uncles, and cousins alike—were shooed away so the women could prepare the food for the following afternoon. Thanksgiving was Abby's favorite day of the year. It was the one day when she felt like she could throw her hair up, slide into a pair of sweats, and just be Abs. No one was judging her. No one cared about her newest album or how much she practiced or what her next career move would be. She didn't worry about looking fat or wearing the latest fashions. There was no need for political correctness. On Thanksgiving, Abby was allowed to be imperfect and she loved it.

She also loved the fit her mom threw when she and her cousins indiscreetly snuck slices of smoked turkey from the huge pan in the middle of the kitchen table. And she loved watching her aunt Vi chop cabbage and gab a mile a minute about her son Antoine's new girlfriend and how she's "too skinny to deliver any good grandkids."

She just loved being there, observing the hustle and bustle of boisterous, satisfied women.

But today, instead of basking in the comfort of her happy holiday haunt, she was across town standing on a cold, slanted stoop in front of her ex-fiancé's mother's house. Abby tossed her hair over her shoulder, simultaneously shaking away the memories of where she was supposed to be, and rang the doorbell.

She was met by silence. There was no commotion—no sign that anyone was home. She gave a small sigh as disappointment began to set in. She reached for the rusted knob and tried to turn it, but as she suspected, it was locked.

She rang the doorbell a second time. Again, no answer. She turned, prepared to leave. Slow, heavy footsteps approached, and her heart rate quickened. The lock turned and the person on the other side cracked the door open and peeped outside.

"Abby!" Dot exclaimed and swung the door wide open to reveal her mammoth body in all its glory. She was wearing a long colorful muumuu. Her hair was loosely rolled in curlers and her left cheek bore the faint imprint of a wrinkled pillowcase. "Look at you," she said, yanking Abby into the warm house and giving her a tight squeeze. "You get more beautiful every time I see you, if that's even possible."

Abby smiled politely, her ego ever-so-slightly inflated. "Thanks. I didn't wake you, did I?" she asked once she'd managed to pry herself from Dot's strong grip.

"Don't be silly," Dot said, dismissing the notion with a wave of her hand. She pulled off Abby's coat and led her into the floral living room. Abby had hated that room since she first stepped into it nearly six years earlier. The green wall-to-wall carpet, uneven, tawdry, rose-patterned wallpaper, and mismatched love seat and ottoman were enough to make her cringe. But all of her offers to help

Dot redecorate had been met with the same response: "This room is perfect just the way it is."

Despite her appalling taste in home decorations, Dot was a special woman. She was saucy, but gentle—jagged in some respects, but smooth and well-rounded in others. To Abby she seemed somewhat of a paradox, a diamond in the rough.

"I have something for you," Abby said. She unzipped her clutch and produced a CD adorned with a satin ribbon.

"Another one?" Dot gasped, her eyes wide and twinkling. "How many is that now? Three in two years?"

Abby beamed proudly as she nodded.

"That's remarkable." Dot removed the ribbon to get a better look at the cover. "Congratulations!"

"Thank you."

"What are your plans for the holiday? How long are you going to be in town?"

"Not long. Probably just through the weekend."

"Why such a short stay?"

"I want to finish a couple of pieces I've been working on before I start promoting the new album. Besides," Abby added jokingly, "four days is all I can take of my family."

Dot shook her head. "You better slow down, Child. You'll be fiddling with that cello and look up one day to find the world's passed you by."

Abby crossed her legs. "My music is my world. It's my life," she said, her chin raised obdurately.

Dot chuckled sagely. "Nothing should be your life," she warned. "Life is life. God is life. Everything else is relative."

Perplexed, Abby watched Dot struggle to hoist herself from the sunken-in cushions of the old couch and shuffle to her TV room, which doubled as an office.

"Do me a favor," she called. "Make an old woman a cup of coffee while I track down my son for you."

"Dot," Abby said, already on her way to the small kitchen. "Don't trouble yourself. I didn't come here to see Jarvis; I came to spend time with you."

"Yeah, yeah," Dot sang. "All of my friends come over at ten in the morning in the dead of winter looking like a cover model off of a fashion magazine."

Abby smiled and searched the stocked cupboards for a mug. She heard the buttons on the cordless beep as Dot punched in a number.

"Hey, Dawn? It's Mom. Where's Jarvis? Well, tell him to get over here. No... No. Would you just tell him to get over here? It's none of your business. Don't worry about it. No, just tell him I've got a surprise."

Twenty minutes and two cups of coffee later, Abby heard Jarvis's raggedy old car sputtering its way up the street. She watched breathlessly from the front window as he bounded up the walkway, dug out the spare key taped inside the mailbox, and unlocked the door.

"Ma!" he shouted, stepping into the house. "What's the sur—," he stopped mid-sentence when he saw Abby. She was just as stunning, just as breathtaking as she was the last time he'd seen her nearly ten months earlier. He was mesmerized by her eyes, touched by her warm smile, and honored to be in her presence. She was gracefully seated on his mom's couch like a cherished, priceless souvenir—a bittersweet reminder of better days long gone.

"Surprise!" she said feebly and stood. He eyed her greedily from head to toe, his gaze lingering a bit longer on her long legs and round hips. She was wearing a dark pair of jeans that clung to her curvaceous figure. Knowing Abby, those jeans cost more than all of the clothes in my closet, he thought.

She had let her hair grow out and it fell in light, layered wisps past her shoulders and framed her face. Her lips were pouty—still dangerously seductive. And her doe-eyes soothingly bore into him and warmed his heart.

"Wow," is all he managed.

She bit her lip sheepishly, walked over to him, and leaned into his chest. Her nose nuzzled his jaw before she hooked her arms around his neck and squeezed. Slowly, he wrapped his arms around her tiny waist and pulled her to him.

They stood in the middle of his mom's living room and held each other. After a few moments, he reluctantly let her go and stepped back to get another look.

"Nothing you haven't seen before," she said flirtatiously.

He shook his head, amazed. "You're beautiful." And it was the truth.

When Jarvis had first laid eyes on Abby, six years earlier, she was just as ravishing—just as resplendent. She had the same magnetic force that pulled everything and everyone into her radiance. He couldn't pinpoint what it was that made her so addictive to him. Years ago, it was probably her innocence—the way she looked at the world and her life, how she harbored unconquerable hope. The sight of her—the sound of her carefree laughter—inspired him and compelled him to acknowledge the promise and possibility of each passing day.

She had big plans for herself and her optimism was enough to motivate him in a way he'd never before experienced. She made him want to strive toward new heights even when he couldn't see his own worth.

She was comfortable with herself. Everything about her seemed real and genuine. He'd spent years looking for someone perfect, jumping in and out of relationships doomed to fail from the start. He'd find a woman who had everything he thought he wanted only to leave her months, sometimes weeks, later for inane reasons—because of the way she walked or chewed her food.

But Abby was different. Things he would have grown to loathe in another woman only made Abby that much more desirable. He adored her smile, how she wore combat boots in the summer, the permanent imprints on the tips of her fingers from her cello strings, the way her hair fell against her back in crazy little ringlets, the contours of her face in the moonlight. Nothing about her was a turnoff. Her quirks made her human; they proved she wasn't a fantasy. She was very real and she belonged to him.

Time passed, however, and eventually excitement was replaced by comfort. Their relationship became familiar and reliable. Jarvis noticed changes in Abby, but he figured that's what people were supposed to do. They lived and they learned and they grew. To expect her to stay the same would've been selfish.

Abby's changes, though, were calculated. They weren't natural; they were necessary. Her life back then, Jarvis had thought, was taking shape nicely. She had a decent job teaching music at a small, private high school. She lived in a nice apartment. She had great friends and a man who loved her. But it wasn't enough. His heart broke as, helplessly, he watched her become progressively unhappy.

"I feel like I'm suffocating," she confessed. They were sprawled out on a blanket on the floor in her apartment. Cartons of Chinese takeout were piled on the coffee table. It was Sunday night and the dread of Monday morning was starting to set in.

"You want to quit?" he asked.

Abby sighed. "I can't afford to quit right now. I have to pay rent."

"It's not that bad."

Abby shot Jarvis a stern look.

"Seriously, Abs, maybe this is a case of the grass being greener."

"I don't think so."

"Six months ago you loved teaching. What changed?"

"Six months ago I was facing eviction. I would've taken a job shoveling manure. Anything to keep from moving back home or borrowing money from my sister." She shook her head. "I'm not a teacher, Jay. I'm better than this. I'm not supposed to be showing people how to play. I'm supposed to be playing."

"I know," he said, reaching for her.

She scooted toward him, her curls bouncing playfully against her cheeks, and rested her head on his chest. "Tell me what to do," she whimpered.

"You should do what makes you happy," he reasoned.

She exhaled loudly. "That's original."

"Abs, if you want to play music, then play. Sacrifice what you have to sacrifice; give what you have to give. Do whatever it takes."

"That's easier said than done, Jay."

"No, it's not. Stop overcomplicating it."

"You don't get it." She stood up and began clearing the table.

"What don't I get?" he asked, propping himself up on one elbow. "You don't think I understand what it feels like to live on a budget? To have to put more effort into paying my bills than into achieving my dreams?"

"You said it, not me." She dumped the empty paper plates and plastic forks into the trash bag sitting in the corner of her tiny kitchen.

"How can you think that, Abby?"

"Well, for starters, you don't have any real bills. You live with your mom."

"So? I still pay rent."

She cocked her head to the side and raised a brow. "It's not the same. If I don't make rent, me and all my stuff will be sitting on the curb in the cold. If you don't make rent, you get scolded."

"So, because I live with my mom, I don't have dreams or goals?" he asked. His pride throbbed.

"I honestly don't know."

He threw his head back in disbelief.

"Don't do this," she pleaded gently. "Don't turn my problem into our problem."

"My girlfriend thinks I have no future. I'm sorry, Abby, that's a problem for me. I have goals. I want to go back to school, earn a business degree. It's not as glamorous as becoming a world-renowned cellist, but it's something."

"You're right," she stood over him. "We've both given up. I planned to produce my first record by the time I was twenty-five and you planned to earn your degree and open your own business. But look at us. You're working part-time at your uncle's dingy gas station and I'm waving a baton in front of angst-ridden teenagers."

"So let's do something about it, Abs."

"Right," she snorted. "I'll go audition for the Chicago Symphony Orchestra while you run off to Harvard."

"Why not? I can't be happy unless you're happy, Abs, and you won't be until you figure this out. So if you won't do it for yourself, then do it for me. Do it for us."

"A solo career is all I've ever wanted," she murmured. "What if I don't have what it takes?"

"How will you know unless you try? If you give it your all, you'll be satisfied knowing you were brave enough to chase what you wanted—that you were strong enough to 'go for it' against all odds. But if you don't—if you hide behind this teaching job—you'll be miserable, always wondering what the outcome would've been."

Apparently those were the words she'd been waiting to hear. Soon after that conversation Abby moved back home with her parents, and for the next year she sank every dime she had into studio time. If she wasn't writing music, she was playing it; and if she wasn't playing it, she was pitching it to someone—anyone who knew any way she could break into the industry. She became distant during those months, the plight of success demanding all of her time and attention. Throughout it all, Jarvis played the role of the supportive boyfriend, but when she stopped by his house one morning to tell him she was going to Chicago that afternoon, he wondered if their relationship would survive.

"How long are you going to be gone?"

She shrugged. "Two weeks, a month at the most."

"You've got to be kidding me. How can an audition take a month?"

"It's not just about the audition. While I'm there, I might as well network. The music business is all about who you know and who knows you. Hannah's going to show me the ropes."

"You'd think you could've told me sooner than the morning you're scheduled to leave."

"It's not like I've been sitting on the tickets for a week and forgot to tell you. I found out last night."

"Was your phone disconnected, Abby?"

"No," she mumbled to the floor.

"Then you could've told me sooner."

"Well, I'm sorry," she huffed. "I didn't know I needed to ask for your permission. You don't want me to go?" It was a statement rather than a question.

"I don't care what you do anymore."

"Jay, I'm this close." She held her index finger and thumb a few inches apart. "I can't pass up this opportunity."

"What has gotten into you? Nothing else matters anymore. I don't matter anymore. We were supposed to go after our dreams for each other, remember?"

"Jarvis, please!" she snapped. "People don't pursue their dreams to make other people happy."

"If it weren't for me, you'd still be conducting high school orchestra. I hate that I ever begged you to do this."

"And I hate that you're the exact same person you were last year and the year before that and the year before that. You were supposed to go back to school, remember? You should be well on your way to earning a business degree by now, but you're working at an arcade in Tel-Twelve Mall. Do you know how old I was the last time I worked in a mall, Jay?"

"Why do you have to be so vicious?"

"Seventeen!" she shrieked, ignoring Jarvis's question. "And you know what happened? I graduated. I went to college. I moved on. But you refuse to do that. You refuse to grow up."

Then she was gone—for three months—and when she came back, she'd been transformed. He didn't recognize her when she emerged from her gate at the airport. Her once curly hair hung down her back in smooth, straight layers and her black, scuffed Dr. Martens and yellow sundress had been replaced with a short blue jean skirt and strappy, high-heeled sandals. The biggest change, though, had taken place within.

"Hey," she said breezily, as if she'd come back from the grocery store instead of a twelve-week gallivant around Chicago.

"Wow, look at you," he ran his fingers through her hair and then scooped her into a hug.

She stiffened and forced a laugh. "I know, isn't it divine?" She squirmed out of his embrace. "Hannah talked me into getting it relaxed. What took me so long to get with the program?"

He shrugged, unsure of what to make of her new look and cool demeanor. "Did Hannah talk you into those clothes too?" He eyed her miniskirt.

She beamed. “It’s Ralph Lauren—three hundred and fifty dollars,” she whispered.

He almost choked. “You paid three hundred and fifty dollars for a blue jean skirt?”

“I thought the same thing at first, but once I tried it on, I was sold. Isn’t it to die for?”

He raised his eyebrows suspiciously. When did she start using words like “divine,” and phrases like, “to die for”? he wondered to himself. Aloud he said, “I don’t know if I’d die for it, but you do look nice.”

“I forgot how simple you were,” she mumbled.

He blinked, stunned and unwilling to trust his ears. “Sorry?”

“Can we go?” she asked, tossing her newly straightened locks over her shoulder. Her smile was broad, but her eyes were hollow and indifferent. She handed him her carry-on bag and sashayed down the long corridor, her hips swaying provocatively from side to side.

That was the beginning of the end.

“Don’t you two look darling?” Dot said as she emerged from her bedroom. Her multicolored muumuu was gone and in its place she sported a baggy turtleneck sweater and a pair of worn but comfortable-looking stretch pants. She’d molded and sprayed her hair into a helmet of stiff curls, and her face was a palate of bright blush and eye shadows. She gave Jarvis a kiss and then tried her best to wipe away the lipstick she’d left behind. “What’re you kids going to do today?”

Jarvis glanced at Abby.

She shrugged. “Who knows—hang out, catch up?” The question was directed at Jarvis.

He nodded eagerly, like a little boy who’d been offered a lifetime supply of candy.

“Have fun and be safe,” Dot directed in typical motherly fashion.

Jarvis grabbed Abby's leather jacket off the coat rack by the door and held it open for her.

Elegantly, she slipped into it.

"If I'd known you were coming, I would've planned something for us to do." He opened the door and escorted her down the snowy front walkway.

"We've never had a problem entertaining ourselves," she said coyly and handed him the key to her rental car.

He smiled and unlocked the passenger side door. Only after Abby was comfortably buckled into her seat did he run around to the driver's side and let himself in.

Abby glanced over at Jarvis as he settled in behind the steering wheel. He was still adorable with his scruffy stubble and eager, hazel eyes. He still bit his nails, still wore the same pair of steel-toed boots, still wanted desperately to please her—to be with her. He still loved her.

"Where to, Jeeves?" Jarvis asked in a hokey British accent.

"I'm hungry," Abby pouted. "Feed me."

"It's half past eleven. Are you in the mood for breakfast or lunch?"

"You have to ask?"

They both smiled as Jarvis took a left onto Seven Mile. He steered them toward JoJo's, a dingy, hole-in-the-wall diner, where they'd shared many impromptu, wee-hour-of-the-morning breakfasts. Throughout their relationship, the diner was their special spot. After head-banging parties on Friday nights or on slow-paced Sunday afternoons, they would go there to cuddle, order platefuls of greasy food, escape the world, and relish each other's company.

JoJo's was open twenty-four hours a day, three hundred sixty-five days a year. While Jarvis and Abby were together, they made a point of eating there at least once a week. Many poignant memories were made sitting across from each other in that restaurant. In fact, it was there, in a small, tattered booth, where they shared their first kiss. It was there that Jarvis professed, for the first time, that he loved her...where they'd fantasized for hours about their future together...where Jarvis proposed. It was also where Abby announced she was moving to Chicago. And where Abby, eventually, returned the ring, and they broke up.

The diner's owner, Jonathan Joseph, Jr., was a squat black man with beady eyes and a bright smile. Dressed in his usual garb—an old, tight, white T-shirt stained with sweat and splattered with grease—Jo was almost always at the diner, grilling or cleaning or ringing up customers. No matter how busy the place got, though, he made sure that Abby and Jarvis were tucked away in their private booth in the back.

Jo was like a father to Jarvis, whose biological father had died years earlier after battling sickle-cell anemia. Jarvis and Jo shared a dynamic that Abby admired.

The first time Jarvis pulled up to Jo's dilapidated diner with Abby, she was reluctant, to say the least, about eating there. The neon sign, flickering against the dark sky read, "J JO'S." The first "O," Abby was told, had burned out years before. In her opinion, the patrons, mostly older black men, with gold teeth and leering eyes, were only slightly more disturbing than the coffee-stained tables and sticky chairs.

"Let's just go to Denny's," Abby pleaded, sticking closely to Jarvis.

"What?" he asked, oblivious to her discomfort. "Why? I'm telling you, the food here is the best."

"Jarvis!" A big voice boomed.

Abby started.

"What're you doing here, Man?"

"I wanted to introduce you to my girl and let her taste some of the best cooking on this side of Detroit."

"Your girl?" Jo asked with one eyebrow raised.

Jarvis stepped back and revealed a timid Abby. Jo looked her up and down approvingly. "Does your girl have a name?"

"Abigail," Jarvis offered.

"Abby," she corrected and extended her hand.

"It talks!" Jo exclaimed.

Jarvis laughed. "Don't let her fool you," he said in a mock whisper. "She's not as innocent as she looks."

"No?" Jo asked, still holding Abby's gaze.

"And let me tell you, she can put away some food."

"You know my motto," Jo said, reaching behind the counter and producing two menus. "If you can eat it, I can cook it. Go on back there." He handed Jarvis the menus. "Pick out anything you want, anything at all. It's on the house."

Jarvis grabbed Abby's hand and all but dragged her to the last booth in the diner.

The food, Abby had to admit, was delicious. Once she got past the restaurant's shabby appearance and somewhat daunting customers, she loosened up. Between the two of them, she and Jarvis ordered enough food for five people.

"I want you to try everything," Jarvis said excitedly. "There's nothing you won't like."

He was right. The French toast and omelet she ordered were the best she'd ever tasted. The bacon was nice and crisp, the hash browns perfectly salted, and the waffles golden and buttery.

By the time all the plates had been cleared away and Jo had poured them each a cup of coffee, Abby thought she was going to roll out of her seat. "I'll never eat again," she groaned and rubbed her distended belly.

"That's what all the first-timers say," Jo said, patting her shoulder. "But the way you cleaned up in here today tells me you'll be back." And she did come back.

"Here we are," Jarvis announced, pulling into the diner's small, deserted parking lot.

"It's been so long," Abby said mostly to herself. Jarvis opened the passenger side door for her and held her hand as they made their way to the entrance.

"Well I'll be," a familiar voice boomed as soon as they stepped in. Abby smiled and looked up to see Jo behind the counter, his big belly peeking beneath his stained, white T-shirt. "I woke up this morning and said to myself, 'Jo Jr., something's special about today.' And it looks like I was right."

Abby walked over to the grill where Jo was standing, a greasy spatula in his hand, and she leaned over the counter and kissed his cheek. "Still looking good, Jo."

"Can't help it," he shrugged. "It's in the genes. I see you managed to drag Mopey out of his den of despair." He pointed at Jarvis. "You moved away and his bottom lip's been dragging on the floor ever since. He was scaring away my customers. Then out of nowhere, he disappeared—forgot how to use a phone."

"Hey, how's it going, Jo?" Jarvis asked.

"I can't complain," he answered. "It's good to see you. I've been calling your ma every other week trying to hunt you down. Why's it been so long since you stopped by to see your dear old uncle Jo?"

Jarvis shrugged. "I been busy working."

Jo nodded. "I've heard of worse things a man can do with his time. How's the cello thing going?" Jo asked, turning his attention back to Abby.

"Good," she smiled. "I just released my third album."

"So Jo," Jarvis interrupted. "We gonna stand around all day and shoot the breeze, or are you gonna feed us?"

Abby grinned. "We're starving."

"Yeah, yeah. What else is new? Go on back there," he said, gesturing toward their booth. "I'll be there after I finish this ticket."

They ordered the usual, which was everything on the breakfast menu, minus the oatmeal and prunes—which wasn't something Abby had planned to let herself do. She'd become much more health conscious over the last year. Her manager had warned her from the beginning that the right look, the right image, was just as important as talent. Nobody wanted to see a fat cellist. Classical music was about elegance and refinement. To let herself balloon into a two-hundred-pound boar would quickly end her short, lucrative stretch as a solo artist.

Her weight wasn't something she'd ever paid much attention to. She'd never been heavy even though she was a self-proclaimed couch potato who didn't watch what she ate. "Life's too short," she'd say after polishing off her third slice of pizza.

Abby's mother had been the same way in her youth, but when she hit forty, all those years of careless eating manifested itself on her hips. These days, she was pushing a size eighteen.

Following her manager's advice, now Abby usually looked for the lowest calorie meal a restaurant had to offer and then asked that no fat, butter, salt, or oil be used in its preparation. But this wasn't just any restaurant with any cook. This was JoJo's, and after her first titillating bite of sugary French toast, with a hint of cinnamon, she knew pretenses were pointless.

"You look like you're in heaven," Jarvis said, as they waited for their second round of grub.

She tilted her head, reached across the table, and stroked his fingers. "I am."

"What's better?" he asked. "The company or the food."

"The food," she answered without missing a beat.

He laughed. "I should've known." His eyes were sparkling. "Nobody comes between you and a meal."

She smiled, stunned by how much she'd missed him. Gently, she tugged his hand.

Knowingly, he got up and joined her on the other side of the booth. Abby gazed at him adoringly.

"Don't look at me like that," he ordered gently. His breath tickled her forehead. "You're making me fall in love with you all over again."

"Had you ever really stopped?" she whispered.

His only response was a tender kiss. Her face was satin soft, his hands firm and sure. Their lips fit together, their breathing fell into sync, and they were swept away. This was familiar. This was home.

She forgot why she gave up—why she left this man who loved her so much, why she skipped out on her chance to live happily ever after.

Their breakfast plates scraped the Formica table with a loud clatter. They both jumped. Jo was standing over them, his ample stomach jiggling from stifled laughter. "No, please!" he said with a smirk. "Don't pry yourselves apart on my account."

Heat rushed to Abby's face and neck as she blushed to a peculiar shade of pink.

Jarvis cleared his throat. "Sorry," he murmured.

"Don't be," Jo said, slapping Jarvis's shoulder. "It's good to see you kids back together."

Abby smiled sheepishly, unable to meet Jo's eyes.

"So," Jo said, trying to fill the awkward silence. "You want to make this order to go?"

Jarvis looked at Abby, who peeked up at Jo and nodded.

Less than an hour later, they were in a hotel room making love.

While away, Abby had still yearned for his kisses, his touch—though she wouldn't admit it. With other ex-boyfriends, once the relationship ended, it was over for good. She refused to turn into one of those couples who broke up and got back together every other month. But with Jarvis, it was different. Despite their opposing lifestyles, their rocky history, and their penchant for mini-drama, she found herself drawn to him again, even if just for a short while.

In the moment, wracked with ecstasy and blinded by lust, he was much more than her ex-fiancé. He was her muse, the unequivocal love of her life. Inspiration and determination were not her motivators. They weren't real enough. They couldn't keep her happy. It was the memory of his face and the echo of his voice that kept her content.

They spent the afternoon and most of the evening talking, spooning, and sleeping. It was almost midnight when Abby rolled over and looked at the clock. "We should get you back to your mom's house," she said groggily.

"We don't have to." He stroked her hair. "I can stay the night."

Abby snorted. "I don't think so."

"Why not?" he asked, his hurt audible.

"Because." She sat up and searched the tousled bedcovers for her brassiere, desperate not to meet his demanding gaze.

"Abs," he said, taking hold of her dainty wrist. "What're we doing?"

"Once I find my bra, I can get dressed, and we'll take you home."

"You know that's not what I mean."

"How can you tell me what I know?" she asked haughtily. The question, even to her own ears, sounded childish. But she split hairs when she felt cornered.

"What's going on between us?" he revised the question. "Every time I see you, we end up at my sister's house or your parents' house or a hotel room doing...well, doing what we ended up doing today."

"And that's a problem for you?"

"It might be."

"Fine," she said, snatching her now wrinkled pair of designer jeans from the lampshade where they had landed in her and Jarvis's whirlwind of frenzied excitement.

"Abby, please," Jarvis begged. The day had been perfect and he didn't want her to ruin it with a tantrum. "I'm just asking you to define our relationship."

"It is what it is," she answered brusquely. "Why do we always have to define everything?"

"Because I need to understand how you can love me one minute and be done with me the next?"

Abby gave up searching for her bra and hugged one of the down pillows to her bare chest. She knew exactly what he was talking about, but she didn't know how to answer him. There were moments when all she wanted was Jarvis. She didn't have to sleep with him or have him hold her—all she needed was to hear his voice, and somehow, she was reassured that all was well. But when she saw him and spent time with him, she was reminded all over again why she left him in the first place—why the negatives so outweighed the positives.

By then, it was usually too late. More likely than not, she was stuck watching him slobber as he slept or listening to him tell one dumb, infantile joke after another. And those things that lured her to him, those attributes she had, mere hours earlier, found irresistible, irritated her to no end.

His tousled hair no longer seemed ruggedly handsome, but boyishly unkempt. His soft lips, once a vision of pillowy perfection, appeared dry and ordinary. And his chunky wool sweater with the hole in the collar that he'd worn faithfully every winter for the past four years was no longer endearingly predictable; it was pathetic and just plain cheap.

Then she thought back to her life in Chicago—her nascent career, adroit friends and brand-new home. She wanted him to be part of it all, but he didn't fit.

They came from almost identical backgrounds. They grew up middle class, both of them the younger of two siblings, both of them dreamers eager to escape the ennui of their ordinary existence. The only difference was that Jarvis opted to wait for opportunity to find him, while Abby went looking for it with brio.

Jarvis had goals and the intellect and raw talent to achieve them. He also had the laziness of a newborn puppy. His apathy is what fed his mediocrity and for Abby, it was infuriating.

She'd explained that to him a hundred times in as many different ways. And each time he'd nod, his eyes misty, and plead for her patience, which she granted without fail. Then they'd set to work, mapping out game plans, researching schools, and comparing contacts. At times, his vigor was enough to banish her doubts.

But the excitement was always short-lived. One by one, he'd drop his classes or he'd quit a series of jobs. He'd bounce around aimlessly until his blazing passion fizzled to a glint and he was back exactly where he started, working part-time and living with his mom.

"Abs, talk to me." Jarvis yanked her from her thoughts.

She slipped her cashmere sweater over her head and sat down on the edge of the bed. "There's nothing to talk about."

Jarvis got up, a sheet wrapped around his waist, and sat down next to her. "Abby, we can't keep doing this."

"Doing what?" She sounded bored.

"This!" He waved his arms around the opulent room. "Spending ten months apart without a phone call, without so much as a letter, but acting like nothing's changed when you decide to visit. I'm tired of wondering if and when I'll see you again."

"Why are you making such a big deal out of this? I'm having fun, aren't you?"

"No. Being at your disposal is not fun." He took her hand. "You know I love you."

She opened her mouth to ask how he could claim to know what she knows, but, as if reading her mind, he added, "and if you don't already know it, I'm telling you now that I do."

She bit the inside of her cheek.

"We were supposed to get married—start a family. I still want that. What happened to all of our plans?"

"A lot." She pulled her hand away. "And if my memory serves me correctly, most of it was your fault."

"Every complaint, every problem you had with me, I fixed. I've changed, Abby."

"Yeah, well, so have I. Sometimes things happen and the timing's just off."

Jarvis shook his head. "The timing is only off if you've fallen out of love with me."

She turned to him, prepared to shatter him with the truth. She was ready to tell him that she didn't want to be with him anymore. She was ready to tell him she was happier—safer—on her own. But when her eyes met his, the words stuck in her throat like viscous molasses. She searched his face for an imperfection—something that would repulse her, something that would trick her into hating the man sitting beside her. But there was nothing. Despite everything, he still meant something to her.

The edges of his lips curled upward into a faint smile. He knew she couldn't do it.

"What changes have you made?" she asked, switching the subject.

"I'm working and saving. I spend less time out. I'm paying Dawn rent—being more responsible."

"Jarvis, you're thirty and you live with your sister and her husband and their two kids. You sleep on a couch in the den. And spending your free time in front of the TV playing Tekken isn't any better than going to a bar or getting drunk at a lame house party."

She examined him closely. His face had grown hard and his stare flinty at her verbal assault. He was angry, but she needed to clear the air—to let him know, once again, why a real relationship between the two of them would never work.

"As for your job," she scoffed. "You load boxes onto the back of a truck. That's not the type of gainful employment I had in mind."

"I'm sorry," he seethed. "We can't all be hotshot musicians."

"See!" she shrieked, her finger aimed at his clenched jaw. "That's another thing. You can't accept the fact that I have a successful career without throwing it in my face every time I mention your latest dead-end job."

Jarvis shook his head. He'd made the mistake of forgetting how callous she could be. Why was he such a glutton for punishment? She wasn't the same Abby he fell deeply in love with six years ago. He knew that. He'd watched her adoring innocence morph into measured sophistication. She'd rid herself of detectable blemishes, polishing and refining one indiscernible layer after another, determined to make herself otherworldly.

And she was. She was truly spectacular—an inscrutable pinnacle of amazing. But the more she fine-tuned her veneer, the more heartlessly aloof she became. He caught glimpses of the old Abby, but they were brief and overshadowed by the hard, arrogant woman she'd constructed to take her place.

"I get it," he muttered.

Abby's face softened. "You're a good man, Jay. But look at our lives. We're headed in opposite directions."

"So I'm a good man; I'm just not good enough for you. Is that it?"

"I love you and I love the time we spend together, but butterflies in my stomach and a few laughs isn't enough to build a family on. I don't want to support my husband and I don't want to be married to a guy whose idea of a romantic evening involves a three-foot sub from Tubby's, a beer bong, and the season finale of The Sopranos. But this," she patted the mattress and looked around the room, "this is what works best for us."

Jarvis cracked his knuckles and stared blankly at the tasteful gold and taupe wallpaper in front of him. "I think you're right." He leaned forward and snatched his boxers, which were sitting on the floor a few feet away.

Abby let out an involuntary sigh of relief. "It's not that late." She grabbed his forearm. She tried to tug him toward the bed. "Let's make up."

He snatched his arm away, shaming her with the repugnance in his eyes. "I mean, I think you're right. It's time for me to go."

They got dressed and checked out of the hotel in silence. Abby stole worried glances at Jarvis with his stiff posture and flared nostrils.

She took a mental inventory of their conversation. She hadn't meant to be so insensitive—so uncouthly superior. But the words had spilled out of her mouth before she'd really analyzed their sting—their potential impact.

He walked a few paces in front of her, taking long, angry strides. His fists were shoved into his pockets. He didn't unlock and open her car door like he'd done earlier. He let himself in first, started the car, fastened his seat belt, and then pushed the automatic unlock button. Before she could sit down and close the door, he revved the gas and sped out of the parking lot. The sudden force threw Abby against her seat.

"Just because you're mad at me doesn't mean you need to take it out on the car."

"Be quiet," he ordered.

"Excuse me? Who do you thi—"

"Shut up!" he shouted. His voice bounced off the windows and echoed within the small space.

Abby looked at him. His eyes were empty and disconnected. Her outrage instantly turned to fear.

Jarvis veered sharply onto the highway ramp. The back tires spun out on the icy road with a loud screech.

"Whoa, okay." Abby scrambled for her seat belt. "You're scaring me."

He didn't respond.

She watched the speedometer rise from fifty miles per hour to seventy miles per hour to ninety miles per hour. Her heart palpitated as she tightly gripped the center console. "Jarvis," she rasped, her knuckles white, "this is crazy."

"You push too hard," he said, his voice trembling. "You just push too hard."

A mixture of snow and mud from the unplowed highway flew through the air and splashed against the windshield, obstructing their view. Jarvis flipped on the wipers but continued to weave in and out of traffic at dangerous speeds. "You're a nasty person, you know that?"

"I know," she managed between nervous pants. "I…I…I shouldn't have…I shouldn't have said…you know, the things I said and I'm sorry. I am. I'm really truly sorry."

"You're really, truly sorry, huh?" His tone was venomous.

"Yes. I am. I swear I am, but please let's talk about it. We can work it out, but not like this. Slow down," she whimpered her plea. "You're scaring me."

The scenery outside was nothing more than bleeding streaks of red, yellow, and green. She held her breath as Jarvis nearly clipped the front of a semi-truck in order to pass a slow car.

"What's the matter?" he goaded nastily. "You can toy with other people's lives, other people's emotions, but you can't take it when someone does it to you?"

"Stop the car!" hysterically, Abby yelled. "Stop the car, now! I want to get out!" Tears streamed down her face.

He was driving so fast that the steering wheel shook.

"But I like this," he mocked. "I like this with you. This is what works best for us. Don't you agree?"

"Please," she begged, her sob guttural. "Please stop."

He only sneered.

And then it happened. A gray minivan pulled into their lane. Jarvis slammed on the brakes, but the car hydroplaned and spun out of control.

Abby screamed and pressed her back against the seat. She watched, horrified, as Jarvis hastily jerked the wheel to the left and tried to regain control of the car. His face was masked in terror.

A strong force threw Abby's body sideways. Her temple slammed against the passenger side window. The blow dazed her and her ears rang. They'd spun across the highway into oncoming traffic.

An SUV, unable to stop, slammed into the car, forcing it to roll onto its driver's side. Disoriented and trembling, Abby wiped the blood from her face and searched desperately for something to hold on to. Broken glass and shards of metal cut her neck and hands.

Jarvis had stopped screaming after the second hit, but she was too scared to look at him—to see if he was okay. She squeezed her eyes shut and waited for the car to stop spinning. The sound of metal scraping concrete was deafening.

Slowly, the car came to a halt. Abby pried her eyes open and tried to blink away the vertigo. In the distance she heard a foghorn. She shook her head and glanced to her left. Jarvis's body was slumped over the steering wheel. The foghorn in the background grew louder and more persistent.

"Jarvis?" Abby croaked. She reached out her lacerated hand and shook him. "Jarvis?"

He groaned.

The foghorn grew even louder.

She heard sirens in the distance. She tried to unfasten her seat belt, but the car, which was in a precarious position, moaned and threatened to roll onto its roof.

Jarvis stirred.

"Don't move," Abby pleaded.

He lifted his head. His nose was bent off center and swollen. "Abby, I—," he began. Suddenly his eyes grew wide and filled with tears. "Oh, God," he whispered.

Abby followed his gaze out the smashed windshield. Her own eyes filled with tears. Coming toward them was a jackknifed eighteen wheeler. The driver was blowing his horn—the foghorn—but they couldn't get out of the way.

The death sentence, cruel and demanding, rapidly barreled down on them. Jarvis screamed a bloodcurdling cry for help. Frantically, he clawed at his door, but it was pinned against the highway's pavement.

Abby sat still, her eyes glued on the gruesome sight before her. Everything fell quiet as her last few seconds moved in slow motion.

She looked at Jarvis. Tears and blood streaked down his face.

She looked at her designer jeans and her cashmere sweater, the beautiful ruby bracelet clinging to her wrist, and her thousand-dollar Fendi clutch.

"It's all relative," she whispered and looked up just in time to see the massive grill of the truck plow into them.

2. *Abby*

"Good morning, Abby. I'm Dr. Rosenbaum. You can call me Paul if you'd like." I turn my head slowly, gingerly to the left. All I can do is blink. My body has been reduced to a raw, undulating blister. The slightest move is excruciating.

"I'm Dennis," my dad says, as he stands and shakes Dr. Rosenbaum's hand. "This is my wife, April."

"Let's have a seat, shall we?" Dr. Rosenbaum retrieves a small, black stool by the window. My parents scoot their chairs around the foot of my bed. The doctor flips open the chart he's holding and sighs.

"Be frank with us," Dad says. "We haven't been able to get any real answers since she's been here. We need to know what's going on."

"Is she paralyzed?" Mom blurts. No doubt the idea has been plaguing her for a while. I want to ask them why they're talking about me like I'm not in the room, like I'm dead, but I can't open my mouth. My brain can't communicate with my muscles and my strength is gone. I'm straddling a thin line between sleep and consciousness and it's all I can do to keep my mind from swimming and my eyelids from drooping.

"No, she's not paralyzed," Dr. Rosenbaum assures them. "But she's got a long path to recovery."

"How bad is it?" Dad asks.

"Abby has a fractured cheekbone, a broken jaw, two broken ribs, and her right knee has been shattered."

I listen closely, silently, my heart racing.

"But what concerns me the most are the extensive burns she's sustained. As I'm sure you've already seen, she's suffered second and third degree burns to her face, neck, and torso."

My dad sits back, one hand over his mouth, both eyebrows furrowed. "What type of long-term disabilities are we talking about?" Dad asks.

"It's too early to say. There's going to be quite a bit of physical therapy involved, and multiple surgeries will be required."

"How could this happen?" Mom asks with a sob. "How could this happen to my baby?"

My dad, at a loss for words, shakes his head. A single tear rolls down his cheek. I close my eyes, dizzy from how quickly my life has changed.

"Listen," Dr. Rosenbaum says. He slides off his glasses. "I've been a doctor for over twenty years now, and if there's one thing I've learned, it's that from a physiological standpoint, the human body is resilient. Bones fuse back together; skin cells multiply. Given enough time, the body will heal itself. Often with burn victims the most debilitating scars are emotional."

"Abby's always been a fighter," Mom says. "She'll pull through the surgeries and the therapy and be back to normal in no time."

"Skin grafting will play a significant role," Dr. Rosenbaum says. "But…"

I open my eyes to see him massaging the bridge of his nose. "Mr. and Mrs. Walker, I need you to have realistic expectations. Even with the most advanced surgical procedures and aggressive physical therapy, your daughter is never going to look the way she used to. The damage is too extensive."

"How can you say that?" my mom asks. "It's been two days. You don't know Abby." Her eyes are brimming with tears. "She's one of the strongest people I know. How many mothers can say that about their children?"

Dr. Rosenbaum nods. "We have a long road ahead of us. In the meantime, the most important thing on everyone's list should be Abby's comfort. We have her on a morphine drip. She shouldn't be feeling any pain." He puts his glasses back on.

Dr. Rosenbaum checks the machines that are beeping and chugging and clicking around me. He marks his observations on my chart.

"Are you in pain?" he asks me. "Blink once for no and twice for yes." I want to tell him that my flesh stings. I want him to know that my body is pulsating, that the heat is trapped underneath my skin and I'm still burning. That I feel exposed and infected, but I can't open my mouth. I blink once.

Dr. Rosenbaum leaves and I watch my parents hold each other and cry at the foot of my bed.

I spend the next few weeks trapped; slipping in and out of a dismal fog. There is always someone in the room when I open my eyes—Dad, Mom, nurses, doctors. They're afraid to leave me alone. They know—like I know—that everything in me wants to shut down.

I don't have the will to live, much less the desire. Why would I? My life as I knew it, as I'd grown to love it, will never, ever be the same. No matter how adept my specialists or skilled my surgeons, no matter how rigorous my physical therapy or extensive the surgeries, the woman I was before I got into that car with Jarvis is gone forever.

My entire reputation, everything I was and everything I'd worked so hard to gain was built around my ability to look beautiful behind a cello. People are pulled in, first, by what they see. Everything else is secondary. Me, seated center stage in a sparkling gown with my hair elegantly fashioned and my skin smooth and dewy is what captured the attention of my audiences, and my flawless performances is what kept them coming back for more.

But who's going to shell out three hundred dollars to watch a singed monstrosity bow music on a worn cello? Some faithful fans might come for a while out of pity, others purely out of curiosity, but neither motivation appeals to me.

The last thing I want is pity. I spent my childhood ensconced in it. Whether it was forced on me by adults who considered me hopelessly inferior to my sister or whether I was drowning in a pool of it that I'd conjured up for myself; I've experienced enough pity for two lifetimes.

And the only thing I want less than pity is to be exploited, which is almost a certainty given my manager who can, and will, spin any debacle into a moneymaking scheme.

"There's no such thing as bad publicity!" hangs on a plaque above his desk in his downtown office. In no time, he'd take my near-death experience and use it to pack one concert hall after the next. People would bring their kids and their cameras; they'd pay double, even triple the price to see Abby Walker: the Melted, One-Woman Wonder. And just like that, I'd become a freak show, a circus act for high society.

I'd rather die. I'd rather be remembered for who I was and what I could have been than live out the rest of my days alone, deformed, and half-human.

But every time I resolve within myself that the life I have waiting for me is a fate worse than death, my chest tightens, and my soul chills. What happens after I take my last breath? Where do I go? Will I be reincarnated, brought back as someone or something else? Will I fall asleep and rest peacefully for all eternity? Is heaven how I've seen it depicted in movies, with white-robed harpists, cotton clouds, impossibly blue skies and pearly gates? And will those gates open for me or will I die only to enter a worse kind of hell than I'd left on earth?

It's my own version of Russian Roulette and as convinced as I am that I want to die, the uncertainty of what comes after death paralyzes me. I'm too terrified to pull the trigger, so I lie still and wait for Fate or Destiny or some other Higher Power to make the decision for me.

In the meantime, Mom spends hours holding my hand and talking about nothing—friends, magazine articles, new recipes. She says things like, "The next time you come to visit, I want to take you to this market your dad and I found off Lahser," and "I've been thinking of reupholstering the couches in the family room. You'll have to help me pick out the fabric when you feel up to it." But I can hear the worry in her voice—the doubt.

Even in my half-lucid state, Mom's worry startles me. She's a strong woman—stubborn and defiant. She's had to be. She was thrust into adulthood at an early age.

Mom and Dad had nothing when they went down to Baton Rouge's city hall to get a marriage license—no money, nowhere to live, no plan. They were a couple of quixotic eighteen year olds with an endless reserve of optimism—and a baby already on the way.

But an unwed, pregnant teenager was more than Mom's parents were prepared to handle. It wasn't so much the pregnant part that sent them over the edge. A child, after all, was a miracle from God. They figured that with a little careful planning they could send Mom away for a while, give the baby up for adoption, and no one would have been the wiser.

The proverbial straw that broke the camel's back, however, rested in my grandparents' belief that life—the rules of attraction, social order, the timeline of love—was etched in stone and my mom's belief that her happiness relied on everything her parents diametrically opposed.

If they said the sky was blue, Mom would say it was purple, and she couldn't be content just pretending that it was purple, she had to prove it. So when her parents said that races shouldn't mix, she, naturally, went out and found my father.

It's a beautiful thing when someone as passionate as my mom takes all of her energy and dedicates it to such a deserving source as my dad. They complemented each other. He gave her focus and drive and she showed him a world beyond the pages in his books. But interracial relationships weren't done in Louisiana—not in her neighborhood, not in her home, not in her family.

Choosing a life with him, she quickly found out, was an even bigger leap into the unknown than she'd expected. It would signal the unfortunate, painful end to a significant chapter in her life.

She was disowned. After all she'd put them through, marrying a black man was just too much insult added to what turned out to be irreparable injury.

So Mom and Dad moved to Detroit where my dad had family. There he'd have a chance to get a good paying factory job, and the opportunity to continue his education.

It was an especially hard time for them. They lived in Dad's uncle's basement. My dad had to be at his first job, mopping hospital floors, at five in the morning; then he was off to class by ten; and if he was lucky, he could stop home for a quick dinner before he had to be at the plastics factory in Novi to work an eight-hour, sometimes ten-hour, shift. He'd get home by one in the morning and be up by five to do it all over again.

Then, one sweltering day in May, Valerie was born. "She was the picture-perfect birth," Mom loved to brag. "I went into the hospital and three hours later there was little Val with a full head of gorgeous hair. The nurses said it was one of the easiest deliveries they'd ever seen."

Of course it was, and ever since, my parents convinced themselves that the sun rose and set by Valerie's smile. Typically, or so I thought, the older sibling was the one used as an example—the one who was expected to rise to any occasion—and the younger sibling was the baby, the one who was loved and coddled superfluously.

Not in my family.

I never had a chance. I was doomed from the moment my mom went into labor—from the moment I refused to nose-dive out of her like dear, precious Val.

"Abigail, on the other hand," Mom usually went on, "was impossible. I nearly died giving birth to her. First she got herself wrapped around the umbilical cord and then she was breach. It was such a struggle. Finally, I'd lost so much blood they decided to give me a cesarean. I must've been in labor for twenty straight hours. When I woke up after surgery, there she was—massive with those shifty little eyes. What were you, Honey, nine pounds?"

At that point everyone would gasp.

"You couldn't tell it now, but Abby was a big newborn. At four weeks, she looked like she was four months and all she wanted to do was eat."

I've always hated those stories, the way she makes it sound like I'd spent my every waking minute in her stomach strategically planning ways to thwart any doctor's attempt to pull me out. Who knows, maybe I did. Maybe I knew that I'd just be crashing a perfect family of three—that all the good roles were taken and that it would be safer to barricade myself in her womb.

They'd come a long way since my dad's floor-mopping days. After Mom had Val, Dad landed a scholarship and started attending college full time. They applied for married student housing, which provided daycare, so Mom was able to secure a job close to campus. They were saving for their own home; Dad had only two more semesters of school left; and even though money was tight, the future looked promising.

In two short years, they'd managed to achieve a precise, delicate balance for their lives, and I, of course, was the one who came tumbling out, all nine pounds of me, and tipped the scales.

3. Jarvis

"Son, I don't have all day," Mr. Kopeky says. He slides a ten-dollar bill across the counter. I look down at it and then back up at the ever-growing line in front of the register. Mr. Kopeky shoves the newspaper he's carrying under his arm and chews on his toothpick.

"Hey, Jo!" yells one of the patrons in line. "What's the deal here? This moron you got behind the counter is going to make me late for work."

Mr. Kopeky's expression softens. "I'll tell you what," he says. "Just keep the change."

I feel Jo's hand grip my shoulder.

"You okay?" he asks.

I nod. "Yeah, I'm fine."

"Maybe you oughta take a break."

"Yeah, maybe." I gladly relinquish my place behind the register.

"Take it easy, Jarvis, and tell your mom I said hi," Mr. Kopeky calls to my retreating back.

I don't answer.

I roll my way to the storage room, prop open the back door, and light a cigarette. I haven't smoked in years—since I met Abby. I'd started as a teenager, typical peer pressure, and the habit stuck with me into my adult years. But Abby didn't like smokers.

"Anyone who smokes is either weak or stupid," she informed me over a burger and fries. We'd only just met. My eleven-year addiction to nicotine hadn't yet been revealed and after that comment, it wasn't going to be.

I ate slowly, desperate to offset my urge to smoke, which would inevitably strike the instant I swallowed my last bite of food. Ordinarily I wouldn't have cared. My general philosophy when it came to women was that there wasn't one worth changing for. Normally, in that situation, the scenario would have played out something like this:

I would have said something like, "Weak or stupid, huh?"

And she would've said, "Yes."

And then, as I dug into my pocket for my half empty pack of Camels, I would've asked, "Which one's worse, weak or stupid?"

And she'd have looked at me quizzically with a hint of a grin, tilted her head to the side, and shrugged. "Stupid, I guess."

And I'd have laughed and said, "That's good."

And of course she would've asked, "Why?"

And I'd lay my cigarettes on the table so she could see them and say something charming like, "Because you already know I'm smart. I'm here with you." Then to seal the deal, I'd look into her eyes sincerely, force a smile and say, "We all have our weaknesses." And in no time, she'd be apologizing profusely for her coarse snap judgment and offer me a light.

Between the human ego's constant need for stroking and the world's permanent shortage of kindness, the right words, I'd discovered early on, peppered with a few compliments and a savvy smile, could win anyone over.

I didn't want to play games with Abby, though. I didn't want to manipulate her or try to trick her into conforming to my set of rules. As unmoving as it sounds, she was different from any woman I'd met in Detroit, and I'd lived in the city my entire life.

I still remember the first time I laid eyes on her.

It was raining outside. My friend Nick and I were stuck at Reed's Music Shop waiting for his sister to finish her piano lessons. I'd been bringing them every Saturday for almost three months—ever since Nick's rusty, '86 Dodge van broke down on the Lodge Freeway and he never bothered to go back and get it. Nick's mom gave me ten bucks, which was incentive enough for me to drag myself out of bed at nine o'clock in the morning because I spent every day, all day, strapped for cash.

But that day, as I pried my sweaty rear end off of a black, plastic piano bench, I was seriously debating whether or not ten measly dollars was worth the hassle. It was ninety-something degrees outside and because of the monsoon-like rainstorm, the air was heavy and humid. It clung to my skin and literally made it hard to breathe.

The guy behind the counter kept insisting the air conditioner was broken, but I wasn't so sure because every time he opened the door to his square, glass office in the corner of the store, a cool rush of air hit my back.

Nick didn't seem to mind. He was across the room fiddling with some dumb guitar he'd had on layaway since layaway was invented.

I bid my time weighing my options. There was no point in going back home. The lesson was only an hour, I reasoned, looking down at my watch. I had forty minutes to wait. What could I do in forty minutes? I could go find an air-conditioned building like a restaurant and hang out there. The only problem was that I'd probably have to buy something if I wanted to lounge around and I only had ten dollars, which had to go toward gas. I could walk to the corner drugstore and buy something cold to drink except it was pouring outside. I looked over at Nick and down at my watch again. Thirty-eight minutes left. I wiped the sweat from my forehead onto my sleeve. Never again, I swore silently.

The bells hanging from the top of the shop's glass door chimed loudly as the most attractive woman I'd ever seen walked in. She was slender with a nice figure—petite and delicate. She was wearing a white halter top that tied behind her neck, leaving much of her smooth, caramel back exposed. Her silky, pastel blue skirt fell to the middle of her calves. It was speckled with wet spots from the rain. Easily, she leaned the big case she was carrying against the wall and then swept her hair, which was clinging to her face and neck in damp curls, into a clip.

"Abby!" the man behind the counter bellowed warmly.

"Si!" she bellowed back.

I looked at him, shocked, as he left his post, walked to the front of the store, and gave her a hug. The guy hadn't said two words to anyone, much less cracked a smile in the twenty-plus minutes I'd been there.

"I didn't see your name in the book. You have a lesson scheduled for today?"

"No, I came to pick up my check and to see if Kat has time to help me with a piece I'm trying finish."

"She's not here," Si said disappointedly. "Give me a minute to check the schedule. I think she's got a student at noon."

"Great." He turned to go to his office. "Hey, Si, what's with the heat?" she asked, fanning herself.

"You hot?"

She nodded.

"No problem, I'll turn the air on." I knew it! "You can wait in my office, if you want, it's cool in there."

She declined. "I want to look at some of your student violins for my cousin."

"Take a look around," he prompted. "I'll see if I have anything special stashed away in the back."

I watched her—this "Abby"—as she perused the cases of instruments, taking time to consider each violin. I put my lines together and waited anxiously for her to make her way down to my end of the shop.

"Hey," I said when she was just a few feet away.

She looked up and nodded. "Hi."

"I didn't mean to overhear, but you know how sometimes something just catches your ear."

She blinked at me, her brow arched.

My palms started to sweat despite the sudden drop in temperature thanks to Si's "broken" air conditioner. "What am I trying to say?" I asked aloud.

"I don't know," she admitted. "What are you trying to say?"

"I just, you know, I thought I heard the guy say that you give lessons or whatever and I've always been kind of interested in taking violin lessons."

Her eyes narrowed. "You?" She smirked.

"What, you don't think it's a good idea?"

"No, no, it's just—well, how old are you?"

"Twenty-four."

She bit her lip. "Don't you think it's a little late to try to learn an instrument?"

"How old are you?" I asked.

"Twenty-three."

"You play, don't you?"

"Yeah, but it's different. I've been playing since I was a kid."

Si emerged from his office. "Good news. I talked to Kat and she said she'd be happy to work with you after her twelve o'clock and before her three o'clock. Does that work for you?"

"Two hours is more than enough time. Thanks, you're the best, Si."

He glowed from her praise.

"While you were back there hunting down Kat for me, I think I found you some new business."

"You did?" he asked, ignoring me completely.

"Our friend—," she paused and looked at me blankly.

"Jarvis," I offered.

She smiled and extended her hand. "I'm Abby, by the way."

"Nice to meet you." I gave her a firm handshake.

"Our friend Jarvis, here, might be interested in taking violin lessons."

Si eyed me doubtfully. "Is that right?" he asked dryly.

Abby smiled. "He's never played before, so Barb would probably be his best bet."

"Actually," I interjected a little too desperately, "I was hoping that you could give me lessons."

The perplexed look on her face quickly gave way to flattery. "Oh, um, I can't, I mean—," she stuttered, her face flushed.

Si rolled his eyes. "That's not possible," he said matter-of-factly.

"Why not?" I snipped, more than just a little tired of his antisocial, holier-than-thou routine.

"Because Abby doesn't play the violin. She plays the cello."

"Okay," I shrugged. "I'll take cello lessons."

"Have you ever played the cello?" Si asked.

"No."

"Then you'd be working with Kat."

"Why can't I have you?" I asked Abby.

She opened her mouth, but nothing came out. Her dark brown eyes softly bore into mine.

"Because," Si answered for her. "Abby is reserved for advanced cellists only."

"That's too bad," I said, still holding her gaze.

"It's a travesty," Si declared glibly. "I take it you're no longer interested."

"Sure I am. Sign me up."

He glared at me and then looked over at Abby who seemed to be stuck in a catatonic-like state. "I'll go get the paperwork," he relented.

"Does this mean I'll get the chance to see you again?" I asked.

"You shouldn't sign up for lessons if you aren't serious about learning how to play."

"Who said I'm not serious?"

"Nobody. It's just that Kat's got a lot going on right now. She gives lessons on the weekends for extra cash, but there are probably a hundred other things she'd rather be doing. So, you know, if you aren't serious..." she said again.

"I need you to fill this out." Si handed me a clipboard. I'll also need a photo I.D., and your deposit of two hundred dollars is due, in full, one week before your first lesson."

"Actually," I said, glancing at Abby, "I'm going to have to hold off on the whole lesson idea after all, maybe another time though."

Si sighed. "Isn't that a shock?"

"Jay, you ready, man?" Nick and his little sister were standing by the door.

"Looks like I have to go."

Abby smiled. "Yeah, looks that way."

"Maybe I'll see you around?" I asked, stalling for time.

"Yeah, maybe."

"I'll get back to you on those cello lessons," I said, making one last attempt to be friendly to Si. No dice.

"Yeah," he scoffed. "I'll be here...holding my breath."

It took me all of a few seconds to decide that I had to see her again and leaving it to chance was not an option. So, as soon as I dropped off Nick and his sister, I headed straight back to Reed's Music Shop.

"Look what the cat dragged in—again," Si announced the instant I walked through the door. "Change your mind about the lessons?"

"No."

"Why did I already know that? I must be psychic," he said to no one in particular.

"Is Abby here?"

"She's in the back."

"Can I see her?"

He shook his head. "Only paying customers are allowed in the practice rooms."

I dug into my pocket and pulled out the soggy ten-dollar bill Nick's mom had given me earlier that morning.

"What do you have for ten dollars?" I asked.

He looked around, amused. "Rosin," he finally offered.

"Okay, give me some of that." I slid the bill across the counter.

"What kind?"

"I don't know. It doesn't matter."

"Well, we carry over fifty different brands," he began slowly, determined to prolong my agony. "I always recommend darker rosins, but a novice, such as yourself, should be aware that they tend to—"

"Give me whatever Abby uses."

He retrieved a small round box from underneath the glass counter, tossed it into a small paper bag, and handed me seven cents. I stared at the nickel and two pennies resting in my palm. That was my gas money.

"You can't be serious," I said, peeking inside the bag, which suddenly seemed very empty. Without looking up, he tossed his thumb over his shoulder.

"She's in Room Four. Enjoy your rosin," he added smugly.

I inched down the long hallway, nine dollars and ninety-three cents poorer than when I first started out, but almost certain that it was worth it.

The corridor echoed with the muted sound of crooning instruments. For some reason I felt like I was trespassing, as though I didn't have a right to be standing there. Searching for someone who probably couldn't care less that I'd just made a forty-minute round trip to see her or that with nothing but hope egging me on, I'd blown all the money I had to get to a room where I knew she would be.

I realized, as I turned the corner, that I was out of my element. If I had any sense, I told myself, I would go home and forget this girl even existed. But I couldn't. I couldn't turn away. I couldn't pretend that she didn't intrigue me—that just being near her, just talking to her, hadn't somehow managed to validate my entire existence.

For that reason alone, I kept walking until I'd reached Room Four.

I watched her through the small Plexiglas square in the door. She was facing me, perched on a folding chair, her eyes closed, and a cello between her legs. Her forehead was wrinkled in concentration as if she was reading the notes in her mind. I stared, mesmerized by the passion I saw in the movement of her fingers, the way her body swayed from side to side, the thoughtful purse of her lips.

I couldn't remember the last time I'd been that passionate about anything. In truth, I didn't know if I'd ever been that passionate about anything.

For a brief moment, I second-guessed myself. What was I doing there? I looked down at the small, expensive bag of rosin—my idea of an endearing gesture that I hoped would be the ticket to a first date. It seemed brilliant only minutes earlier, but under stifling self-doubt it was an embarrassing token that someone as sophisticated as Abby would never appreciate.

The walls of the narrow hall seemed to close in on me and I turned, prepared to leave, when she looked up. An instant smile spread across her face, quelling my fears.

It was there, staring at each other through a small Plexiglas window, where our romance began.

On our very first date, she revealed her deep desire to pursue a music career in Chicago. The thought of losing her, even then, gnawed at my heart, and I secretly resolved to change her mind. I'd be so irresistible, so charming, that if the opportunity ever presented itself, she wouldn't want to go. She wouldn't want to do anything or be anywhere without me by her side. That was how I'd already felt about her.

But as if as she could hear my thoughts, she looked at me, her forehead puckered intensely. "Everything in my life comes second to my music," she warned. "I need you to be okay with that because if you're not, we're both wasting our time."

I gazed into her earnest eyes. Nobody wants to hear that they'll always be second best. But at least she was being up front. I could respect the fact that she had goals and ambition. If anything, her drive made her that much more appealing.

"Of course I'm okay with it," I said, sounding far more certain than I felt.

She grinned and slipped her fingers through mine. Again, her mere presence silenced all of my uncertainties.

Cello or no cello, Chicago or no Chicago, I'd made the right decision, because the truth was, I'd stumbled into something incredible. The truth was that being Abby's second passion would make me better than anything else I could've ever hoped to be.

4. Abby

" 'Stepan Arkadyevitch had learned easily at school, thanks to his excellent abilities, but he had been idle and mischievous, and therefore was one of the lowest in his class.' "

Just like Jarvis, I muse sleepily as I listen to my sister read aloud from *Anna Karenina*. I study her as her eyes dance mechanically across the pages of my favorite novel. She's visited faithfully every week, each time staying for several hours to read assorted literature, including the latest slew of get-well cards forwarded to my parents by my best friend, Hannah.

I don't know what to think of Val's presence. Is it concern or obligation that brings her back every week? My suspicion is that it's a little bit of both.

Most of the time she seems content with the gaping distance between us. We stay in our respective corners only emerging for annual family get-togethers where we smile benignly for distant relatives.

She lives with her husband and kids in suburban utopia and I live alone in the Windy City. Her days are filled with carpools and grocery lists; mine are packed with recordings and rehearsals. Her weekends involve soccer games and Sunday school; mine consist of shoe shopping and late brunches.

Simply put, we're opposites. Always have been.

My sister and I were born exactly two years and six days apart. She was right on time, gracing the world with her presence on her exact due date. While I, on the other hand, was a week late, turned upside down, and bent on strangling myself with the first rope-like object I could find. That, I think, should have been a big indication of things to come.

Genetics was only one of the many cruel ironies that separated me and Val. She inherited Mom's classic beauty. She got the green eyes and the loose, shiny ringlets, the small waist and slender thighs. I, on the other hand, got stuck with plain brown eyes and a Brillo pad for hair.

In addition to beauty, Val was endowed with an exuberant take-charge personality that often left me cast beneath her shadow, hidden by her many achievements.

I wanted to step outside of myself—to command the same kind of attention, the same kind of respect—but I was painfully shy. As sure as Val could be found running for class treasurer or waving her pompoms at the top of a human pyramid in front of the entire student body, I could be found alone in the library with my nose in a book.

People knew me, but they knew me as "Valerie Walker's Little Sister," a title that made me cringe. Still, as desperate as I was for my own identity, I was more terrified of emerging from my shell.

By the time I'd entered junior high, Val had moved on to high school, but not without leaving behind her indelible imprint. The glass cases in the hall housed her track trophies and swim metals. Her smiling face was displayed in mounted pictures of the choir, the yearbook committee, student council, and the Spanish club. And there wasn't a teacher who heard her name who didn't smile and feel obliged to share at least one fond memory of her.

The pressure to measure up to my sister bore down on me daily like a lead anvil. People, my parents included, viewed me with expectancy instead of acceptance. The question on all their minds was, "Will she turn out as well as her sister?" Which translates to: "Will she blossom into the same kind of beauty, will she earn the same high marks, excel at the same sports, attract the same kind of friends, adopt the same interests?"

Val had set the precedent and we all waited with bated breath to see if I could follow suit.

I couldn't.

The things that came naturally to Val didn't come naturally to me. I never made any of the sports teams that I mustered up enough guts to try out for. I couldn't win the good graces of the popular kids, no matter how many clubs I joined or how up-to-date my outfits were. And study as I might, my grades remained just a notch above mediocre.

By thirteen, I'd settled into the bleak realization that I was "the other sister," ordinary and plain, an invisible disappointment.

Oh, what I would've given for just a taste of what my sister experienced—the unbridled success, the adulation. I craved every inch of her existence, but above all, I coveted the proud twinkle in my parents' eyes when they looked at her. It seemed to say, "We love you most."

If ever I were to stumble upon something I was good at, something that would earn me that twinkle, I knew I would never let it go.

Little did I know that thing would be the cello.

I signed up for orchestra at the suggestion of the Girl's A Cappella Choir director, Mrs. Thompson, who regretfully informed me after auditions that I didn't make the cut.

Orchestra was not in my realm of thinking. My objectives were recognition and popularity, and in junior high, joining the band or orchestra was certain to catapult you as far away from both as possible. But I'd grown weary of rejection and the orchestra required no experience. They welcomed any and everyone, and I was at the bottom of my barrel of ideas on how to belong.

The love affair was instant and passionate. Like two destined soul mates who spot each other for the first time across a crowded room, the chemistry between the cello and me was automatic, the lust untamable.

The feel of it resting between my knobby knees, the sensation of the strings beneath my fingertips, the bend of my wrist as it directed my bow—there was no greater joy. There still isn't.

My hard, black cello case quickly became like a fifth limb. Rarely would I be seen without it. I toted it with me to class, to lunch, sometimes even to the bathroom. I ached for it when it was out of my sight. I was incomplete without it.

I excelled quickly, earning and retaining my first-chair position throughout my academic career and into my professional one.

For nearly two years, my gift went unnoticed. Though my skill developed rapidly, I think my family was convinced that my sudden love for the cello was merely a phase. It wasn't until my freshman year in high school when I became an all-state finalist that my parents started to take notice.

The next four years were a whirlwind of recitals, invitationals, competitions, scholarship winnings, private lessons, and state and national championships.

I'd finally done it. After years of searching in vain, I'd finally found my one thing. I'd finally earned the proud twinkle in my parents' eyes.

And Val hated it.

At first, her jealousy manifested itself in snide comments and nasty looks. It wasn't until Dad found Mom's scrapbook of my newspaper clippings neatly stashed at the bottom of our trash can that I realized just how deep her envy ran.

Even so, I made efforts to include her. For years she'd basked in the limelight and, while I hoped against hope that one day I'd know what it felt like, I never once begrudged her of it. We were family, for better or for worse, and I waited dutifully for her to come around. But that day never came.

Instead her attacks grew heavier and more brazen. Like the time I unwittingly convinced Mom and Dad to attend my out-of-state recital instead of her swim meet and she snapped my bow clean in half across her knee.

Over time her jealousy bred a competitive streak a mile long. If I asked to bring home two friends, she'd ask to bring home three. If I said my day was great, hers was better. If I said my day was bad, hers was worse. She worked overtime to steal my thunder as cruelly and as often as possible.

So it shouldn't have been a surprise the day I saw her snuggled cozily under the arm of my so-called boyfriend. The evil glint of delight on her face when she caught me watching them was gut-wrenching.

They were an odd pair. He was a bookish sophomore like me. She was a senior—a popular senior at that. Needless to say, the fling was short-lived. She never wanted him; she just wanted to prove that she could get him.

That marked the end of all civility between Val and me. What once was a silent feud quickly escalated to daily screaming matches, heated accusations, and even a few tussles. In no time at all my anger at her grew into resentment, which eventually hardened into bitterness, which, in time, festered into hatred, until even the mention of her name made my stomach flip and my toes curl.

I welcomed the peaceful environment that settled over the house once she left for college. In my mind, her absence meant that I was officially relinquished from my second-class status. I was free to hog my parents' affection and prance beneath my very own, unique limelight.

Communication between Val and I whittled down to brief hellos on the phone as I passed the receiver to Mom or Dad, and hollow greetings when she came home in the summer and on holidays. That was the status quo for two years.

Then, unexpectedly, her response towards me changed. Instead of immediately asking to speak to Mom when I answered the phone, she inquired about my friends and recitals and classes. When she visited over spring break, she offered me smiles instead of scowls and warm hugs instead of icy brush-offs.

She didn't hesitate to tell me that she loved me or that she was proud of me. She'd often make special trips to attend my competitions, and when she couldn't make it she'd send a card to wish me luck.

I remained skeptical and aloof, however. Val had proven to be conniving and calculating. I just knew, in the back of my mind, that she was only trying to soften me up for the kill. There was an agenda behind her kindness and even though I couldn't figure out what it was, I had no intentions of getting caught with my guard down. Any day now, the malice in her eyes would return, and I would be ready.

But her hate didn't return. Instead, she grew nicer and more gracious. "Jesus changed me," she announced.

Religion had never played a prominent role in our family or in our upbringing. But our parents saw the positive changes in her attitude and in her choices, and so they accepted her Christianity.

But I remained leery, convinced that her nun routine was nothing more than false piety. She'd lost our feud. I'd dethroned her and the only way she could save face was to hide behind her religion—to pretend like she'd suddenly been overcome by God's love and that the past no longer mattered.

I refused to be suckered and I quickly began to resent her religion as much as I resented her. Over time, her attempts to win me over waned and she submitted to the distance of our sisterhood. But I've never taken my suspecting eyes off of her and I'll never forgive her for abandoning me the one time I needed her the most.

"Abby?" I hear someone call my name in the distance. "Abby, are you awake?" I struggle to lift my heavy, uncooperative eyelids.

Val is leaning over me, snapping her finger in my face. "You must've fallen asleep."

I look at her and silently demand her to disappear. "I have to get going," she informs me. Her eyes dart around the room and she shifts her weight nervously from one foot to the other. "But before I go, there's something I want to talk to you about."

My blood pressure rises a notch. I already know what she wants to talk about and it is the absolute last thing in the world I want to hear. How dare she corner me like this, when I'm confined to a bed—unable to speak, my body broken.

"I know we haven't been able to have a real, civilized conversation about this, but I think now, more than ever, it's important for you to understand how much God loves you."

My heart pounds feverishly. I've told her a hundred times that I don't want to hear any of her Jesus malarkey.

"Now that you've had such a close brush with death," she continues, "maybe you realize how crucial it is for you to be right with the Lord. I don't want to see you go to hell, Abby, and I'm not trying to pass judgment. But the Bible says that the only way for any of us to inherit the Kingdom of Heaven is to repent of our sins and to invite Jesus to live in our hearts, and I know you haven't done that. I'm scared for you," she whispers.

My breaths come in heavy, angry spurts. I wish someone, anyone, would walk in, but we remain alone.

"I want to pray with you." She picks up my gauzed hand.

I snatch it away.

She looks up at me, her sharp, green eyes wide with shock.

I glare at her hatefully.

"Abby, please," she begs and reaches for my hand again.

I shout, "No!" but because my jaw is wired shut, what comes out instead is a loud, chilling groan.

She steps back, startled by my vehement refusal.

"Is everything okay?" says a nurse, rushing into the room. I shriek again, all the while holding Valerie's gaze.

"It's okay," the nurse soothes. "Are you in pain?"

I blink once, our signal for no.

"Are you sure?"

I confirm with two more blinks.

She turns to Val. "She should really get some rest."

Val nods. "I love you," she says to me, her tone apologetic.

I close my eyes and turn my face away and when I open them a few seconds later, to my relief, she's gone.

5. *Jarvis*

I light a second cigarette with the butt of my first before flicking it out the back door. Several jolts of pain shoot through both my legs and I grimace.

Phantom pain.

I look down at my lap, still amazed by the absence of my knees, calves, and feet.

"You're lucky to be alive" is what everyone keeps telling me, but I'm not so sure. Yes, I'm breathing, my heart is pumping, my blood is flowing, but I still feel incomplete. I am, after all, literally only half a person.

They've given me pamphlets and statistics. I even went to a support group meeting, but listening to other people moan about the exact same things I was feeling wasn't therapeutic. Hearing people's hopelessness, seeing the same despair in their eyes that I see every time I look in the mirror, only makes me more aware of how permanent—how real—my situation is.

I am never going to walk again.

Prosthetics are the only chance I have of folding up my wheelchair, but financially, that isn't a possibility. My mom has already sacrificed everything but the shirt off her back. I don't have insurance and if it wasn't for Jo the mounting hospital bills would have already wiped us out.

Everyone has been inconvenienced; lives have been disrupted and forever changed because of me—because of my actions. That is the worst part—the guilt of knowing what I did and the ripple effect it has caused.

I can survive without walking. Maybe amputating my legs is an appropriate punishment. Maybe it's a form of cosmic justice—karma's way of exacting reciprocity. But knowing the damage I've caused—knowing that I almost killed Abby—makes me wonder if I'm really lucky to be alive.

Even after everything that's happened, I miss her. If she called and told me that she wanted to be with me, I would pack up everything and move to Chicago. But Abby and I together again is wishful thinking. She doesn't want anything to do with me, and there's more talk of lawsuits than reconciliation.

I've tried to call her dozens of times, but her family's built a fortress around her. I write her letters, apologizing, begging for her forgiveness, but the only responses I receive are brief, curt letters from her lawyer, warning me not to contact his client again. The only person who will talk to me is Val.

"Give it time, Jarvis," she advises. "Abby's got a lot to deal with. We've all got a lot to deal with."

I know she's right, but it doesn't make waking up every morning any easier. It doesn't erase the fact that I've ruined someone else's life—that in an instant, I ripped away Abby's bright future and replaced it with hopelessness.

"I thought you kicked that habit," Jo says, startling me from my thoughts.

I take another long drag. "What can I say?" I blow a thin cloud of smoke from the side of my mouth. "You thought wrong."

He grunts. "You plan on coming back anytime soon? I can't ring up the customers *and* cook."

"I appreciate the job, Jo. It's a nice gesture and I know what you're trying to do, but I don't think I'm cut out to cashier."

" 'Cut out'? It isn't brain surgery, Jay. People hand you their money, you hand them change, and at the end of each week I hand you a paycheck."

I take another drag.

He storms over to me and snatches the cigarette out of my hand. "Give me this." He throws it down and grinds it into the cement floor with the tip of his shoe.

"What's your problem?"

"Smoking is not a cure-all."

"It calms my nerves.'"

"You don't need a cigarette. You need a plan. You need purpose."

I look at him, his heaving stomach and wrinkled hands, his stained white T-shirt and worn jeans. He means well; he always does.

"You got knocked down—roughed up a little. That doesn't mean you're out. You don't just quit."

"Knocked down?" I laugh bitterly. "Jo, look at me!" I point to where my legs used to be. "This is more than knocked down."

He sits on one of the old, dilapidated barstools strewn about the tiny storage room. "I know you think I'm old and don't know which shoe goes on which foot anymore, but I'm telling you, this can't be any more than what you allow it to be. The way I see it, you can continue to feel sorry for yourself and rot away in that wheelchair or you can explore your options and make the most of your handicap."

"How do you make the most out of something like this?" I ask, my lip furled resentfully.

"There are millions of people who can't walk and they live happy, productive lives. Think about the blind and the deaf. You should be praising God that you didn't lose one of your senses.

"You're young. Five years from now, you could look back on everything that's happened and be grateful because it made you a better person. But at the rate you're going, you'll be exactly where you are right now: depressed, sitting in a dark room, growing a tumor from smoking cigarettes, and moping over circumstances you can't change."

"I'm crippled," I say, indignant. "What am I supposed to do?"

"Anything you put your mind to," he answers simply. "You're a bright kid. You know it and so do I."

I grunt skeptically. "I'm a college dropout."

"Don't give me that," he snaps, his eyes narrowed angrily. "You dropped out because you were too lazy to stick with it, not because you aren't smart enough to finish. You pulled the same mess at that special school you tested into—just putzed around pretending to be an idiot."

I shake my head and turn away. He's right.

To this day, I don't know how I captured the interest of the teacher who recommended I be tested for the city's Gifted and Talented program.

I was unruly, with a short attention span and an uncanny affinity for mischief. Most adults assumed that I was a bad seed, but one specific teacher suspected that I was acting out because I wasn't being challenged enough.

I took the test and scored in the ninetieth percentile. Within weeks, I was whisked off to a magnet academy in the suburbs. Embittered about having to leave behind my posse, an eclectic assembly of fellow riffraff, to catch three different buses to a stuffy school that would require twice as much effort and offer half as much fun, I refused to cooperate.

The curriculum was rigorous, yet manageable, the students friendly and diverse, but textbooks and homework simply didn't hold my attention. Learning had always come easy to me. There wasn't enough of a challenge in it. I spent my days gazing wistfully out of the oversized windows dreaming of all the adventures to be had beyond those walls.

My indifference reflected itself in my grades. More than a few times, the powers that be threatened to return me to my old school. But being dumped back into Detroit's failing public school system didn't bother me. I knew I was smart and I didn't need to see an "A" at the top of my tests to tell me that I understood the material.

In the end, I put in just enough effort to stop everyone's incessant complaints and I graduated—barely.

"Jay, you can be anything," Jo says, his words infused with passion. "The time to decide is now. What do you want to do with the rest of your life?"

I sigh and allow myself to dream just long enough to humor Jo. "I don't know. I always thought it would be cool to learn the ropes of business management, maybe supervise a chain of hotels. Who knows? Maybe even own a restaurant someday."

He looks pleased with that answer. "Only way to do that is to go back to school."

"On whose dime?"

"Mine."

"Come on, Jo. Get serious. You're gonna pay for me to go to school?"

"Why not?"

"I don't have the money to pay you back."

"I'm not asking you to."

"Don't waste your money on a guy like me," I say sullenly.

"Jay, you're like my son. If going back to school will give you direction, then I'd be honored to send you. Don't be so content to sit around and watch your life pass you by. Strive for something bigger—something better. The world is your oyster."

"The world *was* my oyster, and like everything else, I screwed it up."

"You can't stop pushing forward every time you make a mistake, Jay. You have to get up, dust yourself off, and keep trying until you get it right—until you reach your potential and find your purpose in life," he counsels.

"Maybe I don't have a purpose."

He shakes his head. "That's not possible. God has a purpose for everyone."

I shrug. "Maybe I slipped through the cracks."

"That's like saying God makes mistakes."

"I don't know the guy. How can I be so sure that He doesn't?"

Jo's eyes swirl with sadness. "Maybe that's the problem."

"Please, don't start with the religion thing."

"I'm not preaching to you. I'm just saying that the only person who can help you up after a fall like this is Jesus. I can try to encourage you and cheer you on as much as I know how, but the solutions I'm able to offer you are only temporary."

"The thing is," I say, "after something like this—something this monumentally devastating—everything except the consequences seems temporary. Solutions don't exist at this level."

"So that's it? You've given up hope?"

I take a moment to reflect. "I haven't given it up; it's just gone. I've lost my bearings and I don't recognize myself anymore. I don't know where I fit."

"Do you remember when Iona passed?" he asks.

Iona is his late wife. She died of breast cancer less than a year before my dad died.

I nod. I was sixteen and I can still picture Jo hunched over her casket, his shoulders heaving with sobs. I watched him helplessly, ashamed to see such a big, grown man break down in front of so many people.

"Everything you're saying, all the confusing emotions you're expressing, I felt those too. I was married to my wife for thirty-seven years and when she died I felt as though my legs had been cut from underneath me. Losing her was like losing the better half of me.

"It doesn't take a car accident or a handicap to know what loss feels like, but in the same breath, sometimes it does take those things to experience gain and, ultimately, growth."

I know, firsthand, that Jo understands the meaning of grief. But looking at him now, I never would have known that he had been broken in such a significant way. If I hadn't been there to witness him, firsthand, at one of his lowest points, I would've assumed that he was always the same happy-go-lucky guy who ran the coolest diner on Seven Mile and told stupid jokes and had a million friends.

"How did you hurdle everything you were feeling?"

"I didn't. You can't hurdle something like that no matter how hard you try. You can trick yourself into thinking that you've cleared it, but eventually, all of the sadness and anger and guilt come flooding back from wherever you had them dammed."

"Then how did you get through it?"

"Do you really have to ask?"

Jo has never been shy about his Christianity. Anyone who knows him also knows that he draws his strength from his faith in Jesus Christ. I respect Jo's beliefs and I know that they make him a wiser, stronger person, but I can't fathom how reading the Bible or getting on my knees to talk to a God I can't see or feel, can help make the world more bearable.

"Don't just take my word for it," Jo says. "The Bible promises that if we seek God, we will find Him. All you have to do is make an effort to get to know Him and He will reveal Himself to you."

A barrage of "what ifs" comes charging to the front of my mind. What if God doesn't exist? What if I'm beyond help? What if I pick myself up only to get knocked down even harder? What if God's love doesn't extend to someone like me?

"I'll think about it" is all I manage.

Jo nods and gets up. "Life comes down to two things, Jay," he says, before heading back to the diner. "Are you smart enough to accept Christ's love, and if so, are you brave enough to allow it to make you great?"

6. *Abby*

My heart races as the alarm clock sitting on my nightstand beeps mercilessly. I pry one eye open and slam my hand down several times, knocking over my glasses and a box of tissues before I finally manage to find the snooze button.

I roll over onto my side, desperate to block out the bright, warm stream of sunlight filtering through my plantation shutters and into my room. Snuggling under my comforter, I try to ignore the dread that is slowly creeping up my body.

Part of me would give anything to stay tucked in bed, safe in the privacy of my home, where no one is allowed to judge me or stare at me and where my insecurities can't eat away at me like acid. But it's half past seven already, and at nine I am expected to be at work, ready to play through the soreness of my bloodshot eyes.

It's becoming harder and harder to get out of bed. I try different tactics every day. Sometimes I coax myself: "You can do it, Abs. Today's a brand new day. Anything's possible." Other times I reprimand myself: "You're acting sophomoric. This is ridiculous. Get up right now!" When all else fails, I barter with myself: "If you go to work, you don't have to practice tomorrow." But even the harshest self-imposed demands and the most extravagant bribes are slowly losing their potency.

Nothing is worth the awkward silences and the uncomfortable stares. No threat is more frightening than the alienation I feel day in and day out.

I make my way to the bathroom. The panels of the hardwood floor send cold shocks through the balls of my feet and I cringe with each step.

Waking up and facing myself in the morning is by far the worst part of every day. I dread entering my bathroom and fighting to avoid my reflection in the oversized mirror I had etched into polished marble.

I used to jokingly call it my "Decadent Wall of Vanity." At the time, I liked the idea of being the first thing I saw in the morning when I awoke and the last thing I saw before I went to bed at night. It seemed innocuous at the time. After all, I'd worked hard to obtain everything I owned. I spent more than my share of years broke, working jobs I didn't want to work, playing gigs I didn't want to play, putting up with people who lacked vision, getting rejection after rejection from labels that weren't even good enough to have me.

I slip into my robe and ponder the irony in someone like me—someone who's spent a significant portion of her life rapt by fame and consumed by an intense need to be recognized and accepted and validated—turning out to be what she's always feared.

I take a deep breath and look at the reflection staring back at me. Even now, nearly a year later, I'm still shocked—still appalled by what I see.

My eyebrows, along with my hairline, have been burned completely away. The top and sides of my scalp are burned so badly, in fact, that I'm not likely to experience any new growth in those areas. Patches of hair hang, unevenly, from certain spots, giving me the look of a chemotherapy patient.

My face is egregiously disfigured. Due to severed tissue, muscles, and nerves, my right eye droops much lower than my left and I'm hardly able to move it. My skin, which used to be smooth and caramel-colored, is now covered with deep, scaly patches, and those areas that have not turned dark brown from scarring are pink and flaky.

There's a pronounced scar on my chin that will fade over the years, I was told, but will never disappear.

My neck is wrinkled and bumpy to the touch, as though I've been clawed open by a wild animal and glued back together by a precocious group of six year olds.

In some areas my skin is shiny, in other places it's dull, in certain spots it's soft and smooth, and in others, it's tough and cracked like leather.

I look like an unfinished lump of clay—as if the sculptor was somehow interrupted during the molding process and forgot to return and finish.

Three years ago, when I moved to Chicago, Hannah had talked me into my first spa day. I knew women did those things—spent gross amounts of money on spoiling themselves with pedicures and facials—but never in my wildest dreams did I think I would be one of them.

The whole concept of spas seemed Epicurean—an experience for well-to-do business women who'd earned the right to a little pampering or rich house-wives whose only real job was to stand on the periphery of their husbands' lives and look impeccably refined.

I didn't fit into either of those categories, so when Hannah rang my door-bell at ten o'clock on a Saturday morning and divulged her big surprise, I was more than a little apprehensive.

"I don't think so, Hannah; spas are not really my kind of thing."

"We'll have a leisurely brunch at the Four Seasons and then we'll meet Mari at twelve thirty," she said, ignoring me.

"Who's Mari?"

"Our spa coordinator."

I laughed. "You say that like it's a normal answer."

"What is wrong with you?" she whined. "It's a beautiful day in the Windy City and all you want to do is lie around in that ridiculous nightgown and play your retarded cello."

I looked down at my pajamas. It was a cotton gown, patterned with little strawberries. The neckline, sleeves, and hem were lined with white, frilly lace that had, over the years, faded to a disturbing shade of gray. Just over my left knee, there was a pencil-sized hole where I snagged it pulling it out of the dyer.

As with many of the articles of clothing I acquired before finally earning enough money to splurge on that crazy thing called fashion, it was a hand-me-down. My sister wore it for all of six months before her breasts, which still have yet to cease growing, out-bloomed the fitted top of the gown and she was forced to give it up.

I loved everything about it—the warmth of the fabric, the way it fit loosely and allowed me to breathe, the familiarity of it. Hannah had a point, it did look ridiculous, but it was one of life's simple pleasures and I couldn't see myself letting go of it anytime soon.

"That retarded cello, you speak of so disrespectfully," I said, flopping down on my couch, "pays my mortgage."

"You know what I mean." She grabbed my arm and forced me to stand back up. "I dance. It's my job and I love it, but I can't do it every hour of every day and every day of every year. That takes the joy out of it."

With her hands on my shoulders, she led me across my living room.

"Where are we going?" I moaned.

She positioned me in front of the large picture window.

"Look at this." She swept her hand over the striking downtown view. "And look at this." She spun me around, and before us was a breathtaking panorama of the downstairs portion of my newly renovated condo. It was one of eight penthouses, two levels with every high-tech amenity available and only half-furnished.

I was what my mother disapprovingly called, "house poor."

"I'm looking at it," I said. The dramatic beauty had worn off a few weeks after I moved in.

"You've arrived!" Hannah exclaimed. "People slave away their whole lives in hopes of achieving this kind of lifestyle and you've got it."

I smiled, subtle excitement creeping down my spine. "Yeah, I know," I relented.

"So, enjoy it already!"

I turned back around and looked outside. It really was a beautiful day. "Okay," I agreed. "Just this once."

And just like that, I became a regular spa-goer. I lived without facials and massages for almost thirty years, pre-Hannah; the words *pore-minimizing* and *exfoliation* were not in my vocabulary. But post-Hannah, Anti-Oxidant Pomegranate Wraps and Himalayan Mineral Baths were as essential as morning coffee.

I dim the lights, disrobe, and step into the shower. It's amazing, I muse, as the scalding water pelts my back, how easily adaptable people are to certain things—how quickly a person can rationalize any reward, no matter how silly.

The tiles I'm standing on, for instance, cost me upwards of six thousand dollars. They were imported from Italy.

There were several patterns that I liked much better. Truthfully, I didn't care at all for most of the imported tiles, but my interior designer assured me that a home of this caliber wouldn't look right with anything other than the best of the best. Apparently, the best of the best could only be found overseas.

So it cost a couple thousand more than your standard tile. In the grand scheme of things, what was a couple thousand dollars? I had to look at the big picture. Besides, I'd earned it, hadn't I?

Next to my shower is a sauna. "Everyone who's anyone, has one," I was assured. I was somebody, wasn't I? My bank account, my car, my home—they screamed, "I'm someone important!" Didn't they? Why should my bathroom be any different?

Except, in the three years I've lived here, I've only been in the sauna once, for about twenty minutes, after which my hair curled up so tightly I had to make an appointment with my stylist the very next day to have it straightened.

The body wraps, the bathroom, the house, the lifestyle—they were easy to justify—easy to accept. And in no time at all, they became a part of who I was. People didn't know me as Abby Walker; they knew me as Abby with the fabulous house. ("You've got to see it!") Or Abby with the incredible master bathroom. ("I heard she went all the way to Italy to buy the tiles!") Or Abby, the glamour girl. ("She swears by her weekly mud baths!")

I was happy to oblige, because being her—being that woman everyone envied—meant that I was special. It meant that, finally, I'd reached the top of the mountain, and victory was sweet.

But as easy as it was to adapt to my new status in life, it has been twice as hard to survive the fall from it. How will I ever get used to the woman I am now when I can't even bear to look at her? Who is she, this grotesque figure who shadows me wherever I go? Am I supposed to dim the lights every time I undress and skulk about in a house with no mirrors so I can live with her? It seems too much like running. But I have no other choice. My fate was sealed the night of the accident.

I push open the heavy glass shower door, resentful of my plush surroundings, and dry myself off. Everything, I figured out too late in the game, is an illusion.

My contractor didn't bother to tell me that along with my twenty-five-foot ceilings and oversized windows, I would also get a jaw-dropping gas bill every month. My interior designer must have forgotten to let me know that my pricey, cast-aluminum, vintage, suede-upholstered couch would cause an exorbitant annual cleaning bill because it has a pesky little habit of picking up more dirt and hair than an industrial vacuum cleaner. And nobody let me know that in the event my face should be disfigured and my money dwindle by any significant measure, most of my friends would disappear.

I still have Hannah, but even our friendship has changed. We speak several times a week. The conversations revolve around her busy schedule and hectic life—the reasons why she hasn't managed to stop by in so long.

A couple of times, she has called me the night after a wild and crazy party to tell me how wild and crazy it was. But she never calls to invite me, never asks how I am doing or if I need anything. Probably because she knows if she invited me anywhere, I wouldn't go, and if she asked me how I was doing, I wouldn't be fine, and that if there's anything I need, it's beyond what she can give.

My eyebrow twitches as I pull my thin, unevenly textured hair into a ponytail. I drape a scarf over the top of my head and tie the two ends at the nape of my neck to hide my singed scalp.

Despite the blazing summer sun, I throw on an oversized sweatshirt, blue jeans, and a pair of boots. I pick up my cello, which is lying on the floor, safely nestled in its case and throw my bag over my shoulder. Longingly, I take one last look at my bed, tromp down the stairs, and head to work.

"No! No! Stop!" Sonya beats her baton against the edge of her stand. "Abby," she glares at me, one hand on her hip, "what are you doing? Where is your head?"

I look up at her, my face is flushed. "Sorry," I mumble.

"I don't need you to be sorry," she snips. "I need you to come in after eight full counts. Not seven, not nine, but eight. And while you're at it, maybe you can find it in your heart to play the right notes."

The musicians on stage shift uncomfortably, a few smirk.

I glance around quickly. Those who aren't amused by my humiliation are shaking their heads in disappointment.

"Sorry," I say again, unable to meet her demanding gaze.

"People," she moans. The nasally vibration of her voice forces the hair on the back of my neck to rise.

"This is unacceptable. How many times do I need to tell you all that this symphony can only be as good as its weakest player? The way some of you show up: late, with attitudes, unprepared, unrehearsed," she ticks off each offense for dramatic effect, "is insulting and disrespectful to those of us who take our jobs seriously and come prepared to work."

I keep my head lowered and hope that her tirade will be over soon.

"Now I need you, and I mean all of you, to focus on what we're doing here. Are we clear?"

There's a low rumble of compliance from the group. I don't bother to respond. Instead, I flip back to the beginning of the piece and wait for her to raise the baton.

I fumble through it, recoiling each time I play a wrong note. Sonya pushes forward and overlooks my constant slips, but I can feel her stares burning holes into my forehead.

I will never give her the satisfaction of saying it, but I know Sonya is right. Over the past few months my conduct has become unprofessional. I'm usually the last person to arrive and set up and one of the first people to leave.

The sense of refuge I used to feel when behind my cello is now, for the first time since my childhood, overshadowed by stifling, paralyzing self-consciousness. I can't concentrate on the notes in front of me. I can't achieve the right tones or land my next shift. I'm too busy stealing glances at the rest of the players. I'm convinced they're all staring at me—judging me.

It's my fishbowl paranoia—the feeling of being turned inside out and put on display for everyone to observe me—that makes coming to rehearsals and playing concerts impossibly difficult.

"Let's take ten, people," Sonya shouts and sets down her baton. "Abby, can I see you for a minute?" she asks.

I lay my cello on its side and follow her backstage, shunning the sympathetic looks I receive along the way.

"Sit down," Sonya says, patting a folding chair she's placed in front of her. She doesn't like me and I don't like her. It's not a secret.

She's had it out for me ever since she was hired as a conductor's assistant. Dr. Wrightman, our principal conductor, adores me. But, at his age and with his busy schedule, he decided he couldn't attend all of the rehearsals and hired Sonya, a snot-nosed know-it-all, who doesn't have half as much experience as the people she's bossing around, to lead our weekly practices.

From the moment she sauntered onto the stage, I knew we were going to butt heads. She tends to nitpick the way I play every piece and I tend to ignore her instruction entirely and do things my own way—the best way.

That's been our relationship for the last year or so—a frustrating, diplomatic tug-of-war. But now that my personal life is so rattled, I don't have the strength to concentrate on how to keep Sonya at bay. There are other, much more intimidating demons I have to fight.

"No," I say and cross my arms. "I think I'll stand."

She shrugs, cavalierly, but her frown betrays her offense. "We need to talk about your performance." Her eyes shift nervously from the floor to the curtain behind me and back to the floor again.

"So talk."

"I'd appreciate a little less attitude and a lot more cooperation. I'm not the enemy here, Abby."

"No, you're not," I agree. "But you're also not my friend. You're a conductor's assistant, who's got to be at least, what?" I ask. "Four, five years younger than me?"

She crosses her legs. "There's no need to be rude."

"You'll have to excuse me if I'm not that open to being chastised by someone who's not even out of grad school yet."

"I'm not the one who's slipping," she says curtly.

I stiffen. "I've had a hard year. Everyone knows that."

"Yes," she sighs. "We all know, but eventually, you're going to have to stop using that as a crutch."

"A crutch?" I screech, furious. "You call this a crutch?" Without thinking, I snatch off my scarf.

She blanches and turns her head away. "Abby, please."

Embarrassed, I fasten the scarf back in place.

"I can't presume to know what you're going through," she says. "But we have a job to do here. You're our principal cellist. It's imperative that you have the music down. When you don't, the pieces threaten to fall apart."

"I'm doing the best I can."

She shakes her head. "That doesn't cut it anymore. If what you're giving me is your best, then you have to find a way to do better."

"If you think it's that easy, why don't you put down your baton and do it yourself?"

"This isn't about me," she declares loudly, her patience spent. "I'm not going to fight with you about this. I don't have to, because whether you like it or not—whether you agree with it or not—I'm in charge here. You get paid to play and I get paid to conduct. It's as simple as that. Your performance is not up to speed. You are not meeting the standard of a symphony cellist. You know it, I know it, and all of your colleagues, who have to pick up your slack, know it."

"Are you firing me?"

"No, but I'm giving you one week to show me some improvement, or else I'm taking the matter to Dr. Wrightman."

I glower at her. "Are we finished?"

"No, we're not," she nips frostily. "There's also the issue of your incessant tardiness and absences. It's unacceptable, Abby."

"I'm on a slew of medications," I explain testily. "They leave me groggy and disoriented, especially in the morning."

"Then maybe you should take some more time off."

"I've used all of my temporary leave."

There's no way I'm going to let her know the truth—that due to incomprehensibly high medical bills, lawyer's fees, a crippling mortgage, and a failing third album, I desperately need the work.

"I don't know what to tell you." She stands. "You've got to find a way to dig deep and get it together."

"Gee thanks," I gush with sarcastic glee. "That puts it all into perspective."

Only after she walks back to the front of the stage do I sit down. I examine my badly scarred, threadbare hands. I don't recognize them.

What am I doing here? I wonder. Playing doesn't make me happy anymore, it confuses and depresses me. Being tested by Sonya on a day-to-day basis doesn't make me stronger or light a fire under me the way it used to; it breaks me into small, indecipherable pieces.

I don't belong here anymore.

"Okay people, let's get going," Sonya shouts over the talking and tuning of instruments.

I sit backstage and continue to stare at my hands. They look exactly how I feel—ruined and useless.

Money isn't important anymore. It never was. The prospect of wealth wasn't what had me squealing into my pillow as a kid. It was the joy of playing the cello. It was the indescribable satisfaction I felt after receiving a standing ovation or looking at the quarterly numbers of my record sales. It was the knowledge that people recognized and appreciated me for my talent, and it was transcending new levels of greatness every time I picked up a bow.

I've lost those feelings. I don't know if they're gone forever, or if they're hidden behind a cloud of trauma and self-doubt, but I know they're gone for the time being and they will not return anytime soon.

Maybe I'll never be on top again. Twenty years from now, someone may utter the name Abigail Walker and people will categorize her life as a tragic shame. She may be remembered only as a promising cellist who peaked in her late twenties and disappeared from the spotlight after a devastating car crash left her searching for something more. But at least I can say I made it to the top—at least, if nothing else, I can say I chased my dream and for a brief second, dipped my toe in the inviting pool of success.

Pull yourself together, Sonya had instructed. Maybe that's better advice than I thought. Pulling myself together means finding my center again. Hours and hours of practicing, rehearsing, and recording aren't it anymore. I need to find a new balance. Money should be the last thing to deter me from restructuring my life. If I have to, I decide, I'll sell my condo—whatever it takes to find peace.

"Abby," Sonya calls impatiently. She's standing by the heavy velvet curtain. "Is there a problem?"

My heart races at the prospect of what I think I am about to do.

"Abby!" she barks. "Everyone else is set up and ready to work. How much longer do you expect us to wait for you?"

I look down at my hands and stand up, overcome with clarity. "Don't bother," I say, breezing past her.

"Don't bother to what?"

"Don't bother waiting."

In front of dozens of curious faces, I pack up my cello and my music.

"What do you think you're doing?" Sonya asks.

Calmly, with my head held high and my chin set, I look her straight in the eye. "I quit."

"Wait a minute," she says, sounding suddenly nervous. "Why don't you talk to Dr. Wrightman first? Abby, Ab—would you wait a second? Abby, wait," she pleads, but my mind is set and I'm on my way.

Grinning at the buzz of murmurs and shocked whispers behind me, I descend the stage steps and without looking back, walk out of the auditorium door.

7. *Jarvis*

The wide linoleum halls of State Hall are swarming with kids who look too young to be in college. Memories of high school bombard me as I make my way past one classroom after another in search of Room 308. The scene seems familiar except that in place of guys tossing footballs and uniform-clad cheerleaders toting rustling pompoms, the students have cell phones glued to their ears and are carrying armfuls of books.

My mom cried, she literally cried—tears, snot, the whole shebang—when I told her I was going back to school. My return to college happened under a whirlwind of coincidences. Jo knew someone who knew someone who knew someone and so went the pattern until finally I was sitting in front of a Wayne State college advisor, flipping through the Fall course catalog.

I could say it all started as soon as I resolved to put the past behind me. I could claim the pieces started to fit together months earlier when Jo offered to fund my college education. But those weren't the catalysts of my new beginning; they were only proof that a new beginning had begun.

Everything was set into motion the Sunday morning Jo showed up at my mom's house boisterously questioning how long it was going to take for me to get ready. I was in bed, asleep, a pillow over my head trying to block out the blazing strip of sunlight beaming right across my face.

"What're you doing?" he shouted, jolting me out of my peaceful slumber. "I told you nine o'clock. Didn't I tell you nine o'clock sharp?"

"It's Sunday," I said, my pulse beating at a dangerously high speed. "I don't work on Sundays."

"We can't be late, otherwise we won't get a seat."

"What are you talking about?" I asked, more blown away by my wicked morning breath than by Jo standing in my room in a suit and tie whining about seats somewhere.

"Sunday," he said simply.

I squinted up at him, my mind still a few paces behind.

"Church?" He lifted a black Bible as if it held all the explanation I needed.

"So?"

"You promised me you'd go."

I groaned and rolled onto my stomach. The conversation I had with Jo the previous Tuesday came flooding back to me. At the time, I was sincere when I said I would go to church, but as with everything else in life, promises fade and I forgot.

"Next Sunday," I mumbled. My eyes were already growing heavy with sleep.

I felt the mattress slant sharply. My body, along with the sheets and comforter, rolled quickly downward. I hit the carpeted floor with a hard thud. Jo was standing over me, an unwavering determination in his eyes.

My palms were damp, my forehead clammy. I grew increasingly nervous on the long, quiet ride to church. My original Sunday plans were what they'd been every Sunday since I'd gotten too old for Mom to drag me to church. I was going to sleep late, wolf down a plate of bacon and eggs, watch bad made-for-TV movies until my brain went numb, and afterwards I'd take a long nap. Instead, I was straightening the tie Jo lent me and hoping against all odds we'd run out of gas or snag a flat tire.

I had grown up going to church, but I went out of ritual. I went because my parents forced me to go—because that's what they told me Sundays were for. Only somewhere between graham crackers and watered-down punch, memorizing Bible verses and passing the offering plate, the meaning—the significance—of sermons, worship, and God was lost until finally church became this thing I used to do, this place I used to go with my parents as a kid.

Given my past and the man I'd become, or maybe more accurately, the man I hadn't become, crossing over any church's threshold seemed shameful and wrong. I felt like a son returning home after having failed at trying to make it in the real world. The last thing I wanted or needed was for people to judge me or assume they knew my story because of the way I spoke and dressed.

My attitude would've been different if the playing field was even—if I could walk into the sanctuary with my head held high, a cocky swagger and a mysterious grin. But I couldn't blend in. I couldn't pretend like I didn't notice the uncomfortable glances and curious stares I received.

"Relax," Jo said. He opened the passenger side door, locked my wheelchair into place, and waited for me to transfer myself from the car using my upper body strength like I'd been taught in physical therapy.

"This is a mistake," I moaned.

"Coming to church is never a mistake." We made our way side by side up a long steep ramp toward the crowded sanctuary.

"I'm uncomfortable." I loosened the tie clinging to my neck and dabbed at my sweaty forehead with my sleeve.

"That's because you're too worried about what you look like and what people are thinking about you. Relax," he said again. "Nobody is paying you any mind. This time is about God. We're here to learn and worship."

And that's exactly what I did. I learned of God's love for me. I learned how Jesus sacrificed Himself so I wouldn't be condemned to hell. I learned that all I had to do was work on the possible and He'd handle the impossible. I learned the meanings of faith and obedience, and in the process, I received joy and hope.

Church every Sunday eventually led to Bible Study every Monday and Wednesday. I like having somewhere to be a couple of nights out of the week, and I've learned more than I ever expected.

I go to bed with questions and wake up with new understanding. I borrow books from Jo on how to pray more effectively and how to maximize misfortune. I've become a sponge, eager to soak in every little truth that comes my way.

The fear of not understanding never crosses my mind because I know God's love will always be beyond my realm of comprehension. I'll never fully know how much or to what extent He loves me, but I can be certain His love will always envelope me. It will always surpass my wildest expectations.

The security I found in God's love gave me the clarity and faith I needed to examine myself through honest eyes. I'm not supposed to be freeloading off my mom. I shouldn't be living in her house or eating her food or forcing her to work twice as hard so she can support both of us. I'm not supposed to be ringing up people's meals all day at Jo's diner. I shouldn't be in my thirties and still without a degree.

Which got me thinking, maybe I'm not even supposed to be in Michigan. Maybe I'm supposed to be in Florida or Ohio or Texas in my own house, with a wife, raising and supporting my own family. Maybe I was never supposed to be in the car with Abby that night. Maybe I was never meant to be an amputee. Who knows where other paths would've led me.

Everyone has a job, a purpose greater than what he is, but how many of us are ever brave enough to explore all we're meant to be? How many of us are able to leave what's comfortable—are able to abandon all uncertainties—and unravel ourselves from worldly restraints so we can glance into God's intended future for us long enough to be inspired?

The man who was intended to find the cure for AIDS could be huddled in a box in an alley somewhere, strung out on drugs, too far removed from what is right to know just how many lives have been tragically affected by his wrong decisions. Or the woman meant to be a peace-keeping envoy could be trapped behind bars for a foolish crime that not only cost her her freedom, but raped an entire country of its liberty and the right to live without fear.

Who am I meant to be? What person or race have I failed because of my doubts and ignorance?

Suddenly, as with the lifting of a veil, I saw everything I could become, all of the years I wasted, all of the excuses, all of the detours, all of the lies, all of the failures and the misses and the lost opportunities—and I cried. I cried like a child and I braced myself as immense sorrow and regret shook my bones.

My new season began that night. Tearful but grateful, I mapped out a plan for my life.

This is the first step, I think as I roll myself around the corner and into my Intermediate Macroeconomics class.

I'm nervous. The classroom looks more like an auditorium with its gigantic media screen, soaring ceilings, and elevated rows of desks. This is education on a grander level than I had ever anticipated.

It's been a long time since I've been a student. What if learning no longer comes as naturally as it did in the past? What if my suspicions are right? What if instead of possessing an untapped source of potential, I'm only disillusioned about what I am and am not capable of doing? What if, despite my sincerest efforts, I fall flat on my face?

I watch a heavyset guy drag himself to a desk in the farthest corner of the room. He looks hot and uninterested.

A few seconds later, in clumps a squat brunette. She's smacking on a wad of gum and chatting loudly into her cell phone. She has no books, no purse, no paper or pen, only a phone, gum, and a loud, annoying voice.

Following behind her is a tall, muscular black guy. He too has no book bag or notebook or writing utensils. He's wearing an oversized jersey, a baseball cap with the bill slanted to the left, and sparkling white tennis shoes. He bounds up the stairs and slips into a seat in the last row.

I turn my attention back to the heavyset guy with the rosy cheeks. His double chin is resting on his heaving chest. He's fast asleep.

I smile as my apprehension quickly evaporates. If people this unmotivated and unprepared can go to college and graduate, I'm going to pass with flying colors.

8. *Abby*

"You what?!" my mother shouts hysterically. I hold the phone away from my ear and wait for her to calm down. "What were you thinking? How could you be so irresponsible? Call that Sonya girl or Dr. Wrightman or whoever it is you need to speak with and tell them that you made a terrible mistake, do you hear me? Hello? Abby, are you listening to me?"

"I'm not calling anyone," I say.

"Excuse me, but if you had any common sense, you'd go beg for your job back."

"Don't you get it? Being there was the opposite of common sense. I was unhappy, Mom. I couldn't even drag myself out of bed and make myself go half the time. It was the right decision."

"You're confusing common sense with personal preference," she says angrily. "You have bills to pay—lots and lots of bills that your father and I can't help you with."

"I know that."

"If you know that, then why are you at home on the phone and not in a rehearsal hall somewhere earning a paycheck?"

"Because I was miserable," I whine.

"So?" she asks, refusing to offer her sympathy. "I don't discount you weren't happy there anymore, but you don't just pack up and quit. There are proper, responsible ways to terminate employment. The proper part involves you giving someone at least two weeks' notice and the responsible part involves you going out and securing another job first."

"I don't need this," I snap.

"You're right," she snaps back. "What you need is a better attitude and a steady source of income."

"Why can't you be supportive?"

"Because I'm sitting here in front of a pile of medical bills that add up to more than I earn in a year and I'm looking at a list of your assets and account balances and I'm very, very worried. You are in serious debt."

My mom, who obtained her accounting degree during Val's senior year in high school, immediately undertook the task of handling my finances when the money from my debut album started rolling in. My dad was not pleased with our arrangement.

"The fastest way to tear apart a family is to get involved with each other's money," he warned us. But in my mind there wasn't a CPA I could trust more. She went above and beyond the call of duty, making sure my taxes were filed and paid and that my money was wisely invested. Much of the time, I didn't know the exact figures, but I trusted her and I knew she would never betray me or let me down.

"How could you let this happen?" I ask, my voice strained with mounting panic.

"I didn't let anything happen," she says sternly. "Your finances are in shambles because of you and no one else."

"What happened to all the stuff you said about making my money work for me?"

"I tried, Abby, but your spending is absurd. You have some sort of aversion to saving money. Trips to Hawaii, Acapulco, St. Barts," she reels off. I can hear her shuffling papers in the background. "A new car last year, a time-share in Martha's Vineyard. I even have a receipt here for a two-thousand-dollar purse. Some of this stuff is preposterous."

"There's nothing left?"

"You have a little, but between your medical bills, taxes, and your mortgage, there's not enough. Everyone has a debt-to-income ratio," she explains. "While you were working, there was enough money coming in to cover your spending, but as soon as you stopped, your debt increased exponentially in a matter of months."

"Maybe I can get a loan to tide me over until I figure out my next move," I suggest.

"Abby, the only thing a bank is going to loan you is a pen to sign bankruptcy papers. You're too much of a liability."

"Okay," I say, willing myself to stay calm. "I'll sell the condo and buy something smaller, or maybe even," I gulp and spit the word out like it's poison, "rent."

The deep sigh on the other end of the phone tells me I'm not going to like what she says next.

"You've already taken a second mortgage out on the condo. If you sell at this point, you won't make enough of a profit to pay both of them off." Breathe, I tell myself. It's not that bad.

"Maybe, Dad and I should come up there," she says gently, her motherly instincts finally kicking in. "We haven't seen you in a while. We could make a weekend of it and discuss your options."

"What options, Mom?" I ask dejectedly. The surge of strength I'd felt mere minutes earlier is gone.

"There's always..." she pauses. "Well, you know, there's always Val and Paul."

If I was a cartoon character, my face would've just turned bright red and thick clouds of white steam would be streaming out of my ears.

"I can't believe you just said that."

"She's your sister and you need her help."

"I'd rather live on the street in a cardboard box."

"At the rate you're going that might just be a possibility."

"Fine," I huff. "Then so be it."

"All of this bitterness and jealousy you're holding onto is going to turn you into your own worst enemy," she warns.

I snort. "Jealousy? I think you're talking to the wrong daughter about jealousy. What does Val have that could ever, in this lifetime or the next, make me jealous?"

"You tell me," she says, her tone challenging.

I'm ready to unleash my resentfulness, let my hurt pour freely, all my memories from the past—all of the betrayals, all of the sabotages, all of the suffering. But my emotions rush forth with unbearable force, flooding my vocal cords and closing my throat.

"Nothing," I say. "I have to go."

"Abby, hang on a second. We have to talk about what you're going to do."

"Just have Dad call me when he gets home from work," I say and hang up.

9. Jarvis

I huff my way up the steep ramp that leads to the Student Union. It's just past noon and the large recreation area is packed with chatting students. Some are fashionably dressed; others are disheveled. Some sport tattoos and piercings and oddly dyed hair; others model pressed slacks and sweater vests. Some are eating alone; others are studying; many are conversing loudly across the long dining tables. It's a diverse group and I'm instantly comfortable as I make my way to the eatery to order lunch before my next class.

The countertops are high and I struggle to relay my order to the cashier who can hardly see me over the elevated shelf. Feeling like a toddler, I throw my head back and ask for a club sandwich, fries, and large lemonade. I strain to reach up and hand her a twenty-dollar bill.

"Let me help you with that," a deep, slow voice offers. I turn around to see a guy with matted ginger hair and squinty eyes. He's wearing a faded AC/DC T-shirt, wrinkled pajama bottoms, and flip-flops. He takes the twenty from me, gives it to the girl behind the counter, and hands me my change. "I'm Charles," he extends his hand. "Charles Campos. Everyone calls me Chas."

"Jay," I introduce myself.

"Where are you sitting?" he asks and picks up both our trays.

I shrug. "Anywhere." We roam around the dense crowd until we find an empty table. "Thanks," I say as Chas sets my food down and moves a folding chair out of the way to make room for my wheelchair.

"I'm in your economics class," he says, while drowning his fries in a crimson pool of ketchup.

"Oh yeah? I didn't see you."

"I was in the back sleeping with the rest of the class."

I laugh. "I was alone up front taking notes."

"I know. You're an intense student. Your pen didn't stop writing once. That's why me and my boys call you, 'Scribble.' "

"Call me what you want," I say. "I'm just trying to graduate."

"You a senior?"

I shake my head. "Freshman."

Chas eyes me curiously. He and I both know I'm way too old to be a traditional freshman.

"I took a couple of detours along the way," I explain.

"What's with the chair? What happened to your legs?"

"Car accident."

He sucks in air through clenched teeth. "That's tough."

I nod.

"What happened?"

I shift uncomfortably. "The police blamed it on bad weather."

"What do you blame it on?"

I look down at my half-eaten sandwich. "I don't believe in blame," I finally answer.

He smiles. "That's cool. I can respect that."

He looks over my shoulder to the Union's entrance. "Nez! Yo, Nez, over here," he shouts.

A few moments later, a round, bald, Latino walks over. His face is kind and when he smiles, his eyes pinch together. He's carrying a large, grease-stained pizza box.

"What's up?" He greets Chas with a complicated-looking handshake.

"You remember Scribble?" Chas says, motioning toward me.

Nez laughs. "I didn't recognize you without your pen and notebook," he jokes, his accent thick.

"How's it going?" I ask around a mouthful of salted fries.

"You know BJ and Lamar?" He juts his thumb behind me.

I turn to see two black guys walking toward us. They're the same height. One wears cornrows, the other, two large diamond studs in either ear. They look mean as they swagger to the table.

"S'up?" they ask simultaneously.

"What's up is that this pizza's getting cold," Nez says. "What took you so long?"

"Rehearsal ran over."

"Lamar and BJ are theater majors," Chas says.

"That's Scribble." Nez points at me. He turns a folding chair backward and straddles its seat.

They nod and give me a quick once-over as we pound fists. "You didn't forget the extra cheese, did you?" Lamar asks. He joins me on my side of the table.

Nez flips open the pizza box to reveal a gooey, steaming pizza, cluttered with layers of toppings.

"I got what I got," Nez says.

"Man, that don't look like extra cheese." Lamar examines the pie with disdain.

"Like I told you last time and all the times before that," Nez says. "Extra cheese ain't a topping."

BJ and Chas snicker.

"How you figure? If the pizza joint has it on their menu as a topping, it's a topping."

"The pizza joint is only trying to make money off the consumer. You ask for extra cheese, you pay them an extra buck fifty and you end up getting the exact same amount of cheese as everyone else."

"I'm trying to enjoy my lunch and you want to argue about a measly dollar and fifty cents?"

"Think of it this way," Nez says, biting into his slice. "I'm adding years onto your life. You eat too much cheese. You're only twenty-five and your arteries are probably already clogged."

"Ain't that the pot talking smack," Lamar says. "Porky Pig's trying to help me eat healthy."

"Oh you got jokes?" Nez asks, his lips spread into a devious grin. "Let me tell you a little somethin' bout yo Mama."

"Bring it on," Lamar grabs a slice of pizza.

BJ and Chas lean forward.

I laugh and shake my head and wait for the challenge to begin.

The five of us sit and talk and laugh. I eat quietly and watch them interact with each other.

Chas and BJ are jokesters. They tease Lamar about the gap between his two front teeth and his bowlegs. They tease me about my "intense" note-taking and my long fingers. They tease each other about girls they've dated in the past. It's all in good fun and I enjoy their humor and their ability to see the lighter side of things.

Nez, who's a political science major, is a talker. He likes to debate. It doesn't matter whether he's arguing with Lamar about extra cheese and why it's not a true topping or with Chas about the Lions and their typical bad season or with BJ about Superman and Spiderman and which one would win if pitted against the Hulk. He's a debater and he's good at it.

Lamar is the voice of reason among the bunch. When Chas and BJ's teasing crosses a line or hits a nerve, he wisely changes the subject by starting a debate with Nez. Or if the debates become too heated, he says something off the wall or cracks a joke to alleviate the tension. He's a peacemaker.

I have fun eating lunch with them and I'm disappointed when Chas and Nez announce they have to get to their next class.

"What's up for tonight?" BJ asks.

"End-of-summer party at Terry's." Chas buses both his tray and mine.

"You should come," Nez invites me. "It's all the way out in Farmington Hills, but I promise you it'll be worth it."

I smile politely. As comfortable as I feel with these guys, I can't picture myself at a rowdy college party complete with kegs and blaring music.

"I already have plans," I say, the disappointment in my voice partially genuine.

Nez tears a piece off the empty pizza box sitting on the table. He writes something down. "Here." He hands me the piece of cardboard.

On it is an address, a phone number, and an illegible map. "In case you change your mind."

The crowd in the Union has thinned out considerably. Once down the ramp, I pull out my campus map and with new vigor and confidence, find my way to my next class.

10. Abby

"Hello?" I press my ear to the phone. I hear muted chattering, laughing, and clamoring mingled with a soft jazz accompaniment in the background. "Hello?" I call again.

"Abby? It's Hannah."

I perk up, happy that she called. "Where are you? I can barely hear you?"

"I'm at another one of those stuffy fund-raisers," she says, trying her best to sound bored.

"That explains the elevator music."

"Yeah."

I wait for her to go on, but she just breathes into the receiver. "Is everything okay?" I ask.

"Yeah, of course. You were on my mind and I thought I should call, you know, check in like a good friend."

I wish she wouldn't make it sound like such an inconvenient obligation. "Right," I say. "Well, I'm fine, everything's fine."

"You sure? You sound like something's wrong."

Her comment raises red flags. Aside from the fact that she's spent the past couple of months dodging the subject of my emotional well-being, Hannah is not that perceptive.

"Why would you say that?" I ask, suspicious.

"I have a sixth sense about these things."

I groan. Her act is veil thin. "You talked to my mom." It's an accusation, not a question.

"Actually," she says slowly. "Val called me."

"Perfect!" I throw up my free hand. "I quit my job and it becomes a family affair."

"You quit your job?!" she gasps, breathless with surprise.

I wince and rap my knuckles against my forehead. "I thought you talked to Val."

"I did. She said you were turning into a hermit and that I should get you out of the house. I was gonna see if you wanted to do brunch this Sunday."

"Don't do me any favors," I murmur, feeling more than ever like a charity case. "I don't need my sister to beg my best friend to spend time with me."

"Abs, what are you talking about?"

"You haven't been by in months," I say. "You hardly ever answer your phone, and when you call me, it's always at times like this, when you're tied up and preoccupied." My sigh is heavy. "I'm not blaming you," I say softly. "I can imagine how hard—how awkward—it must be. I'm not even comfortable around me."

"Oh, Abby," she coos.

"I can live with the late-night calls, and even though I miss being around you, I can accept that you're not comfortable coming to see me anymore, but please, please," I beg gently, "don't invite me out as a favor to my sister."

"Abs, you're my best friend," she declares. "I'm closer to you than I am to my own family. I would never invite you to go anywhere as a favor to anyone."

I don't respond, partially because I'm not sure what to say, but mostly because I don't believe her.

"How long have you felt like this?" she asks, breaking the silence.

"A while," I admit.

"Well, why didn't you say something sooner?"

"What am I supposed to do?" I ask, truly at a loss. "Beg you to be my friend?"

"You never have to beg me for anything," she says, her breaths coming in short, quick spurts.

I can hear the click of her heels as the music and clatter in the background gradually fade away. "I miss spending time with you too, but I didn't want you to feel pressured to get back out there until you were ready."

My lips spread into a relieved, involuntary grin. "After everything that's happened today, I needed to hear that," I confess.

"You mean quitting your job?"

"That and finding out I'm pretty much destitute."

"Do you need to borrow some money?"

I laugh. "What I need is probably twenty times more than you can spare."

"What happened?" Her voice is wrought with worry.

"If you ask my mom, it's a simple case of spending more than I earned, but I can't discount my astronomical hospital bills."

"What about Jarvis? Can't you sue him for your damages?" she asks.

I'd told my parents and Hannah about Jarvis's reckless, ninety-mile-an-hour temper tantrum. All of them insisted I have him prosecuted to the fullest extent of the law.

"You can't let him get away with something like this," Hannah had cried.

"Abby, Honey, she's right," Dad chimed in. "His actions were criminal. If you don't do something about it, you'll send the message that he can get away with this sort of thing. What if he gets angry and does it to someone else? You have the power to cut him off now."

"I never—ever—liked that boy," Mom chanted as she paced from one end of my small hospital room to the other.

I had given it serious thought. I even consulted with my lawyer, but when it came time to take action, I couldn't. Just the thought of a lengthy civil suit followed by an equally lengthy criminal trial made me tired. For my own sanity, I decided to let bygones be bygones.

My behavior that fateful night didn't excuse what Jarvis did by any stretch of the imagination, but I understood his anger. I was too embarrassed to tell anyone how mercilessly hard I had pushed him—how nasty, how cavalier, I'd been with something as precious and fragile as his heart.

I know Jarvis and his family. I love Dot, his sister and her kids, and Jo. And even though Jarvis is the one who messed up, even though my condition is his fault, I knew that if I sued him and won, his family would be the ones to pay.

The more I thought about it, the more I realized that taking him to court would only make a horrible situation that much more catastrophic.

I heard through the grapevine that one or both of his legs had been amputated. It's impossible to say that disfigurement is worse than severed limbs or severed limbs are worse than disfigurement. But I know that both he and I are suffering.

I don't want to care. My mind tells me to hate him. Who would fault me? But my heart won't let me. I haven't forgiven him. I don't know if I'll ever be able to do that, but I can't pretend as though he wasn't, at one time, my only source of inspiration.

"That's not going to work out," I say to Hannah.

"What? Why not?"

"What am I going to get if I sue him? A bag of video games and a pair of steel-toed boots? By the time the whole thing is over, I'll be eighty grand in the hole from lawyer's fees."

"Fine. Forget about the money. At least take him to court on criminal charges. Look at what he's done! You deserve justice!"

"Hannah, he's rolling around Detroit without legs. Lawsuit or no lawsuit, I think justice has been served. Jarvis is the past. I have to figure out a way to salvage my future."

"What're you going to do?"

"Find a way to get rid of some of this debt."

"You could sell your car," she suggests.

I groan, pained at the prospect. After spending the majority of my life bumming rides from family and friends or catching the bus, the idea of giving up my car—my baby—is torturous.

"It's only temporary," Hannah soothes. "Everything's gonna work out."

The doorbell rings. I look at the clock; it's almost midnight.

"How can you be so sure?" I scurry down the vestibule and tentatively crack open the front door.

Hannah is standing in the hallway, festooned in a glittery, floor-length, evening gown, her cell phone pressed against her ear. "Because," she says, pulling me into her arms. "You have me."

"Okay, explain it to me again," Dad asks for the third time. "Hannah is doing what?"

"She's going to move in with me." I speak extra slowly hoping this time it'll sink in. "She's going to help out with the bills."

"You're renting out rooms now?" Mom asks.

I hate when they double-team me and get on the phone at the same time. "We'll be like roommates," I explain. "She'll have her own bedroom and bathroom and she'll pay for half of everything."

"She's going to pay half the mortgage just for one room?" Dad asks, clearly uneasy.

"And half the utilities."

"What's in it for her?" Mom questions.

I shrug. "A great place to stay."

"I'm not sure about this," Mom says. "I think you're digging yourself into a deeper hole. The bills are already more than you can handle living alone. I know this roommate thing sounds great on paper, but expenses always rise when more people are involved."

"And isn't Hannah a bit wild?" Dad asks.

"This isn't about Hannah's character," I say defensively. "This is about taking in a roommate to make ends meet."

"You say that now," Dad cautions. "But what happens if you get into a fight or if she starts to grate on your nerves? You've never had a roommate," he reminds me. "It's not as easy as it sounds."

"I shared a room with Val," I say somewhat testily. "What could be harder than that?"

"Speaking of Val," Mom says.

"April," Dad cuts in abruptly. "This isn't the time."

"It's fine, Dad." I sigh. "What about Val?"

"Well," Mom begins. "I was talking to her yesterday about your problem, and—"

"What problem?" I ask, already livid. "I don't have a problem."

"Abby, don't overreact," Dad instructs.

"She asked me how you were doing," Mom says innocently. "I wasn't going to lie."

"You're my accountant," I say, seething and irritated. "What happened to professionalism? What happened to confidentiality?"

"I'm also your mother," she says. "And Val is your sister. She worries about you."

"I'm sure," I snip, my tone dry and cynical. "It's not enough to have you two scrutinize every single penny I've spent in the past three years and shake your heads disapprovingly; now you've gone and involved Mrs. High-and-Mighty."

"I don't understand where your it's-me-against-the-world mentality comes from," Mom says, unfazed by my outburst.

"Sweetie, we all love you, Val included. No one's shaking their head in disapproval," Dad says, calm as ever. "We know you've been through a lot."

"And we're proud of you," Mom adds.

"You've done very well for yourself," Dad continues. "And no parents could be prouder. But everyone needs help sometimes."

I feel my anger wane. My dad is good at defusing emotional bombs before they explode and leave behind a room full of wounded feelings.

"You haven't even given me a chance to fix it," I say.

"Well, Honey, that's because we don't want you to make it worse," Mom says.

"April," Dad scolds. "That's not helping."

"I really think she should consider Val's offer."

"What offer?" I ask.

There's silence on the other end of the phone as though both of them are suddenly afraid to speak.

"Val talked to Paul," my mother begins slowly. "And if you decide to sell your condo, they'll be more than willing to pay off the remaining balance of your mortgage."

My skin literally tingles. "I'm hanging up now."

"Won't you at least think about it?" Dad beseeches.

"I have to go," I say flatly.

"Well, what should we tell Val?" Mom asks.

I scowl at the phone. "Tell her thanks, but no thanks."

"Good morning, Sleepyhead," Hannah chirps. She's standing behind the island in the kitchen, wearing my favorite sundress, and pouring herself a bowl of cereal.

"Morning," I grumble. My head is throbbing from the discussion I just had with my parents.

"I was going to make us omelets, but you don't have any Eggbeaters."

"That's okay," I say. "I'm not a big breakfast person. Gimme a cup of coffee with a shot of vanilla and I'm good to go."

"I'll remember that for next time, Roomie," she says too enthusiastically for eight-thirty in the morning.

She opens the fridge. "I thought about it all last night, and I can't believe we didn't do this sooner. Who would make better roommates than the two of us?"

She fetches a knife from the wooden block sitting on the counter and a plate, then slices half a banana and dumps it into the bowl. "Think about the amazing parties we could throw."

She grabs another plate and another knife with which she cuts up several strawberries.

"You know I'm not much of a party thrower," I say.

"You cannot have a place like this," she waves the knife around, "and not throw parties."

She retrieves a spoon from the silverware drawer, scoops a small amount of sugar from the glass jar to her left, and sprinkles it evenly over her breakfast. Then, she throws the spoon in the sink along with the two knifes and two plates she's already sullied.

"I guess it would be okay to have a few, small get-togethers," I concede.

She grins devilishly and goes back to the refrigerator.

"What're you looking for?" I ask.

"Soy milk."

My face involuntarily scrunches. "I don't drink soy milk."

"What do you drink?" she asks.

"Vitamin D."

She feigns a gag. "Do you know how much fat is in Vitamin D milk?"

I shake my head. I don't know and I don't care.

"Too much," she says.

I watch, dumbfounded, as she dumps the contents of the bowl into the trash can. "I'll pick something up on my way to work."

I look at the pile of dirty dishes in the sink and the perfectly good cereal and fruit in the trash.

Living with someone is not as easy as it sounds. Dad's words ring in my ears.

I follow her upstairs to her new room. The television and all the lights are on.

"Are you sure this is what you want?" I ask. "You're paying an awful lot of money for one bedroom and bathroom. You could probably get three times more space for half the rent somewhere else."

"It's worth it," she smiles. "You're my friend and you need my help. I want to do this." She slips on my brand-new beige, calfskin Manolo Blahnik sandals. "You have enough to deal with right now. Don't worry about me."

"Uh-huh." I stare at her feet.

"Oh, I hope you don't mind," she says, following my gaze. "I didn't have anything other than the pumps I wore last night and they hurt my feet. I think the heel is too high."

"But those are three-inch heels," I say, pointing at the never-worn, $450 sandals on her feet.

"Hmm," she studies the shoes pensively, "I never would have guessed that."

I take deep, soothing breaths and fight to keep my irritation at bay. The last time I checked, those shoes were in their box—in my closet. Hannah is sweet and well-intentioned, but the vision of her rifling through my belongings and borrowing one of my most expensive pair of shoes without asking has me seeing stars.

"Please be careful with them," I say, gulping down the urge to raise my voice.

"I'll guard them with my life," she says, standing up straight and flashing her version of the Scout's Honor.

She retrieves her keys from her purse. "I'll call you tonight," she says.

I watch her tromp loudly down the stairs.

The television and the lights are still on, her bed is unmade, and the gown in which she arrived last night is haphazardly thrown over the armchair by the window.

An unsettling pang of regret curls up in my stomach. What was I thinking? How am I supposed to live with someone who subsists on soy milk and Eggbeaters and needs three dishes, two knives, and a spoon to fix a bowl of cereal?

My imagination begins to run wild. Images of coming home to a place pulsating with loud, obnoxious music and overrun with skinny, midriff-bearing lushes, forces my blood pressure up.

Roommates automatically come with the price tags of privacy and control and I've never lived with anyone before.

In college, I was fortunate enough to get a single my freshman year, and the year after that I moved into a tiny studio, where I stayed all the way through my Master's program.

I like having my own space. I like making sure things run according to my schedule and are situated my way.

Who am I to tell her she can't dirty as many dishes as she wants or play the television twenty-four hours a day or throw party after party? Yes, I own the condo, but I need her in order to keep it. She knows it and I know it.

My only other option, it seems, is Val. We haven't spoken in a long time. She calls regularly, about once a week, but I never pick up the phone. I do listen to her messages, though, sometimes twice. She never fails to close with, "I love you and I'm praying for you."

After the stunt she pulled in my hospital room, my contempt for her has only grown deeper. But for some reason, I look forward to her messages. There's compassion in her voice and genuine concern. Despite myself and everything that's transpired between us, I feel safe when I listen to her speak—safe and remembered.

Some weeks she just chats breezily, others, she puts my niece and nephew on the phone. "Hi, Auntie Abby," their cheerful voices sing in unison. "We miss you!"

I can't help but smile, and some days—the loneliest days—I'm overcome with regret, just thinking about how much of each other's lives we've missed out on.

But then there are the weeks when she reads me Bible verses or utters long, drawn-out prayers. Those are the messages I erase. Those are the messages that remind me why I resolved to keep her at a distance in the first place.

I can't take money from her and Paul. That would be like accepting charity from two strangers. That's all Val is to me. And I refuse to feel guilty about the rift in our relationship.

She abandoned me first—in the worst way.

For years I waited for her to say something, to stand up for me, to protect me, but she never did. Instead, she turned a blind eye and pretended like nothing happened—like I hadn't told her. She moved forward, carefree, and left me to rot within myself.

Then, even after all of that, after all I'd been forced to survive, she tortured me mercilessly with her spiteful jealousy.

For reasons I've never understood, she begrudged me all happiness. It's as though she wanted to see me broken—as though she wanted to see me fall.

That's why her miraculous change of heart means nothing to me.

If God really exists, if He really changed her like she claimed, then He should have done it sooner, before I lost the will to love her—before the only emotion I could feel toward her was rage.

But He didn't. Instead, He sat on His hands and let her stomp me into dust along with my will to live.

And for that, I can't forgive either of them.

11. Jarvis

I listen and watch Haley as she prays. Her voice is fragile and raspy like a crisp autumn wind. Her tone is shy and faint, but there is strength in her words—strength and simple truth.

Her eyes are closed, her long lashes rest like feathers against the tops of her freckled cheeks. She has short, honey-blond hair, and as she speaks, her breath causes her bangs to rise and fall softly against her forehead, which is wrinkled with concentration.

She's chubby with stumpy, round fingers that somehow manage to fit perfectly into my cupped hand. She's wearing overalls and white sneakers, and even though she's the same age as me, there's an untouchable innocence and youth about her.

She has a slight double chin and a chipped tooth. Her eyes are two different sizes; her love handles protrude from underneath her shirt, and her upper arms are streaked with faint stretch marks.

I don't see an exceptional beauty when I look at her. I see an exceptionally beautiful heart.

She's my prayer partner. I drew her name out of a paper bag two months ago and we've been praying together at Bible Study, and occasionally on the phone, ever since.

I like to hear her pray. There's something captivating about the way she speaks to God, the way she praises and thanks and blesses and asks and intercedes.

Right now, she's praying that I perform well in my classes. She's asking God to give me supernatural wisdom. She thanks Him for me. She thanks Him for giving me the opportunity to go back to college and she asks Him to use me mightily for His purposes. She prays I will make friends who lift me up and encourage my Christian walk. She prays that He will introduce me to people who are able to see what a wonderful person I am. She prays genuinely and thoughtfully.

My prayers are not as long as hers. They're just as sincere, but not as in-depth, not as eloquent.

Her requests are the same every week. She wants more opportunities to witness, daily guidance, and when the time's right, a new job. She wants to see her sister saved and she wants to meet her soul mate. Haley's requests are a mirror of what kind of person she is—uncomplicated and unselfish.

"In Your precious name, amen," she concludes with a warm squeeze of my hand. She's startled when she glances into my already open eyes.

Feeling smarmy, I quickly look away and clear my throat.

"Thanks," I say. "Your prayers are uplifting. They encourage me."

"I'm glad. Your prayers do the same for me." She lets go of my hand and gathers up her Bible and study materials.

The room begins to fill up as sets of prayer partners file in from different secluded spots.

The class is comprised of forty people who range in age from twenty-five to thirty-five. Some are professionals, some are students, and some are parents. We come from different walks of life, we have different goals and are traveling different paths, but we all have two things in common: we are single and we love the Lord.

I look forward to these Bible studies—the people, the lessons, the laughs. All of it focuses me and propels me toward my new life.

"Looks like most of you made it back," Andrew says. He's a young guy, my age, maybe a couple of years older. He's wearing a shirt that reads, "I'm Too Blessed to Be Stressed," faded jeans, and loafers.

His wire-rimmed glasses spend more time sitting on top of his unkempt hair than in front of his dark brown eyes and he has a lisp. He's funny, laid-back, and I think of him more as a friend than a teacher.

"Alright, let me make a couple announcements so we can get out of here," he says over the commotion.

The talking comes to a halt.

"Don't forget the singles' weekend retreat next month. I want to see all of you there—no excuses," Andrew says. "Also don't forget next Monday, we're doing our twenty-four-hour fast. Remember you guys, this is a time for you to focus on your relationship with Christ. And…let's see, what else…" he pauses, glancing down at the open notebook sitting on the desk in front of him. "Ah!" he says, delighted. "Don't forget Jarvis's baptism will take place this Sunday at the 11 a.m. service."

A few people clap.

Haley reaches over and pats my wrist.

"Try to be there," Andrew requests of the class. "And I think that's it. Any comments, questions, or concerns?"

The room is silent.

"Okay, then I'll see you all on Sunday."

A tiny congregation forms around me. Some people just want to congratulate me and shake my hand; others promise to be there for my baptism on Sunday. I thank each of them individually, grateful for their support.

The room is nearly empty by the time I stuff my notebook and Bible into my bag. Haley is standing in the hallway, her tote hanging from her wide shoulder. I look up at her and she smiles.

"You look nervous," she teases. "Are you?"

"A little," I admit. "More so about the testimony than the baptism. I don't do well in front of crowds."

Public speaking has never been my forte, mainly because large groups of people make me skittish. I can think of several humiliating incidents involving me, a speech, and ultimately a room full of cackling onlookers.

"It'll be fine," she says confidently. "If you need someone to pray with or talk to, you can call me anytime."

We make our way down the corridor, through the back of the sanctuary, and out the double doors into the parking lot.

"I guess I'll see you this Sunday," I say, backing away.

"Where are you headed?"

I shrug. "Back inside. The church van doesn't leave for another hour."

"I can give you a ride," she offers.

"Are you sure? It's kind of far."

"Hop in." She points at her little two-door. "I'll take you anywhere you want to go."

I consider her offer and weigh my choices. I could mill around church and be bored for an hour, or I could let Haley give me a ride and get home sooner. Then again, nothing very exciting is waiting for me at home either. I'll just end up forcing down a can of salty soup and studying Professor Leavey's review sheet for my test the following morning. Not exactly an action-packed evening ahead of me, no matter how I slice it.

"My friends are throwing a party tonight," I say. "It's in Farmington Hills. I wasn't going to go, but if you aren't busy, maybe we can go together."

She looks skeptical. "I outgrew the party scene a long time ago."

"I have it on good authority that this get-together is one worth going to."

She tilts her head in consideration.

"Come on," I urge. "We'll just stop by, and if we hate it, we'll leave."

Reluctantly, she agrees.

I open the passenger side door, lock my wheelchair into place, and slide myself, with ease, into her car.

Without my asking, Haley folds the chair and stuffs it into her trunk.

Fastened into my seat, I pull out the grease-stained scrap of pizza box and relay Nez's sketchy directions.

By the time we arrive, the party is in full throttle. It's not the friendly, harmless get-together I anticipated. The decent-sized house is overrun with loud, flailing college kids, most of whom are drunk.

Everywhere we turn there are empty plastic cups, stale popcorn, crushed chips, and beer cans. The furniture is overturned, the music is blaring, and kids are dancing on the couches and gyrating on the coffee table.

Haley sticks close to me, her hand never leaving my wheelchair's handlebar. We make our way through the cluttered living room and into the kitchen. There is a skinny, barefoot girl twirling on top of one of the counters. The tips of her spiked, short blond hair are dyed green. She has a half-empty bottle of something in her left hand and a cigarette in her right. Her cheeks are flushed and she teeters dizzily each time she stops spinning to take a drag or a swig.

I look up at Haley who can't tear her eyes away from the odd sight before us. I'm about to suggest we leave when I spot Chas waving at me from the back porch.

He slides open the screen door and comes over to greet us. "You made it," he smiles broadly.

I nod. "This is a crazy party."

"Yeah, it got a little out of hand. Who's your friend?" He studies Haley. She doesn't match all the other tan, half-naked, half-lucid female guests.

I introduce them.

Haley cautiously shakes his hand. I can see she's uncomfortable and I instantly regret dragging her here.

"Scribble!" Nez's voice exclaims from behind me.

I turn to see him carrying a twelve-pack of beer and a bag of pretzels. His eyes are red and glassy. "This your old lady?" Nez points at Haley and then lets out a loud, foul belch.

Haley steps behind me.

Chas glares at him.

"No," I say. "Just a friend."

"She's cute," he smiles sloppily. "Big, but cute."

The three of us watch him stumble downstairs to the basement.

"That's exactly why I don't drink." Chas points toward the staircase.

I force a laugh.

Haley doesn't respond and a discomfited silence settles between us.

"It's getting late," I say. "I think we should get going."

"No, stay," Chas begs. "You just got here. Join me outside. We got a mad game of poker going."

I glance over at Haley who doesn't look the least bit intrigued. "No, we really have to go, but I'll see you tomorrow."

Chas smiles apologetically at Haley. "Hope we didn't make too bad of a first impression."

"Not too bad," she says politely.

We push our way back through the packed living room and out the front door.

"I'm sorry," I say as soon as we're far enough away from the music for her to hear me. "I didn't know it was going to be so rowdy."

She shrugs. "You live and you learn."

"Let me make it up to you. Are you hungry? We could stop and get something to eat."

"Sure, that sounds good." She unlocks and opens the passenger side door for me.

"What're you in the mood for?" I ask. I hoist myself into the car and wait for her to load my chair in the trunk.

"I'm a simple girl." She situates herself behind the wheel, fastens her seat belt, and pulls away from the curb. "A plain old burger and some fries is as good a meal as any."

"You know what's better than a plain old burger and fries?" I ask.

"What?"

"A free plain old burger and fries."

She laughs. It's a hearty and strangely comforting sound.

"Turn right at the next light," I instruct. "I know a great diner off Seven Mile."

"You're the boss," she says and steers us toward JoJo's.

"Jarvis!" Jo's voice booms across the nearly empty room. Haley looks apprehensive just as Abby did the first time I brought her to the diner.

"This is Haley," I say.

Jo wipes his hands off on his apron and comes around the counter to meet her. "You guys must be hungry."

I smile and try to shake the unwavering sense of déjà vu buzzing around in my head. "A couple of burgers, some fries, and two tall glasses of lemonade should do us," I say.

"You got it. Go on back there—" Jo says, immediately catching his slip. He shoots me a nervous glance. "I mean, sit anywhere you want and I'll have your food to you shortly."

Haley chooses a table in the middle of the diner. "You must come here a lot." She moves a chair out of the way to make room for my wheelchair.

"I've been coming here since I was a kid. This is like a second home and Jo's like family."

"He seems like a stand-up guy."

"He is."

"It's funny," she fidgets with the napkin dispenser, "being prayer partners, we tell each other some pretty intimate things, but I still don't feel like I know you."

"What do you want to know? Ask me anything."

"What's the longest you've ever been in a relationship?"

"Five years," I answer truthfully.

She sits up, visibly more alert. "That's a long time." She sounds impressed. "What happened?"

I shift uncomfortably, not in the mood to pick old scabs, but unable to worm my way out of answering the question. "A lot of things. She moved to Chicago to pursue a music career. I didn't fit into her plans."

"What's her name? Anyone I might have heard of?"

"Abby. Abigail Walker."

Her brows shoot up as her vacant expression gives way to disbelief. "The cellist?"

"That's the one."

"Wow," she muses quietly. "What's it like to date a celebrity?"

I shrug. "She wasn't famous when I met her."

"She's gorgeous," Haley says. "So exotic. I always wanted dark features like hers."

I want to tell her the truth about Abby, about her conniving personality, sharp tongue, vindictive behavior. I want her to know that everything about her, including her straightened hair and capped teeth, is fake—nothing more than an expensive, time-consuming facade. But I'm determined not to be one of those bitter guys who crucifies his ex.

"Here we go," Jo says. He sets two steaming plates of food in front of us along with a pile of napkins and our drinks.

"Thanks," Haley and I chime simultaneously.

We take a minute to say grace.

"So tell me more about her." Haley sprinkles a liberal shower of salt over her fries.

"I haven't seen her in almost two years, but toward the end of our relationship, on a good day, she was..." I remove the onions from my burger and search for the right adjective. "Heartless? Cantankerous? Intolerable? Take your pick."

Haley looks stunned. "Well, what was she in the beginning of your relationship?"

The answer to that question needs no thought. "She was my entire universe."

Haley nods slowly, her mouth arched into a thoughtful frown. "That's even worse," she finally says.

I grab a napkin. "I know."

"Wasn't she in a horrible car accident not too long ago?"

I nearly choke on a mouthful of bread and beef. The subject was bound to come up sooner or later. If it wasn't Haley asking, it would've been a clueless relative I hadn't seen in who knows how long. Abby and the accident aren't erasable.

"Actually," I swallow hard and force my tone to stay even, "*we* got into a horrible accident, and that's another one of the many reasons why we went our separate ways."

Her eyes widen with clarity as she takes in my legs and the wheelchair under a new light. I watch her facial expression change as the tidbits of information she's received come together and create the big picture.

"Jarvis, I—I don't. I mean, my God, how terrible. I'm so—I just..."

I hold up my hand. "You don't have to say anything. It happened. It's the past. She's moved on with her life and I'm trying to move on with mine."

"You two don't see each other anymore?"

I shake my head. "We don't talk, we don't see each other, and as hard as it may be to admit, that's a good thing. There's just too much water under the bridge."

She takes a huge bite of her burger.

I smile.

"What?" she asks, her eyebrows thrown up innocently.

"You have a," I point, "big thing of mayonnaise..."

"Where?" she asks and dabs at the area with her napkin, which does nothing but spread the goop down to her chin. "Did I get it?"

I shake my head. "Here, let me." I reach over with my own napkin.

She blushes as I gently wipe her face clean. I marvel at how different she is from Abby. She's so feminine, so passive and docile. She's attractive, but in a simpler way. She wears overalls and Birkenstocks and she doesn't hide behind a shield of makeup or an army of fancy hairstyles. She's natural and unaffected. There's a vulnerability about her, the way she's unafraid to say what she thinks or how easily she shows emotion.

Abby wasn't emotionless, but sometimes it took the Jaws of Life to get her to open up and reveal what she was feeling. She was stoic and pragmatic and independent to a fault. But because I loved her, I accepted those traits and over time I became accustomed to them. I stopped trying to sit her down and talk about everything. I stopped expecting her to be lachrymose after every rejection letter or botched audition. And eventually I think I stopped feeling needed. Abby didn't need anyone; she tolerated people—she let them come along for the ride—but she didn't need them or even want them. She was born to be a solo act.

If Abby was sitting across from me instead of Haley and I pointed out smeared mayonnaise on her face, she would've rushed to the bathroom to clean it off or grabbed a compact mirror from her supersized, overpriced purse. She wouldn't have trusted me to remove it for her.

Being allowed to wipe food from someone else's mouth is a small, insignificant thing, but I feel grateful for Haley's willingness to let me do it. The mere act erases the ambiguity I've felt for so long about what my role is supposed to be in a relationship and awakens in me the desire to be needed, appreciated, and loved.

"I got it," I say, pulling my arm back.

She smiles kindly and our eyes lock.

"So what's the longest you've ever been in a relationship?" I ask.

"Four years. We were actually engaged for a while," she admits.

"What happened?"

She shakes her head. "I met Jared at a time when I was desperate to be a part of something. I wanted someone to call my own and he seemed as good a guy as any.

"He was attractive—the kind of person not many people really knew, but everyone loved to be around. He had an aura about him, but something was missing. We had comfort, familiarity, trust, love, but there was no spark—no passion.

"I was marrying him because being his wife meant security and stability. And I think he was marrying me because I was a dependable, solid investment."

She sweeps her bangs off her forehead. "It would've been one of those marriages that required both people to sacrifice their happiness for longevity and I couldn't do that."

"Do you ever regret your decision?"

She shakes her head. "Not getting married was the smartest thing I've ever done. My only real regret is not graduating. I was studying interior design. It was my passion and I was good at it. I only had two more semesters to go—twenty-eight credit hours—but I was inundated with caterers and invitations and bridesmaids' gowns and moving.

"I decided to put college on the back burner until things calmed down." She pauses. Her sad, disappointed eyes gaze into mine. "What can I say? Here I am, eight years later, still twenty-eight credits shy of a degree."

"Hey, I'm a thirty-one-year-old college freshman," I say gently. "I know the feeling."

She laughs. "We're a sad pair."

"I kind of like being a sad pair with you."

Her cheeks flush. She lowers her chin. "Thanks."

We talk and steal glances at each other as we polish off our dinners. She's a different caliber of person. She says exactly what she means. There's no conversational undertone or game-playing with her. I don't have to wonder if she's enjoying my company or if accepting my invitation to dinner was part of a bigger agenda.

Best of all, sitting across from her and watching her laugh and tell stories, I'm not afraid to be myself. I don't have to try to beef up my vocabulary or try to act more sophisticated than I really am. The conversation flows freely and steadily and I glow at how good it feels to just be Jay.

"What do you say to some dessert?" I ask.

She rubs her bulging stomach affectionately. "I say, bring it on."

12. *Abby*

I can still see it. There were pink balloons everywhere—floating across the floor, dancing lightly across the ceiling—frilly adornment fit for Val's thirteenth birthday party.

Before this time we had usually had our birthday parties together. After all, our birthdays were only six days apart. But that tradition, to my horrifying dismay, had outlived its short course. Val, it seems, was becoming slightly more allergic to me with the passing of each year. She wasn't a little girl anymore; she was a teenager, and she felt obliged to tell us every chance she got. So, I guess it shouldn't have been a surprise to me when my parents came to the living room one evening after dinner to break the devastating news.

"Hey, Squirt." Dad sat across from me. Mom smiled sympathetically and stood next to him.

"We need to talk, Honey," she said, wringing her hands.

I put down my book and gulped. A conversation that began with "We need to talk" couldn't be a good thing. I mentally reviewed the past week to make sure I hadn't done anything wrong or remotely questionable. Nothing came to mind. I dog-eared the page I was reading and sat up attentively.

"About what?" I asked.

"You know you've got a birthday coming soon."

My face lit up. "I know," I bounced up and down excitedly, "and I have the best idea. You'll never guess what it is."

"I'm sure it's great," Dad said enthusiastically. "But—"

"No, you have to guess," I argued.

Dad sighed, his plan to delicately diffuse the birthday bomb already crumbling around him.

"A pool party?" Mom threw out.

"Nope!" I shrieked. "Guess again."

"The zoo," Dad offered.

I shook my head, ready to burst. "Give up?"

They smiled, relieved, and nodded. "You got us," Dad said.

"A skating party!" I exclaimed. "It's perfect. Nobody I know has ever had a skating party. Tracey Freeman said that she was going to have hers at the new rink off Eight Mile, but it never happened and since her birthday was in March, I figure her parents said 'No.' So, I could be the first person to have a big skating party, and since it's a really big rink—I know because Mark Short went there with his brother last weekend and he said it was gigantic—I could invite all the girls from my class and Val could invite all the girls from hers, which means lots of gifts. And the best part about it is that Val and I could still have our parties together, but not really because I figure that since the place is so big, she and her guests could hang out on one end and me and my guests could hang out on the other." My chest heaved with excitement. "So what do you think?"

"Well," Dad said. "That sounds like it could be a lot of fun."

I squealed and clapped my hands together like a happy little seal.

"But Sweetheart," Mom said, clearly pained that she was the one who had to burst my bubble. "This year is really special for Val. She's not a little girl anymore. She'll officially be a teenager and she wants to do something really special."

"More special than skating?" I asked in disbelief. To my ten-year-old mind, such a thing simply did not exist.

"Not necessarily more special," Dad assured me. "Just different."

I looked at them bewildered. Skating was special and since it was something we'd never done before, it qualified as different also. Was it just me, or did skating still seem as perfect an idea now as it did three minutes ago?

"She'd like to have a coed party," Mom clarified.

"You mean with boys?" I asked, the word "boys," rolling off my tongue like toxin.

"That's right," Dad confirmed.

"Right now, it may seem strange to you, but when you're thirteen, your interests will change too. A couple of years from now when it's your turn to become a teenager, you'll be asking for the same kind of party."

I mulled it over. The whole coed thing threw me for a loop. Why would anyone want to ruin a perfectly good party with boys?

As far as I was concerned they were about as useful as gerbils. Sure, some of them were cute, they were fun to play with, and sometimes they were good for a laugh, but if you stripped those three things away, all you had left was a smelly, hairy rat. Even so, I conceded, they could still skate. If Val wanted to ruin her half of our birthday bash grossed out by cootie-ridden, booger-picking, scabby-kneed boys, that was her problem.

"Okay," I shrugged. "I guess that would work."

They both sighed with relief. "I'm proud of you," Mom glowed.

My dad agreed. "I'm telling you, Abby, you're really maturing. It takes a big person to be so understanding."

I shrugged. "It's no big deal. Val can invite boys to our skating party. It'll still be fun."

Their faces dropped simultaneously. Dad massaged his temples.

"I don't think we're on the same page here," Mom said and sat down next to me. "Sweetie, Val's going to have her own party this year." Her smile was wide, but her eyes were wrought with concern.

"Without me?" I asked.

She nodded.

"We're going to have it here," Dad said softly.

"Not at the new skating rink?" I looked back and forth between them, my eyes brimming with tearful disappointment.

"Not this year." Mom rubbed my knee.

"But why?"

"It's Val's thirteenth birthday," Mom said, her tone patient. "It's a milestone. Do you know what that is?"

I shook my head. "No." And quite frankly I didn't care.

"A milestone is a very special point in a person's life. Val's crossing into her teenage years. Pretty soon she'll be a woman."

Since when did people become adults at thirteen? They weren't pulling the wool over my eyes for a second. There was nothing special about thirteen. It was an odd number customarily reserved for bad luck. The only thing that turning thirteen was going to do for Val was absolve her from being twelve.

This show they were putting on, pretending as though they were beside themselves with regret—tenderly, meekly tiptoeing around me, and showering me with accolades—was as transparent as a jellyfish on a sunny day.

This wasn't about being fair or about Val sprouting into womanhood. This was, once again, about playing favorites. It was about my parents catering to Val's every whim and me being forced to go along for the ride. This was about being the youngest—about having no voice, no options—and it infuriated me.

To make matters worse, the day before the whole thing was set to take place, my parents pulled out their daggers and sliced away another chunk of my happiness. They informed me that at the eleventh hour, Val had decided to turn her birthday bash into a sleepover.

And I was not invited.

"Why don't you get out the school directory and pick a couple of friends?" Dad suggested, despite my miffed insistence that this whole affair was as unfair as the day was long. "Mom and I will call to see if you can stay overnight with one of them."

A couple of friends turned into nine. Nobody was able to take on an extra kid with such short notice. By that evening, desperation had set in.

I propped my elbows up on the kitchen counter and cocked my head to the side while Mom continued to flip through the directory. "I guess it's just me and the couch," I announced sadly. On the inside I was rapt with glee.

"Wait a minute!" Mom snapped her fingers. She flung open one of the kitchen cabinets and pulled out her small cardboard box of phone numbers. "You can stay with Uncle Jimmie and Aunt Bess."

I froze and pinched my thigh to stop the panic from setting in.

Uncle Jimmie and Aunt Bess weren't really family. They were friends of my parents. Dad and Jimmie knew each other from work, although Jimmie had retired shortly after my dad joined his firm; and Bess and Mom met at a dinner party where they hit it off and became instant friends.

Jimmie and Bess used to baby-sit us a few nights out of the week when Mom worked overtime. Both Val and I loved Uncle Jimmie and Aunt Bess and staying with them was like winning a trip to Disney World. They spoiled us with anything our little hearts desired.

But last Spring Break everything changed. I was nine. The day camp that my sister and I were supposed to go to closed at the last minute due to lack of enrollment. We were both disappointed until we found out we'd be spending our vacation with Jimmie and Bess. They had a pool and a dog and a big TV; what more could a kid ask for?

The first couple of days rolled along just fine. We swam and ate jelly beans and watched cartoons until our vision blurred. But the third afternoon changed my life forever.

I was sitting on the floor in the den in my bathing suit with a towel draped over my shoulders, stuffing my face with popcorn and watching Mighty Mouse save the day again.

Val was curled up on the couch, soft, rhythmic snores floating from her lips. We both reeked of chlorine.

"Abby, are you down there?" Uncle Jimmie called.

"Yes."

"I want you to come up to my office for a second."

"Okay." I abandoned my towel and buttery bowl of popcorn.

He was sitting at his desk, a strange, glazed look in his eyes. "Did you have a good time today?" he asked.

I nodded. "A really good time."

"Close the door," he ordered calmly.

I obeyed.

"Come here." He patted his knee.

I put down the remote control I'd accidentally brought with me and climbed into his lap.

"You know something?" he asked. "You and Val are two of my favorite people."

I smiled. "You're our favorite uncle."

"I'm glad to hear you say that. Good friends like us do things for each other," he told me. "Aunt Bess and I would do anything for you and your sister. Whatever you want, we make sure you get it. Isn't that right?"

"Yes," I agreed.

"Well, in every relationship, people give and take. Did your mommy ever tell you that?"

I nodded. "We're always supposed to share."

"That's right. Now I've shared everything I have with you and I think it's time for you to share something with me."

I pondered his request. I didn't have much. There was Chickaboo, my favorite stuffed animal, and I'd saved seven dollars and fifty cents from my allowance, but that was for Mom's birthday present.

"Like what?" I asked, in need of more explanation.

He ran his large callused hand down my leg. "Let me show you."

I closed my eyes and counted as high as I could count. I ignored the burning pain, the nausea, and the tears, and sat still like a limp doll. I kept counting.

"You're such a good girl," he kept whispering, his hot sticky breath scraping my neck.

Sixty-two.

"Just look at how pretty you are."

Ninety-seven.

"Uncle Jimmie loves you."

One hundred and forty-six.

By the time it was all over I'd almost counted to three hundred.

Just as he was rolling up my bathing suit, the door swung open. Val was standing before us with bloodshot eyes and matted hair.

"Do you have the remote?" she snapped.

"Sorry." I picked it up off the desk and handed it to her, my hand trembling. I waited for her to pause, to look around the room, to assess the situation and question why Uncle Jimmie and I were in his office alone with the door closed, my bathing suit bunched up and hanging off my shoulders. But she only turned on her heels and stomped back down to the den.

"You're a good girl, Abby," Uncle Jimmie said. "You know that, right?"

I didn't answer.

"Your parents are proud of you. They love you. You wouldn't want to do anything to ruin that, would you?"

I shook my head. "No," I whispered.

"Something tells me they wouldn't understand how you agreed to share with me. In fact, it might even make them hate you. You don't want them to hate you. That would make me sad. Wouldn't that make you sad?"

"Yes."

"Nobody loves you more than me, but if they found out, there's only so much I could do to protect you. I wouldn't want them to send you away, or even worse, put you up for adoption. I want you to stay part of the family. Isn't that what you want too?"

"Yes."

"Good." He kissed my forehead. "Now go on downstairs with your sister and have some fun. Oh, and Abby," he called.

I turned to look at him, my hero who had in a few short minutes transformed into a frightful monster. "Thank you for sharing with me."

I "shared" with Uncle Jimmie for the rest of our Spring Break. By the time our vacation wound to a close, I'd stopped swimming, stopped eating, and stopped watching TV. Since Jimmie's theory was that I had to share with him as long as he shared with me, I figured the only logical solution was not to accept anything from him so I wouldn't have to give anything in return. But, to my devastation, it wasn't that simple.

I glued myself to Aunt Bess and Val. Wherever either of them went, I was right behind them, dodging Uncle Jimmie to the best of my ability. But he always caught me. It would be when Val fell asleep or when Aunt Bess went to the grocery store. No matter what—in spite of all my strategizing—he was there, waiting with that hungry, depraved look in his eyes.

I never told anyone. I didn't want to be an orphan. I didn't want anyone to be angry with me. There was no doubt in my mind that everything Jimmie said was true. How could my parents not be upset with me when I was upset with myself? How could I expect them not to be ashamed of me when I felt so nasty—so dirty?

Thankfully, school started back up, life grew busy, and we hadn't seen Bess or Jimmie since. But as Mom dialed their number, all of the old feelings crept back into the pit of my stomach. My hands grew sweaty and began to shake uncontrollably. Please God, I begged silently. Please don't make me go.

"Bess? It's April," Mom said cheerily. "We're doing fine. I know it has been a long time. Well, no actually, we were wondering if Abby could stay with you and Jimmie tomorrow. Yeah, Val's having a big birthday party and she's just adamant that having her little sister around will cramp her style. You know how these things go," she whispered conspiratorially, as if I wasn't sitting mere inches away from her.

I held my breath and waited on pins and needles. "Really?" Mom asked, smiling. She gave me the thumbs-up signal, her eyes wide and twinkling with delight.

My heart cracked.

"Wonderful," she said. "You are truly a lifesaver. Nope, anytime before two is fine. Okay, she'll be ready. Okay. Okay. Bye."

"I'm staying over there tomorrow?" I asked, numb with fear.

"Yep, looks like you're one very lucky little girl."

I had only one hope and that was to humble myself before Val and grovel. She was in the bathroom brushing her teeth. Her birthday outfit hung, perfectly ironed, on the door handle.

"Val?" I squeaked.

"Hmm?" She turned to me, a layer of white, frothy toothpaste covering her lips.

"Have you ever...uh, have—have you ever..."

She spit into the sink. "Have I ever what?"

"Have you ever shared with Uncle Jimmie?"

She looked at me, perplexed, her eyebrows furrowed. "Shared what?" she asked, wiping off her mouth and placing her toothbrush back in its porcelain holder.

"Just shared," I said helplessly.

She rolled her eyes and blew past me. "Go away." She stomped down the hall toward our room.

"Val, please," I followed after her, desperate.

"No," she said flopping onto her bed. "I've never shared with Uncle Jimmie. Now, go away."

"Can I please stay here tomorrow?" I begged, choking back my tears.

"Why?" she asked suspiciously.

"Just to be here. I promise I'll stay out of the way. I'll sleep on the couch or outside in the tent and I'll be really quiet. You won't even know that I'm here." The urgency in my voice must have frightened her.

"What's going on?"

"Nothing. I just—I just don't want to share with Uncle Jimmie anymore."

"Share what?"

"Please, Val," I begged. "Please. I promise. I promise I'll do whatever you tell me to do."

"What do you share with Uncle Jimmie?" she asked again.

I shook my head, unwilling, but mostly unable to tell her. "He does stuff to me that I don't like."

"Like what?"

I shrugged, tears spilling down my cheek. "He touches me and stuff."

Her eyes widened in horror.

I felt strangely relieved that she was appalled. For a brief second, it felt as if someone was on my side.

"How could you say something like that about Uncle Jimmie? He's never been anything but nice to us," she snapped. "You shouldn't make up stuff like that, Abby. It's mean."

I stepped back in shock. "I'm—I didn't. I'm not making it up," I stammered.

"Just because you want something doesn't mean you should lie to get it."

"I'm not. I wouldn't."

"I don't want you here tomorrow," she said plainly. "It's my birthday and I say no babies allowed. And just so you know, if you ever try anything like that again, I'm telling Dad."

I stared at the ceiling all night, my chin quivering, and counted down the hours until my impending doom. With sore, bloodshot eyes, I watched the sun rise through our bedroom window. I listened as my dad moved the living room furniture around to create a dance floor and my mom made coffee.

Val bounced about with her hair swept up into a delicate ponytail, her curls fastened loosely with bobby pins. She ate bacon and toast and directed Dad on where to hang the piñata and place the punch bowl.

It was her big day and she was fluttering from one end of the house to the other in a carefree daze as if our conversation the night before had never taken place. I didn't bother to mention it. Instead I watched, detached from the world and myself, as everyone bustled about the house grandly and prepared for the festivities.

The doorbell rang at 1:30. Uncle Jimmie was standing outside, a broad smile on his face. Petrified and defenseless, I threw my book bag over my shoulder.

The last thing I saw as I looked back was Val standing amidst a sea of pink balloons watching me, her eyes saddened with an unsettling mixture of pity and guilt.

13. *Jarvis*

"You looked like you were having fun last night," Jo says. I'm sitting behind the counter reading the paper and eating a poppy seed bagel. The early morning rush has just calmed down and I'm taking a much-needed break before I start preparing for the second stampede of hungry patrons.

I don't bother to look up. "That's because I was."

He pours me a fresh cup of coffee. "So are you going to tell me what's going on between you and Haley or do I have to dock your pay?"

"There's nothing going on. We're just friends."

"She's a good girl. You two would do nicely together. I have a sixth sense about these things."

I chortle and skim over the sports page. "Didn't you say the exact same thing about Abby when you first met her?"

"Don't you like Haley?" Jo passes me the cream.

I put the paper down. "Yeah, I do. She's cool," I say.

"Cool?" he imitates my casual tone. "What does that mean? You forget I'm straddling the fine line between old and geriatric."

"She's my prayer partner from Bible Study. We're in that 'getting to know you' stage."

"It looked like you two knew each other pretty well the way you were hugged up last night."

I roll my eyes. "See, now that's how rumors get started. No one was hugged up. We got out of Bible Study, stopped at a party I was invited to, and then came by here to grab something to eat. End of story."

"She likes you." He smiles. "She likes you a lot."

"Jo, give it a rest."

"What's the problem? You're not attracted to her?"

"She's attractive in her own way. I just—she's not..."

"She's not Abby," Jo says, his voice thick with disappointment.

"It's a lot of things," I confess. "No, she's not Abby, but she's still an amazing person. It's been a long time since I've been able to open up to a woman the way I did with Haley last night. She's got it all: intelligence, humor, compassion, honesty, and a strong Christian walk. But I just don't know if I'm ready to be in a relationship."

"Jay, it's been over two years. You need to get back out there—explore, take chances," Jo coaches.

"That's what I'm trying to do. Dedicating my life to Christ, going back to school, making friends, joining Bible Study, that's all me trying to rebuild my life, but it's going to take time."

"Don't cower away from what you and Haley might have; that's all I ask. Be open to the possibility of a new relationship."

I sigh. "When I was with Abby I spent the majority of our relationship feeling like less than a man. This time around I want to have my life on track. I want to have something to bring to the table."

"And you think finishing college is your answer?"

"I think it's a start."

"Then what?"

"I've been asking myself that a lot lately," I say, turning to face him. "And I know it's a long way off, but I want to run my own restaurant someday, like you. It's the one thing I can see myself still passionate about thirty years from now."

"You need more than passion and good ideas to run your own business. It takes hard work and sacrifice."

"But look at the end result." I glance past him at the diner. "Look at what you've accomplished. JoJo's is practically an institution. You've got customers who would sooner go hungry than eat breakfast anywhere else. They come here and they have regular tables and regular meals and they respect you for that—they're grateful. I want to know what that feels like. I want to re-create the same kind of haven for my generation."

I'm slightly embarrassed to have revealed such an intimate secret—even if it is to Jo. In my life, dreams and aspirations reside on the same plane as singing in the shower; they're exhilarating and private—and potentially humiliating. I stare at the floor and wait for him to give me all the reasons why it would never work.

"Sounds like a good plan."

I peek up at him. His eyes are glistening with approval.

"You really think so?"

"The possibilities are endless," he says. "I know that people made up their minds about you a long time ago, but I always knew this time would come. Never once did I lose faith in you. Never once did I think you'd become anything less than great."

"Thanks, Jo."

"I'm not just saying that." He pats my cheek. "You're special. God's got big things in store for you and don't let anyone convince you otherwise."

The chimes on the front door ring as Mr. Kopeky steps in with his newspaper, indicating the start of the second breakfast rush.

"I'll have the usual." He takes off his hat and shuffles over to his window seat.

I smile, pour him a cup of decaf coffee, and take it to him along with four packets of Equal.

"Morning," he says gruffly. "Why aren't you in class?"

I laugh. "My class doesn't start until two."

He grunts. "How's it goin'? You learnin' anything?"

I shrug. "Let's hope so."

He tosses the front page aside. A loud crash comes from behind the counter. I turn around to see Jo doubled over, eggs splattered all over the tile floor.

"Jo?" I call.

Mr. Kopeky stands up. "You okay?"

"Yeah, yeah, I'm fine," he strains, still bent over. "It's this arthritis. What can I say? I'm getting old."

Mr. Kopeky, satisfied with Jo's explanation, sits back down and turns his attention to dumping the Equal into his coffee.

"Your order will be up in a few minutes," I say and wheel myself across the diner and behind the counter.

Jo's on his knees with a wet towel trying to clean up the mess. His hands are unsteady, his forehead beaded with sweat.

"Can you get this for me?" he asks through shallow puffs of breath.

"Are you sure you're okay?" I ask.

"I'm fine," he wheezes.

"Don't worry about it. I got it." I grab the mop, which is leaning against the wall.

Wobbling, he stands to his feet. "It's just arthritis," he says again. "Don't make something more out of it."

Before I can respond, he unties his apron and disappears into the storage room.

14. Abby

I pry one eye open and will myself to lie absolutely still. My head is throbbing and my shoulders are stiff. I feel as though I've spent the night on a bed of jagged stones. I used to sleep like a baby atop my cushy mattress, surrounded by a fort of luxurious goose down feather pillows. Very few things could tear me away from a peaceful night's rest, but ever since I quit my job I've resorted to napping, which throws off my sleep pattern.

I've spent the past few weeks tossing and turning, waking up in cold sweats to the haunting echo of Uncle Jimmie's grimy old voice.

I sit up and sling my legs, like two lead bats, over the side of the bed. Coffee is the only thing strong enough to take away the persistent pounding at the base of my neck.

The house is quiet, which is a pleasant change. I've always known that Hannah prided herself in maintaining a wilder-than-average nightlife, but lately her ever-so-popular all-night raves have managed to migrate to my place. Twice, the police, responding to annoyed neighbors, came out and pulled the plug.

A large part of me wants to be angry with her. Hannah knows no limitations—no boundaries. The idea of picking up a strange guy at a restaurant and bringing him home, along with six or seven other friends, for a nightcap at three in the morning doesn't strike her as rude or intrusive.

But is she just doing what someone her age with her beauty and her money has the right to do? As perplexing as Hannah's lifestyle is to me, I wonder how much more accepting, how much more tolerant, I would be of it if my circumstances were different—if, instead of hiding in my room with a box of Milk Duds and the TV Guide, I would be downstairs like her, sipping martinis and rubbing elbows with oily-muscled, square-jawed hunks and svelte, trendy, glossy-haired babes. Maybe I would be the one grooving in the middle of a club somewhere screaming for the DJ to turn up the music.

Isn't that how things used to be? Weren't Hannah and I a team at one point in time? I can't remember. Losing myself, watching powerlessly as I morph into a mere shell of the vibrant, confident woman I once knew, is turning out to be, by far, the worst side effect of the accident. Watching Hannah enjoy the type of existence I know I could have—the type of life I've earned—irks me daily.

I make my way down the hall, standing still every few seconds to listen for movement. I'm almost confident she's still asleep until I slip on a huge puddle of water outside her bathroom.

I flip on the light.

The mirror is foggy, the shower still dripping. I can make out a trail of wet footprints leading all the way to her closed bedroom door. Would it have killed her to dry off in the bathroom?

Coffee, I remind myself. I proceed downstairs, but before I can reach the kitchen, I have to tiptoe over and around mounds of Hannah's clothes. She's mistaken the living room floor for her closet. Every day, a new pile starts—in the bathroom, in the living room, on the stairs. Avoiding her strewn wardrobe is a tedious morning ritual dance.

For someone who makes her living as the very embodiment of femininity, fluttering gracefully across stage after stage, I can't understand why she is such a slob. Between the ill-placed clothes I battle every evening and the wet footprints of death I have to dodge every morning, I am starting to feel as if my home is booby-trapped. Hannah and I are going to have to talk—again—I decide just as I stub my toe on one of her stray spike-heeled leather boots.

The kitchen sink is full of dishes, most of which look to be more clean than dirty. Not a big surprise. Hannah needs a different utensil to accomplish every little job. Just last week she was making a tomato sandwich, at one in the morning no less. I watched, speechless, as she used one knife to slice the tomato, another to cut off the crust and another to slice the sandwich in half.

I open the pantry and freeze in alarm at the empty space where my gourmet coffee is supposed to be. The thumping at the base of my neck grows stronger. I rummage through the shelves, pushing aside Hannah's vitamins, soy rice cakes, sugar-free pudding, bran cereal, protein shakes, and all the other healthy, bland-tasting food she chokes down to maintain her physique. There is no coffee in sight, only caffeine-free herbal tea.

"Hey, you." Hannah bounds down the stairs, trampling on her mess along the way.

"Have you seen my coffee?" I ask, my tone decidedly less cheery than hers.

"That chocolate almond stuff in the purple and gold bag?" she asks.

"Yeah."

"I gave that to Mitzy."

I slam the pantry door shut. "Who is Mitzy and why does she have my coffee?" I snap.

Hannah wisely maintains her distance on the other side of the island. "I thought you said you were going to give up caffeine."

"When did I say that?"

"Last week. I was going to the grocery store and I asked you if there was anything you needed and you said 'Coffee,' and I suggested you try herbal tea because it's naturally decaffeinated."

"And what did I say to that, Hannah?" I ask edgily, my voice rising.

"You said 'Okay.' "

"No," I explain, now boiling, and pound my fist on the counter. "I said, 'Okay, I'll keep that in mind.' "

"I was only trying to help, Abby."

"You know what you can do to help? You can pick up all of that stuff so I don't have to worry about breaking my neck every morning." I gesture toward the cluttered living room. "You can stop using five bowls, six plates, and ten spoons every time you eat cereal. You can vacuum every once in a while or do a load of laundry or ask before you invite half of Chicago to my condo."

"Listen," she says, her tone hard. "I'm sorry about the coffee, but you're going a little overboard."

"Overboard!" I shriek. "On which part? Have you looked at this place lately? It's a pit—an actual pigsty—and it only gets worse in the aftermaths of your bi- sometimes tri-weekly get-togethers."

"I work all day!" she shouts. "I don't have time to be a full-time dancer and full-time maid. If the floors need vacuuming or the dishes need washing, then why don't you sacrifice your bi- sometimes tri-daily catnaps and do a little scrubbing of your own?"

"Excuse me?" I ask, adrenaline raging through my body.

"And another thing," she continues. "I'm not an overnight guest or a vagabond you picked up on the highway. I live here. I pay half the mortgage and half of the utilities, so if I feel like inviting half of Chicago or all of Indiana here, I will."

"All you do is get drunk and flaunt yourself," I spit. "You're not a teenager. There's more to life."

Her eyes darken. "You spend every day in sweats and slippers, locked in your room, and glued to the television like an eighty-year-old woman waiting to die. Is that how you want me to be? What would make you happy, Abby? If I suffered with you? Should I come straight home from work, throw on a pair of old jogging pants, and join you and your economy-sized box of Milk Duds in front of the television?" Her usually smooth, pale face is now pink and splotched with anger.

"I'm not suffering," I say, unexpectedly stung by her words.

"Yes, you are," she snaps. "And you're trying to make my life just as insufferable as yours, but it's not going to happen. I'm my own person. You knew that going into this arrangement. You made the choice to withdraw into yourself and block out the world. Don't jump down my throat because you're the only person at your pity party." She snatches an apple from the fruit bowl, stuffs it in her duffel bag, and marches out of the house.

I stare at the closed door, fuming. Who on earth does she think she's dealing with? She must've mistaken me for one of her adoring fans. No one speaks to me that way, especially not in my own house, I think as I fly around the living room snatching up one article of her filth after another. She wants me to do some scrubbing of my own? I'll show her my version of scrubbing.

I grab her baby blue, silk sundress, her black, leather pants, her velour sweat suit, her sparkly camisole, her white designer blazer, several pairs of jeans, a hideous orange miniskirt, and that spike-heeled boot. I continue grabbing everything in sight until my arms can't hold any more and then I carry it all upstairs.

Dumping the load into her bathtub, I turn on the water and watch as almost instantly all of the colors begin to bleed together.

It's still not clean enough, I think spitefully and dash back downstairs almost faster than my feet can carry me to the laundry room, where I grab a big, plastic jug of bleach. En route back upstairs, I pluck a few dirty dishes from the kitchen sink.

I throw the plates and cups into the dark murky mess. The water splashes against the tiles and leaves behind large brown spots. I unscrew the bleach cap and evenly distribute every last drop on top of her clothes.

I nod curtly, satisfied that they are ruined and storm out of the bathroom, slamming the door behind me.

Tying a scarf over my head, I slide into an old pair of sneakers, hop into my car, and speed out of my driveway in search of gourmet coffee.

15. Jarvis

The knot in the back of my throat doubles in size as I look over the balcony at the sea of heads below me. The sanctuary is packed. I see Haley along with a large group from our singles class sitting in the first pew. She looks up, a warm smile on her face, and waves. My jitters dissipate for a brief second as I smile and wave back.

I've written and rewritten what is on the note cards in my hand. There's nothing to be nervous about. In the unlikely event I freeze or lose my place, all I have to do is speak from the heart. It's a testimony, not a book report, I remind myself for the umpteenth time.

I tug at the thin white robe I'm wearing and flip through my notes to make sure they are in order.

"Are you ready, Son?" one of the elders asks. He grips my shoulder firmly.

I glance nervously at the small, shallow pool of clear water in front of me. "I'm as ready as I'm going to get."

"You'll do fine," he says with the confidence I've been searching for since I'd gone to bed last night. "Remember, as soon as the pastor announces your name, Andrew's going to carry you across the water. Don't worry about a thing."

The knot returns. Being the first amputee to be baptized at my church, I had the pastor and his staff stumped as to how I was going to get out into the middle of the pool. Everyone threw out suggestions, desperately in search of a solution.

"My daughter has an inflatable raft. We can float him out on that."

"Is your wheelchair waterproof?"

"We can tie a rope around his waist!"

"Why don't I just carry you out there?" Andrew offered.

The group grew silent and all eyes turned to me for approval.

"Do you think you can do it?" I asked.

"It's no problem. I'll take you out there and you can lean on me for support while you give your testimony. Then we'll go on with the baptism as planned and after you've been submerged I'll carry you back," he explained easily.

The tension in the room eased as the plan settled in with everyone. I didn't argue because I knew it was the best anyone could do. But the idea of someone having to carry me left an uneasy feeling in my stomach.

I want the congregation to listen to my testimony—to understand who I am, how far I've come and how thankful I am for everything that's transpired in my life over the past several months. I don't want pity. I don't want them to look up and see a legless, helpless man being carried across a pool of water. I want them to see a strong man, a changed man, who is publicly proclaiming his love for Christ.

"Whatever it takes," I say, burying my pride.

The piano begins to play as the choir processes down the aisle, swaying in unison. The service is starting.

"Hey, Man, how's it going?" Andrew whispers. He's wearing swim trunks and a white cotton robe identical to mine.

I shake out my clammy hands. "I'm just ready to do this."

"Well, there's someone who wants to see you before you do."

Haley emerges from around the corner. Her cerise lips are glossy and her hair frames her face in deep waves. She's wearing a pastel dress and high heels that accentuate the length of her long legs.

"Hey." I blush, suddenly very aware of how little I'm wearing.

"Here," she says, shoving a thick, rectangular box at me. It's beautifully wrapped in shiny, gold paper. "This is for you."

"You didn't have to get me anything," I say, touched.

"I know, I just—I wanted to."

"Thanks." I listen as the morning announcer finishes up a passage from the Book of Psalms and asks everyone to bow their heads in prayer.

"I saw Jo and I met your mom," Haley tells me. "We thought that if you wanted we'd all take you to lunch after service."

"Sounds good," I say, my nerves making it hard to concentrate. "Why don't I meet you guys downstairs after the service?" I suggest a little too urgently.

The baptismal portion of the service is quickly nearing. Any other day under any other circumstances, I would've enjoyed Haley's presence, but sitting behind stage, mere minutes away from allowing Andrew to carry me, like a child, to the baptismal pool, all I want her to do is leave. I can't let her see me this vulnerable—this fragile.

"Oh, okay." She looks down at the gift she gave me.

"I'm going to open it later when things are less hectic."

She nods. "See you after the service then." She leaves and I let out an involuntary sigh of relief.

"This is a special Sunday," the pastor's deep voice echoes through the massive sanctuary. "Today we're all blessed to witness the baptism of Jarvis Daniels. Many of you over the past few months have gotten to know him simply as 'Jay.' No matter what we call him though, I'm sure those of us who know him all agree he's an extraordinary man from whom we can all learn a great deal."

"Here we go," Andrew says. Wasting no time, he hooks one arm around my waist and the other under my thighs and lifts me out of the chair with ease. I look straight ahead and try my hardest to ignore the lapping water beneath me.

"And now, Jarvis will share his testimony."

The water, which circles my waist, is cool. Thanks to the tall, glass partition, I am confident no one can see Andrew's arm firmly hooked around my back.

"Good morning," I greet everyone.

"Good morning," the crowd replies collectively.

"My name is Jarvis," I begin. "But I guess you already know that."

I look down at my first card. I'm supposed to talk about my childhood, about constantly staying in trouble and my father's death, about having no direction and how Jesus' love saved me. I have it memorized, but all I can think about is getting away from all of these peering eyes. I just want to get back to the safety of my chair, to go back to being invisible.

The longer I stay quiet, the more embarrassing the situation grows. I look out at the enormous crowd. What am I doing? What was I thinking, coming out here and airing all of my dirty laundry, all of my faults and deficiencies?

"Just take your time," Andrew whispers.

I cover the microphone with my hand. "I can't do this," I say.

"Yes, you can," he assures me. "Forget the cards. Just tell them why you love the Lord. Tell them what He means to you."

I turn back to the waiting congregation and as if caught in a powerful magnetic pull, my eyes lock with Haley's.

"I had this whole speech prepared," I say, holding up the note cards. "But I don't want to stand here and tell you something you've all already heard a million times. The long and the short of it is that I'm a sinner. There are things I've done in my past that still haunt me every time I close my eyes—things I'm too ashamed to mention. So in a world where forgiveness is scarce, to have found a God of second, third, and fourth chances, I feel like a new man—like the type of guy I always envied behind closed doors.

"I almost lost my life two years ago in a car accident, but instead I lost my legs. So, quite literally, I'm only half the man I used to be, but waking up every morning and witnessing God's mercy on a daily basis has me feeling more whole than I ever thought possible. It's kind of ironic when you think about it.

"Anyway, I gave my life to Christ in the dark, in the basement of my mom's house. And all I can say is that after too many years of failing myself and others, for the first time in my life, I know I'm worth something because Jesus died on the cross for me. He died to save me, a most unworthy bum, by anyone's account. So thank you for being here to share my rebirth. God bless you." I place the microphone back in its holster.

"Thank you, Jarvis," the pastor says.

I grip Andrew's robe as he carries me to the center of the pool.

"Do you believe that Jesus died on the cross to save you from your sins?"

"I do."

"And have you made the decision to commit yourself to living a holy and separate life with Him?"

I nod. "I have."

He smiles proudly. "Jarvis, I baptize you in the name of the Father and the Son and the Holy Spirit."

With my arms crisscrossed over my chest, I hold my breath as the pastor tilts me back and submerges me underwater. And when I emerge, the sanctuary is filled with thunderous applause.

We're all supposed to go to lunch after church, but Jo's tired, and Mom decides at the last minute to visit her sister in Lansing.

"I guess my lunch plans were a bust," Haley says as we make our way to her car.

"Why? I'm still game."

"Really?" she asks, thrilled.

I nod. "I could eat a horse."

"Well, I'm not sure where we can find any roasted horse, but I do know this neat Chinese restaurant that serves, hands down, the best spring rolls around."

We chat comfortably during the entire ride to Bloomfield Hills. The restaurant is quaint, with cozy round booths tucked into dimly lit enclaves.

We sit side by side, secluded at a small table in the back. Our thighs rest gently against each other as we pick over the menu.

It feels right being here with her, like out of all the cities in all the states in all the continents in the world, sitting beside her in this restaurant, feeding her shrimp toast and sinking into her laughter, is where I'm meant to be.

"Open your present," she demands playfully after the remnants of our appetizers have been cleared away.

"You know you didn't have to get me anything," I say, wiping off my greasy hands on the cloth napkin in my lap.

"You told me that back at church, and like I said, I know I didn't have to. I wanted to."

"It's not a bomb, is it?" I hold the box up to my ear and shake it.

She laughs. "Good thing it isn't, otherwise we'd both be dead."

I tear away the gold wrapping paper and toss the curly ribbons aside. I forgot how exhilarating it is to receive gifts.

Glancing into her bright eyes, I open the box. Inside is a black, leather-bound Bible; my initials are embossed grandly in bold script.

"Haley, this is..." I pause and search for the words.

"You like it?" she asks, her voice saturated in delight.

"It's amazing."

She looks genuinely pleased with herself.

"You're amazing," I say softly.

She blushes and tries her hardest to suppress a grin. "Stop it."

"You know it's true."

"Well," she finally says, her eyes firmly planted on the table, "I'm glad you like it. I saw it and instantly thought of you."

"This means a lot," I say, placing the lid back on the box.

"You mean a lot to me," she mumbles sheepishly.

Her timidity is endearing. It makes her helpless, but in the bravest sense of the word. Buying me the gift, eating and laughing with me, they're all her ways of showing she cares and that whenever I'm ready, she wants something more.

As I look at her smooth neck and her long, thick lashes, I realize I'm truly attracted to her. She isn't the type of woman I usually go for though.

She's heavyset with an awkward shape. Her hands are almost as large as mine and she has a loud, goofy laugh. On top of that she wears frumpy clothes and at times she's painfully soft-spoken, but the more effort I put into knowing her, the more attractive she becomes until I can't see anyone else but her.

Unlike Abby, Haley has earned my attraction. I didn't fall for a short skirt or a little bit of cleavage. What hooked me were her gentle spirit, her kind heart, and her faith in God and in me.

I lean toward her—slowly, cautiously.

Her breath catches.

I stop, just inches away from her face, and wait for her response.

She leans forward, closing the gap between us, and we kiss. It's slow and enjoyable, and when we pull apart, her airy grin mirrors mine.

We eat dinner and we kiss. And we share dessert and we kiss. And we read our fortune cookies and we kiss.

The afternoon is surreal, and as I watch her pull out of my mom's driveway, I smile—almost giddy from the possibility that hangs in the air.

16. Abby

I don't know if the rest of the city has conspired against me or if I'm just in a bigger hurry than usual, but traffic on State Street, for no good reason I can see, is moving at a snail's pace. What are all these people doing out on a Sunday afternoon?

I'm in a very foul, dangerously sour mood. All I want to do is get a bag of coffee and go home. The persistent thumping at the base of my neck, overshadowed by my anger, has long since disappeared. This is no longer about my headache; this is about principle.

My house is not a grocery store. It is not a place for Hannah to invite Mitzy over so she can rummage through my pantry and pilfer my coffee. And furthermore, I'm not switching to herbal tea. I drink coffee in the morning. I'm not concerned about caffeine or its potential health risks. I don't care that green tea will speed up my metabolism or that milk will fortify my bones or that orange juice will boost my immune system. I've had coffee every morning since I was in college and nobody is going to change that.

I resent everything Hannah said to me. Who is she to wallpaper me with insults? Who is she to use my condo, my beautiful home, as her own personal trash can? Who is she to decide that it's okay for Mitzy to drink my coffee instead of me?

I know who she is, I fume, livid, as I make a sharp right turn into the Dominick's parking lot. *She's the woman, like it or not, who makes it possible for me to stay in my home.* There is no way—absolutely no way—I can afford the monthly mortgage without her half. I hate feeling trapped this way, being completely dependent on someone whose values and ideals are so obviously dissimilar from my own.

If things were different, I would've heisted Hannah out on her stuck-up fanny the minute she had the nerve to get indignant. But things aren't different and the reality of my life is that if I evict Hannah, much sooner than later, the bank will evict me.

There are only a handful of customers in the grocery store as I stomp up and down the well-stocked aisles looking for coffee.

At the entrance of aisle seven, a lanky woman sporting cream slacks parks her cart in the middle of my path. Perusing the multiple shelves of spaghetti sauce, she seems indifferent to the fact that she's blocking my way.

"Excuse me," I say, trying to squeeze past. Without turning around, she moves her cart a half an inch to the side and then goes back to her sauce hunt.

"Ma'am, I need to get by," I say testily. She sighs as if I have inconvenienced her in the worst way and moves the cart over another half an inch.

I glare as she picks up a small bottle of Ragu, reads the nutritional label, and then places it back on the shelf. She follows the same routine with a jar of Prego.

I continue to glare.

She continues to ignore me.

Fed up and dangerously close to strangling her, I grab her cart and, with all the force I can muster, shove it down the aisle.

"Hey!" she barks as her cart and all of its contents roll farther and farther away.

"When someone asks you to move, *move!*" I bark back and continue my quest.

Befitting of my already dreadful morning, the brand of coffee I want is nowhere to be found. I search every shelf carefully, reading each label two and three times. It isn't there.

While Mitzy is probably lounging on a chaise somewhere decadently sipping a robust blend of Almond Chocolate Mocha, I have to settle for Hazelnut.

I stand in line, feeling cheated, and wait for the cashier—who seems to move more slowly with every passing minute—to ring me up. *The express lane*, I think with a scoff. *What a joke.*

"Miss, I can take you in this lane," a young man calls to the woman behind me. She, along with the two customers behind her, moves to the next lane over.

On another day, a better day, when I didn't feel like the world was out to get me, I would've let it slide. But how many times am I supposed to sit back silently and get stepped on? When is enough, enough?

"Excuse me," I snap at the young man who's already begun ringing up the woman who, just seconds ago, was behind me. Everyone around us stops what they are doing and turns their attention to me. "You're supposed to take the next person in line."

He laughs nervously.

Wrong response.

"I'm glad you find that amusing. You see this linoleum square?" I point down at the ground. "I've been standing on this square for almost ten minutes because Rainman's sister over there," I gesture at my cashier, "de-de-definitely, can't seem to pick up the pace."

"I apologize." His eyes are wide with uncertainty. "I didn't realize."

"Didn't you have to go through some sort of training? You always serve the next customer in line. That's common sense."

He stares at me, clutching a loaf of whole wheat bread, too petrified to move.

"Give the kid a break, Lady," the man in front of me says. "He said he was sorry."

"Sorry isn't getting me any closer to checking out, now is it?"

"It's people like you who make life unpleasant," someone calls out.

"Is there a problem?" a heavyset man in a red polo shirt asks. He is sporting khaki pants and a name tag that reads "Greg." The manager, I presume.

"There are a couple of problems. First, I've been standing in the same spot for ten minutes." I point at the Express Lane sign swinging above our heads. "The line is not moving. And second, that young man over there opened up his lane and took the last three people in line instead of the next person in line."

He nods sympathetically, prepared to patronize me the way he's been taught in his managerial manual. "I take full responsibility for that," he says. "I do apologize."

"I don't need your apology. I'm in a hurry. What I need is to pay for this coffee," I hold up the bag, "so I can get on with my day."

"That's no problem." He whips out a silver loop crammed with keys. "If you don't mind following me over to the Guest Services counter, I can check you out myself."

Under the disgusted, watchful gaze of everyone who's just witnessed my outburst, I follow Greg to the front of the store where he rings up my coffee as promised.

I'm not the least bit embarrassed as I climb into my car and head back home. I may have been louder than necessary, but I was still right. And besides, I'll never see those people again. They're just an unfortunate part of what is turning out to be an unfortunate day.

Classical music filters softly through my speakers and dances lightly in the small space of my car. I take deep breaths and allow the serene mixture of woodwinds and strings to relax me.

Breathe, I coach myself. *You're almost home.*

My one last nerve—that small, but significant thing absolutely everyone in my path is determined to stomp to death today—begins to repair itself as the tension in my neck and shoulders slowly unwinds.

At a stoplight five blocks away from my condo, a rusted, blue Saturn obliges itself to take up both lanes. The driver of the car, a young woman, is primping in her rearview mirror. With an eyelash curler in one hand and a small black tube in the other, I watch her meticulously apply two coats of mascara to her eyelashes.

The light turns green and I blow my horn, prodding her to drive.

She promptly gives me the finger and putters forward, smoky exhaust pipe and all, to the next red light where she again takes up both lanes.

My neck and shoulders return to their tensed state.

I squeeze into the half of a lane she's left open, determined to get by. When the light turns green, she revs her engine and speeds forward in a spiteful attempt to block me in behind a turning car. Her jalopy, however, is no match for my year-old sports car. Easily, I maneuver in front of her and, for good measure, I flick her off just as she'd done me.

Beeeeeeeeeeeeeeeeeep! I glance into my rearview mirror. The girl is beating on her horn, her free arm flailing dramatically over her head.

Beeeeeeeeeeeeeeeeeeeeep! She shakes her fist at me and suddenly speeds up. Her car spurts forward, only inches away from my bumper.

Beeeeeeeeeeeeeeeeeep! She lurches forward again. Her window is rolled down. She pokes out her head, and with her hair blowing in the wind, she yells a barely audible string of profanities at me. She continues to follow me down the street, attracting the worried stares of other drivers as well as pedestrians.

Beeeeeeeeeeeeeeeeeeeep! She tramps on the gas again. Her car shoots forward, only this time it slams into the back of my car. My body flies forward as smoke pours from the hood of her car. We both sputter to a halt.

I sit still for a few minutes and wait for her to come over, to offer some sort of explanation—some assurance of recompense—but she shows no sign that she plans to emerge from the safety of her car.

Call the police, I order myself. *There are witnesses. Anyone can see she's crazy. Don't do anything you're going to regret.*

But bidding myself to stay calm is a futile attempt at reasoning. I am officially a woman over the edge.

Dizzy with rage, I pop my trunk, which is already ajar from the impact, and throw open the driver's side door.

I pace the length of my car and examine the damage. It's considerable. The young woman in the Saturn still has her seat belt on. She shrugs portentously and smirks. Just as with the young man in the grocery store, that is the wrong response.

I grab my crowbar and stomp the few paces to her smoking Saturn. "Do you have any idea how much that car costs?" I scream and reach for the door handle.

I hear a click as she scrambles and pushes the automatic lock button.

"Hey!" I bang on her driver's side window with my hand. "Hey, I'm talking to you, Little Girl. That car," I point to the expensive heap of crushed metal in front of us, "is worth more than your life!"

She gulps, her eyes wide like a trapped rat and leans toward the other side of the car.

"What happened?" I yell. "Two minutes ago you were Evel Knievel and now you're cowering like a little punk. You wanted a fight. You got one," I promise and slam the crowbar down on the hood of her car.

She jumps and darts over the console into the backseat.

"I'm going to sue you for everything you're worth and more, you hear me?" I swing the crowbar again and crack her windshield.

"Are you listening to me?" I scream, strangely delighted by the fear in her eyes. "You don't know who you're messing with!" I kick the side of her car, leaving behind a grapefruit-sized dent. I raise the crowbar. "You miserable…"

Smash!

"Worthless…"

Smash!

"Piece of trash."

Smash!

"You are going to pay for this!"

By the time her car is dented to my satisfaction, I'm out of breath, my scarf's come untied, exposing my charred scalp, and the palm of my hand is beginning to swell. I don't care. I am furious, blinded by anger, by pride, and by bitterness.

Several cars have pulled over, and a crowd of onlookers has gathered on the sidewalk.

The bleak sky seems to spin, as if at that very moment, someone is turning back the hands of time—as if, at any second, I'll open my eyes and realize that everything that happened today—the fight with Hannah, my tirade at the grocery store, the silly, little girl in her rusted blue Saturn—is nothing more than a vivid dream.

I kneel down in the street, woozy and disoriented. The damaged car is just one more thing I can't afford. It's just one more thing to tack onto my seemingly endless list of permanently damaged goods.

"Everything's going to be fine. The police are on their way," a female voice says gently.

I look up, grateful for the concern, even if it's from a stranger. But she isn't addressing me. She's talking to the girl in the Saturn, whose name, I later find out, is Amber.

Amber, as it turns out, is only seventeen—an exceptional student, fresh out of high school. She is pre-med and was on her way to visit her terminally ill grandfather. She'd received a call saying he'd taken a turn for the worst and was rushing to his bedside when she ran into me.

That's the version she relays to the officer anyway. Her tear-streaked face and quivering voice would've even convinced me had I not witnessed, firsthand, her infuriating display of dirty driving.

There are at least a half a dozen witnesses willing to corroborate her story. It mystifies me the way people practically stampeded over one another to attest to my vicious beating of Amber's raggedy old Saturn, but nobody—not one single person—managed to recollect how she chased me for blocks, blowing her horn and tossing me the finger along with a slew of choice words. It doesn't matter to anyone that she engaged me, unwillingly, in a game of Road Rage Tag, rammed me, and still refuses to offer any remorse.

I spend the rest of the afternoon at the police station in a small white room, sipping watery coffee from a Styrofoam cup. That's all I wanted in the first place—just a cup of coffee.

In the end it only cost me one tub full of bleached clothes, one grocery store full of angry patrons, one badly mangled sports car, one dented Saturn, one swollen hand, and one traumatized seventeen-year-old brat.

Granted, that's a pretty penny to pay for a cup of joe that isn't even gourmet, but I savor each sip regardless.

I continue to savor each sip of my watery coffee and wait patiently as someone somewhere decides whether or not I should be allowed to go home.

All afternoon, I sit and answer questions and fill out papers and sip my coffee until finally the chief of police comes into the room and tells me that Amber's parents are going to press charges.

17. Jarvis

I glare at Professor Leavey, along with all of the other students, as he paces up and down the auditorium's compact, rectangular stage. He's been rambling on about the Baskin Commission and "fixed baskets" for nearly an hour.

I close my notebook and glance at the clock on the wall for the hundredth time. Class will be over in less than twenty minutes and we still haven't received the results of our first exam.

I remember the first day of class: Professor Leavey had waltzed in, a pole of a man, his long thin ponytail a striking contrast to the glaring shine off the top of his bald head. He had a small, oddly shaped face that was hidden behind saucer-sized, thick-framed glasses. The front of his faded T-shirt was tucked in, revealing a huge belt buckle that encased the image of a snarling bull. His wrinkled jeans tapered radically at his ankles and were all but tucked into his scuffed tennis shoes. He looked more like a scrubby student than a professor of economics.

"Looks like a decent bunch," was the very first thing he said. The microphone clipped to his chest caused his voice to echo. "I'm Professor Leavey and this is Intermediate Macroeconomics. I'll start off this class just like I start any other class and that's by giving you what I like to call my 'Definites.' There are four of them and they are my promises to you.

"First, I don't know your names now and I won't know them by the end of this semester. There are far too many of you to get bogged down with names. I have four other classes, each of them this size or larger. Therefore all of my interactions with you, i.e., homework, tests, and quizzes will be done using your student numbers. So for all of you sensitive attention-seekers out there who thrive on a one-on-one relationship with your professors, this may not be the class for you.

"Second, it takes a long time for me to return test scores. Like I said, there are a lot of you. I have hundreds of papers to grade. I also have a wife and children and a life outside of this university, so you'll get your exams back when you get them back. Please don't write me emails or waste my precious office hours to ask about your grades. As soon as I know, you'll know.

"Third, by the time we schedule our midterm review, this room will be half full. That is to say, half, if not more of you, will drop this class. So please, be sure this is the right course for you within the allotted withdrawal deadline. Otherwise you'll be stuck in a class you don't like, I'll be stuck grading subpar papers, and your parents will be stuck footing the bill for your failure. It's truly a waste all the way around.

"And fourth, those of you who do stick it out and put in the work and effort that is most definitely going to be required of you to pass, will walk away with a sound understanding of the impact of international microeconomic development on financial markets and business."

Initially I respected his anti-silver-spoon approach to teaching. He's blunt, honest, and direct, and although his personality isn't everyone's preferred flavor, he is someone I can tolerate.

But as the clock continues to tick away, so does my patience. Hasn't he noticed his students' slow, decisive mutiny? Nearly everyone's stopped taking notes. Half the class doesn't bother to show up anymore, and the other half comes in thirty, sometimes forty, minutes late. I, for one, no longer even bother bringing my textbook.

We sit like stone replicas and block out his breathy, spastic voice.

Professor Leavey, however, doesn't care that the uncertainty of our ability to pass his class is bad for morale. The pattern is set.

At two o'clock every Monday, Wednesday, and Friday afternoon, he begins teaching whether the room is packed or three-quarters empty. He starts at a steady, normal pace, referring every so often to a pile of notes in front of him; then, fifteen minutes into the lecture, he hits a groove and, with spit flying and veins popping, begins gabbing at warp speed.

He speaks as if he's the announcer at a public auction; his words run together and muddle his sentences. He rushes from one point to the next as if he has more material to cover than time to cover it in. And his illegible notes are just as useless as his lectures. By the end of the hour, there may be six or seven words scribbled haphazardly across the projection screen.

My only hope of gaining a sound understanding of macroeconomics, as he so eloquently promised us the first day of class, is through the assigned reading, which would be a viable option were the textbook not written by a sadistic egghead with a penchant for polysyllabic words.

What we need—what I need—is to see my score. I need to see it for peace of mind, to know if I have a future in his class or if, instead of heading to the Student Union with Chas for a quick bite to eat, I need to stop by the Registrar's office and grab a Drop/Add form.

"How're we doing for time?" Professor Leavey asks and looks down at his watch. "We've got about ten minutes left. I'm going to stop here. Tomorrow we'll discuss several different categories of potential bias in using changes in the CPI as a measure of the change in the cost of living. It's exciting stuff."

I roll my eyes and reach for my bag.

"I want to discuss the results of your first exam," he says.

All movement stops. The room falls silent.

"Collectively," he removes his glasses, "your performance was dismal."

My stomach drops.

"I'm not sure the majority of you even have a firm grasp of supply and demand. That is the essence, the very *backbone* of economics.

"I gave all of you fair warning from the very beginning. I won't let you skate by. You must do the readings. You must come to class. If you're not prepared to do those two things then you're wasting my time. Now," he pulls out a thick stack of blue books from his briefcase, "this is how it works. We only have two tests. Your business prospectuses serve as your final exam. Those three grades along with class attendance and the occasional homework assignment will determine your overall score."

Don't panic, I order myself. *You studied for this. You could be the exception.* I try my best to ignore the ominous cloud of self-doubt that's settled over me.

"I encourage a good number of you, and you'll know who you are, to drop this class as soon as possible and do one of two things: Reenroll when you're ready to commit to the work load or take Introduction to Macroeconomics first and try my class again another semester. Now, are there any questions?"

A studious-looking redhead raises her hand.

"Yeah?" Professor Leavey nods at her.

"Do you grade on a curve?" she asks, her voice urgent.

"Most of the time, yes."

She, along with the rest of the room, lets out a grateful sigh.

"But," he says, organizing the tests into four neat piles on his desk, "this was not one of those times."

"Why not?" she half whines, half shrieks. She sounds like a drowning woman who's been thrown a lifesaver only to have it snatched back.

"Because with the extra credit, one of your peers earned a perfect score."

We all groan.

I inspect the auditorium full of anxious college students. Which one of them was heartless enough to score a 100 percent and how much will it cost to have him tutor me?

"The first pile is A through G. The second pile is H through N. The third pile is O through T. And the fourth pile is U through Z," he explains. "Once you get your test, you're free to leave...and don't forget to take advantage of my office hours."

There is no mad dash to the front of the room. Slowly, like a chain gang being escorted down death row, a line forms in the center aisle as one long-faced student after another waits to discover just how dismal his or her grade really is. I sit to the side with Chas and wait for the congestion to thin out.

"I have a plan," he says in his slow, husky voice. Today he's looking especially homeless in his wrinkled Lakers jersey, black sweatpants, and green flip-flops.

"What?" I keep my eye on the stacks of thinning test papers atop Professor Leavey's desk.

"If we come to class every day, do all of the homework assignments, and ace our business prospectus, we can fail both of our exams and still pass the class with a C."

"How are we supposed to get an A on our business prospectus, if we can't even pass the exams?"

"Because everyone knows Professor Leavey's exams are unpassable."

"*Unpassable's* not a word."

"You know what I mean. We can partner up and put everything we have into the final project. I'm telling you, Man, this is foolproof."

I shake my head. "I don't want to fail the exams."

"Better to fail the exams and pass the class."

I ignore him and wheel myself up to Professor Leavey's desk. Only one test remains in the A thru G pile. I grip it in my hand and debate whether or not to open it. To prolong the suspense, I reason, would be masochistic.

Glancing over my shoulder to make sure Chas isn't trying to sneak a peek, I flip to the back of the test booklet.

I stare at the dark red 100 before me. I flip to the front of the book. My name and student number are scribbled across the top. I flip back to the last page of the test. The 100 is still there, shining up at me—a ray of hope. It captivates me and I sit in the middle of the room, immobilized in its trance.

"Mr. Daniels, I presume." Professor Leavey is standing over me. The corners of his thin mouth are turned up. "Impressive. Keep up the good work."

I nod and slide the test into my binder. I'm determined not to be tacky, but otherwise I'd rush to the library, have it laminated, attach a string to it, and wear it around my neck.

Instead I tuck the binder safely, carefully, into my bag and roll proudly out of the room.

18. Abby

As I lie on my bed, staring at yet another exorbitant hospital bill I can't afford to pay, the doorbell rings. The unannounced visitor pounds relentlessly on the front door.

I would ask Hannah to get it, but she hasn't been home since our fight. Her ruined clothes are still soaking in the bathtub. I don't want to do anything—don't want to move. I just want to sit on the edge of my bed, close my eyes, and fade from existence.

Reluctantly, I trudge downstairs.

My mother is standing outside with a suitcase at her feet. Her forehead is wrinkled. She thrusts the *Detroit Free Press* into my hands and blows past me.

I've made headlines.

"Where's Dad?" I ask.

"Parking the car."

"You could've at least called," I say.

"You want to tell me what on earth is going on with you?"

The article is titled, "Where Has All the Music Gone?"

" 'Renowned cellist, Abigail Walker, 30, has traded in her bow for a crowbar,' " I read out loud. " 'Witnesses say Walker pulled a crowbar from the trunk of her sports car and attacked Amber Sheffield, 17, after Sheffield rear-ended her at a stoplight.' " Underneath the article is a picture of me scowling at the infamous blue Saturn, the crowbar raised over my head.

"Whatever happened to responsible journalism?" I ask and toss the paper on the couch with a roll of my eyes.

"So you didn't attack her?"

"No, I didn't attack her." I pause. "I attacked her car."

Mom throws her head back, furious.

"What was I supposed to do? She slammed right into me."

"It was an accident!"

I grunt. "Hardly."

"What're you doing with your life?" she asks. "What possible explanation could there be for your behavior? You're self-destructing. You're reckless. You're miserable."

"No, I'm not," I mumble.

"Then what are you?"

I shrug, admittedly unsure. "I don't know. I'm nothing."

As usual, she's unsympathetic.

"You've had sufficient enough time to sulk. We've all been patient. Reflection time is over. Now you need to come to terms with everything that's happened; accept what is and move on."

"This isn't a passing phase. I'm not going to wake up tomorrow and decide to pick up a cello and start playing again. I'm not going to suddenly grow hair or sprout a brand-new face. This is my life now."

"This is only your life because you're determined to be stuck here. Do you know what Jarvis is doing?"

"Who cares?" I snap with clenched fists.

"I saw Dot a few weeks ago and she tells me that Jarvis is really getting his life together. He's a full-time college student *and* he works full time for Jo."

"I *would* be impressed," I scowl, "if I hadn't graduated from college *ten years* ago."

"Don't be a snot," she scolds. "I'm not defending him. He'll have to answer someday for what he did, but in the meantime he's learned how to pick up the pieces and push forward and so should you."

I don't think about Jarvis often. I tell myself it's because I am too angry. Harping on how he's ruined my life—concentrating on the "what ifs" of that fateful night—is unhealthy. It will ultimately destroy me. But there is a small piece of me, the section closest to my soul and farthest from my heart, that can't be lied to.

It is the part of me that still remembers his mother's phone number, the part of me that slips into his Pistons jersey whenever I can't sleep, the part of me that smiles on those rare occasions when I allow myself to reminisce.

His face has faded from my memory. Having spent so many years with him, I thought the image of his soft eyes and loopy grin would be engrained in my mind forever. I took time to memorize his body, his mannerisms, and his habits. I wanted him to be colorful and absolute and eternal. But now he's only silhouetted against a backdrop of nostalgia, echoing laughter, and tears.

All I can remember is that stupid sweater with the hole and his scuffed steel-toed boots.

I had always assumed that Jarvis was destined to be an unachieved loser. Dancing on the outskirts of mediocrity was his specialty. He did it every day I was with him. The news of his return to college perturbs me. I've long since been to college and started a successful career, but I feel like he's suddenly surpassed me—as if, in a horrifying turn of events, he's risen to an occasion when I haven't. I find myself hoping he fails.

"This has nothing to do with Jarvis," I say coolly.

Dad stumbles through the door with two large suitcases. He goes back into the hall and reenters a few moments later with another suitcase and an overstuffed garment bag.

"Exactly how long are you two planning on staying?"

"That depends on you," Mom says, plucking a tissue from her purse and dusting off my coffee table.

"If it were up to me, you wouldn't be here now."

She looks up, unmoved.

My dad, winded, kisses me on the cheek and joins her on the couch.

"Abby, I don't think you realize how damaging this could be for your career," she says.

"What career?" I ask.

"The press has you pegged as an ogre. Who's going to want to buy an album from the woman notorious for bludgeoning a seventeen-year-old girl's car?"

"Who cares?" I shrug. "I'm not playing anymore."

They blink, confused.

"I've decided to retire," I clarify.

"Please," Mom dismisses my decision with a snort, "you're too broke to retire."

"I think what your mom's trying to say is that, given the state of your finances, retirement may not be an option right now."

"No, I said exactly what I meant," my mother intones, refusing to accept Dad's tactful reconstruction of her last quip. "You're too broke to retire. You *had* to have a penthouse condo in the Loop. You *had* to sleep in the best hotels and eat the finest foods. Well, to play hard you have to work hard, Abby. It's as simple as that."

"I do work hard."

"No, you *used* to work hard. Now, all you do is sit around and pretend like the world owes you something."

"I think we're starting off on the wrong foot," Dad says.

"Why do you baby her, Dennis? If she's as unconscionable as she wants us to believe, then she should be tough enough to hear it straight."

I seethe. "Just get out!"

"Calm down," Dad orders.

"Silly me, I actually thought you were here to show support. But you drove five hours just to judge me."

"Nobody's judging you, Abby."

"You didn't come here to see if I was all right. You didn't ask for my side of the story—you don't even care. What's the first thing you do when you get here? Thrust a newspaper in my face and tell me my career is over."

"I never said anything of the sort," Mom argues.

I ignore her. "I didn't call you. I didn't ask you to come here."

"Honey, we're your parents," Dad says softly. "Put yourself in our shoes. If you picked up the paper one morning and saw what we saw, wouldn't you be concerned?"

"Concerned? Yes, but I wouldn't beam myself to your house bursting with accusations and a pocket full of preconceived notions. I would give you the benefit of the doubt."

Mom chortles nastily. "What explanation could there be, Abby? Unless the crowbar magically developed a mind of its own, jumped into your hand, dragged you to that girl's car, and forced you to beat it, there's no rationalization."

"Tell us what happened," Dad says. "Was she driving erratically? Did she do or say anything?"

"What *didn't* she do?"

I recap the entire incident from start to finish. I tell them about the makeup, how she'd taken up two lanes, the way she jutted forward on three separate occasions and blew her horn. I told them everything and basked in the redemption of my mom's stunned and apologetic gasps.

19. Jarvis

Jo, who is already behind the grill flipping pancakes, tosses me my apron and I go to work taking orders, filling coffee cups, handing out menus, and ringing up satisfied customers. By the end of the second morning rush, I have a generous wad of tips in my back pocket.

Jo joins me at one of the tables where I'm enjoying a blueberry muffin and a glass of orange juice. "Why are you all cheery this morning?" he asks.

I lather my warm muffin with a liberal spread of butter. "I broke the curve."

"What does that mean? You 'broke the curve.' "

"I got a 100 on my economics exam," I say around a mouthful of sweet bread.

He leans back. His toothy smile is congratulations enough.

"I wish you could've been there," I say and take a swig of juice. I recount the previous afternoon, from Professor Leavey's disparaging remarks to the studious redhead to my perfect score.

"What'd your mom say?"

I laugh. "She taped it to the refrigerator."

"She's proud of you. We all are."

We sit in silence for a while, me eating my muffin and Jo staring blankly out of the window.

"I have something I think you should see," he announces suddenly. "But I'm only going to show it to you if you promise not to blow it out of proportion."

"How can I promise not to blow 'it' out of proportion when I don't know what 'it' is?" I ask, amused.

"If it were up to your mom, you would've never found out, but, I don't know, I'm worried about her."

I put my muffin down; my stomach churns nervously. "You're worried about Mom?"

"No, I'm worried about…Abby."

My senses are immediately alerted and I stop chewing. "Why, what happened?"

"It probably sounds worse than it really is. You know how the media likes to create a lot of hype about nothing. She probably didn't even do wh—"

"Jo." Panic balls in the back of my throat. "What happened?"

From his apron he pulls out a neatly folded section of the *Detroit Free Press* and sets it down in front of me. I open it without hesitation. My breath leaves me as I stare, befuddled, at a picture of Abby with a crowbar raised over her head. She's scowling hatefully at the hood of a car.

She's a stranger—angry and unhinged. I read the article over and over again, trying to gain clues, to glean some understanding of what this girl, Amber, could've possibly done to evoke such a response from Abby.

I stare at the picture, at her disfigured face, her angry eyes, her badly scarred hands, and I blame myself.

"What do you think?" Jo asks.

I shake my head. " 'Abigail Walker, former Chicago Symphony Orchestra cellist, resigned unexpectedly last April,' " I read aloud. "She quit her job."

"That doesn't necessarily mean anything. She could be working on another album," he offers.

"Maybe I should call her."

"I don't think that's the solution."

"But she needs someone. Look at her, Jo."

"I agree. She needs someone, but that doesn't mean she needs you."

"Who else is there? Hannah? Val? She'd be better off going on Jerry Springer."

"It's not your responsibility to save her, Jay. This doesn't have anything to do with you."

"This has everything to do with me. This is my fault. You can't see that?"

He tilts his head. "How is this your fault?"

"She quit her job—a job that means everything to her. She's beating up people's cars." I hold the paper up for him to see. "She's completely lost it."

"There could be a million different reasons why."

"There aren't a million reasons. There's one and it's me. I wrecked the car. I threw everything off kilter. I ruined her life."

"Look at you and what you've managed to do with yourself. You lost your legs, Jarvis. Don't overlook that. Don't dismiss it as an unimportant detail. Simple things like getting dressed or fixing yourself something to eat are challenges for you, but you do them. You go to school, you go to church, you work, you struggle through basic routines, and you do it all with a joyful attitude because you've learned to be grateful for who you are despite your circumstances."

"She lost much more than I did though, Jo. I was nothing *with* my legs so it wasn't hard to become something without them. But Abby," I pause as a familiar wave of regret washes over me, "she had everything to lose and she did."

"I understand what you're saying, Son. But, we're all accountable for our own actions. I'm sure she's going through a hard time right now, but misery is a choice."

"I should call her," I say, ignoring Jo's words of wisdom. "I should see if there's anything she needs, if there's anything I can do."

He sighs. "Okay, let's say you call her up and she's happy to hear from you. Say, she needs a shoulder to cry on and she's been thinking about you and wants you to go to her. She wants you to come to Chicago. What do you say?"

"If she needed me, I would go to her."

"What about work? What about school?"

"School and work are always going to be here. Abby's more important."

"What about Haley?" he asks. "I thought the two of you had something."

I shift in my chair. "We do—sort of—but right now, we're technically just friends."

"So you're telling me you'd actually drop everything you've worked for, everything you've sacrificed, to be with Abby if she asked you to?"

"Yes."

Sickened, Jo pushes back his chair, its metal feet scrape loudly against the linoleum floor, and begins to pace.

I stiffen, unsure of how to respond. "Things between Abby and I are complicated—they're different. Regular rules don't apply to us and they never will," I explain.

"Think carefully. Weigh the potential consequences. You've got a good thing going here. Messing with that girl again is going to be the wrench that sends everything grinding to a halt. I guarantee it."

" 'That girl'? Ten minutes ago you were a concerned friend and now she's turned into 'that girl'? What did you think I was going to say when you showed me this?" I toss the newspaper aside. " 'Oh what a shame'?"

"When are you going to let go?" he asks, his voice marked by exasperation.

"I don't know. Maybe never."

The bells hanging from the door chime behind us.

Neither Jo nor I look up.

"It's over, Jay. What's done is done. You and Abby aren't together anymore."

I shake my head. "It's not that cut and dry."

"Why not? What is it? What is it about her that keeps you so drawn to your past—to such a dark and dreary past? There's a bright, promising world staring you in the face and you're willing to shun it for the chance to dive back into an old, destructive relationship with a woman who will never make you happy—a woman who's proven to you time and time again that she'll never put anyone or anything before her own wants."

I throw my hands up. "That's like asking me why there are twenty-four hours in a day or why the grass is green and the sky is blue. I don't know why," I say, my voice rising with each syllable. "That's just the way it is. She's too much a part of me, Jo. We've been through too much just to chalk it up to the past. There will always be a part of me that belongs to Abby."

"It makes no sen—" Jo freezes, the sight of something catching him off guard.

I turn around.

Haley is standing at the entrance of the diner. She's clutching a plastic bag with both hands. Her chin is quivering.

"Hi," she whispers and smiles uneasily. "I, um, I just—well, here." She sets the bag down on the table nearest to her. "It's that book I was telling you about, you know, um, the one on Toronto attractions."

"Haley, I—"

"I have to go," she says to the floor.

"Just let me explain."

"I have to go," she says again and walks out of the door.

Jo looks at me sternly—scornfully. He's thinking, *I told you so*. He's thinking, *why couldn't you let things be?* He's angry and disappointed. But he doesn't say anything. He stares at me for a few seconds; it's a hard, cold, jolting stare. Then with his head shaking, he resumes his place back behind the counter.

I spend the rest of the morning working, but lost in my own thoughts. Half of me, the decent half, the smart half, wants to find Haley and tell her it's all a misunderstanding. I want to apologize and beg for her forgiveness. I want to grovel and plead temporary insanity and pledge my allegiance to her and to our budding relationship.

But the other half, the obdurate half, the curious half, wants to dash to the nearest phone and call Abby. I want to offer my condolences and my help. I want to fix everything that's gone wrong. I want to transform her back into a functional human being. I want to absorb some of her pain and, hopefully, in the process, purge my guilt.

I don't know what to do. I'm torn by two equally convincing arguments and two equally potent women. The confusion and the heaviness follow me from work to school where I barely sit through three lectures and a lab.

By the time I get home and locked into my room, the only thing I'm sure of is that I owe Haley some sort of explanation. I pick up the phone and, with my heart racing, dial her number.

She picks up on the first ring.

"Hey, it's me."

She doesn't respond.

"Please, hear me out."

I hear the television playing softly in the background. "There's no need," she says.

"Yes, there is. I was upset when you saw me. I found out some things and it stirred up old emotions."

"What things?" she asks.

"Abby's gotten herself into some trouble and I feel responsible."

"You feel responsible that your ex-girlfriend, who you haven't seen in two years, attacked a minor with a weapon?"

"It was a crowbar," I say defensively. "And who told you?"

"I read it in the paper like everyone else."

"So then you can imagine how hard this is for her—how hard this is for both of us."

"You know what I think?" she asks. "I think you know you're not responsible. I think you've been waiting for something like this—for anything that might give you license to ride in on your white horse and save the day. Saying you're responsible for what Abby did is like saying it's her fault if you fail a test. What goes awry in her life is not your fault and vice versa. The truth is you want this to be your problem. You want to have a reason—any reason—to see her, to be near her. You're biding your time, pining away for her, hoping someday she'll take you back. I just pray you haven't wasted away too many years of your life before you realize that's not going to happen."

"You don't know what you're talking about," I say frostily.

"I probably don't. Like you said, you two have a lot of history and there will always be a part of you that belongs to her."

"That's right, there will be."

"Then why are you talking to me? What I think shouldn't matter."

"We're supposed to be friends."

She laughs bitterly. "I can't be that girl, Jarvis. I can't straddle the line between friendship and romance. I can't be your security blanket, that person you settle for because you can't have who you really want."

"You'll never be a security blanket," I promise.

"I'll also never be Abby, and right now that's obviously a problem. Listen, we don't know what might've been, and maybe that's a blessing. Maybe that's God saving us from ourselves. I just wish you hadn't led me on."

She sighs. "I mean, you knew I had feelings for you. How hard would it have been to tell me you weren't ready? But instead of being honest, you kissed me."

"I'm just confused, that's all. I don't know what I want—what I should do."

She doesn't respond and we sit in silence listening to each other's shallow breathing.

"I don't think there's anything left to say." Her voice is soft and hurt.

"Haley, there's something between us. I'm not denying that, but I need some time to figure things out."

It's selfish to ask her to wait for me while I wrestle with the possibility of revisiting my relationship with Abby. I don't want to hurt her, but I don't want to make a mistake either. I don't want to say no when I should say yes or turn right when I should turn left. I don't want to look back tomorrow, next week, or a few years from now and regret the decision I made.

But what if not making a choice when I had the chance ends up being the biggest mistake of all?

"Good-bye, Jay," Haley whispers.

"Hello? Haley? Hello?"

I push the Flash button several times. "Haley?" I call. "Hello?"

But it's no use, she's gone.

I decide not to call Abby after all. Haley and Jo are right. She isn't my responsibility anymore. She's the past.

I don't know what happened that morning between Abby and Amber Sheffield. And while part of me feels like I had a hand in pushing her over the edge, the sensible part of me knows that Abby's the one who got herself into the mess and she will have to find her own way out.

God's given me a new lease on life—a new direction. And Jo's sacrificed a lot; he's pulled strings and cut checks. He has a vested interest in me. To flush all of that down the toilet would be wrong and insulting. I have too much going for me. Too many people are depending on me to do the right thing—to finish what I've started and make something of myself. Nobody, including Abby, is worth jeopardizing that long-awaited trust.

It takes less than a week for me to realize I miss Haley. She's switched to a different Bible Study and refuses to return any of my phone calls. There are words I need to say, feelings I need to express, but I can't. She won't let me and I find myself melancholy most of the time. The nights are long and the days are even longer and I have no one to blame but myself.

To get my mind off of her and how I single-handedly massacred our relationship, I immerse myself in class lectures, homework, study groups, and review sessions. They are my life outside of church and work, and it shows.

"Look at this." I toss my calculus exam on the counter. "Excellent!" is scrawled across the top in bright red ink. "I got a 94."

Jo slides on his glasses and skims over the pages of equations and graphs. "Another A," he muses quietly. "You're on your way."

"It was the fourth highest grade in the class," I boast. "Out of sixty students, I got the fourth highest grade."

"You were always bright, just like your Uncle Jo."

"I don't feel bright," I confess.

"That's because you're still nursing a bruised ego."

"It's not ego," I tell him.

"Sure it is. Rejection hurts, even when it's deserved."

"I don't get it. She doesn't want to see me or talk to me. I call her every day, but it's pointless. She hates me."

"What about the trip to Toronto. I thought she was supposed to drive you."

I shrug. "I don't think that's going to happen."

"Is that what you want?"

"What I want is for things to go back to the way they were before this whole Abby mess happened."

Jo shakes his head. "You confuse me. One minute you see Abby's face in the paper and you're ready to dump everything and go to Chicago. Now you're sulking because Haley won't give you the time of day. You don't know who you want to be with."

"I want to be with Haley," I say emphatically.

"Then you have to prove it. For Abby, you were prepared to drop out of school, quit your job, pack your bags, and abandon your life. But Haley doesn't pick up the phone a few times and you're ready to give up. Does that seem right to you?"

"I don't know what to do. How am I supposed to fix this?"

"Take it from a man who spent the better part of his life married, Haley doesn't want to talk to you because there's nothing you can say to make things better. The only way to win her back is to show her you're sincere. Women need to know they're worth fighting for. Show her she's not a passing phase. Show her you'll do whatever it takes to get things with her back on track."

"How'd an old timer like you get to be so smart?" I joke.

He pokes out his chest. "My wife trained me well before she died."

"That she did."

He unties his apron. "If we're done solving your latest love crisis, I think I'm going to sit down for a few minutes."

"Sit down?" I poke fun. "Jo Jr., are you going soft on me?"

He doesn't laugh. "Traffic is slow right now," he says. "Just call if you need me."

I watch him limp slowly to the back room. A frightening uneasiness settles in the pit of my stomach. I've noticed subtle changes—the weight loss, the shaky hands and labored breathing—but he insists it's nothing more than old bones and bad arthritis.

Jo is a headstrong guy, I tell myself, but the worry doesn't ease. If something is wrong, he should tell someone. Or maybe he's tried, the thought occurs, but I've been too wrapped up lately in my own ordeals to pay attention.

"Jo," I call and follow after him.

"Hm?" he moans.

I'm surprised to see he's set up a small, dingy cot by the back door.

He's lying down, his eyes pressed shut.

"What's going on?" I question.

"Just resting my eyes."

"You're a workaholic. You never rest."

"What can I say? I'm getting old."

"You look like you've lost some weight."

He smiles slightly and caresses his round stomach. "Nope, it's all still here."

"Well, what's with the stubble?"

He rubs his chin. "It's nothing."

"Is it the arthritis?"

"What is this, Twenty Questions?"

"Is it the arthritis?" I ask again.

He sighs. "It makes my fingers weak. I can't steady my hands as well as I used to."

"Why didn't you tell me? I can shave you."

He laughs heartily. "Let you near my neck with a sharp razor?" he asks. "Never."

"Jo—"

"It's not a big deal. I was thinking about growing a beard anyway."

"Have you seen a doctor?"

"Jay, go watch the front," he orders.

"You may need X rays or surgery."

"Jay," he pleads. "Everything's fine. The only thing I need right now is for you to watch the front, okay?"

"Yeah, okay."

I examine him as his stomach rises and falls heavily with his strained breaths. He doesn't move—doesn't open his eyes. He lays on the small cot, seemingly paralyzed, his hands balled into tight fists and drifts off to sleep.

20. *Abby*

The truth eventually emerges. Amber was driving on a suspended license and our round of bumper cars turned out to be her fourth accident in two years. She wasn't on her way to bid farewell to her dying grandfather; she was late for a meeting with her parole officer.

Having been arrested all of four months earlier for petty theft and the month before that for drunk driving, she's a juvenile delinquent of the worst kind.

I feel exonerated when the judge informs the Sheffields that their daughter will not be permitted to operate a motor vehicle until her twenty-fourth birthday. *If only all bad drivers were kicked off the road,* I think smugly. *The world would be a better place.*

"As for you, Miss Walker, I'm appalled by your behavior. It's one thing to see our youth fall prey to a dog-eat-dog mentality, but someone of your age—your experience—should have exercised better judgment.

"If violence was the only viable solution you could come up with, you're struggling with some dangerous inner demons. However, when I look at you, I don't see a threat to society. I don't see someone who will benefit from incarceration. I see a woman upon whom tragic circumstances have fallen. I see someone who, with the right kind of help, can become an asset to her community again."

I'm ordered to complete two hundred hours of community service and to attend anger management therapy three times a week for ninety days.

The community service assignment is tolerable. All I have to do is provide cello lessons at an inner-city high school. By my calculations, five students, at one hour each, a day comes to twenty-five hours a week. In two short months, I'll be done.

The anger management therapy, however, is an entirely different story. Everyone knows that therapy only works when the parties involved are willing participants. I am definitely not a willing participant.

I'll admit, beating up Amber's car was not a high point in my life, but losing my temper doesn't automatically make me a candidate for therapy. I resent being forced to go and I would've conveniently forgotten that part of the ruling had the judge not made a point of assuring me I would either attend ninety days of therapy or spend ninety days in jail.

Hannah moves back in the week after my parents leave. She forgives me for the clothes, I forgive her for the coffee, and we make an effort to coexist. It isn't hard. She sticks to her wing of the condo and I stick to mine.

Her late-night soirees occur less frequently with less noise and fewer people. Her clothes no longer litter the halls, there are hardly ever dirty dishes in the sink, and the pantry stays stocked with purple and gold bags of gourmet coffee.

But a strange vibe has settled between us. We're cordial, but uncomfortable, as if each of us knows the other's every move is being scrutinized. Our relationship, after a long stalemate, has made the thorny shift from friends to landlord and tenant. And while I appreciate her efforts to change, the tension between us is unbearable—so I decide to sidestep my principle and do something about it.

I find her outside on the deck, lying on a blue foam mat, contorted into a painful-looking Pilates position.

"Hey," I greet her.

"Hey." She untwists herself.

"Listen, I never got a chance to apologize about your clothes."

"Forget about it." She reaches for her bottled water. "It's over."

I dig out a check from my pocket. "This probably doesn't even begin to pay for it, but it's all I have right now."

She holds up her hand. "I don't want your money."

"What can I do to make it up to you?"

"You don't have to do anything, Abby. Let's pretend like it never happened."

"But it did happen and now things are weird between us and I can't stand it."

She tucks her knees under her chin. "Things aren't *that* weird."

"We spend more time avoiding each other than living together."

She squints up at me. "I moved in here because you love this place and I want to help you keep it. I want you to be happy. You used to be so happy, but now it's like everything and everyone drives you crazy. I honestly don't know what you want me to do or who you want me to be."

"I want you to be yourself."

"How am I supposed to be myself when you snap at me for the most minuscule things?" Her wounded eyes contrast sharply with her glistening, blond hair.

"I know," I pule.

"We used to have the same interests, the same tastes and friends, but things are different now. We live on opposite ends of the spectrum."

"That doesn't mean there isn't a middle ground," I say. "A lot of our problems would be solved if I loosened up and you toned down."

"Yeah," she nods. "I guess you're right."

So that's exactly what we agree to do.

She confines her clutter to her room and I stop hounding her about the way she fixes cereal. She washes the dishes and I play gracious hostess to her guests.

We find a manageable stride and inch back to the way we used to be, maybe even better.

21. *Jarvis*

I take another look at the book Haley gave me. I've thumbed through it, front to back, a dozen times. Each time, it makes me smile.

She's circled and highlighted dozens of events we can do together. I grin at the little notes scribbled next to certain attractions.

"I bet this is beautiful!" is jotted next to a picture of the Royal Botanical Gardens.

"Roller coasters! Yea!" is written below the Ontario Place headline.

"I heard this was really good," she scrawled beside a review of the *Lion King*. "Don't worry—no big ladies with horns in this one. I promise," she added with a smiley face.

I've never been to the theater and it's a running joke with us. She could hardly contain her surprise when I first told her.

"Never? As in never ever?" she asked.

"Never, ever, ever."

"You don't know what you're missing."

"I've seen those big ladies on TV with horns on their hats, wailing at the top of their lungs. That's not my idea of entertainment."

Her head flew back in laughter. "That's the opera," she howled. "Nobody likes opera. Trust me, if you can watch wrestling every Monday and Thursday, which let's face it, is the worst acting possible, you'll love the theater."

I like that about her, the way she takes one of my current interests and couples it with my personality to figure out other things I'd enjoy even when I haven't yet experienced them.

She values me as a person: my opinions, my likes and dislikes, my strengths and weaknesses. She knows I watch wrestling. She knows I like roller coasters. She knows I've never been to the theater. She listens to me. She soaks in every word that comes out of my mouth and processes it with thought and emotion.

That's part of what makes her so remarkable. I know when I'm with her that I am the only person she's thinking of. When we're together, there is no other place either of us would rather be. She leaves no questions lurking in the recesses of my mind. Her wishes—her desires—are true and honest and crystal clear.

But me, I'm as decisive as a leaf blowing in the wind. One minute I'm kissing her and the next I'm shouting my undying affection for Abby. Sunday night I'm confused and Wednesday morning I'm ready to be with her. It's no wonder she doesn't trust me now—after what she overheard me say to Jo—and refuses to listen to my apologies.

Like Jo said, she needs proof—extreme, tangible, irrefutable proof. But before I can show her my dedication to making her happy, I need to get inside of her. I need to compile everything I know about her, everything I love about her, and use it to create something masterful.

I grab a notebook from my nightstand. What do I know about Haley?

I know she's never ridden a train...that she loves jazz music and arcades. I know she enjoys modern art and theater, and she hates malls and shopping. I know she's allergic to shellfish and has a weakness for dark chocolate.

I write feverishly, recounting what I can, all the things she's shared with me. I fill page after page until it's all out—until everything I know about her is staring back at me in black ink. Now what do I do with it?

I don't want to cop out and send her roses or write a generic letter. A couple of flowers and a few sweet words won't express the extremity of my regret. In time, they will fade into nothing and that is not acceptable.

The book of Toronto attractions sits, upside down, on the edge of my bed. My answer's been in front of me the whole time.

I work tirelessly through the evening and into the night, making phone calls, purchasing tickets online, and securing confirmation numbers. I even enlist the help of my mom, who at half-past midnight drives me to the nearest twenty-four-hour convenience store so I can pick up the finishing touches.

By two in the morning, everything is done. I look at the gift I've prepared for her, hopeful and petrified. There's only one more thing that has to be done.

I pick up the phone and dial her number.

"Hello?" A groggy, unpleasant voice answers.

I hesitate.

"Hello?" the voice asks again.

"Haley?"

"Yeah."

"It's Jay."

"What time is it?" she mumbles.

"Two."

"In the morning?"

"I know it's late, but I couldn't wait to call you."

"Is something wrong?"

"I need to see you."

"Now?" she croaks.

"No, tomorrow morning. Can you meet me at the diner? I promise it won't take long."

She sighs. "Give me a second. I'm half asleep." I hear the ruffling of sheets. Her mattress springs creak under her shifting weight.

"It won't take long," I promise again. "I have some things I need to say."

"Can't you just say them now?"

"No, it has to be in person."

"Jarvis, I don't—"

"Please," I beg. "I know it's late and I woke you up and I'm the last person within a fifty-mile radius you want to see. You've done a great job at avoiding me and under any other circumstances I would respect your space, but I can't—not when I know how wrong you are."

"Wrong about what?"

"About me," I say. "About us."

"There is no 'us,' " she snips, her grogginess quickly giving way to irritation.

"All I'm asking for is ten minutes of your time. Please, Haley."

She groans. "It has to be early because I can't be late for work."

"Seven?"

"Fine."

"Great, I'll see you then."

She walks into the diner ten minutes past seven wearing a pinstriped business suit and an apologetic smile.

My palms are sweaty. I was certain she had stood me up.

"Sorry," she says strolling over to me. "I had to get gas."

"You look great," I say.

"What did you want to talk about?"

"Coffee?" I offer.

She shakes her head. "I'm kind of in a hurry."

"You're not going to make this easy for me, are you?"

"Make what easy?"

"I've thought about this and I can't apologize for being confused about Abby. Even if I never talk to her again—never see her again—there will always be a connection there. We almost died together. That's a profound thing to experience with someone. Like I said, we have a lot of history between us, but that's all it is—history."

She sighs. "We've already been over this."

"I want to be with you. I know it took me longer than it should have, but I realize now that what I have with you is special and amazing. This could be it."

She folds her arms across her chest. "I don't believe you."

"I know you don't. Why should you, right? I haven't given you a reason to trust me. I haven't proven myself. All you have from me so far is a handful of empty promises."

"So why am I here?"

"Because I want the chance to prove myself—to show you that I'm not a bad guy, and that contrary to what you might have heard me say about Abby that morning, you're the only woman I want."

Her face softens. "I don't think you're a bad guy."

"But do you know how much I care for you?"

She runs her fingers through her hair and mulls over my question. "No, I guess not."

"Don't move," I order gently.

She watches quizzically as I wheel myself behind the counter and emerge seconds later carrying a large gift bag. I hand it to her.

"What is that?" she asks.

"I call it: *Operation Second Chance*."

She smiles and rifles through the bag's contents.

"These past few weeks have been miserable for me. All I want to do is go back to the way things were, but time travel isn't possible. What I'm left with is now. How do I show you right here, right now, how sorry I am and how much I want this to work? Short of camping out on your front lawn and serenading you, horribly off key, I might add, with sappy ballads, I got nothing."

"You'd be surprised," she jokes. "That might've worked."

"Perhaps. But I think you'll find stronger evidence to back up my words in there," I say, pointing at the bag. "Inside is a train ticket, an itinerary, a couple of disposable cameras, sunscreen, binoculars, candy—everything and anything you'd need to have an incredible trip."

"I don't get it."

"Two days from now we're supposed to be at a single's revival in Toronto. I still want to do that."

She shakes her head. "I already told Andrew I wasn't going."

"I think you should reconsider."

"I can't. I canceled my hotel reservations and I gave my ticket away."

"I bought you another ticket and there's a hotel room booked for you under my name."

Nonplussed, she tilts her head.

"I also went through that book you gave me. I read all of your notes and thought about everything you told me, and you're right, there's a lot to do." I take the bag and hand her my carefully thought-out itinerary.

"I booked us a private tour of the Royal Botanical Gardens, after which we have reservations for lunch at the Garden's Café. Then after that, I thought we could hang out at the JVC Jazz Festival or visit the Toronto Music Garden or we could check out the CN Tower until it is time to go to the first night of the revival."

"Jarvis," she begins, breathless.

I hold up my hand. "Wait. I also got us a couple of tickets to Ontario Place. I checked it out and most of the rides are handicap accessible. So, I thought we'd get up early on Saturday and ride roller coasters until our stomachs cave in. There's a praise and worship service scheduled for three that afternoon. So, I thought we'd go to that, and I made reservations for us to sail around Inner Harbour on a dinner cruise afterward."

"A dinner cruise?" she gasps, her eyes wide.

"There's still Sunday. We'd go to church. And then, since we're not driving out with the rest of the group, I bought us two tickets to see a matinee showing of the *Lion King* at the Princess of Wales Theatre."

She blinks, stunned. She flips through the pages of confirmation numbers and receipts. "You're not joking."

"All you have to do is say yes and I'll have a car pick you up on Friday and take you to the train station."

She beams. "I've never been on a train."

"I know. It's a first experience we can share together. Look, if you end up hating everything, say the *Lion King* is boring, or the dinner cruise makes you sick or, God forbid, I'm not the guy you thought I was, we can come back on Sunday and go our separate ways. But if this goes how I hope it'll go—how I have it planned in my mind—that won't happen. This will be our official beginning."

"No one's ever done anything like this for me."

"Trust me," I plead. "I wouldn't have emptied out half of my savings or spent hours on the phone making reservations or rushed out at midnight to buy sun block and cameras, if I didn't think you were worth it."

"If you didn't think we were worth it," she corrects.

"Are we?" I ask.

She bites her bottom lip and inhales deeply.

I've presented a convincing argument, and although I know the fear of getting hurt is lurking somewhere in the back of her mind, I can see in her eyes that she wants to take this journey with me. She wants to see where this path will lead.

"Yeah," she nods. "I think we are."

22. *Abby*

I moan with dread of my impending three o'clock therapy appointment and roll onto my side. I'm not an angry person. I just lost my temper. Everyone loses their temper. The thought of being locked in a room every other weekday for three months with a pretentious doctor digging around for problems that don't exist, sucks the energy right out of me.

Ninety days in jail suddenly doesn't seem so bad.

It will take a miracle, I resolve, gripping my sheets, *to remove me from my room.*

The aroma of brewing coffee wafts its way under my door and up my nostrils. There's my miracle.

Like black magic, it charms me out of bed and downstairs.

"Morning," Hannah chirps. She's wearing a pair of flannel pajamas and ridiculously fuzzy slippers. Her hair is swept up into a haphazard ponytail, delicate tendrils framing her slender face. "Pineapple?"

I shake my head and make a beeline for the coffeepot. "Why are you so bubbly?" I ask, my voice gritty.

"It's a beautiful day."

I watch as she scoops a healthy amount of fruit into a bowl and sets it in front of me along with a napkin.

"I said I didn't want any."

"That's why you're lethargic. You don't eat breakfast."

"What do you call this?" I ask, holding up my chipped mug.

"Coffee's not breakfast. You need to eat." She hands me a fork. "Just finish what you can."

"Yes, Mommy Dearest."

"So what are we going to do next weekend?" Hannah asks, settling herself on one of the barstools.

"What do you mean?" I stab a pineapple cube and pop it begrudgingly into my mouth. The burst of cold, sweet juice startles my taste buds and makes my stomach growl.

"I was out with Chelsea, Devon, and Riley the other day, and we were thinking maybe we should go big this year. You know, hop a plane to New York and cop some tickets to one of those glitzy, overpriced musicals you love so much."

I nod absently and continue to inhale one forkful of pineapple after another.

"So?" Hannah prods.

I stare disappointedly into my empty bowl.

"Earth to Abby."

"Sounds like a good time to me. I hope you guys have fun."

"What do you mean, you hope we have fun? Obviously, you're coming too."

"Really? I always thought before something could be obvious, it had to be an option. And to be quite honest with you, my flying to New York next weekend, or any other weekend for that matter, is out of the question."

"But it's your birthday," Hannah whines.

"So?"

"So, you're turning thirty-one."

"And that's cause to celebrate because…"

"Because it's your birthday."

"You said that already."

"But it's a milestone."

I lick my fork for stray juice. "Hannah, you call any opportunity to party a milestone."

"That's not true."

"What about the party you threw for that Brian guy?"

"Brian Crystal?"

"Yeah, him. You seriously considered that a milestone."

"Of course. Anyone who passes the bar deserves a proper congratulations."

"But he didn't pass."

"How was I supposed to know?"

"You had a banner made that read, *Fourth Time's a Charm*. You should have had an inkling."

The affair comes to life vividly in my imagination. Brian was a good-looking guy in his late twenties. He had blond hair and flushed cheeks—a stocky build. He looked corn fed and his thick southern drawl gave him away as a bona fide country boy.

Hannah had met him some years earlier at (surprise, surprise) a party that one of her ballet friends had thrown. I got the impression that she was hoping for something more than a friendship to evolve, but Brian, being the dense yet lovable guy he was, never caught on.

Thirty of us hid in her loft, crouched behind furniture and jammed into closets. I thought my legs, which had stopped tingling and had gone completely numb, would suffer permanent damage.

The champagne grew warm, the hors d'oeuvres grew cold, and nearly an hour after the party was supposed to start most of us were ready to call it a bust and go home. But Hannah begged us to stay.

"He probably got hung up in traffic," she said, clicking around the large space in her three-inch throwbacks and wool mini. "Ten more minutes, you guys. This is going to mean so much to him."

Ten minutes turned into another hour. Finally, at around nine o'clock we heard heavy footsteps tromping down the hall. He knocked.

"Sssshhh! Everyone get down."

We all huddled in our designated spots.

Hannah smoothed out her skirt before flinging open the door.

I flipped the light switch. "Congratulations!"

We jumped up just in time to see his vomit project through the air and splatter across Hannah's neck and chest. He was drunk—completely zonked. He cried like a child who'd just been spanked; the tears rolled down his pink cheeks and stained the couch cushions with quiet patters.

I felt sorry for him—I really did—but there was something comical about someone that burly crying over a failed test.

After she cleaned herself up, Hannah went to work consoling him. "I'll never be a lawyer," he sobbed.

"Yes, you will," she rocked him gently back and forth.

"My dad's going to disown me."

"No, he won't."

Trapped, the rest of us looked around the room at each other. Like shadows against a wall, we slinked, one by one, out of the front door and into the safety of the night.

Brian ended up moving back home to Podunk, Mississippi, or wherever he came from, and we never heard from him again.

"That's beside the point," Hannah says, pulling me back to the present. "These are entirely different circumstances."

I snort. "Not different enough."

"Fine, don't think of it as a birthday party. Think of it as an intimate weekend with four of your closest friends."

"Please! It's more like one of my closest friends and three strangers."

"They love you."

"Correction. They *loved* me and only when I was pretty with a limitless cash flow."

"That's not true," she says, her eyes serious.

"I haven't heard from Chelsea since last Christmas. Riley talks to Val more than me; and Devon, I don't even remember what he looks like."

"And why is that?"

"I think the term is 'fair-weather friends.' "

"Give me a break. You turned into a recluse," she accuses.

"My phone number hasn't changed."

"Their numbers haven't changed either," she counters.

I roll my eyes.

"I have a theory," she says. "You want to hear my theory?"

"Lay it on me."

"I'm convinced that there's a book of etiquette floating around out there, and it says that the polite thing to do when a tragedy befalls someone is to back away."

"Interesting. And where might one obtain a copy of this elusive book of etiquette, Doctor?" I jest.

"I have no clue," she shrugs. "See, luckily for you, I've never cared much for etiquette and I wasn't born with very much tact. That's why, after everything, I'm still here, shoving pineapple down your throat and begging to make your thirty-first birthday unforgettable.

"You haven't made it easy, Abby. Not everyone's as persistent as I am. When you give off the vibe that you don't want to be bothered, people back off. You can't turn around three weeks or six months or two years later and chastise the world for neglecting you."

"Even if I believed your theory, I can't go to New York. I can't afford it."

"What kind of friends would we be if we made you pay for your own party?"

"No, I don't mean I can't afford to pay for all of us to go. I can't afford to pay for *myself* to go."

"You give us the go-ahead, and we'll take care of everything. All you have to do is enjoy yourself."

I used to spend nine months out of the year traveling, touring throughout the U.S. and Europe. I miss that—the exhilaration of being away from home, the challenge of language barriers, visiting sites, buying souvenirs, and storing lifetime memories.

I haven't left Chicago in three years. I'm like a dolphin that, after years of experiencing the vast greatness of the ocean, has been captured under circumstances beyond its control and forced to find contentment in the limitations of a man-made tank.

Living locked up in my dream home is tolerable, but it can never compare to what is waiting beyond my front door.

"I'll tell you what," I say, staring into my empty bowl. "You give me another helping of pineapple and I promise you I'll think about it."

Dr. Kessler's office smells like discarded fast food and stale coffee. For the amount of money she charges an hour, one would think she could afford to spruce up the place. The incredibly small, very cluttered room has no windows, no chic, introspective artwork, not even a comfy couch on which I can lie and reminisce about my traumatic childhood. There is only a desk, two folding chairs, a burgundy, vinyl recliner, and oddly placed stacks of files. I stand near the door, feeling apprehensive, literally itching to leave.

Sitting on the metal desk are several ashtrays, each overrun with lipstick-stained cigarette butts. In the corner, on a crate pushed against the cream-colored walls, there is an ancient-looking turntable and a paint-splattered boom box. The shag carpet is a strange shade of brown speckled with orange and yellow. It muffles the creaks of the floorboards as I shift my weight from one Versace-clad foot to the other.

The loud hum of the air conditioner is only outdone by the roar of speeding traffic outside. Through the thin walls, I hear the television playing in the office to the right. Someone is watching a talk show.

A hostile male voice shouts, "That is not my son!"

The statement is followed by a high-pitched voice, choked with devastation, "How can you say that? Look at him! He has your crooked nose and big ears!"

The audience's booing and laughing and clapping perpetuates the screaming match until finally the show's host intervenes as the voice of reason. "Let's find out right now."

"Ms. Walker, it's a pleasure." A tall, muscular woman enters carrying a carton of cigarettes in one hand, a mug of coffee in the other, and a file identical to the ones strewn throughout her office under her arm.

Drawn in by the talk show's web of sensationalism, I strain to hear the results in the next room. Is Mr. Gruff Voice the father of Ms. Devastated's child? I can't make out a reaction one way or the other.

"Sorry about that." Dr. Kessler points a long, slender finger at the noisy wall. "You get used to it."

"I bet," I say, turning my attention to my therapist. If nothing else, she'll be amusing to look at for an hour, three times a week. Her frizzy, badly dyed hair is teased and the top portion flops hideously to one side. She has a chiseled face and large, boxy, white teeth. Her tight, shiny skin appears to have the consistency of fiberglass, giving her the semblance of a storefront mannequin.

Her inverted lips and high cheekbones are plastered with dark rouge, and each time she blinks, she reveals heavy lines of aqua eye shadow streaked unevenly across her lids.

I take in her chunky turquoise rings, her blue blouse and skirt, which are both considerably different shades, her large feet, toned arms, and flat chest. It is all just short of alarming.

"Come in, come in," she says, indicating for me to have a seat. "I'm Dr. Kessler, but feel free to call me Miranda. There's no point in wasting time with formalities. We'll be spending a lot of time together during the next three months."

I grunt. "We'll see."

She sets her cigarettes, and what I can only assume is my file, down on her desk and takes a sip of her coffee. "I want you to feel as comfortable as possible. These sessions can only be as productive as you allow them to be. You have the opportunity to walk away ninety days from now as a different person—a better person.

"Having said that, you should know I'm required to submit weekly progress reports to the courts. If you miss a meeting without calling or without a plausible excuse, I have no choice but to report you AWOL and, more likely than not, Judge Frye will issue a warrant for your arrest."

I don't respond. Instead I cross my legs and try to look bored.

"Listen, Abby. I see the set jaw, the furrowed eyebrows, and the rolling eyes. I'm picking up your hostility loud and clear, but remember, no matter how much you hate it here, you'll hate jail more. My suggestion to you, and it's only a suggestion, is that you take the energy that's fueling your anger and focus it on how to fix what's broken inside of you. It's a much healthier way to live."

I glower at her. "I'm supposed to take advice on healthy living from someone who smokes cigarettes by the carton?" I ask nastily.

"Smoking is definitely unhealthy. I'll give you that." She takes another sip of her coffee. "But it won't get me convicted for aggravated assault."

"I'm not a violent person," I say.

"Are you angry?"

"Not typically."

"People, in general, have a need to define things. They need to define other people, they need to define themselves, and they need to define situations. There always has to be an explanation. That's what keeps us feeling safe. Understanding is control. Definitions facilitate understanding. Therefore when we can't define ourselves, we tend to feel a loss of control."

"I don't feel a loss of control."

"What do you feel? Sitting across from me in this room, right now, what are you feeling?"

"Annoyed and inconvenienced."

"Were you feeling annoyed and inconvenienced the morning Amber Sheffield ran into you?"

I think back to the fight with Hannah, about Mitzy and my coffee, and the incident at the grocery store. "Maybe a little."

"I managed to get my hands on your medical chart. You were in a near-fatal car crash a few years back." She pulls out a legal pad and a pen. "Why don't you tell me about that?"

"My ex-boyfriend was taking me home, the roads were slippery, we crashed, I was burned, he lost his legs, the end," I say dryly.

"Was he your ex-boyfriend at the time?"

"We weren't exactly together. We were more like friends with benefits," I say.

"And the defining begins," she mumbles, scribbling furiously.

"Excuse me?"

" 'Friends with benefits.' There's really no such thing. Every true friendship holds its own set of benefits. Either you were together or you weren't. So your label of 'friends with benefits' is just a nice way of saying that you were sleeping with him. It's a justification."

"No, we weren't dating. Yes, we were sleeping together," I clarify haughtily.

"And why did that make you feel guilty?"

"I never said I felt guilty."

"You wouldn't have felt the need to justify it if you didn't."

I sigh heavily, frustrated by the way she pins me into telling her what she already knows. I've never had the displeasure of encountering someone who could wield a conversation so masterfully.

My initial plan was to supply as little information as possible. I was going to give her the basics—maybe whine about Val a little—but for the most part, all I wanted to do was exhibit my docility. I wanted her to see I didn't have a problem with anger management. I didn't need therapy. But to my great disappointment, I realize that isn't going to happen—not today.

"What does Jarvis have to do with anything?" I ask.

"He was part of the accident and, from what I can piece together, the accident instigated your unraveling."

"I'm not unraveled," I scoff, insulted.

"Abby, what you went through would unravel anyone."

"I've learned to adapt."

"Quitting your job—is that your way of adapting?"

"Playing the cello doesn't make me happy anymore."

"What changed?"

I shrug. "I stopped feeling the music."

"Do you think you stopped feeling the music or do you think you just stopped feeling?"

I roll my head backward, exasperated, but mostly unnerved by her line of questioning. "I know what you're trying to do. You want me to strip off all of my guards and expose my naked soul. You want to light some candles, pass the tissues, and hold hands while I weep all of my sorrows away, but you're wasting your time. That's not who I am."

"Be more specific. Who aren't you?"

"I'm not emotional. I don't cry. I don't fawn over babies or tear up at movies or crumble whenever something doesn't go my way. But that doesn't mean I don't feel things. Everybody deals and expresses their emotions differently. I've just relinquished my rights to be a drama queen."

She smirks. "You're sitting here today because you climbed on the hood of someone else's car and beat the shape out of it with a crowbar. You don't think that's even the slightest bit dramatic?"

"No, I think I was exercising my rights."

"Expound on that for me."

"She had it coming. Who taunts people like that? Who's that bored?"

"She's only seventeen."

I shake my head. "It doesn't matter. All actions have consequences. She had to know that sooner or later, she'd mess with the wrong person. And if she didn't know then, she does now."

"Did you think it was your responsibility to teach her that lesson?"

"It may not have been my responsibility, but given the circumstances, I felt it was my right."

"What right do you have to destroy someone else's property?"

"What right did she have to destroy mine?"

"Is that really what this whole thing's been about?" Dr. Kessler asks, tearing open the carton of cigarettes. "The fact that she smashed into the back of your car?"

"Is that why I flipped out? Yes, absolutely."

She pats herself down for a matchbook, then lights the cigarette, takes a long drag, and exhales deeply.

I watch the gray puff of smoke float its way across the desk and disperse in my face.

"I think you're kidding yourself," she says.

"Do you think maybe you could not do that?' I ask and fan the polluted air in front of me. The room, with no source of ventilation, grows smoggy quickly.

"What?" she asks, innocently batting her aqua-painted eyelids.

"The smoke bothers me."

She takes another long drag. "I'm exercising my right," she says smugly, the cigarette dangling loosely from her fingers.

"The right to choke your clients?"

"No, the right to enjoy a smoke in the privacy of my office."

I rub the back of my neck, which is tense. In fact, my entire body is stiff. A surge of adrenaline floods through me. I crack my knuckles and try not to concentrate on my one tattered nerve that Dr. Kessler has already raked over the coals a record number of times.

"I don't have to tolerate this," I say frostily.

"You do if you don't want to go to jail."

"This is a joke," I say, inhaling a mouthful of stale smoke in the process. "You're a therapist. You're supposed to help people. A little common courtesy would be nice."

"Courtesy is a two-way street, Abby." She grinds the remainder of the cigarette into one of the already full ashtrays on her desk. "Everybody has rights, whether they're God-given or self-imposed or granted under the law. If I sent you outside and had you ask five people to give you a list of their rights, you'd come back with a myriad of answers.

"A right is a very strong, very profound thing. It's a person's ability to exact fairness and justice. But from a psychological standpoint, a person's perceived rights can provide helpful insight into his or her past."

"Okay," I say, admittedly curious.

"Let me give you an example. Say we have a middle-aged man who says emphatically, 'I know it's against the law, but stealing is my God-given right.' What does that tell you about him?"

"He clearly had an improper upbringing."

"Could be. What else?"

"He has no sense of right and wrong."

"But he does, the first thing he told you was that he knows stealing is illegal."

"He's inconsistent."

"What makes you think that?"

"He said it was his God-given right to steal, but doesn't it say somewhere in the Bible, 'Thou shall not steal'?"

"Yes, but don't take 'God-given' so literally. Many people interchange the ideas of God and human nature."

"So he's really saying that it's his nature to steal," I note.

"Good. Now I'll ask you again, what do we know about him?"

"Stealing is a part of his character. He steals not because he wants to but because he has to."

"Good!" she raps her knuckles on her desk. "Now why does he have to steal?"

I shrug. "Maybe he's poor."

"Right. The possible reasons why are infinite. The point is that he's lacking something, whether it is a material need, such as food or clothing, or whether it is an emotional need, like purpose or direction."

I nod slowly. "Makes sense."

"Now, what do you think is the most commonly perceived right among people who have a hard time with anger management?"

"I have no idea."

"The right to mirror emotions—to inflict pain as it's inflicted upon them, to give only when they receive, to deny when they've been denied, to wrong when they've been wronged, and so on and so forth. I call it the 'Tit for Tat' Syndrome.

"You're saying, 'I know it's illegal, Miranda, but it was my God-given right—my nature—to smash up her car like she smashed up mine. She had it coming.' That tells me you hold a clear sense of right and wrong. It tells me you're aware of your actions and even the consequences of your actions. But most importantly it tells me you use your anger to maintain control."

There's something chilling about self-discovery. I slouch in my chair and contemplate the truth of what she's just said. It is frightful to have someone back me into understanding the festering ball of anger that I've become—that I've always been.

"I don't feel like I'm in control of anything," I confess.

"Maybe that's why you're so angry," she suggests. "Control is a funny thing. It's never a problem until you start to lose it."

I dismount my high horse and send it packing along with my attitude. Instead of arguing for argument's sake, I listen closely, my ears perked like an eager dog. I feel like a Bobble Head, sitting across from her, nodding incessantly at every accurate thing she says.

It astounds me how a woman whom I've never before met—someone who, just yesterday, I wouldn't have recognized from any other anonymous face on a crowded street—can describe me like she's known me my entire life. It's as if she's been with me through everything—inside of me processing as I processed, erecting walls as I built them one resentful brick at a time. She knows what I'm feeling and how I came to feel this way. She understands my reasoning, my hang-ups, my mistakes and regrets.

She's mystifying, and as the session winds to a close, I can't find the mismatched, square-jawed, frizzy-haired quack who initially walked through the door. I see someone brilliant—someone who, for reasons unbeknown to me, sympathizes with my hopelessness, my misery.

Oddly, the room doesn't seem quite so small or cluttered. There's no smog, no stench of day-old lunches or acrid smoke. The noise from the next office seems minimal. The whizzing traffic outside is less pronounced. Time is suspended and all of my senses hone in on Miranda.

"Now, for homework," she flips to a fresh sheet of paper. "Don't worry. I don't give it often, and when I do, it's usually entertaining."

I lean forward and try to make out what she's writing.

"Do you have a computer?"

"Sure."

"What about the Internet?"

"I think so."

I know I had it at one time or another. A few years back, my record company set up a website for me. I was supposed to take some time out each week to post notes and answer fan mail. Bach's "Suite No. 1" played in the background and there were interactive icons that linked the viewer to my biography, photographs, and future projects. There was even an online store where people could buy my CDs.

Most of the mail I received, though, wasn't fan mail. My box was packed with long, rambling letters from struggling musicians—many of them not even cellists—who wanted to pick my brain on how to get a foot in the door.

I used to cut and paste the same generic response every time: *Keep practicing! Persistence pays off!*

A couple of the company's executives talked me into doing a live chat where I got more of the same and I haven't visited the site since.

Miranda opens a drawer and pulls out a cellophane-wrapped disk. "I get about ten of these a week." She slides it across the desk.

I look down. It is an AOL disk. "500 Free Hours!" beams up at me in bright yellow.

"If you *don't* already have Internet access, pop that in, have a credit card handy, and you should be good to go."

"What am I looking for on the Internet?" I ask, slipping the disk into my purse.

"Support groups. I want you to find one, preferably for burn victims," she says, feverishly scrawling instructions on her legal pad. "The Internet offers anonymity. We're taking baby steps."

"To what?"

"To claiming back your control."

23. *Jarvis*

Sitting across from each other, tucked away in a cozy, private car, Haley and I agree on the train to Toronto that there will only be two objectives: to praise God and to have fun.

The rocky, emotional weeks prior to our little getaway drained us. Our delicate relationship, be it romantic or platonic, is fragile. Setting expectations and pushing to define things will only complicate matters, and making things more complicated at such a seminal juncture would prove counterproductive.

As always, the conversation flows easily—naturally. We talk about her job as an office coordinator and how she spends more time brokering interoffice peace treaties than coordinating the office.

We talk about Professor Leavey and macroeconomics and Chas and our impending business prospectus.

We talk about our childhoods, our siblings, our families, our friends, our enemies.

We talk about sports and hobbies. We discuss Scripture and debate philosophies. For hours we talk and share and laugh and ride.

With everything she says, every story she tells, every tidbit of information she shares, I feel as though I've peeled back one more delicate layer of her intricate personality.

I watch, captivated, as the gentle rocking of the train lulls her willingly to sleep. Her stomach rises and falls with the heavy rhythm of her breathing. Her left cheek rests on her shoulder, which causes her pink lips to pucker, and her eyelids droop to reveal long, curled lashes.

She looks like a child, safe and unaware.

Unaware that I'm studying her.

Unaware of how breathtaking she is—of how her unconventional beauty has forced me to redefine my standards.

Unaware, just as I am until this very moment, that I've fallen in love with her.

By the time we arrive, the hotel is already swarming with single, young adults geared up for the three-day revival.

Hanging grandly from the ceiling of the hotel's lobby is a long, bright banner that reads, "Faith Tabernacle's 11th Annual Singles' Retreat: Welcome, God Has a Word for You!"

Haley and I make our way to the reception desk where we check in, after which we make plans to meet back in the lobby in fifteen minutes.

I wait for her to cram into the elevator, along with half a dozen other arriving guests and their luggage, before I wheel down the hall to my handicap room on the first floor.

The room is spacious and bright with wide doorways and metal bars attached to the walls by the king-sized bed and in the bathroom. There's a desk and chair, and a television hidden behind a regal armoire. It has all the comforts of home.

I haven't done much traveling in my life thus far. Our family vacations were usually day trips to Lansing or Ohio, and I've been to Canada a few times. The tunnel connecting it to Michigan is less than thirty minutes away from where I lived. As curious teenagers, my friends and I would drive across the border occasionally and take advantage of Canada's drinking age of eighteen. There were a few mornings back then when I'd awakened in my bed after one of our wanton excursions to a Toronto bar without the slightest idea of what had happened or how I got home.

Not surprisingly, there are attractions here that I've never visited, sites I've never seen, restaurants and parks I've never been to sober. Now I'm eager to experience more than just the city's nightlife and I am even happier to do it with Haley.

The first thing on my list, though, is to call Jo. I had to be at the train station early and I wasn't able to stop by the diner before I left. I want to let him know we arrived safely, but mostly, I want to check up on him.

I dial the string of numbers on the back of my phone card and wait to be connected. The phone rings once, twice, then three times, and then four.

I tap my fingers against the nightstand as uneasiness sets in. I hang up and redial.

Again, the phone rings and rings with no answer. Just as I'm about to place the phone back in its cradle, someone picks up. I hear the clattering of dishes and the low murmur of busy conversations in the background.

"JoJo's," answers a male voice that does not belong to Jo.

"Who is this?"

"This is JoJo's."

"No, who are you?"

"Who are you?"

"This is Jarvis."

"Jay!"

"Who is this?" I ask again.

"Saul."

Saul is the third-shift cook. He only works nights and Sundays. I've always liked him. He's clever with a quick, witty cynicism. Tall and very dark, his appearance is striking. And he is as friendly as they come.

"Is Jo there?" I ask.

"No, he took the day off."

My ears siren with alarm. "He took the *whole* day off?"

"Yep. Said he had a doctor's appointment, but you know Jo, he probably won't know what to do with a whole twenty-four hours to himself. Try back in a little while."

"If you see him, tell him I'm trying to reach him."

"Will do," Saul says and hangs up.

I sit by the window and stare at the perfectly manicured lawn before me. Nothing is going to happen to Jo, I reason. He's the strongest man I know. It's a good thing he took time off to see a doctor. That means he recognizes his limitations. It means he isn't afraid to enlist professional help.

So then why am I so worried? What is that gnawing sensation? Why in the midst of such exciting circumstances do I sense something dark and ominous lurking in the shadows?

Part of me wants to put everything on hold and track him down—to barricade myself in my hotel room and dial number after number until I reach him, until I hear his voice. But I can't. This trip with Haley is imperative. The memories we're getting ready to make are necessary and irreplaceable.

The only thing I can do is pray. I can pray for Jo's protection, pray for his health and his safety. I can pray for peace and the faith to relax. I can pray for divine intervention, for miracles and blessings and grace. I can pray for God's will to be done in Jo's life and in mine.

I bow my head and silently pour out my worries and uncertainties. I beg for everything to be okay. And then I throw out praises. I thank God for His provisions. I praise Him for who He is—for His kindness and righteousness and perfect plans.

I open my eyes and see the trees blowing in the wind and I thank Him for that. I see a father waiting to cross the street, his young daughter propped happily on his shoulders, and I thank Him for that. I watch a young couple sitting on a sun-drenched bench share a hot dog from the bellowing street vendor and I thank Him for that. I thank Him for everything because everything is His, including me and including Jo.

I feel better—grateful even—for the easiness that sweeps over me. Strengthened and reassured, I marvel at how simple faith really is. Jo's fine. I'm fine. Everything's fine, and it's because God is in control.

I tug off my sweatshirt, slip on a light polo, and with new confidence head out to the lobby.

Haley's sitting in one of the hotel's many plush chairs, a stack of brochures laid across her lap. She's changed into a T-shirt, a pair of shorts, and sandals. Her sunglasses are situated snugly on top of her head and, along with a map, she's brought the cameras and sunblock I bought her.

"Don't you look like a tourist," I tease.

"Check this out." She thrusts a handful of glossy pamphlets at me. "There's a state-of-the-art arcade inside the CN Tower."

"You want to skip the Botanical Gardens?"

"No, why? Do you?"

"We'll do whatever you want."

"That's just it." She scans the slew of leaflets, brochures, and guides in her hands. "There's too much to choose from. I want to do it all."

"Okay. So then we'll do it all."

"But we're only here for the weekend."

"Then we better get going." I grab her hand and tug her to a standing position.

We hail a cab a block from the hotel. The driver, a round, jolly woman in her mid-forties, kindly loads my wheelchair into the trunk of her car and waits patiently for me to situate myself in the backseat.

"Where to?" she asks, pulling away from the curb.

Haley looks down at our map. "680 Plains Road West."

"The Royal Botanical Gardens," the cabbie says knowingly. "If you're into that sort of stuff, you should go check out the Toronto Music Garden. It's on Queen's Quay West between Bathurst and Spadina."

Haley fumbles for a pen and scribbles the address on the map.

I smile. That's just one more thing to cram into an already packed weekend. We chat back and forth and make small talk with the cabbie until we reach our destination.

Our guide's name is Marcella. She has dark features, a sharply slanted nose, and elfin hands. Her thick accent wraps around each of her syllables and makes ordinary words sound exotic. She greets us with a warm smile and firm handshakes.

Haley and I listen intently as she reviews our schedule.

"Sound good?" she asks.

We nod.

"Our chariot awaits us just through these doors." She walks quickly with short, hasty steps.

We follow.

Parked outside, ready to take us around the expansive grounds, is an old-fashioned trolley bus. Four steep steps leer at me from its entrance. There's no wheelchair lift or ramp, no way to accommodate someone like me.

I slow to a halt. "This isn't going to work."

Haley follows my disappointed stare to the trolley's steps.

"It's not a problem," Marcella says. "We can lift you."

"No way." The vision of strangers gawking at two women lifting me like an invalid is more than my pride can withstand.

"You don't think we can do it?" Haley asks.

"I'm heavier than I look."

"Well, let's at least try."

"No," I say. My tone is firm and definite.

She looks hurt.

"It's not a big deal," I say, relaxing my voice and forcing a grin. "I don't mind waiting around here. Take the tour and you can tell me all about it over lunch."

She turns to Marcella who's standing several feet away. "We'll have to cancel."

"What? No." I grab Haley's hand. "I thought you were looking forward to this."

"I was more excited about spending time with you."

During the long, grueling months of physical therapy following the accident, I had made up my mind that I wouldn't let my condition weaken me. I wouldn't let people pick me up and set me down like a rag doll. I wouldn't allow people to wheel me from point A to point B. I wouldn't become the world's vision of an amputee, and I wouldn't let a physical disability turn into a handicap. I would stay young and healthy for as long as I could. No matter how long it took me—regardless of how many tries—I would always find a way to do it on my own or I wouldn't do it at all.

But as I look into Haley's beseeching eyes, I know this is going to be the exception to my rule. She's the exception to all my rules. Making her happy precedes everything. I'm strong enough to roll myself up steep hills, to hoist myself in and out of cars, to bounce back after a tragic car accident, but I will never be strong enough to deny her what she wants and, surprisingly, I'm okay with that.

"Let's give it a shot," I say.

"We'll be careful," she promises, her smile victorious.

The tour is nice. As planned, we explore the Mediterranean Garden along with many of the outdoor conservations where we learn about the history, meaning, and significance of all types of flowers, plants, and trees. We also visit Dundurn Castle and explore the Interpretive Centre.

Haley keeps her word, carefully lifting me in and out of the trolley with Marcella's help and slowly steering me through one fragrant garden after another. My heartbeat quickens each time she leans forward to whisper into my ear. Her sweet scent, her delicate voice—her *presence*—overtakes the natural beauty around us and I'm drawn further into her.

By the time the trolley drops us off outside of the Garden's Café and we say good-bye to Marcella, I've started to enjoy the leisure of sitting back while Haley wheels me about.

"Are you having fun?" she asks, handing me a menu.

I smile. "I'm glad you talked me into going."

"You looked nervous at first."

I shrug. "You're the first person I've let push my wheelchair."

"I like navigating you around," she says. "It's our way of holding hands."

"I never thought of it that way," I say, quickly settling into the idea.

"That's because you're too busy trying to be self-sufficient. You've got to learn to trust people more."

"I can't let myself become too dependent. I don't want to be weak."

"But everyone's weak sometimes. If we're going to be together, I want us to be honest with each other. I want all of our experiences together to be real and multidimensional. I want to see you and understand you from every angle."

"Losing my legs puts me at a disadvantage," I explain. "A man is expected to be strong and self-reliant. I don't want to have to sacrifice that because I'm in a wheelchair."

She reaches across the table and takes my hand. "You're one of the strongest, most independent men I know."

"But I'll never be able to hold you while we dance or walk you to your door at night." I grip my armrest. "This thing will always be in the way. It'll always keep me from giving you what someone else can. It'll always keep me from being the guy who sweeps you off your feet."

"Jay," she whispers, "you already are that guy. When I look at you, I don't see a wheelchair or an amputee. I don't see someone who's weak or helpless. I see a strong, dedicated, passionately driven man. I see you.

"No, you can't walk me to my front door, but look what you can do. I'm here—we're here—in Toronto, sitting in this gorgeous restaurant, holding hands because of you. Who could ask for more?"

"But what if someday it's not enough? What if *I* end up not being enough?"

"We can't live for someday. All we're promised is now. And right now, you are the only man I want to be with and what you have to offer is above and beyond what I could ask of anyone."

"I feel the same way about you."

"We've got something great here," she says. "Something special. Something extraordinary. But we'll never know how great it really is, if you don't stop doubting yourself."

"I'll try."

"Promise?"

I nod. "I promise."

"Good," she says and opens her menu. "Now, let's eat."

Toronto is like something out of a movie. The city, the people, the weather—it's all like a fantasy, a sweet dream from which I don't want to wake. Haley and I do everything we plan to do and more. We couldn't have invented a better time with three magic wishes and all of the money in the western hemisphere.

We spend every waking minute together. When we aren't with the other singles from the revival, we're off in a whirlwind of fun, checking out the city and all it has to offer.

We have an unforgettable time at Ontario Place, riding the fastest, loopiest roller coasters and stuffing ourselves with junk food. I take Haley's request to heart, and rather than struggling on my own, ask her to guide me through the park.

We spend hours at the Toronto Music Garden where I take pictures of her perched on giant grass steps and she takes pictures of me sitting beneath the huge Weeping Willows. We marvel at the Dawn Redwoods and stroll through the lush grass fields decorated with bright flowers in breathtaking swirled designs.

We visit the Bata Shoe Museum where we learn useless trivia—like the fact that twenty-five percent of bones in the human body are found in the foot and that Judy Garland's ruby slippers from the *Wizard of Oz* were sold at auction for $665,000.

We take a tour of Casa Loma. Haley is captivated by the $3 million castle's soaring ceilings and grand terraces. We listen intently, engrossed by the rise and fall of Sir Henry Pellatt.

We check out Gallery 44 and study all the stunning, timeless snapshots of contemporary photography that hangs from its walls.

We swing by the Hockey Hall of Fame and tromp around the themed arcade in the CN Tower and drink smoothies while we visit the Craft Fair on the Beaches Boardwalk.

We sail around Inner Harbour on our dinner cruise and I feed her my dessert, while we listen to the soulful jazz band and admire other couples, young and old, dancing under the glow of the moonlight.

We lean into each other and watch the *Lion King*, our mouths gaped in amazement as our eyes follow the cast, in their stupendous costumes, up and down the narrow aisles.

By the time we board our train back to Detroit, we're exhausted. The sun's already set and there's nothing but blank darkness outside. Haley snuggles next to me, her head resting on my chest.

I drape my arm across her shoulders. "These were the best three days of my entire life," I whisper and run the tips of my fingers through her hair. "Thank you for coming."

She looks up. "Thank you for inviting me."

"I almost hate to go home." I gaze into her gentle eyes. "Toronto's been like a fairy tale."

"Toronto's not the fairy tale." She strokes my cheek. "We are."

I stretch my neck forward and kiss her. Tenderly sinking into the luscious familiarity of her lips.

"I've been hoping for one of those all weekend," she admits after we pull apart.

"I wanted to make you sweat it out for dramatic effect."

She grins and scoots even closer. "It worked."

We ride in silence for a while just cherishing the nearness of each other. We're an ideal fit.

"Haley," I whisper.

"Hm?" she moans groggily.

"I love you."

She doesn't reply.

"Haley?" I lean forward to see her eyes are closed.

A soft snore escapes her lips. I turn off the overhead light, cover her arms with my jacket, kiss the top of her head, and join her in peaceful slumber.

24. Abby

My home office has a deserted feel to it. The heavy pocket doors rumble as I push them aside. I rarely use the computer. When it became the rage to compose music electronically, I refused. Movies may have been cheapened by fancy technology, but I wouldn't let that happen to my music. Still, I didn't let my old-fashioned principles stop me from rushing out every couple of years to buy the newest, flashiest Mac on the market.

The flat LCD screen, along with the glass desk upon which it is resting, is cloaked in a fine layer of dust. Cobwebs cling in the corners of the half-empty bookshelves.

I blow the grit from the keyboard and squeeze my eyes shut as dust billows toward me in a light brown puff and disperses into the air.

Miranda didn't give me detailed instructions. "Your goal, over the weekend, is to make a friend. Introduce yourself, find a common denominator, and chat. I don't expect you to come back with your future husband or a new business partner," she warned. "All we're trying to do is get you to open yourself up to new people and new experiences and maybe, just maybe, to tap into your ability to empathize and relate with others."

I skim her list of suggested websites and wait for the computer to finish its round of beeping and chugging and scanning. The screen lights up, revealing dozens of icons, most of which I've never used. After a few failed attempts at guessing my password, I call my mom, who advises me to try my birthday.

Bingo!

Seconds later, I am connected to the World Wide Web and ready to make a new friend. I visit several different websites, reading mission statements and looking at pictures of bright-eyed, badly deformed men and women smiling and waving as they hike up grassy hillsides and ride downstream in canoes. It's a bit on the hokey side for me.

I breeze through the Phoenix Society for Burn Survivor's site, which links me to the National Burn Victim Foundation webpage, which links me to SurvivingBurns.org, which links me to the American Burn Association.

I continue to tunnel, without a clear destination, through a maze of information for a good hour.

I click on a Discussion Forum tab. A small gray box requesting my username and password pops on the screen. I click on the Registration button, make up a username, confirm my password, and fill out the lengthy questionnaire.

"Username AWalker is unavailable" scrolls across the screen in red letters. I try AbbyW, AbigailW, AbsWalker, and every other variation of my name that exists. They're all unavailable. I glance around the room for inspiration. Lying, face down, on a wooden tray beside me is a CD of Yo-Yo Ma's, "Six Suites for Unaccompanied Cello."

My username, I decide, will be SuiteMusiq.

Once inside the site's Discussion Forum, I have dozens of topics from which to choose. There's a chat room on Nutrition, one on Coping with Scars, another on Innovative Surgeries, one specifically for family members of burn victims. There are even chats for specific states. I choose the Illinois room.

Lines of dialogue begin to scroll down the screen the instant I enter. DrMom is talking to Curious05 about the benefits of pressure garments. They've done wonders controlling her six-year-old son's contractures. MaiFleur and HottStuf22 are debating whether dermabrasion or collagen injections are more effective when it comes to long-term treatments for scar minimizing. PyroKid911 insists laser treatment is the best for hypertrophic scars.

I follow along, reading as fast as I can. I feel wily, inviting myself to eavesdrop on conversations between strangers—even if it is online.

There is so much I don't know—procedures, medications, therapies I haven't even heard of. With every new line of dialogue my questions mount, but I'm not sure how to throw myself into the groove of things.

Am I supposed to interrupt a conversation already in progress? Should I just start asking questions and wait for a response? Are there certain rules or procedures that need to be followed?

In the middle of my mini-panic, an Instant Message flashes in front of me.

> InfernoLuv: Why so quiet SuiteMusiq?

< SuiteMusiq: Just taking it all in.

> InfernoLuv: New member?

< SuiteMusiq: Is it that obvious?

> InfernoLuv: Lucky guess. a/s/l?

< SuiteMusiq: a/s/l? What does that mean?

> InfernoLuv: Age, Sex, Location?

< SuiteMusiq: 30, female, Chicago. You?

> InfernoLuv: 32, male, Evanston. What brings you by?

< SuiteMusiq: Curious, I guess.

> InfernoLuv: You a burn victim?

< SuiteMusiq: Yeah, you?

> InfernoLuv: Not technically, no.

< SuiteMusiq: Just hang around burn survivor sites for kicks?

> InfernoLuv: My twin sister was burned in an apartment fire. I joined to research, but I stuck around for the support.

< SuiteMusiq: I kind of wish I'd known about this place sooner.

> InfernoLuv: Better late than never.

< SuiteMusiq: My therapist thinks this is a good place to make a friend.

> InfernoLuv: Do you need a friend?

< SuiteMusiq: It wouldn't hurt.

> InfernoLuv: Then you found one. Must be your lucky day.

< SuiteMusiq: Actually, you found me.

> InfernoLuv: I'll split it with you. We found each other.

His name is Sean. He's in pharmaceutical sales. He doesn't have any kids. He's never been married. His dog, Napoleon, is his best friend. He's a self-proclaimed romantic and an agnostic Jew. His favorite cereal is Lucky Charms, his favorite author Wally Lamb. In college he started out as pre-med, but ended up switching his major four times. He graduated with a B.A. in both psychology and theatre. ("I figured that way if I never made it as a doctor, I could at least play one on TV.")

Next to spiders, flying is his biggest fear. He isn't ashamed to admit he still watches cartoons every Saturday morning. ("Popeye's my role model.") He speaks fluent French and a little Hebrew. His adage for life is: "Que Sera, Sera." He believes Listerine is better than Scope, Miracle Whip makes better tuna salad than Hellmanns, and he swears on his life he'll never buy a foreign car or shop at the Gap.

He's savvy and charming and funny with a sharp wit. He's also patient and answers every one of my questions on different types of burns and scars and the best ways to treat them.

> InfernoLuv: Ever heard of Pulsed Dye Laser treatment? My sister had it done about six months ago.

< SuiteMusiq: Did it help?

> InfernoLuv: The scars faded down to practically nothing.

< SuiteMusiq: Yeah right! I don't believe you.

> InfernoLuv: I promise you, with makeup, she almost looks like her old self. I can send you her before-and-after photos if you want to see the difference for yourself.

< SuiteMusiq: You think the treatments would work for me?

> InfernoLuv: Couldn't hurt. What do you have to lose?

What *do* I have to lose? Absolutely nothing!

We "talk" a while longer, my excitement mounting with every word he types, and make plans to meet again in the same chat room the following evening.

I sign off and rush to the downstairs bathroom. Studying my reflection in the mirror, I dare to imagine a smooth, scar-free face. No more wide-brimmed hats or menacing scarves and bandanas. No more dark sunglasses or long-sleeved shirts. I won't have to hide anymore.

Maybe this has all been a test—the ultimate test. The accident, the hospital, the therapy, and the financial troubles—maybe they're all some sort of cosmic pop quiz. But the stars have realigned in my favor. Whoever—whatever—it is that is out there watching over me, watching over everyone, has finally acknowledged my plight, the injustice of it all, and is ready to restore my life.

This changes everything. I can have the laser treatments and then maybe some cosmetic surgery for reshaping—a face lift or cheek implants. I'll undergo a total overhaul, give myself a clean slate.

I can start playing the cello again, go back on tour. That means I won't need Hannah. I'll be able to keep my condo and get my car fixed. No, I won't have to get it fixed. I'll just buy a new one!

To celebrate, I'll go on a shopping spree. The new Abby will need a new image. Forget all that stuff about elegance. I'm young. I want an edge. No more schlepping around my own home in the dark, hunched over in wrinkled, mismatched clothes like a dejected bag lady. Soon I'll be the one stumbling in at 3 a.m. I'll be the one entertaining late-night guests and picking through coveted invitations to exclusive parties.

People will respect me again. I won't be a grotesque "has been." I'm not doomed, after all, to be the once-upon-a-time promising cellist whose name no one can remember.

This thing with Amber Sheffield, it'll blow over. Soon our names won't even be linked. The image of that angry, psychotic woman in the papers will eventually vanish. All of the rumors and the hype will be thrown out like yesterday's trash. But I'll emerge mentally and physically intact. And I have Dr. Kessler and my faceless angel, InfernoLuv, to thank.

For the first time in almost a year, I miss my cello. I can hear the notes, see them masterfully placed in a brilliant composition, and not be reminded of loss.

I've been gorging on a diet of bittersweet nostalgia for a long time. But the spirit of music—the force that whisked me away at the age of thirteen—can never die. It can never be overtaken or ignored into nonexistence. It's a part of me, woven into the fabric of my very being, and without it, I'm incomplete.

I go upstairs to my small practice room, lock the door, and play—releasing months of unexpressed emotion, of unfathomable torture.

Everything's going to be okay. Every note, every stroke of my bow, inches me one step closer to finding my center. I play for hours, through the numbness of my fingers, the soreness of my wrists, the stiffness of my back. I play, not in remembrance of the past, but in anticipation of the future.

Hannah is lying across my bed, her sleek, gangly legs hanging over the edge. She's staring blankly at the ceiling.

"Hey." I flop down beside her.

"I was listening to you play," she says. "You've still got it."

I smile to myself. "It felt good, you know? Better than I remembered."

"It always feels good when you're doing what you were born to do."

"For a while I thought I'd lost it."

"What?"

"My passion. It's everything. That's the beauty of music. It's not about the person with the best technique or the sharpest ear. It's about the artist with the most passion—the one who plays for the love of playing. That's me. It's always been me. I just let myself forget."

"What made you remember?"

"It's more like who."

"Did you meet someone?" She rolls onto her side with a curious smirk.

"Kind of. We ran into each other on the Internet," I confess, suddenly embarrassed.

"We have the Internet?"

"Hannah, focus."

"Sorry, I just—I don't know. Isn't online dating usually a last resort, like for fat women or guys with bad comb-overs?"

"I didn't go online to find a date. I went to join a support group, and this guy Sean was there." I give her the abridged version of my first session with Dr. Kessler, which led to my chance meeting with InfernoLuv.

"Good for you, Abs." She forces a smile and slumps glumly into my pillow.

"Don't sound so excited," I nudge her. "It's only the miracle I've been waiting for."

"Keith dumped me."

"Bartender Keith?"

"No, that's Kyle. Keith's the foot model."

"I didn't even know you guys were dating."

"He called me 'superficial.' Can you believe that? I wanted to go to the gym instead of some stupid fund-raiser, and that automatically makes me shallow?"

"Consider it a favor. You were way out of his league?"

"You think so?"

"Let's just say there's a reason why the man can only model socks."

"I don't know. He had a nice body."

"It wasn't his body; it was his face. He was cockeyed."

She sits up and laughs. "No, he was not."

"He was," I giggle. "I can't believe you didn't notice."

"He did wear sunglasses a lot," she muses.

"Just think, someday he'll grow a crusty corn or develop a nasty foot fungus and end up jobless and on the streets."

"Yeah, and he'll come groveling back to me," she predicts.

"Yep. We'll be out on one of our spa days enjoying a mud wrap," I fantasize. "And he'll burst into the room, his eyes pointed in two different directions, drop to his knees, and beg for your forgiveness."

She snickers. "But it'll be too late."

"That's right. You will have moved on fifty different times by then, I'm sure."

"Do you think I'm shallow?"

I measure my words as I would chemicals for a lab experiment, in careful consideration. "I think you're carefree."

"Is that a good thing? Like am I carefree optimistic or carefree flighty?"

"Optimistic," I lie. "Definitely optimistic. Keith is a loser. If you strip away the muscles and the flashy smile, all you're left with is an ego with pretty feet."

She smiles.

"He called you superficial, so what? Don't let something that dumb make you question yourself."

"Thanks," she says, visibly relieved. "You know, you should take your own advice. Dr. Kessler, Sean, and the laser treatment sound like the miracle you've been waiting for. But if, for any reason, it doesn't work out, you should know that people are going to love you no matter how you look."

She rests her head affectionately on my shoulder. "You don't need a flawless face to play flawless music."

"Thanks," I say, truly appreciative. "I needed to hear that."

The phone rings loudly and echoes through the house.

Hannah jumps up. "I'll get it."

I watch her with newfound respect as she bounds the few steps to my dresser.

"Hello?" she answers brightly. "Hey!"

It's Devon, she mouths to me. "You're kidding," she gasps, her eyes wide. "Front-row seats to *Thoroughly Modern Millie* and *Hairspray?* Both? How did you manage that? Uh-huh, yeah, we talked about it. No, she hasn't given me an answer yet. She seems excited about it though. Uh-huh. Okay, I will. Bye."

"How'd he get front-row seats on such short notice?" I ask.

"He found a dealer online, but you wouldn't believe how much he had to fork over to get them."

"It sounds like he got scalped."

She gives a casual shrug as if being taken advantage of is a small, worthwhile price to pay for such an opportunity as this. "He's holding four tickets to each show with a pretty hefty deposit, so you have twenty-four hours to decide what you want to do."

I shake my head. "I don't like feeling pressured."

"There's no pressure," she assures me, though her wrinkled forehead and the pleading in her eyes tell an entirely different story.

"It could be fun," I toy out loud.

"Fun?" she asks, aghast. "Abigail Walker, amusement parks are fun. Puppies and family reunions are fun. We're talking about making unforgettable memories—good ones. Our children's children's children will be talking about this trip when we're dead and gone."

"I've heard *Thoroughly Modern Millie* is hilarious," I muse.

"I've heard *Hairspray's* even better," she prods.

"And he *did* put down that deposit," I waver.

"And the hotel. Riley and I already made reservations at the W hotel."

"I love that place."

"I know."

"It's really expensive," I say, the realization of all the trouble they've gone through finally catching up with me.

"You're worth it."

"We all are," I note.

"Devon and New York are just seven little digits away."

"Next weekend, right?"

She nods, ecstatic. "Three days, two nights, and four friends in the Big Apple. How can you pass that up?"

I smile; her excitement is infectious. It sounds like nothing but a good time—a well-deserved weekend away. It *is* my birthday and they *are* my friends. *How can you pass this up?* I ask myself.

The answer is palpable. "I can't."

I spend the better part of Sunday morning locked in my small studio playing my cello, stopping only to scribble notes onto a blank music sheet beside me. Afterward, I head to my office with a bucket full of cleaner and disinfectants. The room is pitiful and in need of a thorough scrubbing. I dust and polish and shine until my arms are sore and I've broken into a sweat.

Cleaning the office expands into cleaning the living room, which expands into cleaning the kitchen. My fingers are soggy and wrinkled and my hands smell of bleach. But as I stand back to examine the gleaming floors, I feel proud.

At six o'clock, I drop everything and log into the support group to keep my date with Sean. He's there, as promised, waiting for me.

> InfernoLuv: How was your day?

< SuiteMusiq: Spent most of it cleaning. Yours?

> InfernoLuv: Typical Saturday: me, Napoleon, Popeye, and a bowl of Lucky Charms.

< SuiteMusiq: Sounds more like a circus act.

>InfernoLuv: Hey! Be nice or I won't send you pictures.

My leg bounces up and down nervously as I wait for him to send me the files. When I get the pictures, even if there is no difference, I resolve, I won't let my disappointment cause me to say anything disparaging.

If it ends up a wash, I reason, I'll still walk away with a firmer, broader understanding of what is out there in terms of treatments for burn victims.

Downloading File 1 pops up on my screen and, frame by frame, a photo appears before me.

His sister is attractive despite the thick, dark pink scars that slash her cheeks and chin and the dramatic discoloration on her neck. The damage, however, is not nearly as extensive as mine.

She's staring into the camera somberly, her thin, brown hair pulled back into a ponytail. She's slim—almost underweight, her collarbones protrude dramatically from beneath her skin.

Downloading File 2 pops up, followed by the unfolding of a second picture.

She's staring into the camera looking just as frail. Her hair is pulled back tightly, only her eyes are much wider. She isn't smiling, but the devastation that clouded the first picture is gone. The scars and discoloration that marred her face and neck before are considerably thinner and paler.

Downloading File 3.

She's standing between a rotund woman and an attractive young man. They're outside somewhere, their arms linked. The sun lights up all three of their beaming faces. She looks like a different person. Her cheeks are rounder, healthier, and she's sporting a fun, flirty, pixie haircut. Her scars, though still noticeable, are nowhere near as pronounced as they were in the first photo.

> InfernoLuv: Did you get them?

< SuiteMusiq: The difference is amazing.

> InfernoLuv: Didn't I tell you!

< SuiteMusiq: You were right. She looks like a different person.

> InfernoLuv: FYI, the guy in the last picture is me—in case you were wondering.

I click back to the third download and examine his smiling face more closely. He's handsome in an unconventional sort of way. His short, spiked hair and lazy gray eyes give him a cocky, city slicker look. He has thick eyebrows and a slender nose and his shoulders are broad and boxy.

> InfernoLuv: You there?

< SuiteMusiq: Still here. Just taking a second look at you.

> InfernoLuv: What do you think? On a scale from 1 to 10?

< SuiteMusiq: I'd give you a solid 9.

> InfernoLuv: Yeah. The ladies can't resist the Sean Meister.

< SuiteMusiq: Make that a 6.

> InfernoLuv: Why?

< SuiteMusiq: Because anyone who uses the term "Meister" when referring to himself must lose points.

> InfernoLuv: I'd love to see a picture of you.

< SuiteMusiq: Never gonna happen.

> InfernoLuv: How come?

< SuiteMusiq: You know why.

> InfernoLuv: I'm the last person who would judge you.

< SuiteMusiq: I'll think about it.

> InfernoLuv: That's all the Sean Meister can ask for.

< SuiteMusiq: You just sank to a 3.

I talk to the "Sean Meister" until Hannah comes home and insists I "say bye-bye," so we can watch *Pretty Woman* (again) and eat the tandoori chicken she's ordered.

Sean gives me the name, address, and number of his sister's doctor. "Have fun," he types. "And don't forget to think about what we discussed."

I half-smile, flattered by his curiosity and interest. I tell him I won't, and before parting ways for the night, we make plans to meet at the same time again the following evening.

25. *Jarvis*

Saul is outside locking up JoJo's just as Mom and I pull into the parking lot. The black iron gates and padlock obstruct the tiny storefront, which makes the whole block look foreign—vacant.

I roll down my window. "What's going on?" I ask.

"I gotta go," he fumes. "I've been here all weekend."

"What do you mean? Where's Jo?"

"You tell me, Man. He called me Thursday night and told me he was taking Friday off—said he'd be in first thing on Saturday. Saturday rolled around and he was a no-show. I had to stay here all day until Danny came in at seven. Then Sunday I relieved Danny like usual and now it's Monday and Jo's a no-show again."

"Did you call him?" I ask, panic setting in.

"I don't mind doing the guy a favor," Saul rambles on. "But this is ridiculous. I got another job. I got kids and a wife."

"*Did... You... Call... Him?*" I shout hanging out of the open window.

"Jay, calm down," Mom says. "It's probably just crossed wires."

"Yeah, I called him about a hundred times and so did Danny. He never picks up."

"Why didn't you go over to his house?"

"I'm not a baby-sitter, Jarvis. I'm a cook."

"You're supposed to be his friend."

"I *am* his friend," he spits indignantly. "Why do you think I'm here at seven in the morning when I was supposed to be on a construction site half an hour ago?"

"Did you at least call the police?" I ask.

"For what?"

"What do you mean 'for what,' you moron?" I yell.

"Jay, stop." Mom grips my arm firmly.

"Moron? I'll tell you what. Next time your buddy Jo decides he wants to take an impromptu vacation, *you* can fill in for him. Because as far as I'm concerned, he's no friend of mine." He turns on his heels, his apron tucked under his arm, and in two angry strides, rounds the corner.

"We have to go to his house." I fumble for her cell phone.

"What?" Mom snorts. "You can talk to him later. I have to get to work and I barely have enough time to drop you back at home."

I stare at her in disbelief. "Mom, something's wrong."

"Jay, you're paranoid. You've always been paranoid. I blame your father, quite frankly."

"I'm not joking with you," I snap. "I think he's really sick."

"Jo's never been sick a day in his life."

I dial his number. The phone rings until his voicemail kicks over.

"No, wait! What're you doing? You're going the wrong way!" I glance behind us at the highway ramp.

"I am not taking you all the way to Jo's," she says.

"Please! Mom, I'm telling you something is seriously wrong."

"Jay, he probably just overslept."

"No!' I slam my hand against the glove compartment. "Nobody has heard from him since Friday. That's not like Jo. You know it's not. Something's not right."

"I can't be late for work, Jay," she says apologetically.

"Fine, then just turn around and drop me off at Jo's. I'll get him to give me a ride to campus later."

When we pull up to Jo's house ten minutes later, I can't get out of the car fast enough. His red pickup truck is parked in the driveway. Three newspapers are piled on the front stoop.

"That's weird." Mom nods toward the stuffed mailbox at the end of his bricked walkway. She takes the keys out of the ignition and climbs out of the car.

Frantic with worry, I can hardly wait for Mom to retrieve my chair from the trunk. Hastily I slide into it, wheel myself to the front door, and knock forcefully. "Jo?" I call. "It's Jarvis. Open up." There's no answer. I knock again.

"Jo," Mom echoes, "let us in."

I try to peak inside the front window, but the shrubbery lining the outside of his house is too tall and too thick.

"Can you unlock the gate for me?" I ask my mom. "I know where the spare key is."

She follows me around the side of the house to the back deck where I begin frantically digging through the half a dozen or so potted plants. "It's here somewhere," I mumble.

Mom works her way down the back of the house, cleaning off each window with the side of her fist, and peaks inside.

"Oh God! Oh God!" she pants.

"What? What is it?" I ask. The terror in her eyes turns my hands ice cold.

"Where's my cell phone? Where is it? Where is it!" she screams.

"In the car."

Before I can make any sense of what is going on, she dashes, faster than I've ever seen her move, across the grass and out of the side gate. Abandoning the spare key, I wheel myself to the last window she's dusted clear. The ledge is just above my forehead. I push upward with all my might and the strain causes my arms to shake.

I brace myself for what is on the other side.

The lights are on. One of the dining room chairs is lying beneath the window; its high, wooden back has smashed in one of the glass panel doors of the china cabinet. At the head of the table there's a place mat, linen napkin, and a fork and knife along with a plate of food. A newspaper, still wrapped in plastic, rests to the right of his untouched meal.

"An ambulance is on its way," Mom says, huffing up to me, her chest heaving fiercely from the short jog. "Did you find the key?"

I shake my head. "What's going on?"

"We need the key."

Without answering my question, she moves quickly back to the deck and begins clawing tirelessly through the remaining potted plants. "Why would he plant the spare key?" she asks, her forehead beading with sweat.

"Where is he?" I ask, tearing myself from the window.

"Inside."

"Is he okay?"

"I can't tell."

"What does that mean?"

"Are you sure it's in one of these?" she asks, her voice trembling with angst.

"Mom, wh—"

"I got it!" She yanks out a small plastic bag, showering dark potting soil over her head. She labors to her feet, the knees of her light gray pantsuit soiled from the wet wood, and wheezes her way back around the side of the house and to the front door.

I hear the rescue sirens blaring in the distance as we fumble to slide the key in the lock.

The potent stench of decay wafts into the morning air and hangs low in the front hall. Its intense concentration is forceful and suffocating, invading our nostrils and throats before we even swing open the door.

Several times we try to enter the house, shirts covering our mouths and noses, but the reek is too strong. It overpowers us and, like a brick wall, barricades us outside. It makes no difference. We don't need to go inside to confirm what we already know.

The trees bend to the wind; their limbs creak in agony. The clouds drift sideways in a supernatural migration and mask the sun.

I watch grimly as my bright surroundings turn brown and wilt beneath a low, demanding rumble of thunder.

An ambulance, a fire truck, and three police cars skid to a halt in front of us; their wailing sirens tear through the sad, silence of the morning sky and scrape my ears until they throb.

With ladders and axes and stretchers, they charge across the neat lawn like tardy allies of war, forsaking all to save innocent victims, already ravaged, from the unspeakable devastation of death.

"He's inside," Mom says, her voice small and flat.

They push past us, stomping into the house with their useless tools. Jo's limp body lays collapsed on the living room floor.

I don't look, won't listen, can't feel or accept anything as they roll Jo out of the house, a white sheet covering his decomposed body. I can't answer questions, can't give information, can't understand the montage of words flying at me from strangers who will never understand such loss—such anguish. I can't help.

What I can do—all I can do—is stare at the world before me and try to make sense of it through what feels like clouded eyes.

Logic no longer exists. It has evaporated, along with reason, into invisible shards of despair and I will never know either again. They will hang above me until I too, no longer exist, always taunting, always mocking, always just shy of my reach.

26. *Abby*

The night before my birthday weekend in New York, Devon, Chelsea, and Riley stay with me and Hannah. The five of us barely sleep, ogling over each other's clothes and planning all the things we're going to do when we get to the Big Apple. Being part of a group again is an incredible experience.

Watching Hannah double over in laughter at one of Devon's cheesy jokes, listening to Chelsea leak juicy, behind-the-scenes gossip from the magazine where she works as a fashion editor, laughing at hokey infomercials into the wee hours of the morning—it all makes me feel normal again.

Dr. Kessler encouraged the weekend excursion. She believes part of my anger stems from feeling as if I'm being denied my right to enjoy life like any other thirty year old. Her only request, as our session wound to a close, was that I have fun.

"Don't restrain yourself. Remember, your scars don't define you so they shouldn't have any effect on what you do, where you go, and who you meet. Denying yourself the right to enjoy life—"

"Is a form of self-punishment," I finished the sentence for her.

"Right," she nodded, pleased.

"So, I'll see you Monday?" I asked, my keys in hand.

"I look forward to hearing all about your inhibition-free weekend."

"I'm sure." I turned to leave.

"Hey, Abby," she called after me.

I poked my head back into her office. "Yeah?"

"Happy Birthday."

We arrive at O'Hare airport in style. A long black limousine with tinted windows drops us off in front of our airline. With our noses in the air like five divas, we roll past the backed up economy-class line and make our way to the waiting first-class attendants. Chelsea and Devon go first, then Hannah and Riley.

"Next please," the attendant on the far end calls. I'm nervous, despite her pleasant smile. I look nothing like the woman captured in the small photo on my driver's license. *You should've brought your birth certificate or your passport*, I chastise myself, as the attendant looks at me and then at my license and then back at me.

"And how many bags will you be checking today, Ms. Walker?" she asks while tapping away at the keyboard in front of her.

"Just one," I say, flooded with relief.

After making sure no one has asked me to carry anything on board and that my bags have been in my possession the whole time, she hands me a boarding pass and wishes me a pleasant flight.

There's an odd number of us, and even though I've been assigned a seat next to Devon, I get stuck sitting next to a stranger three rows back while the four of them sit side by side in the bulkhead.

"You don't mind switching with me, right, Hon?" Chelsea asked, her carry-on bag and magazines already occupying my window seat.

"Uh, actually—"

"Thanks!" She grabs a pillow and blanket from the overhead bin. I look at Hannah who shrugs contritely and slides in next to Riley.

When the beverage cart comes down the aisle, I hear Devon's deep voice announce, "Four Bloody Mary's on me!" The four of them erupt in gleeful cheer. I eat my honey-roasted peanuts and drink my Diet Pepsi in silence.

It's only the plane ride, I reassure myself. There are only two seats per aisle. Someone had to be the odd man out. The seating arrangement isn't necessarily going to be indicative of the rest of the trip.

Despite my best efforts to let it roll off my back, though, I'm bothered. The trip is supposed to be in celebration of my birthday and already I'm feeling like a tagalong. *Maybe this is a mistake.*

"Hey," Hannah says. She's standing over me, smiling, a Bloody Mary, replete with celery stick, and napkin in her hand. "Do you want one? Devon's buying."

"No, I'm fine." I sip my soda.

"You're upset," she says. "Is it the seating? Because I'll switch with you."

I shake my head. "It's not a big deal. I just wish Chelsea had asked before she took my seat. I hate the aisles."

"I'll make sure it doesn't happen on the flight back," she promises.

Forty minutes later we taxi into our gate at LaGuardia. Chelsea, Hannah, Riley, and Devon are the first to deplane. They're waiting for me as I make my way out of the long tunnel.

"There she is." Riley points.

Devon and Hannah smile.

Chelsea, with folded arms, taps her foot impatiently.

"Let's go." Devon links his arm through mine.

Once outside, our driver leads us past the long, winding line of people waiting for cabs and down a crosswalk to a black stretch limo.

We drop our luggage on the curb. Riley, who's chatting on her cell phone, is the first to climb in.

"After you." I step back so Chelsea can follow.

"No, no," she says, her voice dry with sarcasm. "After you, Abby. I wouldn't want to take your window seat."

I look at Hannah who looks at Devon who smiles nervously.

"What is your problem?" I ask.

"My problem," Chelsea says, her neck swinging back and forth, "is that you're ungrateful. This trip is a gift. You haven't put a dime toward anything. So you have no right to complain about what seat you get."

"I have every right. Just because you chipped in for a stupid plane ticket doesn't mean you get to treat me like a second-class citizen."

"If it weren't for us you wouldn't even be here."

"None of us would be here if it weren't my birthday," I say with more authority than I feel.

She stares at me, her face blanketed with confusion. "It's your birthday?"

Hannah coughs and signals for her to zip it and get in the car.

"Who cares what brought us here," Devon says a little too cheerfully. "The point is we made it and we're going to have a great time."

"Wait a minute." I look at the three of them. "If this trip isn't for my birthday, then why are we really here?"

"We've done this every summer since I can remember," Chelsea says.

"Who's we?" I ask.

"Me, Devon, Hannah, Riley, and Tasha."

"Tasha couldn't make it this year," Hannah confesses.

"Her sister's getting married," Devon explains.

"We couldn't find anyone else on such short notice, so we invited you," Chelsea says. Her smug grin is a slap in the face.

"Why would you lie?" I ask Hannah, my face flushed.

"I wanted you to do something special for your birthday and since the trip was already paid for and the dates matched up, it seemed perfect."

My face is hot with a mixture of humiliation and fury. "I can pay you for Tasha's portion," I tell Chelsea.

She raises a cynical brow.

"Abby, don't worry about it," Devon says. "Hannah told us about everything you're going through. We're happy you could make it and you don't owe us anything."

"There you go," Hannah says hastily. "Water under the bridge."

Chelsea and Devon join Riley in the back of the limo. Ignoring Hannah's worried gaze, I opt to sit up front with the driver. I am, after all, not really part of the trip. I'm just a last-minute charity case—the bottom of the barrel solution to vacation plans gone awry.

We ride to midtown Manhattan mostly in silence. The tension wedged between us is thick. I can hear them whispering in the back, no doubt kicking themselves for inviting Quasimodo along. I try to block them out by making small talk with the driver, but he's more interested in weaving in and out of the dense traffic at warp speeds than he is in conversing with me.

I watch the passing traffic, or rather the traffic we are passing, and try to devise a way to get home. Had I been thinking, I would've retrieved my luggage from the trunk, turned around right there at the airport, and charged a plane ticket back to Chicago. I can't take anything from these people, not now that I know their true feelings.

The pang of rejection squeezes the back of my eyes, but I blink away the tears. *Don't even think about it*, I order mercilessly. All the hurt feelings in the world are not going to get me to cry, especially not in front of them.

I've braved bigger problems with more important people. I don't break down over stuff like this. I glean from it and use it to make me tougher, I remind myself.

Two bell boys dressed completely in black are standing outside to greet us when we pull up to the W Hotel. Without waiting for the others, I breeze through the stylish front lobby and up to the check-in counter.

A young black woman with thick-rimmed glasses and tiny, neat dreadlocks pulled into a chic bun greets me enthusiastically. Her name tag reads "Danielle."

"I'd like a room for one night."

"Do you have a reservation?" she asks, her eyes bright and pleasant.

"No, is that a problem?"

"Not at all. Is this a single or a double?"

"A single."

She looks down at her computer screen.

"Smoking or non-smoking?"

"Non-smoking."

"Abby, what're you doing?" Hannah asks, rushing up behind me.

"I'm getting a room."

"But that's already taken care of, remember?" she whispers. "I thought you were going to share a room with me."

"And I thought I was coming to New York for the weekend to enjoy my birthday with a few friends," I reply coolly. "So I guess this day's been full of surprises."

"Fine," she says calmly. "But this is an expensive hotel."

"And?"

She leans in closely. "How're you going to pay for this?"

Danielle looks up and takes in my appearance with one, swift, disapproving glance.

"You know what?" I say. "Why don't you make it a suite? After all, it is my birthday."

Danielle looks at me and then at Hannah as if she's waiting for some sort of approval.

"Is there a problem?" I snip and hand her my platinum credit card, which has been tucked away in my wallet, untouched, for over a year.

"No, not at all," Danielle stammers. "Let me just see what we have available."

"Abby, this is ridiculous," Hannah argues.

"The only thing that's ridiculous is you assuming to know what I can and can't afford."

"Ms. Walker," Danielle says. "We've got a lovely suite for you. It's a non-smoking room, very spacious, with a queen-sized bed and a balcony that offers a beautiful view of the city. Also—"

"I'll take it."

"Abby, don't be rash," Hannah petitions.

I don't want to hear it. "Just go away."

"Why are you making such a big production? Like Devon said, we're in New York to have fun. Who cares how we got here?"

I whip around, an unforgiving fierceness in my eyes. "I care."

"So if the weekend's not about you, then you don't want any part of it?"

"Did you see how Chelsea looked at me?" I ask. "Did you see the repulsion?"

"She's like that with everyone."

I shake my head. "She was too quick to throw this trip in my face. I don't want to owe anyone anything. She wants me to crawl on all fours and follow you guys around like a grateful puppy. She wants me to sing her praises and dance a jig while I bask in the radiance of your small, exclusive clique."

"That's not true."

"What you're all forgetting," I continue, "is that I was a part of that clique once upon a time. I may not have been invited to your annual, summer jaunts to New York, but we spent our share of nights partying together. I'm just not good enough anymore, not stylish enough, not rich enough."

Danielle hands me back my card.

"But you know what I'm realizing? I don't need to waste my energy trying to be good enough for Chelsea or Devon or Riley or even you. I'm better than all of you put together, no matter how down-and-out I may seem. Give it time, I'm gonna pull through this.

"But the four of you," I scoff and shake my head. "The four of you will always be reprehensibly superficial and narcissistic. Your actions will always revolve around people's perceptions of you. Your happiness will always be tied to the most frivolous things and the most frivolous people until the day you wake up and realize your lives have no meaning whatsoever."

Danielle hands me my room key.

Hannah, stunned by my harsh words, stares at me as I roll my suitcase the short distance to the elevators.

Through the corner of my eye, I see Devon, Riley, and Chelsea huddled by the front entrance, whispering.

They can have each other. In fact, they deserve each other.

I should've known better, I think, stabbing the elevator button with my index finger. I take a deep breath and try to erase the scowl on my face. All I have to do is get through the night and tomorrow I'll be booked on the first flight out.

The suite is whimsical; its plum and muted earth tones bring immediate relaxation to my tight muscles. I abandon my suitcase and flop down on the expensive-looking couch in the sitting room. It's been a long time since I've been in a room this nice. I take in the simple, clean lines that surround me. It's been a long time since I've been in any room other than the ones in my condo.

I used to live in hotels; touring and promoting my latest projects was eighty percent of the business. The W Hotel was always my favorite. It's modern and hip, with a young, gregarious staff who don't hesitate to bend over backward, and the rooms are packed with the most up-to-date accessories, which made staying away from home less arduous.

Hannah's right, though. All of this service, all of this luxurious convenience, comes at a hefty price. My stomach drops as my mind drifts to just how much the bill will be tomorrow morning. Even if I forego meals, in-room movies, and phone calls, I will probably still be looking at twelve hundred dollars.

Not long ago, I wouldn't have batted a lash at the pricey rate. I would've asked if they had anything nicer. But these are different times and I'm either going to have to beg my parents for the money or spend the next year paying off this one night of bliss in slow, high-interest, monthly increments.

The lesson? Pride is not cheap.

Still, what I did was necessary. I can't let Hannah and her band of arrogant friends turn their noses down at me. To drag behind them for the next three days like an unshakable interloper would be like repeatedly slamming my fingers in a door.

Coming to New York with them was nothing more than a bad case of denial on my part. I hadn't spoken to Chelsea, Devon, or Riley since the accident. They never called, never came by, never wrote. They didn't care. So why on earth, after all this time, would they decide to pull together and plan something for my birthday? It's illogical.

Their lives are a big fast lane of pleasure and anything or anyone who threatens their good times will be discarded without a second thought. That's what happens when good-looking people are paired with lucrative careers. I should know. I used to be just like them.

The hotel phone rings. I hesitate, uninterested in speaking to Hannah or listening to any of the rest of them try to talk me out of my suite. Of course, if they're calling to grovel and apologize for being pond scum, I will make an exception.

"Hello?"

"Ms. Walker?"

"Yes?"

"This is Danielle at the front desk. I'm calling to make sure you've settled in and everything is to your liking."

I look around the room, more aware than ever of how lonely I've become.

I sigh. "Yeah, everything's great."

There's a knock on the door. I roll over, my vision blurred from heavy sleep, and stumble out of bed.

Hannah, Riley, Devon, and Chelsea are standing outside of the room grinning timidly, each of them carrying a bag of delicious-smelling takeout.

Chelsea holds up her bag. "We come in peace."

"We're sorry," they sing in unison.

"What time is it?" I ask.

Riley glances down at her elegant Movado. "Just after six."

"We thought you could use some dinner," Devon says. He holds up a pair of chopsticks.

I step back and wait for them to file in. Like trained servants, they set everything out on the coffee table. There are no plates, so we eat straight from the cartons, passing them to the next person every few minutes.

"This room is incredible," Riley says, crunching on a green pepper.

"Mhmm," Chelsea agrees around a mouthful of shrimp fried rice. "It's much nicer than ours."

"Don't get too attached. I only have it for one night."

"Then what?" Hannah asks.

"Then I'm going back home."

Devon sets down his carton of Szechwan chicken. "Please, don't." His tone is sincere.

"Stay," Hannah begs. "You have to see *Thoroughly Modern Millie*."

"And *Hairspray*," Chelsea adds.

I shake my head. "I can't afford it."

"Enough of this silliness," Riley says. "Tomorrow you'll check out of this room and move into Hannah's. Then the day is ours to kill. We'll go shopping, have lunch, whatever you want. Then, we'll come back, do a quick wardrobe change, and be in our front-row seats by eight. Now, I don't want to hear another thing about it. We're going to have fun or die trying."

The following morning, I splurge on eggs benedict, check out of my suite, and move into Hannah's room. It is much smaller, with fewer amenities, but the joy of not feeling like an outcast is worth the downgrade.

I'm hanging up my clothes when Hannah prances out of the bathroom with her purse and Audrey Hepburn-esque sunglasses in hand.

"Are we leaving already?" I ask.

She freezes and bites her lip guiltily. "I didn't think you would want to go."

"Go where?"

"The girls and I made reservations at Shangari's. It's a spa."

"Why wouldn't I want to go?" I ask, as the all-too-familiar pang of rejection grips the back of my throat.

She smiles awkwardly and searches for a tasteful response. "We scheduled facials and I know how uncomfortable those make you."

She's right. Since the accident, the last thing I want to do is sit back while a woman with flawless skin massages and picks at my scarred face. The point of facials is to leave your skin looking smoother and restored and the only thing that's going to do that for me is a couple of Pulsed Dye Laser treatments and extensive plastic surgery.

"We won't be long," she promises. "A few hours at the most."

"Maybe I'll go see what Devon's up to."

"He already left to meet up with a few of his old college friends."

I think back, perplexed, to the carefully thought-out day Riley had relayed last night over our impromptu dinner. I immediately return to my anxious state.

"So, I'll see you later?" Hannah asks, halfway out the door.

"Yeah, later."

By three o'clock, my definition of "later" has come and gone. I phone each of their rooms, but there's no answer.

I feel so foolish as I pace back and forth. This is starting to become a habit, a very annoying habit.

Hungry, and tired of waiting around, I venture out of the hotel. Down a few blocks and around a couple of corners, I discover an Au Bon Pain. In a secluded booth by the bathrooms, I enjoy a turkey club and skim over the entertainment section of the *USA Today*, which someone has left lying on the table next to me.

Had I gone with my instincts, I think, as I chew my sandwich, I would be sitting in a plane on my way home right now. Better yet, had I gone with my initial instincts, I wouldn't have left Chicago in the first place.

I would be sitting in my office, sipping a cup of aromatic coffee, typing back and forth with Sean.

I sigh contentedly.

Sean and I have "talked" online every evening for the past week. Our effortlessly honest conversations amaze me. How can I feel so at ease with a man I've never met?

There are things I've told him—potentially embarrassing emotions and thoughts—that I haven't had the courage to share with anyone. When I talk to him, I feel like it's okay to open up. Expressing doubt, hopelessness, anger, and self-pity doesn't make me weak; it makes me human.

I'm grateful for his friendship, for the time he takes from his schedule each day to meet with me, for the advice he dispenses, for the jokes he tells, for the philosophies he conveys with no strings attached.

That's why, before I left, I sent him a picture. "It's what I looked like before the accident," I warned.

I went to Walgreens and had a shot from my last album cover scanned onto a floppy disk. In the picture I'm leaning against a brick wall, gazing seductively into the camera; my hair, lengthened with extensions, is draped over my shoulders in chunky layers. I'm wearing a little, black, strapless number and gently cradling the neck of my cello in my left hand.

Even though he's aware of my current situation, part of me knows it was unfair to send him that picture—maybe even a little misleading.

I'm gorgeous in it. My hair, makeup, and pose were all perfected under the watchful eye of a professional photographer. And, given the incredible height of my cheekbones and the sleek contours of my hips and thighs, I think it's safe to assume someone took the liberty of airbrushing a few areas.

< SuiteMusiq: Your turn. On a scale of 1 to 10.

> InfernoLuv: There's no known number. I'm speechless.

< SuiteMusiq: Don't be. I don't look like that anymore.

> InfernoLuv: It doesn't matter. It's still you. Now all I need is to hear your voice.

< SuiteMusiq: Are you being serious?

> InfernoLuv: Why not? There's a lot you can learn from a person's voice. I could be a four-hundred-pound convict named Bertha with snake tattoos and a curly beard and you'd never know it.

< SuiteMusiq: Then how do you explain the picture?

> InfernoLuv: That could've been a photo of my incredibly handsome son.

< SuiteMusiq: I'll take my chances.

> InfernoLuv: Forget Bertha then. I just want to hear the sound of your laughter. Please?

Several minutes of persistent prodding later, I gave him my number. Within moments, my phone was ringing.

The Caller ID read, "Bloomenthal, Sean A." Surprisingly, I wasn't nervous when I pushed the Talk button and lifted the phone to my ear.

"Hello?"

"Is this Abby?" a kind male voice asked.

"That depends on who this is," I replied.

"This is Bertha."

I giggled. "Just who I was hoping for."

We talked for hours about nothing—about everything.

I explained why bowling couldn't possibly be a sport. He explained his theory on how socks disappear on the way from the dryer to the drawer. I told him the secret ingredient to my grandma's potato salad. He gave me the secret ingredient to his Nana's brisket. I explained my passion for the cello—the way it had taken me at an early age. He recounted painful memories from his childhood—bruising events that eventually led to his disbelief in God. Nothing was too big or small, no subject too sensitive, no topic too personal for us to dissect and discuss.

We talked hour after enjoyable hour until, finally, my eyelids grew heavy with sleep.

"It's almost one in the morning," I said. "How are you going to get up for work?"

"I'll make it," he assured me. "As long as I get the chance to talk to you at the end of each day."

"That can definitely be arranged."

And so we began meeting online in the evening when he got home from work and then, only after securing my permission, he would call me and we would talk and laugh on the phone through the night.

I would give anything to hear his soothing voice right now, I think, as I bus my tray and leave the café.

Call him, says a slight but persistent voice. There's nothing stopping me. I know his number by heart and he'd be surprised to hear from me. Talking to Sean is a better way to spend the rest of my afternoon than napping and cursing Hannah and her friends under my breath.

On my way back to the hotel, I stop by a corner Duane Reade and buy a phone card, then I fly the few blocks back to the hotel and up to my empty room.

The light on the phone is flashing. There are two messages. Hannah called to apologize. She, Chelsea, and Riley got on the wrong train and ended up in Hoboken, New Jersey.

"Since we're here," she shouts over loud music, "we decided to hang around and have a few drinks. We'll meet you and Devon outside the theater at a quarter to eight."

The second message is from Devon. He met up with a couple of friends who met up with a couple more friends, and he doesn't want us to wait for him. "The tickets are at Will Call anyway," he says distractedly. "I'll see you guys there."

That gives me plenty of alone time to chat with Sean. Who knows, maybe I'll show them all and not bother to go. Let them experience what it feels like to be stood up.

I slip into a pair of comfortable jean shorts before I dial the string of numbers on the back of the card and follow the prompts.

"Hey, guess who?"

"It's the Birthday Girl!" he exclaims. "I was just thinking about you."

"What're you doing?"

"Nothing much, just rotting a few brain cells in front of the television. You?"

"I'm sitting in a hotel room, by myself, seriously thinking about catching the next flight back to Chicago."

"What happened?"

I give him a very long, very detailed (slightly embellished), one-sided version of everything that's transpired.

"I can't remember the last time I've felt this out of place," I whimper.

"Chelsea sounds like a piece of work."

"They all are."

"So forget New York," he says. "Come home and spend your birthday with me. I bought you a gift. We'll go out to dinner and have a good time."

"That's a very tempting offer."

"Of course it is. What woman can resist food and presents?"

"The food and presents weren't the tempting part," I say coyly.

He grunts like the adorable yet chauvinist pig that he is. "It's all about the Sean Meister."

I laugh. My bad mood already dissipating.

"All joking aside," he says. "If you're not having a good time, then leave. You don't have to put up with that kind of treatment. You deserve better."

I take Sean's words to heart as I change into a pair of hip huggers and a fitted, button-down blouse. Before I make any more rash, costly moves, I decide to have a talk with Hannah. If I can get her away from her airhead friends, long enough to talk some sense into her, I'm certain she'll realize how unforgivably rude she's been the past couple of days.

The doorman hails a cab for me. I stare out of the window at the crowded sidewalks, the trendy storefronts, and the soaring high-rises, while the driver yells at the unyielding cars in front of and around us. I check my watch as we inch our way down the street. Traffic is moving much slower than I anticipated.

I stretch my neck toward the driver. "Excuse me? How much farther away is the theater?"

He glares at me through the rearview window. "I don't know," he snaps.

"Okay," I say, sorry I even asked.

Sinking back into the vinyl seat, I will the bumper-to-bumper traffic to thin out. Fifteen minutes and sixteen dollars plus tip later, I'm standing outside the box office. It's five minutes past eight.

"Hi," I greet the dumpy young man sitting behind the inch-thick partition.

His eyes bulge for a split second as he glimpses my disfigured face. But he recovers quickly, forcing composure.

It's a reaction I experience many times on a daily basis, and yet I still haven't adapted to it. Those nervous, horrified looks, sometimes stares, from strangers are the reason why I dread leaving my house.

"Can I help you?" he asks unenthusiastically.

"I'm supposed to meet some friends here, but I'm running a little late," I explain. "The tickets are supposed to be here at Will Call. Can you see if you're still holding them?"

"Whose name are they under?"

"Devon Russell."

He eyes me suspiciously. "Are you Devon?"

"No. I—"

"If you aren't Devon Russell, I can't give you the tickets."

"I understand."

"Next in line!" he shouts.

The couple behind me steps forward.

I barricade the window with my small body. "The thing is, I don't want you to give me the tickets. I just want to know if you're still holding them."

"Why?" he asks, his eyelids drooping with disinterest.

"Because I'm late," I explain again. "And I want to make sure they haven't already gone in without me."

He stares at me and drums his fingers on the wooden desk. "We're not supposed to do that."

"I understand, and usually I would never ask anyone to bend the rules, but I don't want to stand out here all night waiting for them if they're already inside."

Holding my desperate gaze, he reaches under the desk and pulls out a metal box. I watch his fingers flip quickly through its contents. He pulls out a thin, white envelope. "Devon Russell. All five tickets are still here."

I smile, happy I haven't missed them. "Thank you very much."

I stand by the front door and wait for a familiar face to show up. Cozy couple after cozy couple, eager family after eager family, shoves past me and makes their way into the theater. By nine o'clock, I realize my party isn't coming. Hurt and livid, I catch a cab back to the hotel. Our room is still empty. Everything is just as I left it.

I pack my suitcase. There's no possible explanation, no acceptable excuse that will convince me to stay. I don't need to stick around for two more days of this kind of abuse. I've already put up with too much. To get suckered into any more of this disastrous trip would be asinine.

After I change into my pajamas and stack all of my things by the door, I call Sean to let him know that I'll be back in Chicago sometime tomorrow afternoon, but he isn't home.

Depressed and hungry, I turn on the television and tear into the mini bar, rinsing down a fourteen-dollar can of roasted cashews with a six-dollar bottle of Evian.

Afterwards, cuddled deep under the soft hotel sheets, I stare into the darkness until I drift asleep.

Hannah stumbles in just past four in the morning.

I switch on the lamp, which is bolted onto the wall between the two beds, and try to blink away my dizziness.

She's a mess. There are clumps of amber vomit stuck to the tips of her hair. Her skin is flushed and her bangs are matted to her sweaty forehead.

"Hey," she shrieks and teeters to her bed. "How was your day?"

I shake my head. "You're pathetic."

She belches. "Who me?"

"Go take a shower," I order, turning my nose away from her stench of booze and human bile.

"Don't be mad, Abs," she slurs. "We meant to come back for you."

I turn my back on her.

She transfers her drunk, limp body to my bed. "Really, didn't you get my message? We were stuck in Hokoten."

She giggles uncontrollably at her own blunder. "I mean Kothoken."

More hysterical laughs. "No, what was it? Tokhoben. Well, you know what I mean. We got stuck in New Jersey."

I moan into my pillow. "I don't care, Hannah."

"Tomorrow will be better," she promises and kicks off her shoes. "Tomorrow will be all about you."

"I'm leaving tomorrow."

"You can't leave," she says. Her stomach churns vilely.

"Get off my bed before you throw up," I say, nudging her away with my foot.

Too plastered to catch herself, she sways off the mattress and hits the carpeted floor with a loud thud. Seconds later, she hurls.

I glare at the pile of brownish-orange gunk and then at Hannah who is sprawled on the carpet like a wounded animal.

"Oh, God," she murmurs and upchucks again.

"Unbelievable!" I throw back my comforter and rush to the bathroom for towels.

"Wait, don't leave me," she whines.

"Get up." I toss the towels on my bed and yank her to her feet by her arm. Like a nurse, I undress her, put her in the shower with a bar of soap and go to work scrubbing her regurgitated food and liquor out of the carpet. The cleanup takes forever because the harder I rub the more deeply ingrained the mess becomes.

I place the dirty towels outside in the hall so they won't stink up the room and go back to the bathroom to retrieve Hannah. When I pull back the curtain, I am annoyed to see her curled up against the tile fast asleep. The soap is still in its box; the shampoo and conditioner are unopened.

What I should do is stomp over to Chelsea and Riley's room and force them to come deal with Hannah, but they're probably just as smashed as she is. It's a wonder they even made it back to the hotel. As angry and revolted as I am though, I can't just leave her there, naked, shaking, and splattered in her own vomit.

She's heavy. Her lithe, one-hundred-pound frame proves difficult to move as dead weight. I sit her up straight enough to wash and rinse her hair. Then I fill the tub with warm soapy water and let her soak like a pile of dirty laundry. I scrub her neck, back, arms, legs, and stomach until the strong, putrid odor clinging to her body disappears.

Then, using my body as support, I half drag, half carry, her into the bedroom where I dry her off as best I can, dress her in the first pair of night clothes I come across in her drawer and tuck her under the comforter.

I hate this part of our friendship. She'll probably wake up late tomorrow afternoon with a splitting headache and question how she got cleaned up and into bed. She's barreling toward something horrible, an unforeseen but unavoidable fate. It's only a matter of time before her destructive lifestyle and flagrant irresponsibility slams her, at full throttle, into a concrete wall.

But that isn't my problem. I don't have the time or the desire to baby-sit Hannah. I have my own dilemmas, my own tragedies to endure, my own mistakes to clean up. In the grand scheme of things, Hannah is just a distraction, just one more added complication to an already treacherous journey.

She snores and grunts and mumbles her way through the night, waking up only once to beg me for a glass of water.

My eyes are red and my nerves frazzled by the time I give up on sleep and trudge to the bathroom to get dressed.

Hannah is lying on her stomach with a huge down pillow fastened securely to the back of her head.

I don't leave her a note or say good-bye. I just go. It's something I should've done much sooner. If I had, maybe I wouldn't be nearly fifteen hundred dollars in the hole for a mini-vacation that turned out to be a full-blown nightmare.

The grimy towels are still lying just outside the door, contaminating the hallway with a sour, eye-watering stench.

Disgusted, I step over them and make my way downstairs and into the first cab I can find.

I'm overjoyed to be back home. My condo seems more beautiful than when I left it. The ceilings are higher, the walls are brighter, the rooms are sunnier, and the floors are shinier. I'm grateful to have a place of my own—four permanent walls behind which I will always feel welcome.

The first thing I do when I step through the door is call Sean. "I did it," I say. "I packed up and caught the first available flight home."

"I'm sorry your birthday didn't work out the way you'd planned."

"It's okay. As badly as it ended, I think getting out of the house was good for me. I feel renewed."

"That's it? You aren't going to try to salvage the rest of the weekend?"

"No, I've had enough partying for a while. I'm going to hang around the house and relax."

"I'm sorry," he says. "But, no."

"What's wrong with a little R & R?"

"Why don't you let me take you out?" he asks.

My mind races to come up with a viable excuse. "Because I'm jet-lagged."

"C'mon, Abby, live a little."

"I'm just not comfortable with the idea of meeting you yet."

"Are you afraid?"

"Yeah, a little," I confess. "Of what your reaction will be. I'm not the woman you saw in the pictures."

"You are on the inside, and that's all that matters."

"Sean, I like you, and even though we've never met, your opinion of me matters."

"Abs, I want to spend your birthday with you. I want to make you laugh and listen to you talk and look into your eyes. I want to be near you. If what you look like doesn't matter to me, then why should it matter to you?"

I smile, my battered, deflated ego is long overdo for a good pumping up. "I really am jet-lagged," I say.

"Fine, we'll hang in. All I want to do is spend time with you."

"How long will it take you to get here?"

"Just say the word and I can be there in less than an hour."

I ignore the nervous fluttering in my stomach long enough to give him detailed directions to my place. When I hang up the phone, my clammy hands are trembling.

My first instinct is to run upstairs and primp. I need to shower, shave, moisturize, and accessorize.

The right makeup paired with flattering lighting, in addition to a short skirt, low top, and high heels, is all I used to need to lasso a man.

Instead, I settle for a fresh coat of lip gloss, a knee-length jean skirt, a white tank top, and flip flops. Makeup and revealing clothing and dim lighting won't hide my scars. I'm the way I am by no fault of my own and Sean knows that. If he wants me, he'll have to want all of me, just as I am.

An hour and a half later, the doorbell rings. I'm in the kitchen with rubber gloves on, scrubbing the already pristine countertops and trying to forget that an incredibly handsome, charming man is on his way to come see me. I don't bother to check my reflection in the foyer mirror.

I smooth out my skirt, tilt my head back, and summon all of my mettle into a wide, radiant smile as I open the door.

He's dressed in pressed slacks and a crisp, white, button-down shirt. His sleeves are rolled up past his elbows and the only thing more blinding than his smile is the huge bouquet of tulips he's carrying.

I wait for him to recoil—for even the slightest flinch—as he looks at me with his soft, pale-gray eyes.

"Happy Birthday," he says and pulls me into a long, warm hug.

I take in his soothing scent of soap, vanilla, and spearmint. His arms are firm but gentle against my back, and I miss his closeness even before he pulls away.

"Now, let's see what we have here," he says and twirls me around.

I laugh. "What do you think?"

His face falls serious as he examines me the way an art connoisseur examines a one-of-a-kind sculpture for flaws. He shakes his head.

My heart stops.

"Gorgeous." He smiles. "Absolutely mind-boggling."

"You're not so bad yourself," I tease.

He straightens his collar. "I do what I can."

"Would you like to come in?" I ask.

He peers into the marble vestibule before stepping inside.

I give him the grand tour. He seems keenly interested as I throw in interesting tidbits about the imported Venetian tile and custom-made furniture.

"So this is how the other half lives," he says as we settle into the living room couch. "No wonder you like to stay at home so much."

My heel taps quickly against the hardwood floor. "Do you want something to drink?" I ask, too nervous to look him in the eyes.

"No, I'm fine," he says softly.

I feel the warmth of his smile brush my neck.

"Talk to me." He pulls aside a strand of my hair.

"What do you want to talk about?" I ask, my eyes downcast.

His fingers feel dry and coarse as they hook under my chin and turn my face toward his.

Our eyes meet.

"Relax." His tone is gentle.

I sigh and shake out my jittery hands. "I'm trying."

"Is it me?" he asks. "Do I make you nervous?"

"It's all of *this*," I say, motioning at my scalp, face, and neck.

He pushes my hair out of my face and off my shoulders until my skin is fully exposed. Gingerly, he traces the tracks of my scars with his fingertips.

My face hasn't been touched by anyone other than me in nearly three years. I close my eyes to keep from shuddering.

The sensation of human contact overwhelms me to tears and I bite the inside of my cheek to keep them from spilling forth.

He runs his hands across my forehead, over my nose, down my cheeks, across my ears, and under my chin. He runs them down my neck, across my collarbone and back up my neck. He continues to caress my skin and trace the contours of my scarred, misshapen neck and face until I relax, until his hands stop feeling scary and foreign.

When I open my eyes, he's gazing at me, not with confusion, not with pity, but with approval and admiration.

"Beautiful," he whispers. "You're absolutely beautiful."

We eat pasta on my living room floor and listen to Sinatra while we talk like old friends and profess over and over how happy we are, at last, to have finally met.

I make up one of the guest rooms for him and he spends the night. The following morning he makes me Belgian waffles and coffee, and I play the cello for him, and he reads me sections of the morning paper. Our time together is enchanting.

He's all I can think about as I make my way to Dr. Kessler's office on Monday. I haven't felt this light and carefree since I first met Jarvis. I don't know if it's love or just the euphoria of being appreciated, but after my day with Sean, recovery seems less like a myth and more of a possibility.

Dr. Kessler is sitting behind her desk, blowing away the steam rising from her mug. "You're late," she says.

I smile. "There's a very good explanation."

Intrigued, she sets down her coffee. "I take it your inhibition-free weekend in New York went well?"

"Not exactly," I say and delve into a long, breathy recap of the botched birthday trip and Hannah's shenanigans.

Dr. Kessler nods and takes notes. "I must say, after all that's happened, you're in a much better place than I would've expected."

"That's not the good part," I say and delve into an equally long, equally breathy recap of my time with Sean.

As I continue to talk, her smile fades and her massive, square jaw locks into a disapproving frown.

My enthusiasm wanes quickly.

"What were you thinking?" she asks when I'm finished.

"You told me to make a friend."

"I said take baby steps. Meeting a man online and then, a week later, inviting him to stay the night at your house is ludicrous behavior."

"I thought you would be happy for me."

"Abby, this is therapy—mandatory anger management therapy at that. I'm not running a dating service. The homework exercises are serious and pertinent to your rehabilitation."

"What rehabilitation? I'm fine; there's nothing wrong with me."

"Do you think bashing in a car hood is the proper way to handle a fender bender? Do you think inviting a stranger over to your empty house to spend the night is a normal response to a bad vacation? Your reasoning process is warped and very extreme."

I fold my arms across my chest. "My reasoning process is just fine."

She flips open my file and reads her notes. "You're emotionally needy, but you'd sooner self-destruct than become too intimate with someone. You're non-communicative and detached. You're hostile and angry, particularly toward your family." She sighs and turns the page. "You exhibit all the signs of someone who's suffered sexual abuse."

I dig my fingernails into the chair's wooden armrest as fury and shame churn and boil within me. "You're wrong," I snap. My eyes shoot daggers.

"You need to talk about it, Abby. The tighter you hold on to it, the more likely it is to destroy you."

"You're way off base. There's nothing to talk about."

"I'm not here to judge; I'm here to help. You're scuffling with some serious issues and the biggest one is denial. You have to talk about it. I know what's best for you."

"With all due respect, Dr. Kessler, I think I'm the only person qualified to decide what's best for me."

"How old were you when it first happened?" she asks.

My nostrils flare and suddenly I feel claustrophobic. The ceiling hangs much lower than I remember; my shirt feels tighter; the air is smoggier. My chest labors heavily and my forehead instantly grows damp.

"Breathe in through your nose and out through your mouth," she instructs.

Her voice grows faint as the small room begins to spin out of control. She walks around her desk. Her mouth is moving. She's talking to me, but I can only concentrate on my rapidly depleting source of air.

"Breathe in through your nose," Dr. Kessler says. She's holding my hand.

I obey.

"Good girl. Now, blow it out through your mouth."

I do as she says until my heart rate resumes its normal pace and the room stands still.

"You're okay," she says over and over. "Just keep breathing."

She sends me down the hall to the bathroom where I splash water on my face and try to pull myself together.

When I return, she wants to focus the rest of the session on Sean and all the reasons why I need to call things off.

"You're in a fragile state," she says. "You aren't ready for a relationship. If something were to happen—if he suddenly decides he doesn't want a girlfriend or it turns out that every word out of his mouth's been a lie—you'll be crushed and ill-equipped to handle that kind of disappointment. A man is not going to make your troubles go away, Abby. You can't keep making other people responsible for your happiness."

I hear her speaking, but I don't listen to her words. I stare at her and work to block out the sound of her voice.

She doesn't know Sean like I do. She hasn't heard his laughter over the phone. She wasn't there when he ran his hands down my face—when he said I was beautiful. Everything about him is genuine. Sean is what's best for me. He's the only person who makes me feel worthwhile.

I don't need to talk about Jimmie or Val or all the reasons why I am the way I am. What's done is done. I've made it this far without rehashing my childhood and I'll continue to push forward long after my time is up with Dr. Kessler.

I can't go back. I have to focus on what's good in my life. Sean is what's good. Sean and the Pulsed Dye Laser treatment are the only things I need, to have a new beginning.

"I hope we're clear," Dr. Kessler says.

I look past her at the round clock hanging on the wall. "Time's up," I say.

She purses her lips. There's more she wants to say, more analyzing to be done, more explanations to unearth, but not today. Today I've paid my emotional dues and I'm going home.

She doesn't try to stop me as I gladly leave her office. She doesn't try to dispense any last-minute trinkets of wisdom. She doesn't force the issue of my past, but we both know it's there. We both know my secret.

27. *Jarvis*

"Jo's lungs collapsed" was the doctor's verdict. Apparently that is a common side effect of pulmonary congestion—a condition he began battling before I was even born.

His medicine cabinet, nightstand drawer, and kitchen counter are cluttered with varying sizes of orange prescription bottles. He never had arthritis. He never made an appointment with his doctor. He didn't have to. He knew he was dying.

At night, I close my eyes and hold my breath until my chest burns and my head spins. I want to know what it feels like to suffocate to death. I want to know what Jo must've experienced during his last painful minutes alive. If I was braver, I would've held my breath until my spirit broke—until my insides melted and my organs gave way to the pressure.

But I'm not brave, and just as I feel myself slipping into darkness, I open my mouth and inhale greedily. And then I cry. I cry because I'm still here and Jo isn't. I cry because without him life's impossibilities seem so much greater than what I can conquer alone. I cry because I miss him—because he's irreplaceable.

Then I hold my breath and try again—try to push myself past the edge, try to follow Jo to wherever he is. But the result is always the same. Eventually, I open my mouth and breathe greedily and weep all over again for all the same reasons.

Mom and I arrange his funeral. We're the only family he has left. The small sanctuary is packed with mourners. They fill the pews, stand against the walls, huddle miserably in the back, and even litter the hallways outside.

I sit in the front row with Mom and my sister and Haley and pretend to listen to the proceedings. I've been pretending all week. Pretending to study, pretending to sleep and eat, pretending to smile, pretending to care.

But I don't care. Such courage does not exist in me. How can it? By the age of thirty-two, I've lost two fathers. Misery, I've concluded, is imminent. God is merciless. Life is futile and no one is safe.

Who will be next and for what reason? What is the point in slaving day in and day out to become something or *someone* of worth when life—when human existence—is so senselessly fragile, so random and arbitrary?

My motivation is gone. It's been stolen from me with vicious guile and is now forever buried underground with Jo. I'll just go back to being nothing, to being nobody. That's truly all I ever was and anyone who thought differently was only blinded by the glare of false hope.

But not me. Not anymore. I'll sooner pluck out my eyes and block out the world entirely than be blinded by hope again. I won't make the mistake of stepping away from what is real—what's certain.

I sulk in the corner of our house with my arms folded bitterly, angrily, across my chest and stare at the people milling around like ants.

Haley crosses the room carrying a plate of food and cup of red punch. "Hey," she greets me cautiously, her eyes alert. "I brought you something to nibble on."

I shake my head. My arms remain folded across my chest. "I'm not hungry."

She sets the rejected sustenance on the table in front of me. "Don't you think you should eat something?"

"No."

"Is there anything I can get you?"

"No."

She sighs. "Do you want me to go away?"

"I don't care.

"Why are you so angry with me?" she whispers, her chin trembling.

"I'm not angry with you," I reply flatly. "I'm not anything."

"Jay, you have to take it to God. He's the on—"

"Don't," I warn. "Don't talk to me about God."

She winces, troubled pity pours from her eyes. "That's not the answer."

"There are no answers," I announce like a true defeatist.

"So you're just going to forget everything God's done for you? Is that supposed to make you feel better?"

"Yes," I hiss defiantly.

"How? Shutting out God won't bring Jo back."

"Letting Him in won't either."

"Turning into a hateful cynic is not what Jo would want for you."

"How would you know?" I snap. "You barely knew him."

"I didn't have to know him to see how much he loved you."

"Yeah, he loved me so much that he lied to me. Arthritis..." I shake my head. "He knew I was stupid enough to believe it."

"He didn't want you to worry. There was nothing anybody could do."

"How do we know that? There are other doctors, other hospitals, better ones in bigger cities. Why was he working fifteen-hour days when he should have been at home or in a hospital? Why wasn't he on a respirator or a transplant list?"

She shakes her head, unable to offer any answers. "Those were his choices, his decisions to make."

"What about me? Don't I get choices?"

"You get to choose how this experience impacts your life. You get to decide what direction to go from here."

"I have no idea," I confess.

"Ask God." She reaches for my hand.

I pull away. "Don't."

She looks at me, her head tilted to the side, her eyes red-rimmed and brimming with tears. A voice inside of me begs me to stop. *Stop hurting her;*

stop pushing her away; stop shunning her attempts to be supportive; stop trying to destroy one of the only meaningful relationships you have left.

"He's the only way," she says unapologetically.

I don't respond. Deep down, I know she's right. Too much has transpired over the past few months. Undeniable—some would even say miraculous—things have gripped my life and turned it completely around. But in the aftermath of Jo's death, it all seems unimportant and irrelevant, like dunking the winning basket after the buzzer. It's just too little, too late.

"I'm going to lie down." I back away from the table.

"If you need anything—," she starts. But I am already on my way down the hall toward my bedroom. I close the door, yank off my coat and tie, and climb onto my bed. Haley's words echo in my mind. *You get to decide what direction to go from here.*

I gaze up at my eggshell ceiling and consider my options.

One path is plain and ordinary. It's predictable and I've spent most of my life traveling down it effortlessly. Sure it's the road of common men, trampled by anyone who's grown to cherish the ease of mediocrity. There's no excitement on that path, no growth, no chance for glory. But it is brightly lit and there's no need for maps, no fear of getting lost. It is characterized by flat, simple terrain. It is unmistakably certain.

Then there's the other path, which is shadowed by ambiguity. There are deep gullies and soaring hills. There are narrow, unexpected turns, thick forests, jagged cliffs, and every other imaginable impediment. I'm not familiar with that path. In fact, I've spent a substantial amount of energy running from it. Yes, it offers excitement and growth and the chance for glory, but at a cost, and I fear I'm too weak to navigate that path successfully.

I lie in bed and stare at the wall, pondering all that hangs in the balance, all the ramifications of choosing one path over another. Time, for me, will continue to stand still until I make my decision. But I'm too much of a coward. If I'd reached this dilemma under different circumstances and Jo was still alive, he would have the answer and a perfectly logical explanation to back that answer up.

He always had the gift of perspective. While most of us operate from a palate of black and white with fourteen shades of gray in between, Jo viewed the world in color. He saw things exactly as they were, no interpretation needed.

Who would help me now? Who would listen while I unloaded my confusion, and more importantly, who could understand it?

I hear the storm door creak open and closed. The house is clearing out slowly as one by one the guests depart to their cars and back to their lives. There's a light, tentative rap at my door.

I roll onto my side. "Come in."

Haley appears; her purse hangs from her shoulder. "I'm getting ready to leave," she says.

"Already?"

"It's been a long day and my feet hurt."

"Okay."

I want to say more—to apologize for being so callous, to explain the overwhelmingly complex emotions roiling in my chest, to thank her for being patient and empathetic. I want to say more, but the words cling to the back of my throat. She senses my hesitation. "Can I bring you anything before I go?"

I peer at her concerned face and draw comfort from her softness. "Can you just sit with me for a while?" I ask, my voice cracking.

"Sure."

I prop a pillow up beside me and watch as she removes her shoes and sinks tiredly against the headboard.

"I knew something was wrong," I say after a few moments of silence. "I sensed it."

She nods. "You couldn't have done anything."

"At the diner, he'd set up a cot in the back," I say, tears spilling down my cheeks. "He dropped dishes. He messed up orders. He could barely breathe."

"He'd been sick for a long time."

"His heart was failing," I choke back a sob, "and all I could talk about was me, *my* problems, *my* wants, *my* needs."

"It's not your fault."

"I was in Toronto having the time of my life and he was writhing on the floor, alone, fighting for air." I look up, ashamed and guilty, to see her own tears drip shamelessly from her chin.

"It's not your fault," she says again.

I shake my head and weep. My shoulders convulse violently and my body shakes, raked by the loss of a second father. "I don't understand," I sputter. "I prayed for protection. In Toronto, I prayed that Jo would be okay, and God gave me peace. Why?" I croak. "Why did He give me peace when Jo was already dead? Why did He betray me?"

"Ssssshhhh," Haley soothes. She pulls me into the warmth of her arms and strokes my back. "Jay, listen to me," she pleads. "God didn't betray you. He gave you peace because everything is okay. Jo's in an eternal paradise with a perfect body. He's not sick anymore. He'll never be sick again."

"He didn't deserve to die, not like that," I gulp. "He was a good man."

She rocks me slowly back and forth. "It was his time."

"Why is God punishing me?"

"He's not," she says. "But God's children aren't exempt from pain, Jay. People live and they die. That's the rhythm and the cycle of life. You have to take comfort in knowing that Jesus holds the keys to life and death. He's in control of absolutely everything. We may not understand His timing or His methods, but we can always fall back on our faith in His perfect will."

"I don't know what to do." I rest my head in her lap. "I don't know which way is up."

"You will," she promises. "God won't let you fall and neither will I."

"When do the hits stop coming?" I sob, unable to glean comfort from her words.

"He gives us times of rest. He sends people to encourage us and to help us resolve seemingly hopeless situations. He loves you so much, Jay."

I cry into her lap. My tears bleed through her black skirt, but she doesn't move. She doesn't complain. She continues to stroke my back and whisper prayers into my ear. "Show him, Father," she pleads. "Bathe him in understanding and peace."

I soak in her words. *Please, God,* I beg silently. *Give me understanding. Give me peace.*

"Jarvis," Mom calls. She swings open my bedroom door. "Oh!" She takes in the scene of tears and sniffling on my bed. "I'm sorry. I didn't know Haley was still here."

"It's fine," I say, struggling to straighten myself out. "What do you need?"

"There's someone here to see you. Says his name's Victor Wright."

"What does he want?"

She shrugs. "He wants to talk to you."

I sigh, lethargic from emotions run amuck. "Yeah, okay. Just give me a few minutes."

"Take your time. When you're ready, he's in the living room."

Haley wipes the tears from my face with the back of her hand. "You're okay," she says, examining me.

I sniffle. "I know."

"You had too much bottled up inside." She blinks back a fresh wave of tears.

I brush her bangs from her forehead. "Why are you crying?"

"I hate that you have to go through this. I love you so much and I can't do anything to make it better."

I smile, perhaps for the first time since Jo's death. *She loves me*, I muse. The odd combination of euphoria and sorrow is somehow stabilizing.

"You just did."

She nestles closer to me.

"I better go see what this Victor guy wants."

Reluctantly, she pulls away. I yank my shirt straight and smooth out my pants before sliding into my wheelchair.

Perched on the edge of my bed, Haley tugs her shoes back on. "Should I wait here?"

I kiss her hand. "Come with me."

She slings herself up and we make our way to the living room where Mr. Wright has made himself at home on our floral love seat. He's holding a steaming bowl of peach cobbler.

"Mr. Daniels!" he exclaims. He has a jovial countenance; his double chin wags from side to side when he smiles. I note his gray hair and protruding stomach. He's tall with a broad nose, lanky arms, and husky shoulders.

"*Jarvis* is fine." I shake his hand. "This is Haley."

"It's a pleasure." Mr. Wright nods and smiles warmly. He places the bowl of cobbler on the coffee table and sits back down.

Haley joins Mom on the couch.

"What can we do for you?" I ask.

"You don't know me," he says. "But Jo spoke of you fondly."

"You were friends?"

He nods solemnly. "We were best men at each other's weddings. He was there when both my children were born, and I was JoJo's first official customer." He reaches for the black leather briefcase by his feet. "I'm also the executor of his estate."

"His estate?" I ask puzzled. "You mean the diner?"

He pulls out a manila file and hands it to me.

"The diner, his house, several properties in northern Michigan, Chicago, Indiana, and Ohio—not to mention his trusts, his life insurance policies, and stocks. He left all of his assets to you."

Mom gasps. She and Haley grip each other's hands, their eyes wide with shock.

I shake my head, dismayed. "What assets? All Jo had was the diner."

"Son, that diner alone grosses nearly a million dollars a year."

It was my turn to remove my jaw from my lap. "That can't be."

He points at the folder in my hand. "It's all there. Jo had no debt. Everything he had, he owned outright."

"How—how much does it all come to?" Mom asks.

"About three and a half million dollars."

"Three million dollars!" I choke.

"Give or take." Mr. Wright smiles.

I shake my head. "I—I can't take this money."

Haley's face drops.

Mr. Wright scratches his chin.

Mom glares. "Why not?" she asks.

"I didn't earn it."

"It's a gift," Haley argues.

I hold up the folder. "This is sweat—Jo's sweat. He worked his entire life to earn this. I can't take it. I don't deserve it."

"You have to," Mom says. "It's yours. He gave it to you."

"I don't have to do anything." Defiantly, I hand the manila folder back to Mr. Wright.

"Jarvis is right," he says disappointedly. "He doesn't have to take it."

"If he doesn't want it, then who gets it?" Mom asks.

"It's seized by the state of Michigan."

"What'll happen to the diner?" Haley asks.

"It'll either be sold at private auction or shut down."

All six of their eyes burrow into me.

Three million dollars is a lot of money, more than I ever expected to see in my lifetime. But I don't feel right taking Jo's money. The diner isn't mine; it's his. It will always be his.

Love, sacrifice, vision, and hard work went into making JoJo's what it is. Whatever stock he acquired, whatever trusts or investments he made, also belonged to him. I didn't have anything to do with it.

Even if I accept the inheritance just to save the diner from closing, how am I supposed to manage three million dollars? I'm a lowly college freshman by day and a waiter by night. How am I supposed to run a business? I don't know the first thing about ordering supplies, or keeping books, or paying taxes. Under my supervision, the diner will probably end up closing anyway.

On the other hand, with the right advisement, three million dollars can go a long way. There's so much we need, so much we've gone without. I could easily afford to finish school. I could buy mom a brand-new house. I could afford to see a specialist and explore my options with prosthetics. I could invest it and, when the time was right, use the return to start my own business.

"Maybe you need to sleep on it," Mom suggests, desperation in her voice.

Haley nods in agreement. "It's a big decision. You should make it when your judgment isn't clouded by grief."

"There's no rush," Mr. Wright says.

"I need to pray about," I finally decide.

The tension in the room eases.

"I just want to do the right thing," I explain.

Mr. Wright nods. "I understand. In fact, I think that's very responsible of you."

"Three million dollars," I say aloud. "Why would he leave it all to me?"

"Who else would he leave it to?" Mr. Wright asks.

I shrug. "You?"

He shakes his head. "I'm an old man. I can't carry on his legacy the way you can."

"He could've left it to my mom or given it to his church."

"With his wife gone," Mr. Wright explains, "you were his family. You were his son. He wouldn't see this money—his business—go to anyone but you."

I don't know how to respond. Jo was like a father to me. I respected and admired him just as much as my biological father. He had faith in me. He ignored my endless faults and ignited within me the will to persevere. He taught me not to ascribe to anyone else's image of who I'm supposed to be.

Now, after blessing me with purpose and guidance, he's also giving me all of his worldly possessions. Even from the grave, he's spurring me on. He won't let me backslide—won't let me use sadness as an excuse to take the common man's path.

But what if I don't have it in me? What if I jump in headfirst and squander it all down to the very last penny? What if, in six months, I run JoJo's into the ground? I won't just be failing myself, I'll be failing Jo. I don't know if I can take that chance.

"Sleep on it, pray on it, talk about it. Do whatever it takes to come to a decision you can live with," Mr. Wright says. He hands the folder back. "Look it over. Consider what it entails."

I tuck it under my arm.

"Is there a number where we can reach you?" Mom asks.

Mr. Wright flips open a small, flat, gold-plated box and hands all three of us his business card. "It's got both my home and office numbers on it."

"Thank you for stopping by." I extend my hand.

"It was an honor." He gathers his coat jacket and briefcase.

Mom gets up. "I'll show you out."

He turns to face me. "If I may say one more thing?"

I nod.

"I knew Jo better than anyone. Maybe even better than his wife." He chuckles nostalgically. "I knew him and all of his business affairs inside and out. I knew his character, his morals, his values, and I promise you—I *promise* you—he would never have left you his estate if he didn't think you were capable of handling it."

I lower my head. Tears threaten to spill from my eyes. "Thank you."

"Be it his choice or your destiny, you are his son," he says firmly. "That will never change, no matter what you decide."

28. *Abby*

Sean and I sit at the coffee table. It's the fourth consecutive weekend we've spent together. We're in the middle of our third hand of Go Fish. It's the only card game I know how to play besides War—and I'm wiping the floor with him.

He grabs a handful of popcorn and eyes me distrustfully.

I grin and bat my lashes.

"Got any nines?"

"Go fish."

"Got any sixes?" I ask.

Begrudgingly, he hands me two. "Any fours?"

"Go fish."

"That's it!" He throws down his hand and reaches across the table in an attempt to snatch my cards.

I shriek with delight and leap behind the sofa. "Don't be such a sore loser!"

"Come here." He chases me from one end of the living room to the other. "You're cheating! I know you are!"

I dash left in a last-minute attempt to barricade myself behind the love seat, but he's too quick and catches me by my wrist.

"Gotcha," he says, tugging me into his chest.

We tumble to the ground.

"Let me see your hand."

I laugh and tighten my grip on my cards. "Never!"

He tries to pry open my fingers. "If you aren't cheating then you have nothing to hide."

"Face it; I'm just better at this game than you are."

"Are you going to let me see your hand?"

"Nope." I giggle.

He sighs. "Then you leave me no choice."

Before I can get away, he begins to tickle me—first my stomach, then my feet, then my neck. Tears trickle down my cheeks as I cackle and squirm on the floor.

"Quit! Please! Cut it out," I beg.

"Not until you give me the cards."

"Okay, okay," I say, my chest heaving.

He loosens his grip on my legs. I jerk forward and try to crawl away, but before I know it he's got me pinned against the floor again and is tickling me mercilessly.

He laughs at my agony. "Some people are too hard-headed for their own good."

"Am I interrupting?" someone asks.

Sean and I leap apart. Hannah is standing in the front hall; her gym bag rests by her feet. She's wearing ridiculously short spandex shorts and her arms and shoulders are glistening with sweat.

I sit up and straighten out my T-shirt while Sean makes every attempt to keep from gawking at my roommate.

"We were just playing around," I say, standing to my feet. "You remember Sean?"

She smiles politely and approaches with her hand extended. "How could I forget?"

"How's it going?" he asks, dusting his palms off on his jeans before shaking her hand. "Hannah, right?"

"You remember?" Her coy laugh is irking and I cringe.

Sean nods eagerly. "I never forget a name...or a face," he adds.

"Me neither," Hannah says. "Especially not one as cute as yours."

"Don't you have a date tonight?" I ask.

"He canceled."

"Oh, so you have a boyfriend?" Sean asks. I sense disappointment in his voice and it's heart-wrenching.

"No, just drinks with a colleague."

"Well, we don't have any plans tonight if you want to hang around with us."

Hannah looks at me.

I shoot her the evil eye—a silent but firm warning for her to back off.

"No, I think I'll call it a night, maybe take in a good book."

"There's no reason to be locked up in your room by yourself when there's perfectly good company downstairs, right?" He turns to me, his eyes hopeful.

I quickly erase the murderous glare from my face and nod. "Sure, why not?"

"Okay," Hannah chirps. "But instead of hanging around here, why don't we go to dinner and then catch a late movie?"

"What do you say, Abs?" Sean asks. "You up for it?"

"I can't." My tone is short and definite. "I have to be up early tomorrow for school."

"That's right," Hannah says. "I forgot about that whole community service thing."

I shove my hands in my pockets to keep from lunging at her.

"Community service?" Sean asks.

"Abs has to teach a bunch of inner-city hoodlums on the south side how to play music."

"It's court ordered," I say, too embarrassed to look up.

He gives my shoulders a squeeze. "Doesn't sound so bad."

I gain profound satisfaction from Hannah's envious stare.

"Fine. Dinner and a movie are out. How about Scrabble and a frozen pizza?" Hannah suggests.

Sean shrugs. "Sounds good to me."

"You know what?" I toss my cards onto the coffee table. "I think maybe I'm the one who should call it a night."

"What's wrong?" Sean asks.

I shake my head. "I'm tired and three's a crowd."

Hannah folds her arms across her chest and rolls her eyes.

"Good night." I make my way to my room and close the door. I can't compete with Hannah and her perfect skin and long legs and itty bitty waist. All the giggling and flirting in the world won't make me as stunning as she is—it won't hide my abnormalities.

The worst part is that she doesn't really want Sean; she just doesn't want me to have him. In that way, she's just like my sister.

Hannah is a man-hunter. She chases men and dumps them for sport. She doesn't care that Sean's the only person since the accident who's been able to make me laugh—I mean, really laugh, the kind of laughter that forces me to forget my problems.

Never mind that he understands me better than people I've known my whole life or that in the middle of the night when I wake up cold and shivering, the vision of his face is the only thing that can calm me back to sleep.

Forget my heart and my feelings. Forget that I'm falling in love with him.

Sean knocks softly and cracks open the door. "Hey," he inches forward, "what's going on?"

"Nothing." I brush past him and into my bathroom. "I'm getting ready for bed."

"It's six o'clock."

I shrug. "Like I told you. I have an early day tomorrow."

He sits on my ottoman. "Should I go home?"

"No, please, by all means, go have fun with Hannah."

"I didn't drive all the way out here to see Hannah. I came to spend time with you."

"Could've fooled me."

"We were just playing cards. I didn't think you'd mind if she tagged along."

"I'm sure her miniature shorts and sports bra had nothing to do with your invitation. I saw you. You couldn't take your eyes off her."

"She's your roommate."

"She's evil," I snap.

He laughs. "Where is this coming from?"

"She's always been this way," I gripe. "Whenever anything or anyone good comes my way, she swoops in with her perfect body and bubbly laugh and steals it right from underneath me."

"I guess that, coupled with the whole New York fiasco, doesn't make her your favorite person."

"Not exactly."

"If it's any consolation, she's not going to steal me away. Yes, she's beautiful, and yes, maybe I was concentrating a little too hard on her shorts, but trust me when I say, she's got nothing on you."

I gaze into his earnest eyes. He enthralls me. We've only been in each other's lives for a month and still I'm confident he's my soul mate. I want to be with him, to know what it's like to kiss him, to be enveloped in his arms. But he hasn't made any moves—hasn't given any signs that he's ready to take our friendship to the next level.

"Get your pajamas on," he orders. "And come downstairs and watch a movie with us."

Channel 7 is running a Demi Moore marathon and *Ghost* is just starting. We settle ourselves in the living room around a table of chips, popcorn, mini tacos, and a very fruity, very alcoholic punch Sean concocted with a half gallon of orange juice, lemons, and a pint of vodka.

Hannah and I sit on opposite ends of the couch and Sean curls up on the love seat. I keep my eye on both of them. They seem to be engrossed in the movie, but I can't help noticing that each time Hannah repositions herself, her robe hikes up a few more inches.

During one of the commercials, Hannah offers to refill our cups with ice. I watch as she bends over farther than necessary, revealing an ample amount of cleavage, gathers the cups, and saunters into the kitchen.

"Did you see that?" I ask as soon as she's out of earshot.

He smiles. "I plead the fifth."

I chuck a pillow at him. "Pig."

"Would you feel better sitting over here with me?"

My stomach flutters. "Yes."

He scoots to the right and makes a spot just big enough for me.

I scuttle over, my socks pattering against the hardwood floor, and slide in next to him. It's snug but a perfect fit.

"Comfy?" he asks, pulling his blanket over my shoulders.

"Mmm-hmmm," I purr, like the proverbial cat who got the milk.

Hannah returns; a dark shadow crosses her face as she takes in our new seating arrangement. She sets down the cups. "You know something? I just remembered I have a really important call to make. It's for work."

"At this hour?" Sean asks.

She nods. "I can't believe it slipped my mind."

I smile. "We'll be here."

The movie comes back on, but instead of turning my attention to the television, I watch Hannah schlep dejectedly up the staircase and to her room.

I grin victoriously and only after she shuts her door do I relax and snuggle closer to Sean.

The parking lot is overrun with chrome-rimmed jalopies, blaring profane rap music. The boys who aren't checking out the cars are checking out the girls; and the girls, in their stilettos and low-cut shirts, are pretending not to enjoy the catcalls they receive as they strut their overly developed, overly exposed bodies through the crowds of other milling students and into the school.

I smooth out my skirt before stepping out of my car and make my way around the corner to a less crowded entrance. Security guards meet me as I step in line and wait my turn to walk through the metal detector. A rather burly officer takes my purse and empties its contents, tampons and all, onto a long table.

"What is that?" he asks, pointing at the large, black case resting beside me.

"It's a cello."

He grunts. "Step through."

I obey.

He stuffs my belongings back into my purse and turns his attention to the next person in line.

The halls are just as crowded as the parking lot. I grip my things tightly to my chest and push my way down one locker-lined corridor after another until I find the office.

"Can I help you?" the woman manning the front desk asks. Her small work space is scattered with memos and files. She looks to be my age, with dark, rich skin and high cheekbones. Her hair is pulled back with a beaded headband and her wool sweater hangs loosely from her shoulders.

"I'm looking for Amanda Vine."

"And you are?"

"Abigail Walker, the new cello instructor."

She smiles. "Let me get her. You can have a seat if you want."

I survey the badly spotted couch behind me and opt to stand.

An older woman steps from the corner office. She has a slight hunch and her gray-streaked hair falls in stiff, brittle strands down her back. Her glasses dangle from a chain around her neck and her lips turn down in such a way that she has a permanent scowl.

She sniffs disapprovingly at my maroon silk skirt and matching blazer before speaking.

"Ms. Walker, I presume?"

I smile.

"I'm Amanda Vine. We're glad to have you here," she says, her steely tone sounding the furthest thing from glad.

"I'm glad to be here," I lie.

She gives me a curt nod as well as another seift once-over.

"Good," she says, after sizing me up to her satisfaction. "Orchestra meets third period.

This is our handbook." She shoves the thick, monstrosity into my hands. "Learn it, love it. And lastly, here are your keys. This one's for the storage room, this one's for your desk, and this one's for the classroom. I strongly advise you to lock up everything at the end of each day. Questions?"

"What period will I be giving lessons?"

She eyes me suspiciously. "You won't be giving lessons. You're the new music teacher."

I blink and try my best not to choke on the shock that is rapidly setting in. "That's not possible."

"I beg your pardon?"

"I'm a cellist, Mrs. Vine, not a conductor, and certainly not a teacher."

She purses her thin, cracked lips. "Your resumé says you can play all string instruments."

I smile graciously. "Yes, but—"

"Then what's the problem?"

"Judge Frye ordered me to provide private cello lessons and that's what I've come prepared to do."

Mrs. Vine shoves her tinted, square glasses up the bridge of her nose. "I've already spoken with Judge Frye. I have permission to implement your services where they are most needed, and right now I don't need a private tutor; I need someone to teach third period."

"This is crazy!" I exclaim. "I haven't taught in years."

Mrs. Vine smirks. "Don't worry. It's like riding a bike. You never really forget."

"But—"

"This is the attendance sheet," Mrs. Vine cuts in, ignoring my protests, and hands me a four-page printout. "Gail will show you to your classroom."

"Hold on a second," I call to her retreating back. "There's been some sort of mistake."

Gail stands from behind her desk. She's wearing a sympathetic smile.

"There's no way. Isn't there someone I can talk to? She has a boss. She has to have a boss."

"You'll be fine," Gail assures me and leads me back into the crowded hallway.

"This is a disaster. I can't teach. I don't even like kids."

She laughs. "Your classroom is on the third floor. You can take the elevator," she points to a defaced set of metal doors in front of us, "but the stairs are your safest bet."

She steps quickly and I follow closely behind. There are students bouncing basketballs and chugging soda and shouting and laughing and teasing. Some look shy; others are definitely bully material. A few students are bogged down with books; most are toting what looks like empty book bags.

I avoid the curious stares and keep my eyes straight ahead.

"Here we are," Gail says, flipping on the lights. The room is cluttered with folding chairs and rusted, lopsided stands.

KiKi Loves Chico is scrawled across both chalkboards and the ceiling is stained with large, brown water spots.

The air is hot and muggy and the bars on the windows block out the sunlight and make the large space feel more like a concentration camp than a music room.

A whimper escapes my lips.

Gail grips my arm. "It's going to be fine. Listen to me. Are you listening?"

I face her.

"All you have to do is hold your ground. These kids will only run over you if they think they can get away with it. Take next period to get your game face on. It's the first day of classes. Nobody expects you to have a lesson planned. Introduce yourself, take attendance, and establish the ground rules. That's all you have to do."

I nod, though I feel like I should be taking notes.

"Go ahead and get settled in," Gail says. "If things get out of hand, you know where to find me. I'll stop by and check on you at lunch."

I gulp.

"Remember," she says, "you're the boss."

I'm the boss. I'm the boss. I'm the boss. Those three little words become my mantra and I repeat them to myself over and over again as I wipe down the chalkboard and clear away the trash.

I sit at my desk and scan the long list of names printed on the attendance sheet. There are at least seventy kids in the orchestra. How did I go from giving one-on-one private lessons to teaching and conducting seventy students? What am I supposed to do with seventy ornery teenagers for ninety minutes, every day, five days a week?

Had Judge Frye told me this was going to happen, I might have taken my chances in jail.

I'm the boss, I remind myself in a vain attempt to banish the persistent lump of panic loitering in my stomach.

"Take it slow," I coach myself. "All you have to do is introduce yourself, take attendance, and establish the ground rules."

I spend the rest of first and second period skimming the massive handbook so I know what ground rules to establish.

The bell signaling the end of ssecond period rings. *Introduce yourself, take attendance, establish the ground rules. You're the boss.*

The students begin to stroll in. Some are carrying instruments; others have brought nothing more than a frown and a tired face.

"Hello," I greet them with a forced smile.

A few students look up, but the majority of them ignore me and continue conversing with their peers.

"Uh, excuse me? It's time to take your seats so we can get started."

The room grows noisier as they continue to pretend like I don't exist.

"Hey!" I shout, banging my fist on the desk.

The racket gradually dies down and the room eventually grows silent.

"That's much better."

"Who are you?" a voice calls from the group.

"My name is Ms. Walker and I guess I'm your new substitute."

"You guess?" another student asks.

I study their faces, their body language, their posture. Corpses are more enthusiastic.

"Titles aren't important to me," I say. "What matters is that I'm here to teach you music. It's my passion and, hopefully, if it's not already yours, it will be."

A sneeze, two coughs, and one hundred forty blinking eyes are the only responses I get.

"I'm not an educator by definition," I continue. "So you'll probably find my teaching style a little unorthodox. But if at any point you feel like I'm moving too fast or something is unclear, don't be afraid to tell me."

More silence. A young man in the back fastens a set of headphones to his ears and closes his eyes.

I'm the boss.

"Okay, now for a few ground rules. First and foremost, you must be on time. If you're late more than three times this semester or you have more than two unexcused absences, you will be removed from the music program and placed in study hall. That's their rule," I wave the handbook, "not mine.

"Second, you must bring your instruments, music, notebooks, and a pencil or an erasable pen with you to class every day. If you forget one of those four things, don't bother coming.

"And third, every Friday, each of you will be required to play an excerpt from whatever piece we're learning. Your performance will not only factor into your grade, but will also determine what chair you place. So practice as much as you can. Are there any questions?"

A stout young man with cornrows and a pronounced scar across his left cheek raises his hand.

"I got one," his baritone voice rumbles.

"Yes?"

"What happened to your face?"

Some of the students crow; many cast incredulous glances at those sitting around them.

I fold my arms across my chest. "Are there any pertinent questions?"

"I think that's pertinent," he says, his eyes daring.

"What is your name?" I ask, my words chopped with anger.

"Terrance." He smirks obnoxiously. "But you can call me Terry."

"Well, *Terrance*, contrary to what you might think, my appearance has nothing to do with how I teach or how well you learn to play music. Do you understand?"

He shrugs. "I disagree. I don't think I want to learn anything from you unless I know you have a good reason for looking that ugly."

I blink, stunned by his boldness.

The class sits quietly and waits for my response.

My first instinct is to tell him off, toss him out, and let Mrs. Vine deal with him. Or better yet, I can just pack up my stuff and leave. But that's what he wants. I can see it in his icy stare and clamped jaw. He's desperate to get under my skin, to crack me, to prove to everyone witnessing our standoff that he's in control.

I'm in this situation because of a horrible lapse in judgment—because I let my anger get the best of me. I can't make the same mistake twice, especially not over a sixteen-year-old showboat with a smart mouth and a chip on his shoulder.

Our eyes lock. He flashes a daring sneer and stretches his legs out in true mongrel fashion.

"If *your* scar doesn't keep me from teaching, then why should my scars keep you from learning?" I ask.

He sits up and points his index finger at me. "My scar is none of your business."

"Likewise," I seethe.

"I know what happened to her face," a young girl announces. She's sitting down front next to a window. A violin case rests in her lap. "You're Abby Walker," she says.

I nod. "That's right."

"I'm Kendra," she introduces herself. Her voice is husky and thick with an exotic accent. "I have your CD."

"You have a CD?" someone asks.

"I have three." I feel my cool points rise a notch.

"So what happened?" another student calls.

"She was in a car accident," Kendra answers.

The rest of the class turns to me for confirmation.

"That's what happened to my face," I say to Terrance.

He doesn't flinch.

"I heard you retired and moved out of the country," Kendra continues. "But then I saw you in the paper this summer."

"Why were you in the paper?" a young man asks.

I shake my head. "It's not important."

"She beat up some girl," Kendra says.

The room immediately livens up with fascinated murmurs.

"For real?" one student calls.

"What'd she do?" someone else asks.

A heavyset Latino boy chuckles to himself. "You must've lost."

"Whoa, whoa." I wave my hands and signal for them to pipe down. "I didn't beat anyone up. It was an over-publicized fender bender at best."

They grumble in collective disappointment.

"Hey, yeah," a petite girl in a skin-tight halter wags her finger wildly, "I remember. You're the crazy lady with the crowbar."

"That was *you*?" someone asked.

"Wait, what happened?" another student yells.

My heart races. *How did we get stuck on this topic?*

They stare at me intently, their eyes wide and their ears keenly awaiting a violent tale of road rage.

I sigh and throw up my hands. "She rammed into the back of my car and I lost it."

"That's it?" a young man asks.

I feel like a standup comedian who's bombing miserably in front of a tough crowd.

"It was a brand-new Porsche," I explain.

"What!" The boys especially nod in understanding.

"I would've beat her up too," one of them empathizes.

"She had it coming."

"Nobody had anything coming," I say, desperate to regain control. The last thing I need is a rumor floating around that instead of conducting the high school's orchestra, I was instructing its wayward members to fight anyone who rubs them the wrong way. "It was an unfortunate mishap and now it's over."

"So how come you aren't in jail?" inquired another student.

"This isn't punishment enough?" I joke.

The students laugh and the mood in the room eases.

"Y'all think that's funny?" Terrance asks, his lip curled into a snarl. "She just called us a prison sentence."

"Don't put words in my mouth. That's not what I said."

"I'm just translating."

"It was a joke."

"You're the joke."

"What exactly is your problem, Terrance?"

"My problem is that I'm tired of being treated like garbage. They could've hired a real teacher, but instead, they chose you; a bourgy convict with a background in music. Why? Because you're free and we don't matter."

"I'm a professional cellist. How much more qualified do I need to be? Most students will never get the opportunity to study under an established artist."

"So, you want us to be grateful that we're your community service?"

I shrug. "I don't care."

"Why should you? In a few weeks your debt to society will be paid and you'll be out of here faster than you came."

"Listen, regardless of the circumstances that landed me here, I'm here. Now you can either take advantage of what I have to offer or you can miss out. The decision is yours."

"I'll gladly take advantage of you any day of the week, Baby." Indecently, he licks his lips and eyes me from head to toe.

"I've had about enough of you," I warn.

"Right back at you."

"That's easy enough to solve," I say. "Get out."

He snatches his backpack and stomps down the aisle, banging into his peers and knocking over stands on his way. Without turning around, he slams the door behind him. The loud bang resonates and we all sit in silence.

"Does anyone else feel that way?" I ask. "If so, you can follow him."

There's no movement, only stares.

"Good, then let's get started."

One by one, I have the students stand, introduce themselves, tell what instrument they play, and share one interesting fact about themselves that most people don't know.

I answer questions and take suggestions and address concerns. By the time third period is over, I feel like I've just boxed twelve full rounds.

I smile and nod as the kids exit the classroom just as unenthusiastically as they entered. Once the room is empty, I lock everything up and brave the congested halls in search of the only friendly face I know.

Gail is in the Teacher's Lounge, flipping through an old issue of *Reader's Digest*. A half-eaten cherry danish and a mug of steaming tea sit on the table in front of her.

She looks up. "You survived."

"Barely."

"Sit. Take a load off." She pats the worn cushion beside her.

I groan and flop down on the couch. "They're monsters. When did children turn so hostile?"

"Went that well, huh?"

"Depends on your definition of 'well.' This one kid, Terrance, had it out for me from the start."

"They're just testing their boundaries."

I shake my head. "It was more than that. You should've seen this kid—animosity was seeping from his pores."

I recount his rude questions and cutting retorts, how he contorted my words in a fierce attempt to turn me into the enemy. "Everything I said was wrong. He wouldn't be reasoned with."

She sips her tea quietly. "You know what it sounds like to me?"

I kick off my pumps. "What?"

"The kids aren't the only ones who can gain from this situation. You told them to take advantage of your presence—to take in as much as they could because very few students get the opportunity to study under someone like you."

I nod. "Right."

"How many professional cellists get the opportunity to mold minds in such a powerful way? The young men and women out in those halls are the future. You're here for a reason."

I snort. "Yeah, because I have to be."

"That's your problem right there," she points at my derisive sneer. "Nobody wants to feel like an obligation, like a punishment—even persnickety teenagers. How do you expect these kids to open up to you or respect anything you have to offer when you've made it perfectly clear they don't matter?"

"I never said that."

"You don't have to. You think this school and these kids are beneath you. Your nose was in the air before you pulled into the parking lot."

"That's a little judgmental."

She shakes her head. "I like you, Abby. I really do. The difference between you and me is I don't have to drive a fancy car or wear silk suits in order to like myself."

"And I don't need to battle snot-nosed brats every day of my life to feel like what I do makes a difference," I say, openly offended.

"I've been here eight years and counting. I've watched aimless kids find direction; I've watched promising students fall prey to the streets; I've cheered on graduates and even cried at a couple of funerals; but every day, every minute, I've been in this place I consider time well-spent.

"That's what I want for you when you leave. I want you to look back on this experience and know it was worth every early morning, every parent-teacher conference, every missed lunch or late-night practice. If you let them, these kids will change you in ways you can't even imagine."

"I'm not cut out for this," I grumble.

"Give it a fair try," Gail says. "You'll be surprised. Sometimes just showing up is half the battle. Ask yourself, 'If these kids walk away having learned only one thing this semester, what should it be?' "

"That's easy. A love for music."

"There you go." She stands and rinses her empty mug in the small, stainless-steel sink. "Make it about the music and you can't go wrong."

Four hours after the first day of school has ended and the students and most of the faculty have gone home, I'm in my new classroom, rummaging through the former music teacher's file cabinets.

The material is unorganized and uninspired. There are mostly beginner and intermediate scales and random Suzuki volumes, which are rudimentary and boring. It's no wonder my students filed in looking as if they were about to have a root canal.

I slam the bottom cabinet shut. *Think, Abby, think.* How did my teachers get me to fall in love with music? What did it feel like? What pieces did we play? What challenged me? What did I hate and what did I look forward to?

I glance around the dismal room, frustrated. Tomorrow will be just like today and so will the day after that and the day after that unless I can gain their trust and ignite in them a desire to learn.

My cello is resting on its side next to my desk. Even now in my lowest moment—with no paying job, no guarantees, no plans for the future—it makes me feel secure. It's nothing more than carved wood and wire strings and polish, but there's an unspeakable splendor in knowing it produces melodies that can evoke emotion, alter moods, and heal invisible wounds.

I pick it up, rosin my bow, and play. I know hundreds of pieces, but right now I improvise from the heart. I close my eyes and become my own patient. The notes whisk me out of the room and down the halls and outside, past the trees and into the skies with the clouds and the birds and the sunshine where I'm safe.

Suddenly I'm in a magical place where scars and roommates and mortgages and students and worries don't exist. The only thing that matters is the music; the next beat, the next rhythm. There is no right and wrong, no mistakes, no starting over, no doing it better the next time.

I want to stay in this place. I want to live in this fantasy where I'm perfect by default—where understanding transcends knowledge and dreams are real.

I hold the last note for as long as I can, and when I open my eyes, Kendra is sitting across from me, smiling.

She claps. "That was tight—just like being at a private concert."

"It's late. What're you doing here?"

She shrugs. "Detention. What're you doing here?"

"Trying to pick out music for the orchestra."

"What's wrong with what you were playing?"

I chuckle. "That wasn't music. That was me messing around."

"I might have something." She reaches into her bag and hands me a score for Brandenburg Concerto and the Four Orchestral Suites.

"Where'd you get this?"

"The library."

"This is pretty advanced stuff. Can you play this?"

Her eyes light up. "You wanna hear?"

"Sure." I place my cello in its case and wait for her to set up.

Her posture is atrocious, her technique sloppy. There's no set beat or key. She puts more effort into looking at her fingers than into reading the music. Her arm is stiff and her bow glides everywhere but between the bridge and the fingerboard. She shifts awkwardly and plays the entire excerpt in crescendo.

I fold my hands on my lap and try not to flinch as she screeches to a finish.

"So?" she asks, her face beaming with anticipation.

"It was—well, you know, it was a little rough."

Her smile fades.

"But at the same time, it was also good, really, really good," I add hastily.

"No, you're right. I've been playing for three years now and I haven't gotten any better."

"With practice and the right direction, I have no doubts you can play this piece, but why don't you start off with something simpler?"

She locks her violin in its case. "I play what I can find."

"I have something for you," I say, walking to the filing cabinet. I hand her the third book in the Suzuki collection. "I think you'll like this. Give it a try and if you want we can set up some private, after-school lessons. I'll work with you on your problem areas."

She shakes her head and hands the book back. "I can't afford private lessons."

"I'm your teacher," I say. "You don't have to pay me."

"Nothing's free."

"I tell you what." I hand the book back. "You can make it up to me by practicing. For every private lesson you get, you have to practice an extra hour."

She looks leery of my altruism, but takes the book. "Okay. I can handle that."

"First lesson tomorrow at three?"

She nods.

I wag my finger at her in buoyant scorn. "That means no more detention."

She laughs. "Okay. Thanks, Ms. Walker."

She bounds out of the room, her violin in tow, and as I watch her, I can't decide what's scarier: the fact that I feel like a teacher or the fact that I like it.

29. *Jarvis*

"Another one?" Chas asks, a twinge of jealousy in his voice. "You aren't human. How do you do it?"

I look down at the exam booklet resting in my lap, the bright red *A* beams up just as brightly as the first one did. "I study and I do the readings and I come to class."

"I come to class," Chas says.

"Yeah, but I stay awake."

"Like I said, you aren't human." He tosses his *D-* exam in the trash can outside of the classroom.

"I'll catch you later," I say, eager to get to the library to cram a little more for my Conceptual Physics midterm.

"We're supposed to talk about our business prospectus."

"There's plenty of time for that," I say.

"Jay, I have to get at least a ninety on this to pass."

"You'll pass," I promise.

"Most teams are writing their rough drafts. We haven't even come up with an idea."

I sigh. My resolve to study gives way to guilt at the panicked expression on his face. "Twenty minutes," I say. "Then I've got to go study."

The Student Union is more crowded than usual thanks to Free Burger Friday. Every student on campus, it seems, is lined up to buy one sandwich and get another one for free. Chas and I find a small table over by the bathrooms.

I study my note cards while he bogarts his way through the dense crowd to get to the vending machines on the other side of the room.

He returns a few minutes later carrying three bags of chips, two sodas, and an assortment of candy. "Brainstorming food," he says.

"Do you have any ideas?" I ask.

He shrugs. "Whatever will impress Professor Leavey. It's got to be something that will stand out."

"How about a car wash?" I suggest.

"A car wash?" he moans, unimpressed.

"It'll be easy to find a location, to determine our target clientele, to figure out our start-up costs…"

"It's also boring."

"It's a business prospectus, not a bachelor party. What difference does it make?"

"My grade is hinging on this," he reminds me. "We can't go in there with the same prospectus as a half a dozen other teams. We have to be original."

"How about a deli?"

"Come on, Jay," he says, chomping loudly on a handful of barbeque-flavored corn chips. "There are a thousand delis in Detroit. A deli won't get me an *A*."

"What will get you an *A* then? Give me something to work with."

"What if we had an auto repair shop that also doubled as a daycare?" he asks.

"What?"

"Yeah, think about it. People could drop off their cars *and* their kids. It's brilliant. You need a tune-up, but you also have other errands to run and you don't want to take the children along. What do you do? Leave them at the shop." He stares upward as though the vision is before him.

"How are people supposed to run errands when their cars are in the shop?" I ask.

"True," he murmurs. He waves a barbeque-stained index finger at me. "Or maybe we're thinking too small. Maybe it's a place for the whole family. There could be an area for the men with big couches and big-screen televisions and burgers. And there could be an area for the women like a salon where they would get their hair and nails done. We could even have a dog groomer!" he exclaims. "It would be a luxurious family center for mom, dad, the kids, Fido, and the car."

"Get serious," I say, throwing him a steely glance and ripping open a packet of peanut M&Ms.

We sit and think in silence. "I got it!" he explodes.

I brace myself for another one of his "epiphanies".

"We can do your car wash idea."

I breathe a sigh of relief.

"But it can also be a deli. A car wash deli. Get your car washed while you grab a quick bite to eat."

I crumple the empty candy wrapper and stuff my note cards into my book bag.

"Where are you going? You said twenty minutes."

"Close enough," I say without looking at my watch.

"But we still haven't come up with an idea."

"I don't have time for this right now," I say, my patience short. "I need to study."

"How about tonight?"

I shake my head. "I've got that thing tonight. You're still coming, aren't you?"

"I don't know." He tilts his head back and raises a brow. "Are you planning on being as surly as you are now?"

"Did you just call me *surly*?" I ask. "Who uses that word anymore?"

"I could think of a different, more accurate word," he says. "But I wouldn't want to taint your Christian ears."

"*And* you need my help to pass Professor Leavey's class," I add.

"That too. But seriously," he says, "are you okay?"

Am I okay? People have been asking me that for weeks now and I still don't know the answer. Am I surviving? Yes, but barely.

I'm too overwhelmed to grieve. I've got three midterms this week. Haley's dragging me house hunting tomorrow. I start physical therapy next Thursday, and now Chas is hounding me about our stupid business prospectus.

I scratch my head. "I'm hanging in there."

"You know what? Forget about this. I'll figure something out," he says.

I shake my head. "We're partners. Give me a couple of weeks. Write your ideas down as they come to you; I'll do the same, and as soon as things calm down, we'll get together, pick the best one, and work out the kinks."

He looks skeptical, but agrees.

"I'm not going to let you down," I say, swiping the last bag of chips. "Everything's going to work out. You'll get your *A*."

Mom taps her glass with her fork and stands.

"Speech! Speech!"

She holds up her hand and the noise from the intimate, merry crowd of friends and family falls to a hush.

"I have one of the best sons in the entire world." She looks at me with tears in her eyes. "I'm honored to be your mother and so proud of the man you've become."

I smile, embarrassed, but touched.

"This place was Jo's dream," she says.

We all glance around the small diner.

"And he's passed that dream on to you. I know you'll live up to his expectations. You've already lived up to all of mine. God's blessings."

Everyone holds up their glasses. "God's blessings!"

Dinner is delicious. My plate stays full as random guests cruise by to offer their congratulations and an extra taste of their special homemade dish. I smile politely, grateful to be surrounded by so many people who care.

I answer twenty variations of the same question as I have a taste of meatloaf and then barbeque chicken and then smothered potatoes and then collard greens.

"How are you doing?"

"Are you feeling all right?"

"You getting along okay?"

"How's life treating you?"

"You holdin' up okay?"

My answer doesn't change. "I'm okay. Everything's okay."

Haley stays by my side. She looks beautiful tonight in her purple and white strapless dress and beaded sandals. Her hair is swept back, accentuating her soft neck, and her cheeks are naturally flushed.

I squeeze her hand under the table every now and then because feeling her—just knowing she's there—makes the day's happenings less wearying.

"Penny for your thoughts," Haley says to Chas, who's staring blankly ahead. A huge, untouched piece of tiramisu sits on a plate in front of him.

"I was just thinking how great this place is going to be."

Haley nods. "It's got a lot of possibilities. I can't wait to see what he does with it."

"I'm not doing anything to it." I dig my fork into Chas's dessert.

"You aren't serious?" he asks and flicks my hand away.

"You've got to do some revamping," Haley says. "Look at it."

"If it was good enough for Jo, it's good enough for me," I say, making an effort to keep my voice even.

Chas examines the walls. "You could at least give it a fresh coat of paint."

"This place needs way more than paint," Haley says. "It needs a complete overhaul."

Chas nods. "It's in tatters."

I stiffen. "That's because it's older than I am."

"Exactly," Haley says. "It's time for a change. The whole greasy spoon look is out. People don't want to sit on shredded vinyl or eat off coffee-stained tables."

I turn to her, hurt and offended. "You said you loved JoJo's."

"I think it was great for Jo and his customers."

"Jo's customers are my customers now."

"But you can expand—try to target a younger, more diverse clientele."

"She's right," Chas says. "This place has a lot of potential."

I swipe another forkful of his tiramisu. "The diner grosses a million dollars a year. I think its potential has been recognized."

"You could build an addition," Chas says.

Haley points to the front of the diner. "Maybe make that part a little lounge area."

"He'd need an updated POS," Chas adds.

I polish off the last of his delicious dessert.

"New chairs and countertops and a brand-new menu," Haley continues.

"You know what I'm thinking?" Chas asks.

I shrug. "We need more tiramisu?"

He looks down at his empty plate and frowns. "This is it," he says. "This is our business prospectus."

"This is *not* going to be our business prospectus."

"It's perfect. Everyone else is going to have a bland report and a couple of mundane pie charts, but we'll have floor plans and photos, maybe even permits. This is how we stand out. This is how I get my *A*."

"This is not a game, Chas. This is real life—my life. I'm not turning it into a stupid homework assignment so you can pass Macroeconomics." I grimace at the harshness of my tone.

"I'm gonna get another piece," Chas says. He grabs his plate and walks away.

Haley rubs my arm. "What's going on with you? You're snippy tonight."

"I'm not changing anything," I say.

"Do what you feel is best."

"JoJo's has been around for decades, so Jo must've been doing something right. Doesn't that deserve to be remembered?"

"Of course, but everything changes, Jay. You're so busy trying to preserve Jo's memory that you're afraid to give the diner your own flare."

"He has regulars. People who are counting on me to keep things running as smoothly as he did."

"Updating the registers and adding a lounge area won't keep the diner from running smoothly," she says.

"I could end up in a hole if I invest in a bunch of high-end improvements and sales stay the same."

"With the right marketing that won't happen."

"Everything sounds good in theory."

"I can't tell you what to do," she says. "No one can. All I ask is that you make your decisions based on what's best for the diner and not what's less frightening for you."

I huff. "I'm not frightened."

"Then what's stopping you from moving forward?"

She picks up our empty plates and glasses and leaves me with my thoughts.

I look around the small, crowded space. Not long ago, I worked here. I served coffee and wiped down tables and rang up orders, and now it's all mine. The tattered seats and stained tables, which Haley and Chas find so offensive, belong to me.

There was a time, not long ago, when I had my own ideas on how to make JoJo's better; more stylish, more up-to-date. But that was when Jo was still alive—when the future of the diner rested in his hands and my visions were nothing more than harmless daydreams.

Haley and Mom pose for a picture. Their faces are glowing, their smiles wide. My aunt says something and they throw their heads back in laughter, while everyone around them claps. Chas is engrossed in conversation with a woman from my Bible Study. Mr. Wright and Mr. Kopeky sit with their wives and sip coffee. By the end of the evening there are no strangers in the room.

I mingle with everyone and laugh at jokes and listen to stories about Jo and Mom and my dad and eat too many pieces of pie. I make an effort to be engaging and I set aside my grief long enough to enjoy my surroundings.

But alone in my room in the dark, when there are no more distractions and the silence is haunting, I have to answer the question.

What's stopping you from moving forward?

30. *Abby*

The school parking lot is empty when I arrive the next morning. It's the earliest I've been up and functioning since I quit my last job.

Armed with excitement and a plan, I make my way down the bright halls toward my classroom. Last night, as I was dozing off, it hit me! The way to make these kids fall in love with music is to push them to a new level—to show them I have faith in their ability to excel.

High school is not where I honed my craft. I didn't start making money playing music until I was halfway through college. I don't have to turn them into overnight prodigies. I just need to inspire them.

First, I dig through the dusty storage room and take inventory of the school's instruments. Many of them need repairs and are unusable. After sifting through everything, there are only fourteen violins, nine violas, four cellos, and one bass.

Next, I rearrange the room, positioning the cellists on my right, the violinists on my left, and the violists in the center. Then I head to the main office where I photocopy the music Kendra gave me.

"Ms. Walker," Mrs. Vine nods curtly. "How was your first day?"

"Fine, just fine, I say, manufacturing a grin." We introduced ourselves, went over the handbook. They're bright kids."

"Especially that Terry. He's quite gifted. Hopefully, you'll be able to give him some direction."

Surely, she isn't talking about the same combative, disrespectful punk I threw out yesterday. "Terrance, the young man with the scar?"

"Such a shame." She shakes her head. "He was trying to stop a domestic dispute between his mother and her boyfriend. The boyfriend slashed his face. The whole thing was devastating—set him back a year."

I nod earnestly. "That's unfortunate."

She pats my arm. "Well, if there's anything you need, you know where my office is."

"Actually, I was going through the storage room this morning and discovered that we don't have enough instruments."

"Funding is hard to get, especially for extracurricular programs," she says, as if that's an acceptable explanation.

"But how am I supposed to teach my students how to play music if they don't have instruments?"

"Many of the students have their own instruments."

"Yes, but many of them don't."

She grins sadly, her eyes rueful. "Welcome to the public education system. You'll have to do the best you can with what you have."

By the beginning of third period, I'm still angry and appalled by Mrs. Vine's apathy toward the music program, but I shove my feelings aside and put on a brave face for my students as they file into the classroom.

To my great relief, most of them are toting their own instruments. Terry, I notice, walks in with nothing more than a scowl.

"Good afternoon," I greet them.

"What's up, Ms. W?" a few call back.

"I've got some music for us." I hold up a small portion of what I spent all morning copying.

They seem enthusiastic.

"I want my cellists and bassists here, my violists here, and my violinists here." I point to their designated spots and wait for them to shuffle into order.

"First violinists?" Half the violin section raises their hand and I pass the music out accordingly.

"Second violinists?" The other half, which includes Kendra, raises their hands and I give them their music. I follow suit with the violas.

"First cellists?" Out of the group of eleven, Terry raises his hand. I pass his music back. "Anyone else?"

I smile at him. "Looks like you're the only one."

He glares. "Looks that way."

"Okay," I address the class. "Let's get these instruments passed out."

"Hold up," someone shouts. An unhappy buzz has taken over the room.

"We can't play this," another says with a shake of his head. "Look at it. We don't know what these notes are."

"That's what you're here to learn."

"Yo, you must be confused. This ain't the Chicago Symphony Orchestra."

I sense a mutiny coming on as several of the students fold their music in half and cross their arms defiantly.

"How do you know you can't play it if you haven't tried?" I ask.

"I don't need to jump off a roof to prove I can't fly," a young man sitting to the left of me says.

"I'm not asking you guys to jump off a roof. I want you to broaden your horizons—discover your potential."

"How do you know what our potential is? You don't even know us."

"I've been in the music business a long time and I know talent when I come across it," I say brightly, settling the issue for the moment at least.

My palms sweat as I read down the attendance sheet. The meager supply of instruments quickly dwindles, but so far, has proven sufficient. With two names left on the list, I have three violins and one viola left.

"Beatrice Rodriguez?"

A stringy-haired girl with muted, hazel eyes stands. She plays the viola.

I exhale loudly, relieved.

She comes to the front of the room and retrieves her instrument.

"And last, but not least, Terrance Wallace."

My heart sinks as I look at the angry young man in the back. His gaze is hard. "I'm sorry, Terry, it seems we've run out of cellos."

He shrugs. "Guess I'm off to study hall."

My own childhood experience comes to mind. Terrance and I are a lot alike, both underdogs, both searching for an escape, both mired by circumstances beyond our control. Had I not found the cello as a little girl, I would've bypassed my only opportunity to become somebody extraordinary. I couldn't send Terry down such a dark and miserable road.

"Why don't you use mine?"

The hatred from his eyes gives way to stunned disbelief. "For real?"

I gulp, terrified, as I imagine all the possible ways he could destroy it. "Sure. I can't have my only first cellist warming the bench."

He pulls up his sagging pants and comes to the front of the room. I hold out my cased cello—my life's worth, my baby. We both look down at my shaking hand.

"Don't worry, Ms. Walker, I'll take good care of it."

Once everyone's tuned up and situated, I raise my baton and hope for the best. What I get, is a different story.

They are, by far, the worst orchestra I've ever heard. Each of them plays as if he's the only member. There is no musicianship and no cohesiveness. As I study them, one by one, I realize that a good number of them don't know how to read music, most of them have difficulty with mixed combinations of syncopated patterns and dotted rhythms, and the rest must be tone deaf.

I beat my baton against the stand in front of me. "Stop! Stop!"

They look up, quiet and embarrassed, and wait for my barrage of criticisms.

"Not bad, but why don't we take it slower. We'll go section by section, okay?"

They nod.

"Terry, let me hear you from the top, first eight measures."

I count off four beats.

His posture is impeccable, his vibrato strong, his shifting precise. I stare, amazed, as he breezes through the short excerpt.

"Wonderful," I praise him. "Better than wonderful. It was perfect."

31. Jarvis

"This is one of my favorites," Debbie says.

We pull up to the fifth house on our list. So far she's shown us two houses out of my price range, one with three levels, and another that sits on an acre of land. Climbing in and out of her big, shiny SUV is starting to take its toll on me, but I concentrate on refereeing between her and Haley, who's one more wrong property away from blowing her lid.

"She doesn't listen," Haley hisses as we follow Debbie up the long walkway. "I said two-bedroom, one-and-a-half-bath ranches in Southfield on a zero lot. How hard is that?"

"Not hard," I whisper.

"Then why haven't we seen one house that fits that description?" She bores holes into our real estate agent's back.

Debbie unlocks the door and leads us inside. "It has three bedrooms, two bathrooms, and hardwood floors throughout. The seller is very motivated."

"He doesn't need three bedrooms," Haley says, her voice chilly.

She smiles. "You never know. He might want to turn one into an office."

I squeeze Haley's hand. "Let's just have a look."

We stroll through the house. The rooms are spacious, it has a nice-sized kitchen, and all the doorways are wide enough to accommodate my chair.

"And just through here is the den," Debbie says, turning to her right. "Watch your step."

Haley stops, as do I, on the elevated platform. "He's in a wheelchair," she snaps. "I specifically said no stairs."

Debbie ignores her and turns to me. "What d'ya think?"

"Don't get me wrong, it's a very nice house—"

"But it's not what he's looking for," Haley says.

Debbie purses her lips. "I think that's a decision for Mr. Daniels to make."

"I gave you his specifications over the phone. Nothing you've shown us so far matches."

"I make it my business to offer my clients variety."

"You don't listen," Haley says, her voice rising. "This is Livonia. We aren't even in the right city."

Debbie taps her clipboard. "I did a lot of research to put these properties together."

"Well, maybe if you'd listened harder and researched less, we would've found something by now."

I raise my hand. "Okay. Time out, time out. Calm down, both of you." I turn to Debbie. "Listen, I appreciate all the work you've put into this."

She grins, though her eyes are flamed with anger.

"But Haley's right, I have certain limitations. So what I really need is something smaller, on one level, and it absolutely has to be in Southfield. Do you have anything like that?"

Debbie flips through her list.

Haley glares and taps her foot impatiently.

"One," Debbie says. "It's a condo off Franklin Road."

"Can we see that one next?" I ask.

She sighs. "I'll have to call. We aren't scheduled to be there until three."

"We'll wait outside," Haley says and tramps loudly down the hall to the front door.

I follow, perplexed, by her unusual display of animosity. "What's going on with you?"

She paces the length of the yard. "She's had two weeks to get this together."

"I'll find a place to live. These things take time."

"You've been through so much over the past couple of months and I wanted this process to be as painless as possible."

"And I love you for that, but jumping down Debbie's throat is not the solution."

"I don't like that woman."

"She's trying to do her job."

Haley snorts. "She's trying to rake in a big commission. Do you know how much this place costs?"

"Let's just enjoy spending the day together."

"Jay, that's sweet, but you don't have time to waste. It takes at least sixty days to close on a house and you said you wanted everything to be situated by the time you were done with therapy."

"Well yeah." I tilt my head and sigh. "But that might not have been the smartest plan."

Her eyebrows furrow. "Which part?"

"Okay," Debbie says, emerging from the house. Her cheerful demeanor is back. "We're set."

"I'll sit up front this time," I say.

Haley follows my cue and climbs into the backseat.

"Get excited." Debbie peels away from the curb. "I have a good feeling about this one."

We pull into a quiet, gated community just off Northwestern Highway. A large red and white banner reads, "Models Open."

We make our way down a neat, tree-lined street and park at the end of a cul-de-sac.

"This looks nice," I say.

"It's a detached condominium," Debbie informs me.

The property's quaint. A short, brick walkway leads to a covered stoop. There's a small lawn, and well-manicured shrubbery lines the outside.

Haley, who didn't utter a word on the ride over, walks silently beside me.

Debbie unlocks the door. "This has carpet in the two bedrooms, hardwood floors in the common areas, slate in the bathrooms, and tile in the kitchen."

The living room is bright and airy. The ceilings soar above us, and our voices echo in the large, empty space.

We examine the modest-sized home, "ooooing" and "awwwing" at all of its features and fancy appliances.

"As you can see, you've got a lot of space to work with," Debbie says, as our tour comes to an end.

Haley smiles. "It's gorgeous."

Debbie hands me a sheet of paper. "This is a list of all the possible upgrades. Because this is a new construction, the developer is very flexible."

"Look," I say, holding the list out to Haley, "I can have a fireplace put into the living room."

"Or even a screened porch out back," she notes.

"The real beauty is that you don't have to worry about maintaining the property. Your monthly assessment covers sidewalk shoveling, trash pickup, and landscaping."

Haley squeezes my shoulder. "It sounds perfect."

"Can you give us a few minutes?" I ask Debbie. "I want to go through one more time."

She nods. "Take your time. In fact, I'll run to the sales office and see if they have an information packet to give you. Just meet me over there when you're done."

"It's everything you want," Haley says once Debbie leaves.

I nod. "And more."

"All it needs is a woman's touch. I'm thinking pink paint and floral print curtains." She spans her hand across the bare white walls, like an artist testing her vision on a blank canvas.

"I'm thinking more of a black and white motif," I say. "It's simple yet masculine."

She laughs. "That's redundant. How about *yellow* and black?"

"Brown and gray?"

"Have you always been this devoid of taste?"

"Is that any way to speak to the man whose house you want to decorate?"

"I know." She says with a demure smile. "Why don't you let me surprise you?"

"No way! I've seen your apartment. What will it look like when Chas comes over to watch football and we have to squeeze between the stuffed animals on the couch?"

"You'll look like a man who's deeply in touch with his feminine side."

I smile. "*If* I get the place, our safest bet is to decorate it together."

"Like you're going to have any time to shop for furniture. Between school and therapy, I'll be lucky to see you on the weekends."

I sigh. "So then, maybe now's not the best time for me to be out of commission."

"Jay, you can do this. I know it's a lot, but if there's anyone who can pull it off, it's you."

"I've thought about it, all the possible avenues I can take, and I think I should hold off on the prosthetics."

"That's crazy. It's just your nerves talking."

"I decided to expand the diner like you suggested. That's what I was trying to tell you earlier. I've already talked it over with Mr. Wright. Chas knows too."

"What does the diner have to do with your walking again?"

"Something has to give. I'm not Superman. How am I supposed to rebuild JoJo's *and* go through grueling physical therapy *and* move into a new house *and* pass my classes?"

"You put something on the back burner. You prioritize."

"That's what I'm doing."

"Why is it, of all the balls you are juggling in the air, the only one you're willing to drop is the one that matters?"

"I'm not dropping the ball, Haley. I'm postponing my physical therapy until I can find time to dedicate myself to it."

"You can be such a coward," she says, her nostrils flaring. "You're actually willing to forgo your chance at a better quality of life just so old men with too much time on their hands can shuffle down to a new-and-improved JoJo's at six in the morning and get a cup of coffee and a plate of corned beef hash?"

"Drop it."

"No, I will not drop it." Her eyes are sharp, her jaws clenched. "What is so hard about a couple hours of physical therapy every day?"

"I'm a bilateral transfemoral amputee, Haley. I haven't used my residual limbs in over three years. Do you even know what that means? Do you?" I ask sternly.

She shakes her head. "No."

"Exactly! You have no idea what I'm up against."

She steps back.

"I'm in over my head here," I say, my voice lower. "Two months ago I was a handicapped, college freshman who waited tables part time for extra cash. I didn't have much, but my life made sense. Now, I'm a business owner and a home owner. I have bank accounts and stocks and insurance. I have more money than I care to have or know what to do with and I'm figuring it all out as I go."

"I know," she says. "It's more than most people can handle."

"Then don't label me a coward just because I've made a decision you don't agree with."

"I'm sorry," she says softly. "I just..." She kneels down in front of me so our eyes are level. "You do so much for other people. You want to get the diner running again for Jo. You won't take a semester off because you don't want to disappoint your mom. And I know you, you're going to spend more time than you should putting together a stellar business prospectus so Chas won't fail Economics. But what're you doing for Jay?"

"Look around you. This condo isn't free."

She shakes her head. "This is drywall, glass, and a little bit of paint. If it burns down tomorrow, there are hundreds more like it ready to be bought. Having the freedom to walk to class, to come and go as you please—that's special."

I caress her cheek. "I just can't do it all."

"I'll help you," she says. "I'll put the house together. I'll work with Chas on the prospectus. I'll scrub toilets, take orders—whatever you need me to do."

"You've got your own life, your own job to tend to."

"I'll quit."

I search her eyes; they're intense and serious and determined. *Who is this woman?*, I wonder. *Where did she come from, and is she really mine?*

I feel sorry for any man who isn't me because I'm utterly convinced that the only woman worth having, is kneeling in front of me, begging to carry a portion of my burdens.

"You can't quit your job, Haley. How're you going to pay your bills?"

"I'll work for you. Pay me what you think is fair."

"I'm flattered, really I am, but—"

"You don't think I can do it? You don't trust me?"

"The situation's not that crucial. I've been in a wheelchair for this long. I can hang on for a few more months."

"That makes one of us," she mumbles.

As I watch her walk down the hall, it finally dawns on me: Prosthetics are more than my ticket to independence; they're my chance for a normal relationship. As much as I've tried to compensate for my handicap, Haley's forfeited many of the rewards of being a woman. Walking again wouldn't be for me; it would be for us.

I find her in the master bedroom gazing out of the window. "Sometimes it takes me a while to catch on," I say.

She sighs. "No, it's me. I'm being selfish."

"Tell me what you want."

"I want you to be able to do it all: the diner, school, physical therapy. And I want to be there to help you every step of the way."

"Are you sure that quitting your job is a smart move?"

"I hate my job. If I'm going to be overworked and underpaid, I at least want to do it for someone I love."

"Do me a favor. Pray about it and if you still feel the same way, then we'll do it."

She smiles. "Really?"

"Don't think you're going to be getting any special privileges," I chastise playfully.

She shakes her head and makes her way toward me. "Of course not."

"When I'm in boss mode, you won't be able to win me over with that beautiful smile."

"I know."

"And I don't want to hear any complaining."

She hovers over me. "You won't."

I smile. "Good."

She leans in and kisses me. It's gentle and soft and when she pulls away there are tears in her eyes.

"Thank you," she whispers.

I cup her chin in my hand. "No, thank *you*."

32. *Abby*

"Abby!" Hannah yells.

"What?"

"Phone."

It's nine o'clock in the morning—far too early for anyone to be calling on a Saturday. "Take a message!" I yell, but there's no reply. "Hannah?" I call as loudly as my raspy morning voice will allow. "Hannah!"

I pull myself, with much effort and resentment, into a sitting position. The room is blurred and it takes a few seconds for my eyes to focus. I yawn and stretch and comb my fingers through my hair.

"Phone!" Hannah screams again.

I pick up and groan.

"Abby!" an overzealous voice says.

"Yes?" My tone is decidedly less enthusiastic.

"This is Chuck."

"Who?" I bark.

"Chuck Ritter from Magnolia Records."

I ditch my attitude and try to sound as perky as I can in the absence of a strong, much-needed cup of coffee. "Chuck! How are you?"

"Just fine. I didn't wake you, did I?"

"Of course not," I say, my voice miraculously clear and alert. "I've been up for hours. I get my best composing done in the morning."

"That's good." There's a brief silence. "Well, I'm calling to see if you're free for lunch Monday."

"Monday?" I ask, my senses heightened. A call from an executive at my record label on a Saturday morning?

"I'm going to be in Chicago for a board meeting," he explains. "And I figure, while I'm there, we might discuss a few things."

"Actually, my Monday's packed."

"How about Tuesday?" he asks.

"Hold on a second, let me check my calendar." I grab a fashion magazine lying on my nightstand and flip through the pages noisily. "Uh, nope, it looks like my week is pretty full."

"How about next week?"

"Next week?" I set down the magazine. "That's a pretty long board meeting, Chuck."

"I'm willing to extend my stay," he says. His jovial timbre is gone and the conversation has taken on a serious undertone. "Or if necessary, I'll make another trip."

"Why don't you save yourself the inconvenience and tell me what's on your mind right now?"

He sighs. "I think it's better if we have this talk in person. This is not a conversation I wanted to have over the phone."

"It's okay," I say, fighting to keep my voice steady. "Just tell me."

"Your sales are down, Abby. Way down. We're sensitive to your situation and we've tried to cater to your needs, but maybe it's time for you to split from Magnolia and go your separate way."

"I almost died," I say. "Do you have any idea what that's like?"

"I can only imagine Abby, but—"

"No, you can't," I say, my voice a whisper. "You can't begin to imagine."

"You've cancelled appearances, you failed to promote the third album, you haven't made any plans to record a fourth one, and in light of this latest incident with Amber Sheffield, we've decided your name is not one we wish to be associated with our label."

"You haven't given me a chance to make a comeback. I've got new stuff—good stuff. You've got to at least hear it."

"I know you do," he says kindly. "You're a talented artist. I'm sure you'll have no problems finding work."

"But I have a contract. You can't just cut me loose."

"Your contract expires at the end of next month." His pity pours through the receiver along with his smooth, calm voice.

I scrape the bottom of my reserves of dignity and brace myself as I prepare to serve the last of it to Mr. Ritter on a silver platter. "Isn't there anything you can do?" I ask, humbled and desperate.

"I'm sorry," he says. "The decision's been made."

"Anything at all?" I plead.

"Take care of yourself, Abby, and good luck with your career."

Dr. Kessler is wearing a pantsuit. Her hair looks extra frizzy, her eye shadow is extra aqua, and her jaw extra square. I'm not in the mood to listen to her psychobabble.

She takes a sip of coffee. "How was your week?"

"Fine."

"Anything eventful happen?"

"No."

"How's Terry?"

"Good."

"And Gail?"

I shrug. "Same, I guess."

"You're upset. What's wrong?"

"I don't want to talk about it."

"What *do* you want to talk about?"

"I don't want to talk about anything," I say, inexplicably hostile. "What does talking do? Is talking going to transform me back to normal?"

She leans back. "I don't know. What is normal?"

"Anything but this. Anything but a beastly old maid with no friends, no job, no recording contract, no money, no options! What did I do that was so wrong? Who deserves this?"

"Do you really believe bad things only happen to bad people?"

"I've lost myself, Miranda. For a while I thought I could get back on track, but I'm not so sure anymore."

"How have you lost yourself?"

"I don't know who I am anymore."

She stares at me for a moment, her eyes intense and searching, then opens her desk drawer and pulls out a notepad. "Here," she says and hands me a pen. "Write down everything you used to be—all the words you feel describe the old you—the Abby you can no longer find."

I glance at the clean sheet of paper. All the words that come to mind shame me.

I toss the pad and pen back on her desk. "I don't feel like it."

We sit in silence—me concentrating on the dull hum of the air-conditioner, Miranda sipping a cup of coffee and studying me carefully.

"There is something I've been meaning to talk to you about," she finally says. "Our time together is coming to an end soon and that means we need to schedule your family session."

"If that involves me and my sister being in the same room, you can count me out."

"Why? You've got a lot to say to her. Don't continue to repress your anger."

"Why open up Pandora's box?"

"Because I truly believe that's the only way you're going to find closure."

I roll my eyes. "Everything can't be fixed with a heart-to-heart and a hug."

"She's your sister, Abby."

"And I hate her. I hate everything about her and everything she stands for and everything she believes in."

"That's harsh, especially when she might be suffering just as much as you are."

I scoff bitterly. "Val's too perfect to suffer. She's too likeable and personable and exceptional in every way. Just ask her. She'll tell you."

"You were molested by a trusted friend and yet you're projecting that anger onto your sister. Don't you think it's best to figure out why?"

"I'm not projecting. I don't like her because she was horrible to me."

"Yes, when you were kids, but from what you've told me, she's done nothing but reach out to you throughout your adult years."

I shrug. "Too little, too late."

"I'm not buying this 'callously indifferent' routine you're trying to sell me."

"There's no routine with me. What you see is what you get."

"You care about your sister," she says.

"A couple of degrees don't qualify you to tell me how I feel."

"When people expend this much energy trying not to care, common sense tells me they do."

"Why are we having this discussion? I said no."

"I'm not asking you. I'm telling you, your family session will be Friday morning."

"No!" I exclaim with a resolute shake of my head.

"It's part of the program. I've already spoken with your parents and your sister."

I glare. "What happened to confidentiality? Maybe I don't want my family to know everything about my past."

"I haven't told them anything. What they learn on Friday will be completely up to you."

I knock on Mrs. Vine's closed door.

"Come in."

She's sitting behind her desk, a lipstick-stained tuna sandwich rests on a napkin in front of her. "Ms. Walker," she smiles. "You caught me trying to sneak in lunch."

"I can come back," I say.

"Have a seat. What can I do for you?"

"I need to take Friday off."

"Do you mind if I ask why?"

"I have to go to a family therapy session. It's part of my court ruling."

She nods. "And it's going to take all day?"

"That's the thing. I have no idea. I would hate to commit to being here and get tied up."

She studies me for a moment. "Gail tells me you're researching college music programs for Terrance Wallace."

I search her stern face carefully before I answer. "Um, yes. I'm looking into it."

"Any luck so far?"

"I have contacts at Northwestern and the University of Chicago and Gail knows a couple of people at DePaul, but we haven't heard back from anyone yet."

She hands me a manila envelope from a stack of paperwork on her desk. "Those are Mr. Wallace's transcripts. They might help."

"Thank you."

"Nobody's been able to reach him the way you have," she says.

I smile. "He's a bright kid. Gifted too. I wasn't nearly as good a player at his age."

"It's bigger than that. His whole attitude's changed. He has more confidence, more drive. All your students do."

"They love to play music. I just facilitate that."

"You're an encourager," she says. "You give these kids hope."

I smile. "They do the same for me."

"Have you thought about teaching as a career?"

I laugh nervously, caught off guard by her question.

"I guess not," she says. "You've got your music to think about."

"Actually, I've decided to retire."

Mrs. Vine leans back in her chair, a strange look of delight in her eyes. "Would you consider a permanent position here?" she asks.

"Are you offering me one?"

She nods. "Absolutely. You'd be a greatly needed asset."

I'll admit, I love teaching. I even love my students, but something in me can't stomach the demotion from platinum recording artist to high school orchestra conductor. And that something is good, old-fashioned pride.

"Can I think about it?" I ask. "Weigh all my options and get back to you?"

"Sure, take your time."

"Thanks again for this," I say, waving Terry's file.

"Don't mention it. Oh, and, Abby?"

"Yes?"

"Enjoy your day off."

33. *Jarvis*

I study my physiotherapist and my prosthetist as they huddle around my chart. Ordinarily, they would be intimidating with their white lab coats and their pocket protectors and their fancy, medical jargon. But they're extra kind, their smiles extra wide; their ears are tuned, and their voices keen.

We've become comfortable with each other over the past couple of months. We refer to one another by our first names; we sip coffee, and discuss sports and weather. The sad thing is that I know they wouldn't be this accommodating if I didn't have money.

Rick faces me. "Okay, Jay. What I'm going to do today is familiarize you with all the parts of your prosthetics. We'll get them on, see how they feel, and then Janice," he nods to my physiotherapist, "will take you down to the rehabilitation ward where you'll work on balance and gait training."

I nod, ready to see what I'm made of. Janice helps me onto the tall examining table. The stiff, white paper cover crackles and snaps under my shifting weight.

She squeezes my forearm. "I'll check back in about a half an hour." Her tan, thick-soled shoes squeak loudly against the pristine linoleum floor as she leaves the room.

"I know we've been over this before," Rick says, "but I always like to go through everything twice just to make sure there aren't any last-minute questions."

I watch, excited, as he produces a blue aluminum tube from a long box setting on the floor next to his chair.

"There are four parts to your prosthetics. First, you have the liners. They're relatively soft and flexible." He holds one out for me to feel. "It's silicone. This is going to protect the skin of your residual limb. Once you roll this on, you'll slide your leg into the hard socket."

He pulls out a hollow, semi-thick, conical pole. "The hard socket then attaches to this," he says and holds up what looks like an industrial-size door hinge.

"That's one of my knees?" I ask.

He nods and screws it onto the end of the hard socket. "It attaches to this tube, which attaches, last but not least, to this." He reveals a brown, plastic foot. "What's great about these," he adds, "is that the heel is adjustable, so they'll fit into almost any shoe."

I stare at the expensive makeshift leg in front of me.

"I know it looks complicated," Rick says. "But once you've had some time to play with it and get comfortable donning and doffing, it'll be second nature."

I nod.

"What I want to do now is get these on and see how they fit. If you feel any friction or rubbing, it's important that you let me know. The last thing we want is to create sores or bruising."

I watch him set to work, rolling and stuffing and screwing and snapping everything into place. "How does that feel?" he asks periodically.

"Fine," I say. The truth is, they feel heavy and foreign and I wonder how I'll ever lift them enough to walk. I can't tear my eyes away from them. I feel like a much scrawnier version of the Terminator.

Rick checks one last time to make sure the socket fits snugly before he starts to leave. "How do they feel?" he asks.

I shrug. "Weird."

"Good. Weird is what you feel right before you start to feel great."

"Aarrrghhh!" I growl and press my lips together. My eyes are squeezed shut, my shirt damp with sweat.

"Better," Janice says.

I shoot her a flinty glance. I'm crippled, not delusional.

My arms wobble and threaten to give out. "I want to sit down."

"You only have a few more steps left. Don't stop. Push!"

I'm tired and each of my legs feels as though it's been strapped down with a stack of phone books.

"AARRGHHH!" I try to step, but I don't have the strength, and my artificial foot crashes down in front of me. "I want to sit down now!"

Janice hooks her arm around my waist and helps me to my wheelchair.

I pant uncontrollably and will my heart rate to slow to normal.

"I know it can be frustrating, but you're doing a good job," she says. Her smile is warm.

"Please, don't patronize me."

"I would never do that."

"Insisting I'm improving, when clearly I'm not, is patronizing."

I shift uncomfortably under her searching stare.

She kneels beside me. "Listen, nobody said this was going to be a walk in the park. Physical rehab is taxing and it's going to take a lot of effort and dedication on both our parts. It's going to take cooperation."

She pauses, perhaps expecting a reply, but I remain silent. "I'm a professional, Mr. Daniels. I know what I'm doing here, and before we go any further, you need to figure out what your role in this is going to be.

"If you want my help, I suggest you hand over the reins so our time together will be productive."

"Nice speech," I say dryly.

"Thanks," she smiles, undeterred by my negative demeanor. "Now, I want you to start from this end of the parallel bars and work your way down to that end."

I shake my head. "I can't."

"Stop telling yourself that! The more you say it, the more you believe it."

"Then what am I supposed to say?"

"I think I can. I think I can. I think I can," she chugs annoyingly.

"I'm not the '*Little Red Engine That Could*.' I'm an amputee trying to do the impossible."

"Impossible? Do you know how many people, some with greater odds to beat than you, have wheeled in here and walked out on their own? The only thing stopping you from joining them is your attitude."

I pause and remember that mom has dubbed me the Comeback King. "My son's a living, breathing miracle," she tells anyone who'll listen. I try to be that guy, the one who's constantly overcoming, who, even in the midst of paralyzing circumstances, pulls a last- minute trick from his bag of surprising capabilities and beguiles his loved ones with another tale of triumph.

But my stamina is waning. I have a demanding class load of eighteen credits. If I did nothing but go to school, study, and sleep, I'd still feel unprepared for the slew of homework, labs, and projects that all seem to fall due at the same time. Therapy five days a week and revamping JoJo's to boot is a slow, painful form of suicide.

I'm frustrated, I feel trapped, and half the time I'm tempted to forget it all and concentrate on what I want to do. But then I think of Haley and Chas and Mom and how I'm knee-deep in their expectations and I'm reminded that quitting is not an option.

"Can you—can I just have a minute?" I ask. "You know, to regroup."

She nods. "I'll go get you some water."

I look down at my hands resting in my lap. They seem smaller than usual, helpless and breakable.

I bow my head.

Father, I need You. I feel like I'm failing and I want to give up. But You aren't a God of failure and I'm Your creation—Your son. I can do nothing in my own strength. If this is Your will, if this is where You want me to be and what You want me to do, then help me. Your path is the only one I want to be on. Your desires are the only ones I want in my heart.

Bind my flesh and take my weaknesses and use them to have Your way. You are the true Comeback King. I'm only Your servant and I need You now. Touch me. Fill me. Speak to me. Lift me.

The devil is a liar. He's a thief and a discourager who's out to rob me of my joy. He wants me to believe You don't care. But I speak death to his schemes.

I want to be safe and secure in You, Lord. Adjust my attitude and my heart and I'll be sure to give You all the glory and all the praise. Amen.

I don't feel stronger. I'm still exhausted. I still have a test to study for and a lab to finish. I still have contractors to ride and furniture to pick out. I still have to traverse the parallel bars with what feels like ten-ton legs, but I know my prayer has been heard. I know, somehow, He'll make a way.

Janice returns and hands me a sweating bottle of water. "Ready to get back on the horse?" she asks.

I empty the bottle in several quick gulps and set it down on the floor. "Let's do it."

"We have a surprise for you," Haley says. She and Chas are sitting on paint buckets in the middle of the diner, which is in a frightfully gutted state of disarray.

I lower my square of sandpaper. "What is it?"

"We finished the prospectus," Chas says.

I smile, half expecting them to scream, "Just kidding!"

"It's not due for another three weeks."

"It's only a rough draft," Haley says, passing me a bound report. I flip through the project slowly. It's well written and put together. There are charts, blueprints, photographs, and a convincing final analysis.

Given Chas's incurable case of computer illiteracy, I know Haley must have put a lot of work and time into it.

She had her resignation typed and ready to hand in the day after we talked in the condo. Although I had agreed to it, I didn't have a good feeling about hiring her as an employee. There's truth in the saying, "Don't mix business with pleasure."

Haley and I have the same values, and I appreciate her vision and enthusiasm, but she's also emotional and excitable and my biggest fear is that she will forget that during the day, I'm her boss.

So far, she's proven me wrong. She's organized and prompt and on top of everything and everyone. Most of the time I don't even need to ask her to do certain things. If she sees a task that needs to get done, she rolls up her sleeves and digs in, no matter how grueling or unglamorous.

Because I have so much on my plate, most of the grunt work falls on her. She spends her mornings arguing with the finicky contractors and battling the city for the proper permits; she shops for furniture in the afternoon, and still manages to pick me up from physical therapy every evening.

We aren't just a couple anymore; we're a team, and I love that. I depend on it and draw strength from it.

Chas has been worth his weight in gold too. A few weeks ago, he helped my mom move into Jo's house so I could get some much-needed sleep and then cram for a calculus exam. He also spent all day figuring out how to put up handrails in my new bathrooms, kitchen, and bedroom.

"This is better than anything I could've done," I say, flipping the booklet shut.

They look genuinely pleased with themselves. "One more surprise," Chas says.

"Close your eyes," Haley orders.

I laugh and listen as they scramble around and whisper.

"Okay, take a look."

They're holding up a huge poster. Bold yellow and red diagonal stripes play the backdrop to the letters, "JD's," which leap from the center of the bright design in bold black letters.

I smile. "It's nice," I say. "You know, very…colorful. It's, uh, well…it's… what is it exactly?"

"We were thinking it could be your new menu design."

"That's great guys, but what's 'JD's'?"

"Your initials," Chas says.

"Haven't we been down this road—a couple of times?" I ask, turning back to my partially sanded wood cabinet.

"The diner's under new management," Chas says. "It only makes sense for it to have a new name."

"And what about all this work you're having done?" Haley asks. "This isn't going to look like JoJo's when you're finished."

"Are you two bored or something? Because if making posters and pestering me is all you guys have on your plates, I got lots of sandpaper."

Haley puts the poster down and blows me a kiss. "Your living room set is being delivered today," she says; her tone's apologetic, but her smile gives away her relief. "I'll see you later."

Chas slings his book bag over his shoulder. "She's my ride."

"Take it easy."

I return to sanding the varnish off the old cabinets, but my eyes keep gravitating toward the vivid poster beside me. It's a great design; modern, bold, and eye-catching like I want the diner to be.

"JD's" is a stupid name for a diner. "Come on, let's go to JD's," I say, testing it aloud. "You want to go to JD's for lunch? JD's is the place to be."

I laugh and shake my head and try to ignore how easily the name rolls off my tongue.

34. Abby

My parents, Val, and Dr. Kessler are sitting in a small circle in the middle of Dr. Kessler's office. They're chatting quietly when I walk in.

"Abby," Dr. Kessler says and glances at her watch, "you're fifteen minutes late."

"Traffic."

"Say hi to everyone and take a seat so we can get started."

Mom is the first to stand. "Look at you," she says, giving my waist a small pinch. "You're getting plump."

I shoot Dr. Kessler my somebody's-going-to-die-today look.

She winks reassuringly and takes a sip of her coffee.

Dad wraps his arms around me and kisses the top of my head.

"You look great," Val says, walking toward me.

I stiffen but allow her to give me a brief hug for argument's sake.

Mom and Dad both smile radiantly, the sight of their girls locked in a loving embrace almost more than they can bear.

I take the seat next to Val. It's the only chair left.

"I've been working with Abby over the last several months, addressing some of her internal conflicts, and I have to say, she's made leaps and bounds."

My parents nod, puckering their foreheads as they hang on to each of Dr. Kessler's words.

"Our goal today is not to solve all your problems, but to open healthy lines of communication."

"Abby and I have always had great communication," Mom says proudly, her chest poked out. "I talk to her several times a week."

"No." I shake my head. "You talk at me several times a week."

Her smile fades quickly.

"What do you mean by that, Abby?" Dr. Kessler asks.

"She calls me every other day just to remind me that I'm still a failure."

Mom gasps, instantly gripping her chest, and shoots Dr. Kessler a worried glance. "That's not true."

"Tuesday she called to let me know her best friend's daughter bought her a house in Tuscany. And then she said, 'Maybe someday, if you can get, yourself together, you'll be able to do something like that for your father and me.' "

Mom laughs nervously. "I was joking."

I roll my eyes. "No, you weren't."

"What about your dad?" Dr. Kessler asks. "How is communication between the two of you?"

"Dad doesn't talk," I say. "He mediates."

My father clears his throat. "Is that bad?"

I shrug. "I want to share things with you. Stuff I wouldn't feel comfortable telling anyone else, but I don't because I know that instead of listening you'll try to handle me."

"That's because you're so unpredictable," Mom accuses. "If our advice isn't what you want to hear, you blow up."

"That's true," Val says.

I glare at her. "You don't even know me."

"And whose fault is that?"

"Let's not get off track," Dr. Kessler says. "Valerie, can you elaborate? An example would be helpful."

She glances at me as though she's scared to speak—scared I might pummel her if she says the wrong thing. "Abby's in debt," she begins slowly. "Major debt. After the accident, she couldn't work and her bills piled up. She cried to Mom about it for weeks. But when Mom told her about my offer to help, she screamed at her and hung up in her face."

I shoot daggers at my mother. "I did not scream at you. And this is why I hate talking to you," I say, throwing my hands up. "Because you always run and tell Val."

Mom frowns. "She's your sister."

"Why does everyone keep saying that, like it obligates me to her? Val and I share the same DNA. That's it!"

"That was unnecessary," Dad says, his voice stern.

"Yeah, well," I lean back, my arms folded across my chest, and stare straight into Val's pained eyes, "she abandoned me first."

She blinks and looks away as a solitary tear glides down her cheek.

"Are you proud of yourself?" Mom spits, her nostrils flared as though my presence is too great a stench to bear. "Your jealousy has burdened all of us. What has your sister ever done to you?"

I turn to Dr. Kessler. "I told you this was a bad idea."

"It's a valid question," Dad says.

"You guys don't know anything," I say to my parents.

"Then tell us, Abby." Dad says. "We're here to learn."

I shake my head and lower my eyes. "What's the point?"

The discussion lulls as Mom, Dad, Val, and I retreat to our respective thoughts.

"I have an idea," Dr. Kessler says. "Let's do a bit of role-playing. Abby, you be your mother, and April, you be Abby."

"I'll start," Mom says, jumping right in.

She flips her hair dramatically, sticks her nose in the air, and bats her lashes. "I'm Abby," she says, her voice haughty and affected. "And my world revolves entirely around me."

"That's not me," I say, appalled by my mother's imitation.

Dr. Kessler holds up her hand, silencing me, and motions for Mom to continue.

"I don't need anyone because my way is the only way that makes sense. But beneath all the glitz and glamour, I'm really lonely and scared, especially now that I've lost everything, and I realize I never acquired what really matters in life, like a husband and children and true friends—all the things my older sister, Val, has."

I grit my teeth. "You've got to be kidding."

"That's why I lash out. I had everything, but they were all the wrong things, and now my life seems meaningless."

She lowers her nose and looks at me. "What I don't understand," she says, her tone decidedly gentler, "is that the people I insist on pushing away are the ones who don't need to be impressed. They're the ones who are proud of me no matter how big my house is or what kind of car I drive. They're my family and they love me unconditionally."

"Abby," Miranda nods at me. "Your turn."

I sit as straight as possible, cross my legs, and primly fold my hands in my lap. "My name is April Walker and I'm *clueless* as to what my daughter, Abby, has been through in the past thirty years. I say I love her, no questions asked—that she doesn't need to prove her worth to me—but the truth is she'll never fit my idealized version of what a daughter should be.

"She's not married; she hasn't given me grandkids. Simply put," I glare at her, "she's not Val. All she does, all she's ever wanted to do, is fiddle around with that worthless cello." I shake my head disapprovingly.

"I don't understand Abby. At times I don't even like her, but she's my daughter, and I pretend to accept her because I have to—because she's my cross to bear. And every family has one."

Mom stares at me with hurt stamped on every attribute. "I—That's not fair. Anyone will tell you," she says to Dr. Kessler, "I love my daughters equally."

"*I* know," Dr. Kessler says. "But do they?"

"I think I need a break," Dad says, his voice quivering.

Dr. Kessler nods. "That's a good idea. I'd like to speak to the girls privately. Why don't you take a walk—get some fresh air—and come back, in say, twenty minutes."

Mom takes my father's hand with a squeeze as they stand and leave.

"Valerie, what're you thinking?" Dr. Kessler asks.

Her face crumples, squeezing big tears from the corner of her eyes. "I hate that Abby's so angry—that she feels so ostracized. I know it's my fault," she says, her words thick with mucus.

I stare at her, perplexed and nervous in equal measure. "I know why you are the way you are." She hiccups. "I was twelve and you were ten and it was my job to protect you, but..." she shakes her head and unceremoniously swipes at her tears with her sleeve.

I fold and unfold my arms, combating the dampness in my own eyes.

"I didn't know what to do," she says.

"It was a long time ago," I whisper, my anger at Val overtaken by the sight of her so obviously riddled with guilt. "Forget about it. I have."

"No, you haven't," she weeps into her hands. "You can't. You never forget. Trust me." She looks up at me, her face flushed, her shoulders hunched. "I know."

Time stands still as the reality of her words sink in. I'd just assumed that she left me alone to suffer at Jimmie's hands, when really she was being victimized in the exact same way. She couldn't protect me. She couldn't even protect herself. "Why didn't you tell me?" I ask.

She stares into her lap, unable to meet my gentle, questioning gaze. "I was humiliated." She sniffles. "And scared. I was just a kid."

"But we could've stuck together," I argue. "We could've helped each other. Instead you tortured me."

She glances up at me, her eyes pleading. "I'm so sorry, Abby. I was full of rage and you were just there." She wrings her hands. "I should have been a better sister."

I study her small, folded body—the anguish in her face, the strain in her voice. I see myself in her—empty and violated.

"Me too," I say, reaching for her.

At my touch, she falls to her knees, rests her head in my lap, and wails.

I look at Dr. Kessler, uncertain of what to do, but she remains silent, only offering to watch us from the other side of the circle.

It has been decades since I've shown my sister affection, since I've let myself feel anything toward her other than anger and resentment. I'm not sure how to touch her—how to comfort her.

"Don't cry," I plead gently and stroke her hair. "Please don't cry. We'll figure it out," I promise. But nothing I say seems to quell her steady sobs.

I kiss the back of her head. "What can I do?" I whisper into her ear. "What can I do to make it better?"

"Forgive me," she moans into my damp skirt.

My chest tightens at her simple request. "Of course I forgive you," I say, choking back tears. "Of course."

Slowly, her sobs subside. Then, without warning, she lifts her face and presses her wet, tear-streaked cheek to mine. "I love you," she says hugging me painfully tight.

I hesitate for a moment. She has spoken those words to me a thousand times over the years, but not once do I recall saying them back.

"I love you, too," I whisper and return her hug.

Reluctantly she pulls away. "It doesn't have to be like this," she says. "I can help you reach past the bitterness—past the hurt."

I scan my sister. Right now, in this office, with her smeared mascara and her running nose, I feel connected to her in an unprecedented way. I don't want to leave this moment—to lose this bond, this understanding. But I know the next words out of her mouth are going to trump everything that's just happened.

"Val, don't," I beg.

"Christ is the only way," she says. "He loves you. He knows your pain even better than I do and He can take it away. He can make you whole again."

"Why do you do this?" I ask, my anger returning as quickly as it left. "Why does every conversation have to come down to God?"

"Because Jesus is the answer to everything," she says, still kneeling in front of me.

I shake my head. "I'm not like you. I don't need mythology and fairy tales to make my life bearable."

"He's not a fairy tale," she says. "He's very real. You just have to open yourself to knowing Him."

"I don't want to know Him!" I bark, leaning away from her. "I don't want to believe in a God who let's ten and twelve year olds get molested. I don't want to know a God who lets innocent people get into car accidents and come out looking like this." I point at my face. "I don't need a God like that, Val."

She examines me with palpable grief. "You need Him more than anything," she says, returning to her seat.

"This is why we don't talk," I say to Dr. Kessler. "She's delusional."

"That's presumptuous," Dr. Kessler says. "A lot of people rely on their faith in God to see them through life's journeys."

"Yeah, well," I fold my arms defiantly, "not me." I turn to Val. "Why can't you just back off?"

"I love you too much to back off," she says. "Jesus is the only permanent source of healing and joy. He's the only reason life is worth living and until you understand that—until you accept it—you'll continue to be miserable."

"I can't do this," I say, snatching my purse. "I'm done."

"Abby," Dr. Kessler says calmly, "don't be rash."

"Please don't go," Val says, grabbing my wrist. "Don't run away."

Despite my irritation, I don't snatch my arm away. I'm too tired to fight. "Why can't you accept me the way I am?"

"I do," she says, lacing her fingers through mine. "I just want you to be happy. I want more for you than what I see in front of me."

"I'm not a Christian," I say matter-of-factly. "And I don't want to be. Can you accept that?"

She eyes me, her face fraught with uncertainty. "No," she says. "But I can love you, regardless."

I shake my head and untwine our fingers. "I don't want love without acceptance," I say. "One without the other turns them both hollow."

She blinks back a fresh batch of tears, but says nothing.

We're separated by a precipice of fundamental belief and neither of us can come any closer than we already have for fear of a terrible fall.

"Tell my parents I'm sorry," I say to Dr. Kessler, "I had to go."

"You two could work this out," she says, disappointed. "If you really wanted to."

I glance at Val, saddened, but hopeful. "Maybe someday we will," I say and walk out of the door, closing it behind me.

Sean's car is parked in the desolate guest lot when I get home. My spirits lift for a brief moment until I realize, he can't be here to see me.

It's eleven on a Friday morning. I should be at school printing out attendance sheets and cleaning off chalkboards.

There are a million different reasons why he might've stopped by at such a strange hour, but only one makes sense.

I take the elevator up to my floor and pause just outside of my door. I don't hear anything, but I slide my shoes off, just in case, and quietly slip into the front hall.

Hannah's playful laughter is followed by Sean's deep, muffled voice.

I tiptoe through the study and peek around the corner, but the living room is empty.

"Here, taste this," Hannah says. They're in the kitchen.

"What is it?" Sean asks.

"It's a soy burger. No fat."

"Mmmm," he moans. "That's actually really good."

"I know. Abby won't even try them. She lives off a strict diet of Milk Duds and Sprite. That's why she's getting so fat."

"I wouldn't call her fat," Sean says.

I smile.

"She definitely doesn't have your body though."

Hannah giggles. "There's a lot I have that Abby doesn't."

"Like what?"

"Wouldn't you like to know?" she teases.

"Yeah, I would." His voice is serious. "Look at you. What guy wouldn't want to get to know you? You're funny and smart."

And blonde, with legs that go on for days, I think, rolling my eyes.

"I thought you and Abby had something going."

I hear the refrigerator door open and a wrapper crinkling.

"We're just friends," Sean says.

"Give me a break. I walk into a room and you guys are all over each other."

"We play around a lot," he says, his words distorted by a mouthful of food. "She's a nice girl and everything, but there's no chemistry."

Hannah laughs. "How can anyone have chemistry with someone who looks like that?"

"Don't say that. Abby has a beautiful heart."

"Maybe. But I'm the total package."

"Yes, you are," Sean says. "So let's go out this weekend."

Hannah titters. "That'll go over real well with Abby."

"She doesn't have to know. We'll meet somewhere or you can come to my house."

"I have tickets to the Cubs game on Sunday," Hannah says.

"I was thinking we could do something a little more intimate."

"Like what?" she asks, her voice suddenly husky.

"Like this."

Silence follows, but I have no problem imagining what they're doing. I sit down on the couch, too blown away by the day's dreadful events to storm into the kitchen and break up their make-out fest.

How can this be happening to me? How can life be this unfair—this cruel? Haven't I endured enough for one day? For an entire lifetime?

"That was incredible," Hannah says. "You have soft lips."

Their shadows grow progressively larger as they leave the kitchen and walk toward the living room. My first inclination is to scramble away. I don't want them to see me like this—to think, for even a second, that they've broken me.

But this is my home, my living room, my kitchen. I won't run anymore. So what if they see me cry? I can't keep pretending like I'm made of steel. I have to stop lying to them. I have to stop lying to myself.

Hannah is the first one to enter. She's carrying a bag of chips and a movie.

They both stop abruptly at the sight of me on the couch. Hannah's evenly tanned skin turns pasty. Her eyes are cast with worry. "What're you doing here?" she asks.

"I live here."

She points at Sean, who's holding two bottled waters. "We were just...this isn't...He came over to see you and, uh, you weren't here. So you know, I was just, um...I was just entertaining him until you got home."

"Really?" I look at Sean. "You came to visit me at home on a Friday morning when you knew I'd be at work?"

He swallows hard. "Uh...yeah."

I nod. "Okay, well, here I am. What do you need?"

His laugh is strained. "Do I ever need an excuse to come and see you?"

"Yeah," I say flatly. "This time you do."

"Let's not make more out of this than it is," Hannah says, donning a stiff, plastic smile. "Now we can all watch the movie."

"I'll get another drink," Sean says, quickly disappearing back into the kitchen.

Hannah tries to pass me the bowl of chips.

"Oh no, I couldn't," I say, waving it away. "I live off a strict diet of Milk Duds and Sprite."

Her eyes grow wide and her face drops.

"Here we go," Sean says, handing me a bottle of water.

"What're we watching?" I ask.

Sean holds up the movie case. "A Beautiful Mind."

"You're covered all the way around, aren't you? Russell Crowe has the beautiful mind, I have the beautiful heart, and Hannah is the total package."

He freezes. "What?"

"You heard me. Or does lack of chemistry cause lack of hearing?"

He sets the movie down and turns to me. "Let's talk about this. Give me a chance to explain."

I shake my head and groan. "You have no idea how tired I am of talking."

"Abby, you're an incredible woman."

"Spare me," I say, standing up.

"It's not like he's your boyfriend," Hannah says.

I nod. "You're right. He isn't. And you aren't my friend. This arrangement's been milked dry. It's time for you to move out."

"That's a little drastic, don't you think?" Sean asks.

Hannah stands. "No, she's right. We used to be so in sync with each other." She turns to me, her forehead wrinkled with superficial concern. "But I look at you now and I don't know who you are anymore."

"I don't either," I whisper.

"Then let me help you." She cautiously approaches me, her arms outstretched.

I shake my head and step back. "Being in this house with you is like ingesting poison on a daily basis."

Her brows furrow. "So that's it?" She shrugs. "Are you forgetting about the mortgage? You need me."

"I'll sell the condo. I don't care anymore. I just want you out."

She puts down the remote control and scours the floor until she locates her missing sandal.

"Don't forget your boy toy." I point to Sean.

Quietly, they gather their belongings.

Hannah eases cautiously past me.

Sean casts me apologetic glances, but I keep my head turned.

A somber mood settles after they've gone.

I grab the bag of chips resting on the coffee table and plod upstairs to drown myself in processed food and overacted daytime television.

It is inevitable—a fundamental rule, in fact—that something good will eventually always fall prey to something bad. The greater the good, the greater the bad. That is a principle of life, a truth that has existed since the beginning of time. They're supposed to make us stronger, these quintessential peaks and valleys. They're supposed to build depth of character, intensify perspective, and cultivate empathy. Without them, we would be unable to relate, unable to understand and feel, unable to grow.

The problem is that every so often a person can be stretched beyond his natural limits. He's unable to withstand the agony of a hard fall is ill-equipped to endure for an extended amount of time in the dark without hope. When that happens, he has no choice but to crack. It is involuntary. It is reflex. Maybe the mind is just too fragile, maybe the heart too weak. Who can judge? The point is that when enough pressure is applied, enough battles lost, enough victories usurped, enough effort exerted in vain, the human spirit will perish.

That's my theory anyway. Like everything else, it's just speculation, a tactic to explain away life's unexpected and undeserved hardships. Jimmie, Val, my entire childhood—they were all part of one long, insufferable valley called adolescence. But I survived. I survived to become a very talented, very successful cellist. A seemingly endless reserve of money, notoriety, and clout, there was no higher peak.

Some would say there was nowhere else to go but down—and down I went, one snowy night in Michigan with my ex-lover. Another valley.

I should've seen it coming under my theory, but that's the thing with soaring peaks; you can't see the bottom of the hill through the clouds, much less envision yourself down there. And so I've been waiting, my body and mind scraped over one harsh, unforgiving rock after another for three excruciating years.

I've wanted to quit, to put down my weapons, fold my arms, and refuse to fight. After all, how can life continue to wage war on someone so weary, so defeated? Isn't mercy every man's one, undeniable right. Aren't we all, at any given time, allowed to hand in our time-out cards and crawl into our shells until it's safe to come out again?

I haven't given in, though; never called a time-out. I was certain if I hung on long enough, a peak was on the horizon. And sure enough, I met Dr. Kessler, who inadvertently led me to Sean, who held the name and number of the man who, with time and a laser gun, might be able to restore some of what I've lost.

A fortuitous chain of events? I think not. Fate, luck, chance, they play no part. The pattern's been set. I brazened the valley and I'm due a peak.

But I'm discovering that there's a fatal flaw in my theory—a simple, but crucial oversight—which is the inability to ensure fairness. There's no trial, no judge and jury, no enforceable law that says every valley must be followed by a peak and every peak by a valley.

Who is there to blame when one valley is followed by another and then another and then another until you're writhing in a troth, lost somewhere deep in the burrows of the earth where no human arm extends far enough to reach you? There's no one.

Some people find favor and spend most of their lives floating on clouds atop the highest peaks of the highest mountains. Then there are those in the middle, where most people reside, bouncing back and forth between moderate highs and temperate lows. And still yet, there are those born into misfortune, slaves doomed to inexplicably deep, never-ending valleys that can quickly erase even the most optimistic man's hopes of salvation. That's just life and I've been okay with it up until now—until I somehow fell into the bottom category.

The promise of one more peak has always been enough to drive me on—to give me, sometimes, just enough energy to keep from crashing. But another peak, I finally realize, is never going to come. And so by instinct, by reflex, my spirit is ready to shut down and I am prepared to let it.

"Hello?" I croak.

"You cannot still be sleeping," Gail's cheerful voice says.

"What time is it?" I peel one eye open.

"Just after one. Get up. I want to go to lunch."

My room is dark, but rays of bright sunlight peer through the sides of my half-open shutters. "Not today."

"You must've had some day off," she says.

"Unforgettable."

"Good for you, but now it's time to get back to work."

"It's Saturday." I roll onto my back.

"I talked to my friend, the one at DePaul, and I think I might have some good news."

"What is it?"

"Meet me at Nookies in an hour and I'll tell you."

"Gail!" I moan.

"One hour. Don't be late," she says and hangs up.

My bed is covered with melted Milk Duds and chip crumbs. Both my pillows are smeared with my lipstick and foundation.

I look down at myself. I'm still wearing my pleated khaki skirt and jean jacket.

Nobody called last night—not my parents, not Val, not even Sean. I don't know why I was expecting them to chase after me, why I watched four sappy Lifetime originals and went through a shamefully large box of candy waiting for the phone to ring.

I sling myself out of bed and stumble to the bathroom. My mascara has dried in thick, dark lines down my face.

The water from the shower beats strongly against my back. I suck the steam in through my mouth and nose and pretend it's cleansing my insides.

I'll sell the condo, rent an apartment somewhere. If I take the teaching job, I'll get a place close to the school. I'll sell my Porsche and get something more practical. I can put some of the money toward my Pulsed Dye Laser treatments. I'll join a gym, maybe buy a dog.

It won't be that bad. There's life after fame. I won't be in the spotlight, but I'll be training young men and women to follow in my footsteps. I'll be a big fish in a little pond. My students appreciate me. Mrs. Vine and Gail appreciate me.

I'm already on my way to rebuilding—to making a new life for myself—a less demanding, more satisfying life.

You'll see, Abs. It'll be great.

I beat my fists against the cold tile and sob. Who am I kidding? Things will never be the same. I will never be the same, and though that's not entirely bad, it frightens me. I don't have an identity outside of "Abigail Walker, Renowned Cellist," and the part of me that worked so hard to get where I am, doesn't want to let it go.

I slide to the floor, tuck my knees to my chest, and rock myself. I wish I wasn't the only person I could turn to. I wish there was someone else's arms around me, someone else's voice soothing my throbbing heart.

You're okay. Everything's okay, I tell myself. I say it over and over again, but I can't get myself to believe it.

"You look terrible," Gail says.

She's sitting at one of the sidewalk tables reading the *Tribune*.

I smile weakly. "You got me out of bed to tell me that?"

"Have you been crying?" she asks.

I breathe deeply, my shoulders slumped. "No," I murmur.

She puts the paper down and pours me a cup of coffee. "What happened?"

"Where do I start?"

She pats my hand. "From the beginning."

I tell her about my expired recording contract, about my emotionally draining family session, and Hannah and Sean. I tell her about my debt and about Mrs. Vine's offer. I unload everything, letting my tears flow freely, despite the nervous glances of curious strangers.

"What makes you happy?" she asks, handing me a stack of napkins.

I shake my head. "I honestly don't know anymore."

"It sounds like even when you had your music deal, you were miserable."

"Yeah, I was," I say, dabbing my eyes.

"Then this is your chance to do things over again. You dumped that Hannah girl, so you're already ahead of the game. And as for Sean, it's his loss, and believe me, he knows it."

"What about my family? They'll probably never speak to me again."

"Do you want to mend your relationship with them?"

"I want them to accept me for who I am."

"Then you have to accept them for who they are, Abby. Your sister is a Christian. Your dad's a mediator. Your mom's—well, she's nuts."

I laugh. "Yeah, but in a good way."

"I believe there is no greater blessing than to love someone and to be loved in return."

I sniffle. "That's true."

"People show love differently. Your dad trying to fix all your problems and your mom trying to propel you forward and your sister trying to share her religion—that's them loving you."

I smile. "What're you doing working in a school office?" I ask. "You should be charging emotional head cases like me a hundred bucks an hour for your pearls of wisdom."

Her cheeks glow. "I'm a woman of many talents," she says. "And so are you."

"What can I do besides pluck a few fancy tunes on a cello?"

She smiles and pulls a scrap of paper from her shirt pocket. "This," she says, handing it to me.

"What is it?"

"The number to the director of DePaul's music program. He was so impressed with the audition tape you helped Terry make that he wants to set up an interview. We could be looking at a full scholarship," she squeals.

I gasp. "But what about his grades? Mrs. Vine gave me his transcripts and his GPA is less than stellar."

"He has to score well on his standardized aptitude test," she says simply. "He's got to apply himself."

"He can do it," I assure her. "No, he's *going* to do it, even if I have to ride him for the rest of the year."

"Does that mean you're staying?" she asks.

I grin. "Where else am I going to go?"

She hands me a menu, and as I skim over the pages, I'm exhilarated by the freedom of choice.

All my life I've been confined by image, trapped by the lure of money and success and what both would require of me.

Now that I don't have either, I'm free to figure out who I am, free to experience the world like everyone else—through trial and error.

For the first time ever, I can choose to enjoy life.

"What're you going to have?" Gail asks.

I smile, giddy. "I don't know. Everything looks good."

35. Jarvis

I, Jarvis Daniels, a self-professed gutter-bound, jack-of-no-trades, am about to become a college graduate. I'm about to become the first in my family to earn a degree, and Mom and Haley are on their feet screaming like wild banshees. But that's okay. They're *my* wild banshees.

I walk (yes, walk!), with the assistance of my cane, across the stage of higher learning, shake hands with the president of Wayne State University, and accept my diploma.

"Over here, Jay. Look at me, over here!" my mom yells over the cheering crowd of parents and students.

I transfer my tassel from the right side of my cap to the left and give her a huge, toothy smile.

Flash! Flash! Flash! She starts snapping pictures as if I'm marching off to war and might not make it back home.

Haley blows me a kiss.

William, Mom's new husband, tips his hat proudly and that's it. My moment has come and gone. But the feeling, the sheer elation of my accomplishment, will stay with me for a long time, maybe even forever.

I walk down the stage steps, take my seat, and cheer on my friends as, one by one, they too graduate. This, I realize gaily, is a reward of taking the path less traveled—of throwing away maps, chucking flashlights and compasses out of the window, spurning doubt, binding fear, closing my eyes, and stepping into the unknown with faith.

This is a job well done. This is happiness. This is *my* life.

Without Christ, I would not be where I am. I would not be who I am. I wouldn't know His infinite love or His limitless power. I wouldn't know courage or strength. He's become my lifeline, my reason for being, and I know that everything I've achieved so far and everything I'll achieve in the future is because of Him. And I'm grateful.

Mom bounds toward me, her arms outstretched, a camera swinging from her neck. "Congratulations!" she says, hurling herself at me. "I'm so proud of you."

"It was a fine ceremony," William says.

I smile. "It's been a good day."

"We have to get to the house," Mom says. "People are probably starting to arrive."

"You guys go ahead without me. I'm going to wait for Chas."

Haley hooks her arm through mine. "He's catching a ride with Janelle. You can see him later."

"No, I really need to talk to him. It's about the restaurant. We've got to tie some things up."

"Today?" Mom asks. "You can't work today."

"I have to," I say. "It's important."

Haley's face grows heavy with disappointment. "It can't wait until tomorrow?"

"I fly out tonight." I shrug, apologetic. "I'll meet you guys at the house in a little bit."

She frowns and walks away.

I know she's upset. Between finals and running JD's and preparing for the opening of Treasures, my new restaurant in Chicago, we hardly see each other anymore.

Looking for Chas is not easy. Old professors and friends stop me every few minutes to congratulate me and ask about my future plans. I chat as politely and quickly as possible. I pose for a few photos and exchange numbers with a couple of business grads looking to break into the restaurant business.

Finally, I find him. Janelle's sitting on his lap, and they're talking to a group of our friends.

"Jay!" he says, a big smile on his face. "Congrats."

"Same to you," I say.

Janelle plants a friendly peck on my cheek. "We were all just about to head to your house."

I point at Chas. "Can I steal him for a minute?"

She laughs. "You can take him for longer than that."

"I'll meet you there?" Chas says.

Chas and I walk a ways in silence. The sky is overcast; the campus is nearly deserted. We find a dry bench and sit.

"I'm going to do it," I say. "I'm going to ask her."

Chas smiles. "Good. You're not going to find anyone better than Haley."

"I don't want to rush her, though. Maybe she's not ready."

"Jay, you've been together for four years. Trust me, she's past ready."

"She's been acting funny lately. Every time I mention Chicago, she gets this look on her face."

"What kind of look?"

"I don't know. Kind of an angry scowl."

"Well, can you blame her?" he asks.

"I know I've been distant lately with all that's going on, but she's usually so supportive."

"You're moving to Chicago. You've bought a place. You've got your restaurant. You've set up a whole new life and you haven't given her any indication she's going to be part of it."

I nod. "Makes sense."

"So how are you going to do it?" he asks.

"I'm going to say, 'Haley, will you marry me?' "

"What about the ring? What about the setting and the mood?"

"Who are you, Martha Stewart?"

"I think you should go all out. Make it a grand gesture. You could rent one of those planes, you know, the ones with the banners."

I laugh. "People don't do that in real life."

"What about a billboard?"

I shake my head. "Too public."

"Have you asked her parents for their blessing?"

I look at him. "Do you think I should?"

"Of course, Man. That's a given. You always want to start a relationship with your in-laws off on the right foot."

I nod. "I need to give this some more thought."

"Yeah, but don't overthink it," he says. "Because then you'll chicken out, and I meant what I said before. You won't find anyone better than Haley."

My meetings run smoothly, and more importantly, on time. By three in the afternoon, I've approved the guest list, sampled and selected the desserts, and met my new staff.

I reschedule the walk-through of my new condo and catch an earlier flight home.

The next seventy-two hours of my life will be dedicated to finding the perfect engagement ring and planning an unforgettable proposal.

Mom picks me up from the airport. She's wearing a long, fuchsia dress. Her hair is set in large rollers.

I give her a hug. "This is a new look."

She twirls around. "Will's taking me dancing. How was your trip? Everything coming along nicely?"

"Better than expected," I say, tossing my bag in the backseat. "We're actually ahead of schedule for once. It's nice to have some breathing room."

"Good. You can relax now, take a little vacation."

We ride down Telegraph and listen to gospel music. The windows are down, the sun is out, and there's not a cloud in sight.

"What do you think about Haley?" I ask.

"She's precious," Mom says.

"What do you think about having her as a daughter-in-law?"

She lets out a hearty laugh and pounds her steering wheel. "I think that would make me one of the luckiest mothers in the world."

I smile. "That's good to know."

"Have you bought the ring?"

"Not yet. Chas and I are going to look tomorrow."

She reaches over and pats my cheek. "You two are going to have a great life together."

We make it to the condo around a quarter to six. Mom comes in to use the bathroom and I pick up the phone and dial Haley.

"How was your day?" she asks.

"Great. How did things go at the diner?"

"The usual." She pauses. "I miss you."

"I miss you too. I'll be home the day after tomorrow and then we have an anniversary to celebrate."

"It better be good too," she says in her baby voice. "You've been neglecting me lately."

"Jay," Mom calls. "I'm gone."

I grimace and put my hand over the phone.

"Who was that?" Haley asks.

"I didn't hear anything."

"It sounded like a woman."

"Oh! Yeah, that was just the TV."

"Really?" she sounds unconvinced. "I could've sworn someone called your name."

"Nope. I'm the only one here."

"Jay!" Mom shouts again.

I bury the phone and poke my head out of the door. "See ya." I call in a loud whisper.

"Call me tomorrow," she says and lets herself out.

"Jay? Hello?" Haley's distant voice calls from underneath my blankets.

"Sorry. I had another call."

"I heard voices," she says.

"Um…speakerphone."

"You're acting weird. Are you okay?"

I let out a fake yawn. "I'm just tired."

"I won't keep you then."

"I'll give you a call sometime tomorrow."

"Sleep well."

I hang up the phone and flop down on my bed. My forehead beads with sweat. *I'm not cut out for this.*

I smile. But if I survive the next few days and everything goes as planned, I'll be the happiest man in the world.

"You going to Bible Study with Haley tonight?" Chas asks.

I shake my head. "She thinks I'm still in Chicago."

We're in a small jewelry shop in Dearborn, surveying their many rows of encased diamond rings.

"Be careful," Chas warns. "Sneaking around, even for a good cause, can be dangerous."

"Well, I had to set everything up. What was I supposed to say, 'Sweetie, I won't be able to see you tomorrow because I need to pick out your engagement ring'?"

"You figured out how you're going to do it?"

I examine a glistening marquise, displayed on a velvet pad. It's stunning, but not quite what I'm looking for. "Everything's been arranged."

"Look at this one," Chas says, pointing to a gaudy cluster of diamonds on a thick gold band.

"I think that's a cocktail ring."

He shrugs. "So, how's it going down?"

I smile. "Our anniversary is on Tuesday. I'm taking her to this little Chinese restaurant in Bloomfield Hills. It's where we had our first kiss. I talked to the manager and he's going to make me a special fortune cookie. So after dinner she'll crack open her dessert and the fortune will read, 'Haley, will you marry me?' "

"Smooth," he says. "Real smooth."

"All I need now is the ring."

"How about that one?" He points to a hideous combination of baguettes and rubies.

"Can I help you gentlemen?" a saleswoman asks.

"I'm looking for an engagement ring."

"What's your price range?"

I shrug. "I don't have one. I'll know it when I see it."

"Do you know what size?"

"Seven."

"How do you know that?" Chas asks.

"Her mom told me. I took your advice and called her parents."

"And?"

"They couldn't have been happier."

He leans against one of the cases. "Wow," he muses. "You're really going to do this."

I nod. "I love her. We've been through a lot together. I can't see myself with anyone else."

The saleswoman returns. "This is a lovely one. It's a pear cut, one and a half carats."

It's nice, but unimpressive. "I want something bigger," I say. "Something that'll stand out."

She nods and slides back the glass cabinet door to her right. "This one's two and a half carats. The center stone is a classic round cut."

I look at Chas. "What do you think?"

Clasping his hands beneath his chin, he casts his eyes to the ceiling and bats his lashes demurely. "I'm not a three-stone kind of guy," he jokes.

"Yeah, I think I want to stick with solitaires."

We look at dozens of rings, but none of them are good enough. None of them match what I have in my head. I'm going to ask Haley to marry me, to be my wife, to spend the rest of her life with me.

The ring has to be worthy of that type of commitment. When I open the case and she lays eyes on it for the first time, I want her to know I put a lot of thought into it. With this ring, I want her to know how much I love her, how much she means to me.

"It's nice," I say, examining the diamond band she's brought out. "But it doesn't have that something special. It's too..."

"Ordinary?" Chas offers.

"Yeah, don't you have anything custom? Something one of a kind?"

The saleswoman eyes me carefully. Her long, slender neck and pointed nose make her look regal and distinguished.

"I've got something," she says. "A customer had it made a few months ago, but the engagement fell through."

"Let's see it," Chas says.

She disappears behind a swinging door marked "Employees Only" and returns a few minutes later carrying a small, black velvet bag.

"It's a four and a half carat solitaire set in white gold."

"That's it," Chas whispers, jabbing my arm.

I examine the ring. The diamond sparkles up at me in all its brilliance. It's perfect.

The saleswoman hands me a small magnifying glass. "The detail on the band was all done by hand," she says. "A lot of time and consideration went into this ring."

"How much?" I ask.

She jots a number down on a business card and passes it to me.

Chas looks over my shoulder and coughs. "I guess time and consideration don't come cheap," he says.

It's a lot of money, more than I ever anticipated spending, but I can't take my eyes off of it, and this is a once-in-a-lifetime purchase.

"We can size it and have it ready for you by tomorrow," the saleswoman says.

I glance at the price and then back at the ring. "I'll take it."

"Good morning," I say and hand Haley a bouquet of roses.

She snatches them from my hand, tosses them onto the counter, and returns to counting down the registers.

I stand for a minute, stunned by her insolence. "What's going on?"

"You tell me."

"I just got in and I wanted to stop by and surprise you."

She glares up at me. "You just got in from where?"

"From Chicago."

She slams the register shut. “You just got in from Chicago?”

“Yes, now would you please tell me what the problem is?”

“I called you back at your hotel yesterday and they told me you checked out two days ago. Two days ago, Jay!”

“Okay, calm down. There’s a perfectly good explanation.”

“What is it?” she asks, her nostrils flaring.

“I can’t tell you, not yet.”

“What is going on with you?” she yells. “I don’t even feel like I have a boyfriend anymore. You’re never around and now you’re lying and keeping secrets.”

“I know it’s been a rough few months,” I say. “And you have every right to be upset, but I need you to trust me.”

“Are you seeing someone else?” she asks bluntly.

I step back, my eyebrows furrowed. “What kind of question is that?”

“Are you? Because that’s the only thing that makes sense.”

“You’re being ridiculous.”

“Is it Abby?” she asks.

I stare at her, dumbfounded. “Abby?”

“Yes, your ex-girlfriend, Abby. The one who conveniently happens to live in Chicago.”

I laugh. “I haven’t thought about Abby in ages. I don’t even remember what she looks like.”

“I find that hard to believe considering she was the love of your life.”

“*You’re* the love of my life,” I say.

Her features soften and her shoulders ease, but her gaze remains demanding. “Then where were you?”

“I was busy making plans for tomorrow.”

“What kind of plans?”

I walk around to the other side of the counter. "It's an anniversary surprise."

She peeks up at me, her irritation giving way to curiosity. "Really?"

"I want tonight to be perfect," I say. "And you're a hard woman to please."

She smiles. "I am not."

"I like that about you. It means I can never be lazy." I graze her forehead with a kiss. "You keep me on my toes."

I feel every last drop of irritation and anger wane from her muscles as she leans into me.

"I shouldn't have thrown your roses."

We both glance down at the pile of petals, leaves, and baby's breath strewn over the counter. "They're beautiful," she says.

I fold my arms around her and squeeze her to me tightly. "It's almost over. Just bear with me for a few more weeks."

"Things are changing so quickly," she says.

"Aren't you the one always talking about how change is good?"

"Yeah, but you'll be in Chicago and I'll be here. How are we supposed to make it work?"

I smile. "We'll talk every day and see each other on the weekends."

"It's not going to be the same," she whines.

"We'll only be five hours away by car and one hour away by plane."

"Do you have to go?" she asks.

I take a step back and look into her pleading eyes. "Haley, I've come too far to turn around now. Think of how much money I'll lose."

"Let Chas go and you can stay here with me and run JD's."

I shake my head. "Treasures is my project. It's my dream and it's God's will for my life. He's opened too many doors to allow this to happen."

She sighs and pulls away. "Then I guess you have to go."

"Hey, come on now. Don't be like that. This is supposed to be a happy day."

She nods. "I'm happy."

"Can I get a smile?"

She grins half heartedly.

"With teeth?"

The bells on the door chime and Chas walks in. He smiles. "How're you kids doing this morning?"

"Fine." Haley uses the distraction to put some distance between us. She grabs a pile of clean dish towels and slips into the back room.

"Tension much?" Chas asks.

"She found out I wasn't in Chicago yesterday," I whisper.

He shakes his head. "Didn't I tell you all that sneaking around was going to catch up with you?"

"Sssssshhh," I hiss and motion him outside.

Seven Mile is congested with morning rush hour and we strain to hear each other over the honking horns and noisy engines.

"She doesn't want me to go to Chicago," I say.

"That's because you haven't asked her to go with you yet."

I shake my head. "She asked me to stay in Detroit with her and run JD's."

"What about Treasures?"

"She wants you to take it over."

"Is that what you want?"

"No, and even if it was, it's too late now. I've sold my old condo and closed on my new one. I've got food critics lined up, the press is coming, the invitations have been sent—this is it. There's no turning back."

"Then tell her that. She'll understand."

I rub my jaw and sigh. "I don't think she will."

"Wait a minute, you're still—you aren't thinking about backing out of the proposal are you?"

"It just seems like now may not be the best time. There's too much commotion."

"Haley loves you. She would follow you to the ends of the earth."

"You're right," I say, drawing strength from his words.

"But if you leave without letting her know where she fits into your future," he adds, his tone solemn, "you might lose her."

"What if she says no?"

"That won't happen. She's going to open her fortune cookie, take one look at that huge diamond you bought, start bawling and say, 'Yes.' And you're going to call me tomorrow, relieved and excited to be engaged to the woman of your dreams."

"You're a good friend," I say. "I want you to be my best man."

He laughs. "There's plenty of time for that. Why don't you get your bride first?"

I glance at my watch. "I'll see you later."

"Wait, where are you going?" he calls after me.

"To go pick up the ring!"

The restaurant is dimly lit. Most of the tables are occupied by cozy, starry-eyed couples.

"Good evening," the hostess greets us and gives me a less than subtle wink. Haley doesn't notice. She glances around our romantic surroundings distractedly.

The manager personally escorts us to the secluded booth I reserved days earlier. "Enjoy," he says, handing us our menus.

"Is everything okay?"

She unfolds her napkin and places it in her lap. "Fine. Why do you ask?"

"You're quiet tonight."

"It's been a long day."

"For me too," I say.

"Is that why you left so abruptly this morning?"

"Tea?" our waiter asks. He's short with gray hair and round glasses.

We turn over our cups and wait for him to fill them with the steaming, aromatic brew from his kettle.

"I'm sorry about that," I say once he's gone. "I forgot I promised my mom I'd help her move some stuff out of the garage."

"Chas said you were late for an appointment."

I sip my water. "He must've been mistaken."

"I called you at home. I paged you. I left two messages on your cell phone. Why didn't you call me back?"

"Today's been hectic. I haven't had a chance to check my voicemails."

"Whatever." She opens her menu and looks over her choices.

"Why are you trying to pick a fight? We're supposed to be enjoying each other's company."

She closes her eyes and sighs.

"Hey," I lower her menu. "Talk to me."

"This morning you said you have to go to Chicago because Treasures is your dream, and I have to admit, that crushed me."

"I didn't mean to"

She shakes her head. "You also said it's God's will for your life, and that got me thinking. What is His will for my life? What are my dreams? Once upon a time, I wanted to be an interior designer. I was good at it too. And I realize now, it's not too late."

"So what're you saying? You want to go back to school?"

"I'm moving to New York, Jay."

I look at her and wait—wait for her to crack a smile, to tell me she's only kidding, that she would never put that kind of distance between us. But she only returns my gaze, her chin set.

"That's absurd."

"Not really. Where better to study interior design than in New York? I'm sick of Detroit."

"Then come to Chicago. You can go to school there."

"I don't want to move to Chicago."

My heart drops. "Are we—are you breaking up with me?"

"I've sat on the sidelines for four years and rooted you on while you fulfilled your dreams. Now it's time for you to do the same for me."

Our waiter returns smiling, his eyes pleasant. "Ready to order?"

"Sesame chicken," Haley says.

"And for you, Sir?"

"Uh..." I open my closed menu and pick out the first thing I see. "Seafood delight."

"That has mushrooms," Haley says.

"What?"

"Mushrooms. You're allergic."

"Right." I scan over the menu again, but the words are blurred. My mind is racing and my palms are sweaty. I'm not hungry anymore. I'm too nauseous with panic at the thought of losing my future wife.

"Give him the pepper steak," Haley says.

The waiter nods. "Good choice." He collects our menus and shuffles around the corner.

"See?" I smile. "You can't move to New York. What would I do without you?" I reach for her hand but she pulls away.

"I can't spend the rest of my life ordering your food. Or working at the diner for that matter."

"I understand that, but we have lots of options. Why New York? You can study interior design anywhere."

She shrugs. "You could've opened your restaurant anywhere. Why Chicago?"

"Are you punishing me? Is that what this is? I spent an entire year praying for wisdom and guidance, researching and deliberating, before I chose Chicago."

"I need to find myself, Jarvis; to figure out who I am."

"Why can't we do that together?"

"You don't have time for me anymore."

"Don't say that. I'll make time. I'll do whatever it takes."

"I want space," she says. "I think we should take a break."

I blink back tears. The ring feels like a two-ton boulder in my pocket. "Please," I beg. "Don't do this."

"We're in different places now. It's time to let go and move on."

We pick over our dinners in silence. The mood is heavy with loss. I don't look at her—I can't. I'm angry and deflated, but mostly I'm confused.

How did I get broadsided like this? When did our relationship take such a drastic turn for the worst? Had I really grown that detached, become so preoccupied, that I couldn't see her drifting away?

I bought an engagement ring and purchased a house. I've been slaving for months, flying back and forth between Detroit and Chicago, building Treasures from the ground up, not for me, for us.

But she doesn't want a life with me. She wants to move to New York to find herself. Four years, wasted.

The manager comes over; his smile is broad. "We have a very special dessert for the happy couple."

My heart skips a beat. "No, we won't be needing dessert tonight."

He and Haley toss me peculiar glances.

"Yes, yes," the manager insists. "Very special dessert for a special evening."

"No, really." My eyes are wide and desperate. "We'll pass."

"But we prepare especially for you."

"Look," I say, my voice coarse, "maybe next time."

"Jay, just let him bring the dessert," Haley orders. Her tone is one of exasperation.

"I don't feel like dessert. Let's just go."

The manager claps his hands twice and one of the waitresses appears from the kitchen carrying two fortune cookies on a gold saucer.

"For you," she says, placing the rigged cookies in front of Haley.

She smiles. "Thank you."

The manager and waitress bustle to the front of the restaurant to watch the magical moment unfold from afar.

Haley looks down at the saucer, her forehead wrinkled. "What's so special about fortune cookies?"

"Nothing," I say, snatching both of them.

"I think one of those is for me."

I chuck them both under the table.

She glares. "What's the matter with you?"

"You mean besides the fact that my girlfriend dumped me on the night of our four-year anniversary?" I bark.

"You don't have to be mean," she says.

"No," I mumble. "You're mean enough for the both of us."

"Throwing cookies on the floor and yelling at me isn't going to get us back on track."

"Who says I even want to?"

Her eyes brim with tears. "All I asked for was time."

I toss forty dollars on the table. "Take all the time you need. I'll be outside."

I snatch my cane, ignoring the curious glances of the expectant staff, and storm out of the restaurant. I feel foolish as I pace up and down the deserted sidewalk, my punctured pride throbbing. It's a fierce, constant pain that makes my eyes water and my blood boil.

Haley walks out. Her face is sad, her eyes red.

She cries as we walk to the car, and with each sob, my anger gives way to shame.

I take her elbow gently. "Haley, I'm sorry. I shouldn't have gone off."

She shrugs me away. "Just take me home."

"Can we at least talk about it?"

"Take me home," she says, refusing to look at me.

The ride back to her apartment is agonizing. Haley curls close to the passenger side door and swipes at the tears rolling down her cheeks.

I watch her from the corner of my eye and scrape my mind for something to say, anything that might repair the damage caused.

She's hurt, we both are, but I love her. I love her and I want us to work.

Tell her! I prod myself. *Open your mouth. Say something.* But there are no words in my vocabulary to express the extremity of my regret. No sentence, no coin of phrase poignant enough to draw her back to me.

She lets herself out and rushes up the front lawn and into her apartment without looking back or saying good-bye.

I sit on my kitchen counter, wrapping my plates in tissue paper and dropping them carelessly into a box on the floor.

Chas rummages through my poorly stocked refrigerator.

"Let me get this straight," he says. "You didn't propose and you broke up."

"And she's moving to New York," I add.

"That wasn't the plan."

I groan. "Everything that could've gone wrong went wrong. It was like having a tooth extracted with a dull knife."

I abandon my packing project and hobble, in the absence of my cane, to the living room, where I lie down on the couch, my face toward the ceiling, and wish for an immediate, quick, and painless death.

Chas follows me. "How did it end?" he asks, scooping my chunky peanut butter straight from the jar with his finger.

"I drove her home. She was crying." I put a pillow over my head and try to erase the heart-wrenching sight of Haley's red nose and tear-stained cheeks from my mind.

"You can fix this, Jay. Find her and tell her the truth."

"Which is what?" My voice is muffled.

"You love her more than anything," he says. "She's the one—the only one—and you want to make her happy for the rest of her life."

I sigh and toss the pillow onto the floor. "Maybe last night was God's way of telling me she's not the one. She said she didn't want to move to Chicago, and I know, without a doubt, that's where He's called me to be."

"If you had proposed and she said no, I would buy that, but you didn't even have the guts to pop the question," Chas says, wagging an accusatory, peanut butter-smeared finger.

"She dumped me."

"Obviously, she was protecting herself," Chas says. "You're moving in two weeks. You made a life for yourself in another city."

I sit up. "I made a life for us."

"Yeah, without telling her."

"It's over, Chas."

"Fine," he shakes his head and sighs. "What're you going to do?"

"Pick up the pieces and start over in Chicago."

My last two weeks in Detroit move in slow motion. I occupy my time labeling boxes and sifting through old yearbooks and photo albums—anything to keep me from calling Haley.

I don't visit JD's. Chas and I say our good-byes at the airport.

"I'll see you at the opening," I say.

He's disappointed in me. He thinks I gave up too easily, that I should charge gallantly to her apartment, my heart and an engagement ring in hand, and sacrifice myself one last time on the altar of love.

He wants to lecture me, to remind me who I'm leaving behind. But instead he hugs me.

"Take care of yourself."

"I will," I say and head down the concourse with my bag, my boarding pass, and a broken heart.

36. *Abby*

I look at the sluggish, sulking group sitting before me. It's the end of the year; finals are over, and the only thing standing between them and summer vacation is two measly days. Their minds are on sunny beaches and house parties, and it shows in their performance.

"Come on," I say. "At least act like you're trying."

"It's Senior Day," Marissa bleats.

Carlos plucks his bass. "If they get to skip, why don't we?"

I smile, sympathetic to the plight of the underclassmen. "Because none of you are seniors."

"Listen to that." Layla points to the door. Students are in the halls, laughing and talking loudly. "All the other teachers let *their* classes out early."

I glance at the clock. There's only forty minutes left and they've given me their all this year.

Montez taps his bow against his stand. "We know this stuff."

"Come on, Ms. W, have a heart," Eddie begs. They all moan and offer their most pathetic puppy dog faces.

I laugh and throw up my hands. "Good-bye."

They jump out of their seats and cheer, segueing from hopelessly burnt-out, high school musicians to triumphant, master negotiators.

"This means I expect a killer performance tomorrow night," I yell over their clatter.

They toss their instruments in their cases, oblivious of me, and all but stampede out of the door and into the crowded halls.

I turn off the lights and make my way downstairs to the teacher's lounge. The usually empty room is packed with my colleagues who take one look at me and erupt into disappointed mutters.

I find Gail. "Is it something I said?"

Marvin, who teaches advanced chemistry and biology, hands her a wad of money.

"Thank you," she says smugly, plucking the cash from his hand.

"What's that for?" I ask.

"We had a pool going on what time you'd let your students go. With the ceremony tomorrow and your track record, most of them bet you'd make them play it out to the bitter end, but I know that beneath that veneer of iron will, there lurks a big softie."

I laugh. "You should've seen them beg. They get better at it every year."

"Can you really blame them?" she asks. "Two months of freedom is just around the bend."

I watch my fellow educators mill around the small lounge. There's a buzz of excitement among them. School's almost out and that means they can enjoy their lives and their loved ones. Some are going to see their children and grandchildren; others are planning romantic getaways with their spouses. A few ramble on and on about family reunions. Gail's going on a cruise with her two sisters in July.

I have nowhere to go and no one to see. I have the number to Giordano's Pizza, an unopened DVD, and a stale box of chocolate chunk cookies tucked away in the back of my sock drawer.

My students are now my passion, my one and only passion. In the beginning I told myself that teaching would only be an interim, something to pay the bills, to tide me over until my next big break. But the semesters flew by and one year led to the next until I'd become comfortable where I was—not happy, but able to survive, capable of filling my days and my voids.

The time I meant to spend writing new music, I spent giving after-school lessons. The money I was supposed to spend recording a demo, I invested in my

Pulsed Dye Laser treatments. The energy I should've applied to finding a new record label, I used to push the school board for better funding.

In the past, I was Abigail Walker; during school hours I'm Ms. W; but what am I going to be tomorrow once school is out, once my reason for getting up every morning is gone for eight weeks?

I open the festive tin of cookies on the table in front of me and pick out a cranberry oatmeal one.

"What are you doing?" Gail asks.

"Drowning my misery."

She snatches the cookie just as I'm about to sink my teeth into it. "I thought we said no carbs."

"What's the point?" I ask. "Why deprive ourselves? We're all going to die anyway. I'd rather be fifteen pounds heavier and happy."

"This cookie," she says, eyeing the moist, tempting morsel in her hand, "isn't going to make you happy."

I snatch it back. "I'm willing to give it a shot."

She shrugs and grabs a sugar cookie from the tin. "We'll start back on our diet tomorrow."

Gail is right. The cookie doesn't make me feel better. It's sweet and soft and warm, but it's only in my mouth for a few seconds and then it's gone. I take another one and wolf it down, this time not bothering to taste it. I just want to fill myself. It's not hunger; it's emptiness.

"Slow down," Gail says, as I reach for my third cookie. "You want to talk about it?"

"Do you think life is pointless? You know, like nothing we do or say or believe matters?"

"Are you going through some sort of existential crisis?" she asks.

I sigh. "No, just the summer blues."

"How many times have I asked you to cruise to the Bahamas with my sisters and me?"

"I can't afford it."

"What about your family? Go spend time with them."

"My parents are in Europe," I say. "And my sister, I don't know. We're still working things out."

"Well, you can't sit around for eight weeks and get fat off cookies."

"I was thinking of offering lessons, thirty dollars an hour, all ages, all levels."

She shakes her head. "That defeats the purpose of having a summer vacation. We're going to lounge around like the lazy old hags we are and enjoy our freedom."

"And when July rolls around and you're off hooting at buff, oily Bahamians, what am I supposed to do?"

"Read a good book? Clean out your closet? Tape my soaps for me?"

I scrunch my face.

She hands me another cookie. "We'll think of something."

"I feel so alone."

"You've got a great job, making a difference doing something you're good at. Your students love you; your boss adores you. What more is there?"

"Someone to go home to," I say.

"I've been down that road—worst three years of my life."

"I almost got married once. He was so nervous, he stuttered through the whole proposal. It was a rainy afternoon. We were in the back of this dingy diner and he pulled out a cheap, silver band and he asked me to be his wife."

"What happened?"

I shake my head. "It was a long time ago. We were too young, too different."

"Did you love him?" she asks.

I close my eyes and search the darkness for his face, but I can't find it. "Not enough."

I hang my keys on the hook by the door and drop my bags in the living room. My apartment is more like a five-hundred-square-foot cell. The walls are bare, the ceiling low, the carpet shaggy, the furniture sparse.

Anyone who's ever been by asks why I don't hang pictures or paint the kitchen cabinets or update the light fixtures. I tell them I don't have the money or the time. I tell them simplicity doesn't bother me, that I like my plain apartment.

The truth is, I never meant to be here this long. I didn't want to get comfortable, to admit this was my new station in life. Selling my house, filing for bankruptcy, losing my recording contract—they were just setbacks, character-building obstacles that would make my return to stardom that much more of an accomplishment.

But here I am, four years later, my walls still white, my cabinets still unpainted, my light fixtures still old, and no closer to leaving, no closer to moving forward, no closer to reviving my career.

I walk the few paces to my kitchen and check my answering machine. The light is not flashing, but I push the play button anyway. You have no messages.

The sink is overflowing with dirty dishes. I bypass them and pour myself a glass of orange juice. Then I make my way to my bedroom where I rummage through my dresser drawers in search of my emergency stash of Milk Duds.

I lie on my bed and pop one ball of chewy chocolate after another and watch my ceiling fan rotate.

Is this it? I wonder. *Is this as good as it gets?*

The funny thing is, I don't remember my old life. I mean, I can envision my old condo, old restaurants and hangouts, old friends. But I don't remember what it felt like to be the woman who lived in that condo and went to those restaurants and hangouts and associated with those friends. I remember feeling normal, but never complete.

Come to think of it, I don't remember being happy or satisfied at any stage of my life. That's not to say I didn't have fun or make memories. I celebrated and laughed and enjoyed myself when those moments came and the experiences were gratifying, but when they were all over and the spotlight had been taken away, I wasn't content enough to be still—to wind down and reflect. I had to get out there and recreate it, only more spectacular, with a bigger, longer spotlight and greater recognition.

I knew what I was doing when I buried myself underneath an impossible schedule of tour dates and special appearances and album recordings; I just didn't know what I was running from, what hidden fear kept me dancing so frantically.

As I sit up and survey my cubicle of a bedroom, I realize the only thing I was running from was myself. I wouldn't have to confront the scared, unsure, cruel, unfeeling tyrant I'd become. But I couldn't dance forever, no one can, and now I'm suffering the consequences of an unbridled life.

I live alone in a tiny, fifth-floor walk-up. I conduct high school kids in the daytime and I organize and reorganize my movie collection at night. I eat TV dinners and spoon ice cream straight from the tub. I spend Saturdays in my robe and Sundays watching all-day marathons and grading music theory tests.

I shake my head and tilt the box of Milk Duds upside down; it's empty. There's a White Hen Pantry a few blocks up. Maybe I can burn off the calories from my first box of Milk Duds on my way to get another one.

I slip into a pair of old sneakers and clomp down five flights of stairs and outside onto the sidewalk. The sky's a refreshing shade of blue, despite the muggy temperature.

There's hardly any traffic as I cross the street and head down Clark. I walk slowly, not at all eager to get back to my gloomy apartment.

The shop windows display sleek, faceless mannequins in bright, tiny outfits. I pass by a boutique with a big "Going Out of Business" sign taped to its door. "Everything Must Go" and "75% off" beam out at me.

My closets are already jammed, and more importantly, I can't afford anything new, but I end up searching through their racks of clothes anyway. It's mostly vintage items that smell like mothballs.

"Everything in that bin is ten dollars," the owner, a heavyset woman with jiggling arms, says. "And if it has a yellow tag, it's five."

Four bins' worth of funky accessories and two racks of bell bottoms later, I come across a simple black dress. It's wrinkled and in dire need of a lint brush, but it's classic and just might be my size.

The dressing room is really a corner with a patterned sheet tacked to the walls as a divider. I take off my clothes and slide the dress on. It's lined with a soft, satiny fabric, which feels like cool water against my skin.

It fits, snugly hugging my body. I turn to the mirror and study my reflection beneath the dim lighting.

After three costly laser treatments, my face and neck remain hidden behind a range of disfiguring scars. My left eye still droops dramatically; my mottled skin still looks cracked and old like worn leather. People still look the other way, embarrassed for me, or blink back their disgusted shock, or grin uneasily with pity in their eyes.

Small children still cry and older kids still point in bewilderment. But I've gotten used to myself by now. This is who I am. This is how I look. And all of the cosmetic surgeries and laser treatments in the world can't change that.

Sometimes, when my day's been especially rough, or my week unusually lonely, I start to feel sorry for myself. I cower in my small apartment, unable to conjure the mettle to go out and face the world. Simple activities like running to the post office or going to lunch with a friend are chores because I know people are judging me by what they see on the outside.

But then Monday rolls around and I remember my students—how they depend on me, how they accept me, scars and all. I think of their hard effort and their young enthusiasm for music—for life. And the next thing I know, I'm up and pushing again, motivated by their motivation.

They give me strength and courage, but mostly, they give me focus beyond myself.

"How much is this?" I ask, emerging from behind the sheet, the dress draped over my arm.

"Seven bucks."

I pay for it, along with a darling pair of earrings, and exit the shop with my gold finds safely tucked under my arm. Then I stroll the two blocks left to the White Hen Pantry where I splurge on two boxes of Milk Duds and a pack of Skittles.

Students, parents, and teachers cheer as I lower my baton and the orchestra members stand and take their bows.

"Excellent," I whisper and smile at my students who are glowing from a job well done.

Mrs. Vine steps up to the podium and taps the microphone several times. "Before you leave this afternoon, we have one last special presentation."

I tiptoe down the stage steps and join Gail who's saved me a seat in the front row.

"Every year we hand out a Most Valued Teacher award. It's who you," she points into the crowd, "the student body vote for. This year I'm proud to present our Most Valued Teacher award to..." She pauses for dramatic effect. "Abigail Walker."

The students and faculty, including Gail, jump to their feet and clap wildly.

I'm stunned, but flattered, as I stand and join Mrs. Vine behind the podium.

She holds up a silver statuette of a hand waving a baton. My name, the date, and a thank-you message are inscribed elegantly into its wooden base.

"When Ms. Walker first arrived here, she was wearing a miniskirt and a diamond necklace that probably cost more than my car," Mrs. Vine says.

Laughter spreads throughout the large auditorium.

"She was obnoxious, among other things, and frightened, and I had my doubts about whether she would make it. But here she is, four years later, standing strong and transforming our high school one student at a time.

"Before she joined us, funding and enrollment for the performing arts programs were at an all-time low. We had fewer instruments than students to give them to, insufficient learning materials, and no foreseeable way to fix those problems.

"Ms. Walker has pushed and fought an upward battle for more money, better instruments, and better music. She sat in board meetings, wrote letters, organized fund-raisers, and solicited help from neighboring colleges and universities. She's sacrificed countless weekends and holidays and it's paid off.

"Her dedication doesn't end with music. She's also implemented the *B or Better Program,* where members of the orchestra sign a contract at the beginning of each year promising to keep their GPAs at or above a 3.0.

"And she started the *Scholarship Search Program* and the annual *ACT/SAT Review* to give our kids a better shot at college."

She turns to me. "Your passion and tenacity and undying faith in your students and this school, have been invaluable. I'm honored to present you with this award."

She hands me the trophy and gives me a quick, stiff hug.

Gail rushes forward and takes control of the microphone. "We have a last-minute surprise for Ms. Walker," she says.

The cheering crowd falls silent as a lanky man with a familiar scar across his left cheek walks down the aisle.

"My name is Terrance Wallace," he says after taking his place behind the podium. "I was one of Ms. Walker's first students. Four years ago, I was seventeen with a lot of problems. I was ready to drop out and start hustling full-time; and then Ms. Walker entered the picture like Mrs. Vine said, with a phat diamond necklace and an itty bitty skirt."

I laugh along with the crowd.

"I hated her and she wasn't too fond of me either," Terry continues. "First day of class, she kicked me out. But then she turned around the next day and gave me her cello because the school had run out.

"I tell everyone: *That* was the moment that changed my life. She saw something in me that everyone else ignored, and for the rest of the year she road me. She even came to my house one Saturday to get on me about my college application essay.

"Sometimes I wanted her to disappear, sometimes we fought, but she saw me through to the end, and I'll be graduating from DePaul in December."

I hug him, grateful for his kind words and equally proud of his accomplishment.

"You're far more than this year's Most Valued Teacher," he whispers in my ear. "You're my true-life hero."

The trophy looks big and out of place in my ordinary apartment. First I put it on top of my attaché and then on top of the television and then on my bookcase. It brightens the room no matter where it rests, and when I look at it, I can't help but smile. Maybe I'm not a hapless failure. Maybe people really do appreciate me and what I do really does make a difference.

I change into my pajamas, and even though I'm not thirsty, walk to the kitchen to get a glass of water so I can pass by my award again.

The phone rings.

"What're you doing?" Gail asks.

"Nothing."

"Stop staring at your big, shiny trophy and get dressed."

I smile at how well she knows me. "For what?"

"We're going out tonight."

I glance at the two Blockbuster cases and the stack of takeout menus on my coffee table. "I don't feel like going out," I say.

"You're not staying home on the first official weekend of summer vacation. We're two gorgeous, single hot mamas. Let's act like it for a change."

"What'd you have in mind?"

"A friend of mine was supposed to go to a restaurant opening, but he can't make it so he gave me his invitation."

I groan. "That sounds boring."

"Come on, live a little. We'll get gussied up and go rub elbows with the rich and famous, stuff ourselves with gourmet appetizers. Who knows? You might meet a very rich, handsome man and live happily ever after."

I laugh. "That would be a first."

"I'll swing by and pick you up at eight?"

"Okay," I say and scuttle off to my room to find my new black dress.

37. Hello Again

Jarvis dusts the sleeve of his sports jacket and mingles confidently with his guests. All those months of no sleep and missed deadlines and catching red-eyes to and from Chicago have paid off. The opening is a success.

The food is delectable, the servers professional and efficient, the live music appropriately upbeat, the setting intimate, and the critics impressed.

"Jarvis, this is marvelous, absolutely splendid," a shrill voice exclaims. He looks over his shoulder to see an older woman smiling up at him. "You must be so pleased." She takes his arm. Her hands are cold and her fingers weighed down with several flashy rings.

He smiles, unable to place her face or remember her name. "I am," he says.

"Have you had a chance to meet my daughter?"

"I don't believe so."

"Let me introduce you," she says, tugging him through the dense crowd to the other side of the restaurant.

A young woman is waiting for them by the bar. She twirls her necklace nervously.

"This is Elizabeth," the woman says, pointing proudly at her daughter. "She's finishing her last year of med school here in Chicago."

"Liz," the young woman says as she shakes Jarvis's hand. "Thanks for inviting us."

He nods and tries to recall how he knows the mother and daughter team. "You're welcome."

She smiles. "It's a great place. I'll be sure to tell my friends."

"Well, thanks for coming. I appreciate it. Enjoy yourself," he says, turning to leave.

Liz grabs two glasses of champagne from a passing waiter. "Have a drink with me," she says.

Jarvis holds up his hand. "No, thank you."

Liz and her mother exchange offended glances.

"I don't drink," he explains kindly.

"Oh! Of course!" Liz says, quickly setting both glasses down on the bar. "I'm not a big drinker myself."

"Look," Liz's mother points, "I think I see Dale and Nita. I should go say hi." She gives her daughter a good luck wink and waddles back into the party.

Cornered, Jarvis makes small talk with Liz, who expends more energy flipping her hair and flashing her cleavage, than conversing.

"I kind of always knew I wanted to be a doctor," she says. "But I also model on the side. I don't know what I'd do if I ever had to choose between the two."

Jarvis canvasses the room for a familiar face. "Yeah, I see how that could be tough," he says, indulging her for the sake of politeness.

"You're lucky to be so young and settled. Have you always wanted to be a restaurateur?"

His eyes freeze on Chas, who's followed by his mom and then William. Jarvis holds his breath and continues to stare at the door.

Haley walks in shaking the rain from her hair.

"Will you excuse me?" he says to Liz, who's droning on about her true life's ambition, which is to be a talk show host.

"Jay!" Chas says. "This looks great."

"You're late. I was afraid you guys weren't coming."

"And miss my baby's big debut?" his mom says. "Never."

Jarvis smiles sheepishly at Haley and nods. "Hi."

She nods back, her face flushed. "Hi."

"We'll be testing out your food if you need us," William says grabbing his wife's elbow and leading her toward the nearest table.

"Me too," Chas says. "We'll talk later."

Haley and Jarvis stand quietly, neither sure of what to say. The last time they saw or spoke to each another was that awful night at the Chinese restaurant.

"You came," he says.

"I had to see what all the fuss was about."

"What do you think?" he asks, stepping aside and sweeping his arm across the posh restaurant.

"It's amazing, Jay." She smiles. "Really, it's fantastic. Congratulations, you got everything you wanted."

He scans her face—those sad eyes and that trembling chin. "No, I didn't. Not everything."

The cab pulls up outside the restaurant. Abby is not happy as the valet opens her door and she and Gail scurry, in the rain, to the covered entrance.

Gail came to pick her up at eight as planned, but she took one look at Abby's sexy outfit and insisted on going back to her place so she could change.

"What difference does it make?" Abby asked. "It's not like anyone's going to know who we are."

"It won't take long," Gail said, flailing her arm wildly at a cabbie who zoomed right past her.

Abby pointed to Gail's fitted maroon slacks and sheer, embroidered top. "You look fine," she argued.

"Yeah, I look fine and you look gorgeous."

Abby wrapped her shawl tightly around her shoulders. "Gail, it's windy and I think it's going to rain."

A raggedy cab pulled to a halt in front of them. "Twenty minutes," Gail promised.

Twenty minutes turned into an hour and a half. Gail raided her closet, twice, coming up with several different outfits, all equally stylish, only to end up settling on the same maroon slacks and embroidered top she'd started out in.

It took another ten minutes to hail a cab and another fifteen minutes to fight the downtown traffic, and just as they were nearing their destination, it started to pour.

"Invitations?" requests a pleasant woman wearing a blazer and tie.

Gail hands the woman a soggy piece of paper.

"Miles and Amanda Schneider?" the woman reads aloud, her eyebrows furrowed. Gail laughs nervously and hooks her arm through Abby's. "My friends call me *Mimi*."

Abby shrugs as the hostess studies her, a peculiar look on her face.

"Well, welcome to Treasures and enjoy your evening."

Safe inside, Gail nudges Abby, "This looks pretty cool, huh."

Abby glares and dabs at her wet arms with a cloth napkin.

"You need a drink," Gail says. "I'll be right back."

Abby takes in her surroundings. The restaurant is nice, high-end, but not stuffy—the type of place she used to frequent. She sways gently to the jazz music in the background and surveys the rest of the guests.

A short balding man in a tight turtleneck spots her across the room and shoves his way through the crowd toward her.

She whips around, grabs a plate, and piles it with an assortment of hors d'oeuvres, praying the guy will take a hint and get lost.

"Excuse me?" a voice squawks behind her.

Abby turns to see the dreaded bald man standing before her. "Hi," she says.

"I couldn't help but notice you when you came in."

She grins, feeling awkward, and shoves a miniature crab cake into her mouth. "Thanks."

"You look familiar," the man says. "Do I know you from somewhere?"

She shakes her head. "Doubt it."

"What do you do?" he asks.

She hates that question. "I'm a retired cellist," she says. "I teach music now."

"Yes, yes, I remember you." He snaps his piggy, little fingers. "Starts with an A," he says.

"Abigail."

"Right!" He snaps. "Abigail Walker. Are you here to play?"

"No," she says, trying her best to remain pleasant. "I'm here to have a good time like everyone else."

"I've never met a celebrity before," he says. "My name's Henry."

Gail teeters her way back across the room, two glasses of wine sloshing in her hands.

"It was nice meeting you," Abby says, sidestepping him. "What did you have to do?" she asks, relieving Gail of one of the glasses. "Run to Italy and stomp the grapes yourself?"

"Testy, testy," Gail says, sipping her wine. "I see we're still cranky, but Auntie Gail just saw something that will alleviate any woman's bad mood."

She turns Abby around and points to a tall gentleman by the bar. He's having a lively conversation with two other guests. Abby's grip tightens around her glass as she peers more closely.

He's handsome in his stylish sports coat and neatly pressed slacks. Though he's leaning on a cane, his stance is wide and confident, his shoulders broad. His short haircut and trimmed goatee give him an air of sophistication.

An older woman walks up behind him and grips his shoulder. She's short and wide and she looks very familiar.

"Oh my God," Abby whispers, her heart racing uncontrollably.

Gail purrs. " 'Oh my God' is right."

"You should have seen Mr. Kopeky's face when he found out you'd moved without saying good-bye," Chas says. "He threw a fit right in the middle of the diner. 'What's wrong with that boy?' Chas mimics Mr. Kopeky's shaky, gruff voice. " 'Next time I see him, I'm gonna have to learn him some manners.' "

Jarvis laughs and shakes his head.

"It's true," Haley says. "The only thing that would calm him down was free raisin-cinnamon oatmeal and a cup of coffee."

"I'll give him a call as soon as everything dies down."

"You did good," Chas says, glancing around the two-story restaurant. "I'm proud of you."

"We all are," Haley adds.

Jarvis smiles. "So when are you moving to New York?"

"Oh," she says, her eyes firmly planted on the floor. "That kind of fell through."

Jarvis glances at Chas who shrugs.

"Jay, the food is unbelievable," Jarvis's mother says, gripping his shoulder.

He turns to see her and William, both carrying overflowing plates.

"Hm, try this," she offers, holding out a raspberry tart.

"Ma, I've tried everything on the menu fifteen times, at least. If I never have another tart, it'll..."

Jarvis catches a glimpse of someone standing by the tables. He cranes his neck and focuses on the woman looking back at him. He freezes. Their eyes lock and she mirrors his slight grin, but neither of them move.

Abby is stunning, despite her piebald skin and prominent scars. She's gained weight. She looks different—healthier and older—but still kept, still breathtakingly regal with her hair swept back. Her eyes, though uneven, are still soft and intense, her lips, though framed by wrinkles, still pout seductively.

She's wearing a strapless black dress that clings to her body and accentuates her hips.

"What is it?" his mom asks.

Haley touches his arm. "Jay, what's wrong?"

They all follow his gaze into the crowd.

Jarvis's mom gasps. "Oh my word!" She shoves her plate at William. "I don't believe it," she exclaims and rushes across the room, bumping into curious guests along the way.

"Who is that?" Chas asks.

Haley looks up at Jarvis who's still frozen, still mesmerized.

"It's Abby."

"You know her?" Gail asks as she and Abby watch the mammoth woman with outstretched arms bound toward them.

She hands Gail her glass of wine. "Yeah, I do."

"What a surprise!" Dot says, pulling Abby into a tight warm hug.

Abby embraces her and tries to maintain her composure. "What're you doing here?" she asks.

Dot swipes at her tears and smiles. "This is all Jarvis's," she announces grandly.

Abby blinks back disbelief. "He owns this restaurant?" she asks.

"Yeah, you know Jo passed away."

Abby nods. "I heard about it."

"Well, he left Jarvis the diner, which is now 'JD's,' and a bunch of other real estate properties, including this one. Jay took one look at it, and ten months later, Treasures was born."

"That's great," Abby says. "He deserves it."

Dot grabs her hand. "Come over and say hi."

"You know, I really shouldn't. I'm here with a friend," she points at Gail, who's standing quietly behind them trying desperately not to look like she's eavesdropping.

"You have to," Dot says, her eyes still misty. "It's been too long."

Abby ignores her lightheadedness and tries to control her breathing as Dot leads her over to the bar where Jarvis and his two friends are all waiting and staring. Gail follows behind them, still toting both glasses of wine.

It's been seven years since that night in Michigan. Seven years since their lives changed so drastically. And now, as she and Jarvis stand in front of each other, mere inches apart, words escape them.

A single tear rolls down Abby's cheek. "Hey," she whispers.

Jarvis wraps his arms around her and pulls her into him. His grip is tight and sincere, his scent familiar and comforting.

She squeezes her eyes shut and cries freely as he quietly repeats the same three words.

"I'm so sorry," Jarvis whispers into Abby's ear. "I'm so sorry. I'm so sorry."

"It's okay, Jay," she says, choking back sobs. "It's okay."

Jarvis tightens his grip around Abby's waist as she clings tightly to him. He knows people are watching. Haley is standing next to him. He doesn't want to hurt her, but he can't let Abby go. Nobody knows what they went through. Nobody knows how long he's waited to beg for her forgiveness.

He holds her in front of his parents, his best friend, ex-girlfriend, and one hundred and twenty guests. He holds her and cries, squeezing his eyes shut and sinking into the words he's yearned to hear her say for so, so long.

"It's okay, Jay. It's okay."

It amazes him how, after all this time, the feel of her in his arms, of their bodies pressed together, seems right—how her hands on the back of his neck and her breath against his cheek feel safe, as if he'd been displaced and now with her resting snugly against his chest, he's come home.

He kisses her cheek and reluctantly releases her. "You look good," they both say at the same time.

Jarvis wipes his eyes and laughs. "Thanks."

Abby points to his legs. "I thought you—you know, I heard you were…"

Jarvis lifts his left pant leg and taps the metal tube with his cane. "Prosthetics."

"Wow." She smiles.

"Look at you," he says, running his thumb across her chin.

Abby breathes deeply, aware of the people staring at them. "I can't believe this is all yours," she says, shifting the focus by gesturing around the restaurant. "You've done well for yourself."

"I've been getting by," Jarvis says humbly. "How about you?" he asks. "What're you up to these days?"

Abby's grateful for the dim lighting. She feels the heat of humiliation trail up her neck and flush her face. She scampers for a truthful yet vague answer.

"I'm retired now, so…"

Jarvis nods. "Well, you've earned it, right?"

"Don't be so modest," Gail chimes in. "Abby conducts high school orchestra. You should see her with the kids; she's inspirational. In fact, she just won our Most Valued Teacher of the Year Award."

"That's wonderful," Dot says.

Abby winces at her throbbing pride. "It's just something I fell into." She tosses Gail a steely glance and silently tallies up all the ways she's going to hurt her as soon as they leave.

"I guess we should make some introductions," Jarvis says. "This is William, my stepfather."

Abby smiles warmly at the gray-bearded man standing next to Dot and shakes his hand.

"This is Chas, surrogate brother and business partner extraordinaire. And that's Haley."

Abby nods first at the tall sloppy redhead with the sleepy eyes and dorky bow tie, and then at the portly, rather homely woman with stringy blond hair and rosy cheeks in front of her.

"After all the emotional hellos, I don't want to feel left out," Chas says, reaching for a hug.

Everyone laughs. Haley folds her arms across her chest and looks away.

"This is Gail." Abby steps aside to reveal her talkative, dark-skinned companion. "She's a good friend and colleague, if you hadn't already guessed."

They all say hello and the group goes quiet.

"Why don't I give you the grand tour?" Jarvis offers.

The plump girl, whom Abby noticed, Jarvis neglected to give a title, glowers at them and leans forward as if she might pounce at a moment's notice.

"Um, are you sure?" Abby asks. "I don't want to pull you away on your special night."

Jarvis takes her hand and entwines their fingers. "It's fine," he says and leads her away just as Haley storms off.

Jarvis escorts Abby around both levels of the restaurant, the offices, the kitchen, and the two patios. He's excited to show off his completed dream, especially with Abby.

They end up on the terrace. The rain has stopped and left behind a clear, dark blue sky speckled with stars and warm breezes.

"Do you want to sit?" Jarvis asks, pointing to a wrought-iron bench behind them.

"Sure."

"Wait, hold on." He takes off his sports coat and lays it down for Abby to sit on. "There you go."

"Thanks," Abby says, smiling. "When did you get so chivalrous?"

"I've grown up—done a lot of changing."

She sighs and gazes at the magnificent view before them. "Yeah, everything's changed."

"Not you," he says. "You're still amazing."

Abby chuckles. "Yeah, if your definition of amazing is broke, lonely, and miserable."

"What are you talking about?"

He listens as Abby recounts bits and pieces of the last seven years—about Hannah and Amber Sheffield and Dr. Kessler and Val and Magnolia Records and bankruptcy. As she talks her shoulders slump and her voice loses its vibrancy, and he sees for the first time tonight how tired and defeated she is. "I feel like I'm in a maze," she says. "And all I want to do is find my way out and get on with my life, but every turn I make is the wrong turn. And every wrong turn just gets me more lost."

Jarvis takes her hand in his.

"How did you do it?" she asks, gazing into his eyes. "How did you get here—to this point?"

"That's easy," he says. "I gave my life to Christ."

Abby pulls her hand away. "Forget I asked," she says, her stomach churning.

"You said you're in a maze," Jarvis says. "I know exactly how you feel. I was in one too, but I can't tell you the right way to turn because every maze is different and personal. God's the only one who has the aerial view."

Abby shakes her head. "I don't believe in God."

"Why not?"

"There are too many things that don't make sense in the world."

"But how do you know following Christ won't help the world make more sense?"

She sighs. "I don't want to get into a philosophical debate about it."

"Abs, you know me better than most people. Did you ever think this would be me?"

She smiles. "No, never."

"Me either, but I'm here and just as joyful as I can be and it has nothing to do with the restaurant or my family or even you. It's Christ within me who makes me whole."

"But tomorrow Treasures could burn down or you could die suddenly and all of this would be for nothing."

"Have you ever heard of Solomon?" Jarvis asks.

Abby shakes her head. "No."

"He writes about the pointlessness of life in Ecclesiastes. He says that men toil under the sun to gain pleasures in life only to die empty-handed. He likened it to grasping for the wind."

Abby shrugs. "Sounds about right."

"He was a great ruler—wise and wealthy and powerful—but he found that nothing apart from God made him happy or satisfied him."

"So? What's your point?"

"You've tried everything. You've been rich, had fame, you've been down and out, you've had a condo and now an apartment, you've played sold-out concerts, you've taught high school kids. You've tried everything and nothing makes you happy."

"Yeah, but God's not the answer, Jay. Trust me."

"How do you know when you haven't made an effort to get to know Him?"

"Get to know Him? He's not real!"

"Prove it," he says, throwing his hands up with a shrug. "Buy a Bible and read one chapter every day. Pray, talk to Him as freely as you talk to me. Go to church; I'll even go with you and just see what happens. What do you have to lose?"

She considers Jarvis's challenge. It's the only time in her entire life she's entertained the idea of God existing. But she looks at Jarvis—his mannerisms, the way he speaks, the man he's become—and she knows his transformation is nothing short of a miracle.

What do I have to lose? she asks herself. Sleepless nights and lonely weekends? An apartment she hates? A job she's not meant to do? She has nothing to lose. She has nothing, period.

"Okay," she relents reluctantly. "What's the worst that could happen?"

Jarvis looks pleased.

"I'm not making any promises, though," she adds.

He chuckles. "It's going to feel good, on so many levels, when you call me up in a couple of months and tell me how right I am."

Jarvis marvels at how easily he and Abby share with each another. They sit side by side and catch up like two old chums. Their past doesn't hang over them; it doesn't even come up.

She tells him about her award and brags about Terry and the rest of her students, both new and old.

He tells her about Chas and college, about Jo's death and the transformation from JoJo's into JD's. They sit, just the two of them, in front of a Chicago cityscape, and bare their souls.

Abby turns her body so she's facing Jarvis. "Can I ask you a question?"

"Shoot."

"How do you know Haley?" she asks.

Jarvis shrugs. "She's a friend."

"She was glaring kinda hard just to be a friend."

"She's my ex."

"How long were you guys together?"

"Four years."

Abby blinks, somewhat surprised. "That's a long time."

He nods. "She's seen me through a lot. I was planning to propose," he shrugs. "But it didn't work out."

Abby pokes him playfully. "You and your botched engagements," she teases.

He sighs. "Yeah."

"So what happened?"

He tells her about the months of nonstop traveling and the distancing and the ring and the Chinese restaurant and the fortune cookies and the fight that ended it all. "Wasn't meant to be, I guess."

"It sounds like you two are good for each other," Abby says.

He tilts his head sadly. "I thought so too."

Abby studies his long face and regretful eyes. "You really love her," she says.

Jarvis nods. "More than anything."

"Then what're you doing out here with me?" Abby asks. "You had a fight. You're both angry and embarrassed. Let it go. If there's one thing the both of us know, it's that life's short and tomorrow's not guaranteed."

Jarvis searches Abby's face. "Maybe God stopped me from proposing because He knew I would see you here, tonight. Maybe Haley's not the one I'm supposed to be with."

Abby rubs his arm. "That's not going to happen," she says, resting her temple on his shoulder. "We weren't meant to be."

"How can you be sure?"

"Because you're madly in love with a woman who's obviously just as madly in love with you, even if neither one of you is big enough to admit it right now."

They sit in reflective silence for a while.

Abby hugs herself. "Can I see the ring?"

Jarvis smiles. "What makes you think I have it?"

"I know you," she says. "A diehard romantic to the core."

Jarvis pulls the black velvet box from his pants pocket and hands it to her.

Abby holds it gingerly in her palm and opens it. She feels an uneasy mixture of envy and sorrow. But she's happy for Jarvis and knows he's made a wise choice in Haley. "It's beautiful," she says, gazing down at the ring. "She's going to love it."

Jarvis stands and offers his arm. "But first she has to see it."

Abby stands and hands him his damp sports jacket. "I'm going to stay out here for a few more minutes."

"Okay." He rubs her bare shoulders and kisses the top of her head. "I'll see you in there?"

Abby nods and holds her breath as the one-time love of her life disappears into the night to find his soul mate.

The jazz band has been replaced by a DJ and the dance floor is loaded with sweating, dancing bodies.

"Where have you been?" Gail asks, her shoes off and her hair pulled back.

"Tying up loose ends," Abby says.

"Well, are you done? Because I need a partner." Gail ushers her toward the dancing crowd.

"Hey," Abby shouts over the heavy bass. "Do you think maybe you'd want to go to church with me on Sunday?"

Gail smiles and hooks her arm through Abby's. "I'd love to."

They squeeze and shove their way to the middle of the floor and start bouncing and swaying and bumping to the pulse of the music.

Abby throws her head back in laughter and hoots as Gail spins and dips her.

She still has nothing more than an unimpressive apartment waiting for her. She still has no summer plans, no money, no one to go home to. She's still trapped in her maze.

But she feels lighter, her mind is less fogged, her soul strangely burden-free, and so she dances, unconcerned and unaware of who's watching. She dances and laughs and celebrates the possibilities that lie ahead.